Talented

Sophie Davis

DEDICATION

To my father, Henry. I love you, Dad.

ACKNOWLEDGMENTS

I would like to thank Bear and Irish for all of their hard work and dedication. I would like to thank Bear for all of her hard work editing; without her help, this book would be seriously lacking in the word "that." I would like to thank Irish for her patience, and all the late night texts asking her advice on story changes, which led to her having dreams about the characters. I would like to thank my mother for all of her support and advice. I would like to thank my father for repeatedly asking whether the book included sex. I would also like to thank Burner for indulging me by reading the book in one of its earliest renditions.

Chapter One

An earsplitting wail punctured the silent night, shattering the illusions of my dream world and bringing me back to reality. My eyes popped open, becoming instantly alert as the sound reverberated through the dark cabin again. I bolted upright in my bed. Terror seized me. I knew that noise. In school, I had done monthly drills in response to *that* noise. Emphasis on drills. I'd never heard the sirens for real. I'd hoped I never would either. Even now, as the warning bells blared through the speakers in the clearing outside of my cabin, I prayed it was just a test.

I could only see the parts of my room illuminated by the ribbons of artificial lights streaming through the slits of the wooden blinds covering the windows. In the short time I'd been awake, my swollen eyes had adjusted to the darkness. Hastily, I threw the blanket back as my trained eyes darted around the cabin. The other two beds were empty. Crap. Henri and Erik, my cabin mates, must have heard the invasion sirens and run out immediately. How had I slept through that? Why didn't they wake me up? Assholes.

I didn't waste time putting on real clothes, or even shoes. I flung the cabin door open with my mind before I was fully out of my bed. Running into the night; pajamas, bare feet and all, I sprinted straight into the center of Hunters Village. I stopped abruptly; for all of the training drills I'd taken part in at school, there had yet to be a single drill since my arrival at Elite Headquarters two weeks ago. I had no idea where I was supposed to go, or what I was supposed to do. *Breathe, Talia,* I reminded myself. *Just breathe.*

The night air was unseasonably warm for late September, but a chill ran through my body, all the way to my bones, as panic gripped and twisted my insides. The sirens sounded again. We were under attack. Someone was attacking Elite Headquarters. *Calm down. You need to breathe,* I ordered myself. I forcibly inhaled the warm air through my nose and then blew it out, unsteadily, through clenched teeth.

Slowly, I turned and pivoted in a three-hundred-and-sixty-degree circle. Chaos was the only way to describe the scene surrounding me. Pledges streamed from the cabins around Hunters Village. Panicked screams pierced the silence between siren blasts. I dug my nails sharply into my palms to prevent my own fear-driven yelps from escaping. *Clear your mind. Focus. Concentrate your energy,* I coached myself. Trying to obey my own commands, I closed my eyes and forced my mind to go blank.

My hypersensitive ears immediately registered a faint whizzing sound from above. I tilted my head back as I opened my eyes. The night sky looked as if it were falling, one star at a time. It took several seconds for my mind to process what my eyes were seeing; stars weren't falling out of the night sky, but bombs were. Swallowing over the lump in my throat, I forced the unpleasantness clawing its way to my mouth back down. *The people who panic in a crisis are the people who die*, I reminded myself.

The bombs exploded, expelling bright neon liquid when they made contact with the ground. One landed several feet in front of where I stood. Fear got the better of me and I screamed as the bomb burst and several drops of the glowing liquid hit my bare skin. I wiped at my calves, frantically smearing the fluid with my palms. I rubbed my hands on my thin t-shirt and it instantly began to glow. I waited for pain that never came. I stared, wide-eyed, as bomb after bomb detonated on the ground, leaving neon puddles in their wake. Pledges ran with hands over their heads in an attempt to protect their faces.

I needed to do something, anything, besides standing here waiting for another bomb to hit me. I concentrated all of my considerable mental energy on the falling explosives and focused on slowing their descent. After several seconds, the bombs froze in mid-air. I let out a breath I wasn't aware I had been holding as I strained with the effort of holding them in place.

Opening my mind, I felt a flood of mixed emotions. The panic radiating from the other Pledges' brains mirrored my own. Strangely, I also felt enjoyment, laughter even, mingled with the fear and anxiety. Confusion engulfed my other emotions.

What was going on? *Donavon*, I thought. I needed to find Donavon; he would know what was going on. I pulled some of my mental focus away from holding the bombs and sought out Donavon's mind. It took me only seconds to find him, but once I did, I was even more perplexed.

Donavon was laughing. I could feel his glee as he watched the scene I was currently starring into from a different vantage point. I honed in on his exact location; he was close. Concentrating harder, I slipped deeper in to his head. Finally, I saw Hunters Village through his eyes. I knew exactly where he was standing - on a small hill that overlooked the Village.

"*Donavon?*" I mentally called out to him.

"*Welcome to the Hunters, Tal,*" he laughed.

"*WHAT?!?*" my mental voice screamed at him. Was he joking?? This was an initiation ritual?? Irritation quickly replaced my fear and confusion.

I narrowed my eyes in his general direction; I had a feeling he could see me from his perch, even though I couldn't see him. I was so annoyed at being dragged out of bed in the middle of the night that I let my mental hold on the "bombs" slip, causing one that had been hovering not far over my head to hit me square in the face. I opened my mouth to scream and the neon liquid nearly choked me. Accidentally swallowing a huge gulp, I began to gag. I fell to my knees, retching, and willed myself to throw up the unknown substance.

Donavon's laughter filled my head again, "*It's just colored water, Tal.*"

He clearly found the situation hysterical, and himself clever. Anger washed over me. The last two weeks had been the most physically demanding of my life and now I was being roused from bed in the middle of the night to have faux bombs launched at me??? *So* not funny.

I concentrated on what I now knew to be water balloons – I picked that detail out of Donavon's mind – and refocused my energy to freeze them in mid-fall again. I honed in on Donavon's mind and forced the balloons back through the air to their origin, to Donavon and his group of cohorts. Not waiting for his reaction, I turned on my heel and walked back into my cabin, slamming the door, and crawled back into bed, not caring that I still looked radioactive.

I had the covers pulled over my head when I heard the door open, accompanied by loud laughter.

"Talia," Erik called, "come out and play."

"Leave me alone, you ass," I snapped. Three distinct sets of laughter chorused in response. I felt the covers being yanked back. I clung to the soft fabric of my white comforter, but I was no match for the three boys. I kicked and punched as Donavon leaned over me. His dark blonde hair was soaked with the neon liquid, making me feel a little better.

"Don't be a spoil sport, Tal," he laughed. "This is your formal welcome into Hunters Pledging."

He wanted to see a spoil sport? I would show him a spoil sport. I kicked him in the stomach, hard, and he grunted. I flashed him a wicked smile. Erik pinned my legs down, giving Donavon the opportunity to scoop me up off my bed. I continued to squirm as he carried me across the cabin and back out into the night. He had over a foot and close to a hundred pounds on me, so my efforts were in vain.

"Come on, Talia, it's almost over," Erik whispered as he walked next to us. I craned my neck to face him and gave him a nasty look. He just laughed; I was hardly a threat at the moment.

Donavon carried me over to where a group of other Pledges had already begun to congregate. He placed me on my bare feet in the wet grass but kept his hands firmly on my upper arms. Mentally I sent him a string of angry expletives. I didn't have to see his face to know he was smiling; he was enjoying my discomfort way too much.

"For those of you who don't know me, my name is Henri Reich," an extremely tall, lean boy said, quieting all of the side conversations taking place among those gathered. "This is a little something we at the Hunters like to do as a welcome to the new

Pledges. I know you guys have all been working really hard these past two weeks. Making it this far means you've passed the initial phase of training and are well on your way to graduating and becoming full-fledged Hunters. Congratulations."

When Henri stopped talking, Donavon released my arms. He stepped back so quickly I stumbled, nearly falling over. Donavon was not the only one who had retreated, all of the older Hunters had moved away from us, leaving me and the other Pledges standing in the center of a new circle. More balloons rained down on the small group of us before I could register what was happening. These balloons were filled with a thick, gooey liquid in varying colors: paint. I used my hands to shield my head, but it didn't actually help.

When the color assault finally ended, I removed my hands and looked around at the older Hunters. Some were doubled over, they were laughing so hard. Even the most serious of the group were shaking with silent laughter. I scowled, hoping this was the only welcoming gesture they'd planned for us.

Donavon materialized behind me, wrapping his arms around my waist. "Are you mad at me?" he whispered into my ear. I reached my paint-covered hands up to his face and smeared squiggles down his cheeks. Then I ran my fingers through his damp, blonde hair, leaving most of the paint behind.

"Not at all," I smiled sweetly.

"Enough, enough. I can't take all the cuteness," Erik joked, coming over to us. "Congrats. Tal, you made it through your first round of training, and now you are officially a member of the most awesome Hunting team ever - mine," he said, smiling broadly. Erik had smears of turquoise paint, the same color as his eyes, across each of his high cheekbones; the color complemented his tan skin nicely. He leaned down to hug me and I noticed flecks of purple and red paint decorating his thick black hair. I gave him a half-hearted hug in return.

"Talia, I'm glad to have you as part of our team," Henri said as he wrapped one of his long arms around my shoulders.

"Thank you," I said sincerely. "I'm really glad to be here." I was. This was what I'd been working towards since I'd started attending the McDonough School for the Talented seven years ago.

At the end of their junior year, students selected the top three divisions of the Agency in which they wanted to work after graduation. Then a Placement Committee – consisting of each division head, the Director of the Agency and McDonough's headmistress – reviewed each student's test scores, their Talent and their Talent ranking, and assigned them to a division. Students spent their senior, or pledge, year as the Agency termed it, working and training with their designated department. Not every student scored high enough to be rewarded with one of his top three choices, those students were randomly doled out to the less desirable divisions. The Hunters had been my top choice - my only choice. I knew I wanted, *needed,* to be a Hunter from my very first day.

For most, it's an easy decision; they go with other Talents of their kind. Others, like me, want to do something different; their particular ability does not have a niche. It's not unheard of for Talents besides Morphers, Light Manipulators, or Telekinetics to become Hunters, but I am one of the few who actually did. Most non-morphing Hunters aren't assigned to a team, but serve as "floaters" instead. Floaters are Hunters that join individual Hunting teams on a short-term basis, usually for just one Hunting mission, to lend their individual specialty when it's needed.

"The food and drinks are on their way out, so please take advantage. As a special treat, curfew for the night has been lifted.

And there will no training until after lunchtime tomorrow, so enjoy yourselves," Henri called to the entire group.

Upon arriving at Elite Headquarters to start our Pledge year, each Pledge was assigned to a Hunting team with a vacancy. Hunting teams have three members, but when one member left– for whatever reason – the Agency replaced him, or her, with a Pledge. Part of what made the Hunters such a competitive division was the fact that they only took as many Pledges as there were vacant Hunting positions. This year only fifteen of us were accepted, much less than most years.

I'd been assigned to Henri Reich and Erik Kelley's Hunting team. Henri was the oldest, and the leader of our trio. He stood almost two feet taller than me and was all lean muscle. His eyes were a warm, light brown, and he wore his hair just a little longer than most Hunters would have. Henri had been kind and patient in my short time working with him.

Erik was his polar opposite. He was only a couple of years younger than Henri, but was much more immature. It had amazed me to learn they were such good friends; regularly hanging out in their free time. Erik was shorter – somewhere right in the middle of Henri's height and mine – and more muscular than Henri, but by no means bulky. His thick, dark hair naturally fell to one side, and was long enough that he used a bandana to keep it out of his face when we practiced. He had extraordinary turquoise eyes; peculiar eye colors were a byproduct of the same nuclear spill that had caused our Talents. My own unnatural purplish-blue eyes were a result of the same catastrophe.

Several more Hunters came over to welcome me and offer their congratulations. Graciously, I thanked them. Donavon grabbed my hand and led me away from the group after a short, squat boy with dark brown hair, whose name might have been Lenyx, had extended his felicitations.

"Thanks," I mentally sent him.

I wasn't exactly what you would call social. For most of my life, I've had only one friend: Donavon. My parents had hired private tutors for me since we had never stayed in one place long enough for me to go to school and I rarely had the opportunity to spend time with other children. Donavon was a social butterfly, but he knew that large groups of people make me uncomfortable.

"I figured you might want to get away."

"What makes you think I want to get away with you?" I teased him. He pulled me close, wrapping one arm around my waist, and lifted me off of my feet until our lips met. I wrapped my arms around his neck and kissed him back; I could never stay mad at him for very long.

"Told you that you wanted to get away with me," he whispered in my ear, setting me back on my bare feet. His breath tickled my ear, and I giggled in spite of myself.

He took my hand and led me behind the semi-circle of cabins, known at Headquarters as Hunters Village, and into the woods. We followed a short dirt path through the trees and into another small clearing. There was a small fire already blazing in the center of the clearing, and blankets and pillows were spread out next to it.

"It's been so long since we spent time alone together. I thought that since you don't have a curfew tonight, maybe we could sleep under the stars." His mental voice sounded tentative. I could tell he was afraid that I'd say no.

We hadn't spent much time together, just the two of us, in nearly a year. Since I was younger than Donavon, I still had to complete my time at school while he'd come to Headquarters. The time apart had been hard on both of us. I'd seen him on holidays, and the occasional weekend he'd been allowed to leave, and we'd talked daily, but it had been a huge change from seeing each other in classes and at every meal. One of the things I'd been looking forward to the most was being around him again.

I strode confidently towards the blankets and sat down. I patted a spot on the fabric next to me. Donavon gave me a huge smile and took a seat, folding his long legs underneath him.

"Donavon...," I mentally began, looking at my hands uncomfortably. I *did* want to spend the night with him out here, under the stars, but I also didn't want him to get the wrong idea.

He lifted my chin, forcing me to meet his clear blue eyes.

"I know, Tal. No pressure. I just want to spend time with you." His mental voice was soft.

"Thank you," I said out loud, giving him an appreciative half-grin. Donavon was only a year older than me, but that year seemed to make all the difference when it came to taking the next step in our relationship.

We both lay down with our heads on the pillows, facing each other. Donavon draped one arm over my small waist and extended the other one under my head. We stayed like that for the rest of the night. Nobody walking by would have been able to overhear our conversation, even though we talked until just before sunrise. Our entire exchange took place mentally. We rarely spoke "normally", not since that first summer when we met.

Donavon pulled me in closer, and I buried my face in his broad chest feeling comfortable, and relaxed for the first time since arriving at Elite Headquarters.

I drifted off to sleep as the sky turned from the dark of night to the pink of morning.

Chapter Two

The Great Contamination, as the history books called it, occurred a little over one hundred years ago. It started with natural disasters – earthquakes, tsunamis, hurricanes, and tornados. Those catastrophes destroyed small coastal fishing villages and devastated large industrial nations alike. The above-ground damage was extensive; entire towns were washed away. Millions, world-wide, lost everything, including their lives. Within weeks of the initial string of disasters, the world received another shocking blow. The nuclear reactors buried deep in the Earth's surface had begun to leak. Originally, the governments of the most powerful nations in the world banded together in an attempt to contain the waste. They called in world-renowned scientists, but nobody could figure out how to prevent the spread of the nuclear material.

In less than one year, all of the world's oceans were officially declared contaminated. The decimation of marine life was just the first step on the path to the destruction of the world's ecosystem. Governments all over the world issued massive health warnings; swimming in the world's oceans became prohibited, and the remaining sea life and land animals were deemed unsafe to eat.

As if the initial effects of the disasters were not bad enough, several years after the contamination the long-term ramifications became apparent. Any and all animals that survived the spill were rounded up and bred in an effort to rebuild the populations slowly. But the animals born in captivity weren't normal. Horses were born with horns, dogs with feathers instead of fur, fish with three eyes, and even two-headed pigs were reported.

Quickly, it became evident that the anomalies weren't specific to animal life. The change in animals was followed closely by changes in plant life. Leaves began to glow at night, and the bark on trees grew a fuzzy coating, stinging anything that touched it. Even insects began to exhibit changes in color, size, and the number of appendages.

However, the most drastic effects of the contamination weren't observed until the first post-contamination children were born. Most afflicted children were born with unnatural eyes, white-blonde hair ,or an extra finger or toe here and there. A large percentage were also born with a little something extra – something more serious.

As the first post-contamination-era children reached the age of five, parents started to notice that the kids were – in a word – weird. Some parents hid their children's abnormalities or, as they are now called, Talents. Other adults weren't able to hide the fact that their child changed into an animal at will. It soon became obvious that these Talents were as varied as they were prevalent.

Morphing is the most common Talent. Some children can morph into multiple animals – called polymorphs – while others were limited to only one or two creatures – mono or dimorphs. Telekinesis, telepathy, compulsion, higher reasoning, viewing, and visions were also among the first recorded Talents. Eventually light manipulators, electrical manipulators and mental manipulators were also discovered.

Of course, not all children were born with Talents. Many appeared and acted just as ordinary as their parents. Scientists studied both types of post-contamination-era children, desperately seeking answers as to why some were born "normal" while others were not. Experts experimented on the kids for years following the spill, but their efforts were to no avail. They were unable to isolate any single gene mutation that would account for the variation. Researchers were baffled. There was only one hypothesis that they all agreed on: the Talented were a direct result of the world's nuclear contamination.

Some Talents were revered while others were feared. Visionaries were among those prized. Everybody in the world wanted to believe a better life was on the horizon, and any child who claimed to see a brighter future was placed on a pedestal. On the other hand, telepaths and mental manipulators were among those feared; nobody liked the idea of children who could influence the minds of others.

The contamination levels remained extremely high for several decades after the initial breakdown of the nuclear reactors, so the first few generations of offspring were heavily saturated with Talented children. As time passed, the filtration systems became more advanced, and scientists developed chemicals to counteract the effects on the human body, resulting in fewer and fewer children born with a Talent. The rarest Talents petered out early on while the more common ones still remain over a century later.

Presently, less than a quarter of the population is born with a Talent. While there is no doubt that originally the Talents were a result of the nuclear contamination, today the cause is less certain. Some believe that children born with Talents now are the descendants of the first generation of children born in the post-contamination era. Others believe that some individuals always possessed abilities, even before the spill, and the genetic irregularities that cause Talents were just enhanced by the nuclear material. Still others believe that it's all chance, and being Talented is a fluke.

What do I believe? Some days, I feel as though I am cursed: cursed with an affliction that cannot be healed; cursed to explore the mundane minds of those surrounding me; cursed to know what people honestly think about me; cursed to be burdened with other people's darkest secrets. Other days, I believe that I won the genetic lottery because, after all, who wants to be ordinary?

Chapter Three

"It's rude to stare at people while they're sleeping," I slurred drowsily to Donavon as I dragged myself out of sleep. I still had my eyes closed, but could feel him watching me. I could also feel the warm sun on my face and knew it must be mid-morning. I smiled. I didn't usually have the luxury of sleeping much past sunrise.

"It's time to get up, sleepyhead," he teased.

"Shhh. Sleeping," I shot back, still grinning.

"I snagged some stuff for breakfast, and if you get up now, we can eat together before you need to head back for your afternoon practices," he tempted. He knew the fastest way to wake me up was promising me food.

"Ugh," I groaned loudly. Despite waking up with the birds for nearly half of my life, I was definitely not a morning person. I finally opened my eyes, and sure enough, Donavon's face was only inches from mine. His hair was cut short, so even after a night of sleeping outside, he looked fresh and unaffected. I had a feeling that I didn't look quite so good. My thoughts were confirmed when he reached out and gently detangled leaves and twigs from my wild dark curls.

The few female Hunters that I'd met wore their hair short so it was easy to conceal on missions. I'd briefly contemplated cutting my hair short, but when you're cursed with thick and curly hair, short is not a good look. Instead, I usually threaded my long brown curls into a braid that reached halfway down my back.

"How bad is it?" I cringed, not sure I wanted to know the truth.

"You look like an earth goddess," he joked. I pushed him hard, causing him to fall over on to his back, laughing.

"Feed me, please," I said, still groggy.

I sat up and blinked several times, trying to clear the last vestiges of sleep from my otherwise perfect vision. The late morning light streamed into our makeshift campground through the tops of the surrounding trees. Donavon must have gotten up during the night to stoke the fire because it was still burning strong. He reached into a cooler sitting on the far side of his black-and-red-checkered blanket and pulled out several containers. The first was a shiny, metal thermos that he warmed in the fire. The next contained bright red raspberries. The last plastic container held thick slices of a white, spicy cracked-pepper cheese. Finally, Donavon pulled out a loaf of bread with a crusty brown exterior and a soft white center. He used a Swiss Army knife to cut the bread, and used tongs to place it in the fire for just long enough to warm it. I watched, feeling extremely lazy as he poured the dark-brown liquid from the thermos into two ceramic cups he pulled from a black canvas bag, and handed one to me. I held it under my nose, inhaling the rich aroma, as the steam pouring off the top warmed my face. He handed me half of the loaf of bread. I took it gratefully and spread several slices of the cheese along the length of the baguette, chewing happily. I popped sweet, juicy berries in between mouthfuls of spicy, cheesy bread.

"*Good?*" Donavon asked, watching me with an amused smirk. I beamed in return trying to keep all the food in with my mouth closed.

"*It'll do,*" I replied in the most off-hand tone that I could manage mentally. I didn't want him to be too satisfied with the amazing and delicious breakfast he'd arranged. In truth, mornings like this with Donavon were what I lived for. Sitting here, alone with him, reminded me of when we were children, before life became so complicated.

After we had finished eating, we packed up our campsite, extinguished the fire, and walked the short distance back to Hunters Village and our respective cabins. We paused when we entered the cluster of small houses. Donavon leaned down and kissed me good bye.

"*Have a good day,*" he grinned.

"*You, too.*" I was still barefoot, so I walked carefully through the grassy area, still checkered with splashes of paint and neon dye from the night before.

I gently opened the door to the cabin I shared with Erik and Henri. Both were, thankfully, still in bed. I glanced longingly toward my empty bed, still a mess of sheets and pillows from the night before when I'd been so rudely awakened. Tiptoeing across the wooden floor towards the bathroom, I silently prayed that the ancient boards wouldn't creak. I had one hand on the doorknob to the bathroom when I heard a voice from behind me.

"Late night, Talia?" Erik's tousled black haired head was just visible over the top of his dark green blanket. His turquoise eyes were shining with amusement. The streaks of paint were still on his face.

"None of your business," I retorted, trying to hide my quickly-reddening cheeks.

"Actually, it is my business. We're a team. You, me, and Henri. Our lives depend on each other, so anything and everything that affects one of us affects all of us," he lectured me, with mock seriousness.

"You're still a Pledge, and I'm the leader of this team, so you have to do what I say; and I say you tell us where you were last night," Henri chimed in. Great, they were both awake. I glared at him.

"You both know exactly where I was," I squeaked. I sounded like a child getting caught doing something wrong, instead of an adult who had every right to spend the night with her boyfriend, which, of course, was what I had been going for.

"I wanna hear you say it," Erik taunted.

"Why?" I demanded.

"So we can see you blush," Erik laughed. Too late. The heat from my face was already spreading down my neck. Thank God the room was still somewhat dark.

I mentally shoved the bathroom door open and quickly stumbled through, willing it to close shut behind me. The door slammed hard enough to shake the wooden walls of the cabin. I heard Erik and Henri's laughter even after I turned on the shower water.

I took my time in the bathroom, not wanting to face Erik or Henri sooner than I had to. There weren't many girls who chose to become Hunters; most favored other divisions of the TOXIC Agency after graduating from *The McDonough School for the Talented*. I had always wondered why, and now I knew. Most girls were too smart to subject themselves to shared living quarters with teenage boys.

When the water finally ran cold, and I had succeeded in removing all the paint, and likely the top layer of my skin, I turned the silvery knobs to their respective off positions and carefully climbed out of the shower. I toweled myself dry and selected a set of standard issue workout clothes, stretchy black pants and a stretchy black tank top, from my designated bathroom drawers.

I used the towel to clear the layer of steam from the small oval mirror over the sink. I closely examined my reflection, searching for traces of the previous night. Mercifully, my mundane reflection was the only thing staring back at me. My damp curls looked black instead of brown from the water. My pupils were dilated so only a rim of purple was visible between the black center and the white sclera. My normally olive-toned skin was bright red, from the heat of the shower water and my vigorous scrubbing. I tapped my index finger on the pointy, slightly upturned end of my nose as if that would help to flatten it down a little. I rubbed at the smattering of tiny brown dots that covered the bridge of my nose and my cheekbones; they didn't go anywhere, assuring me they were all my own freckles and not lingering dirt. Finally, when I couldn't find any additional ways to prolong my bathroom time, I wrapped the towel around my hair and opened the door into the main room of the cabin.

"Took you long enough," Erik exclaimed impatiently. "You do realize that we all have to shower, right?"

"I thought you took your weekly shower three days ago," I shot back.

"I did, but I have a hot lunch date with one of the Brains, so I don't want to smell." Brain was a kind of slang term for a Higher-Reasoning Talent because their minds analyzed data faster than any computer. Erik wiggled his eyebrows at me, his trademark move, and then lifted his arm and sniffed.

"Charming," I rolled my eyes.

"Do I smell, Tals? Maybe I don't need to shower after all," he asked, walking toward me and putting his armpit in my face.

"Eww, Erik! Honestly, if the girls that line up to go out with you had to spend as much time with you as I do, they would definitely reconsider."

"No way. Every girl here considers *you* the luckiest girl alive." I looked over at Henri and gave him an "is-he-serious?" look. He just shook his head. Erik and Henri had been friends and teammates for two years; I guess he was used to Erik's bravado.

Erik finally went into the bathroom to take a shower himself, and I sat down on my unmade bed. I counted to ten, and then, as if on cue, Erik screamed my name followed by a long list of expletives; he'd discovered that I'd taken all the hot water. I smiled in satisfaction.

Chapter Four

In the decades following the Great Contamination, it became clear to the "powers that be" that the Talented were a new breed of children and posed many potential threats. The question of how to deal with these children was the most hotly debated topic at global summits. Fear of the unknown drove many nations to demand that the children be locked up "for their own safety," but imprisoning Talents was actually for the peace of mind of scared politicians. Some extremist nations even argued in favor of the eradication of any and all persons exhibiting paranormal abilities. In the end, no satisfactory global solution was reached; instead each country was left to handle the situation in a manner that best served their individual interests.

Margaret Anne McDonough was the seventy-fifth president of the United States of America and also grandmother to tow-headed, five-year old Daniel McDonough – an exceptionally strong mind manipulator. President McDonough believed children born with abilities needed to be nurtured, and taught to use their Talents. She converted a military facility located in western Maryland, previously a presidential bunker, into a training facility that soon became known as *The McDonough School for the Talented*.

The McDonough School for the Talented doesn't only play host to American children. Since many other countries aren't as forward thinking when it comes to Talents, the School welcomed all gifted kids from anywhere in the world. I, like many of the children there, wasn't born in the US; I was born in Capri, Italy. Even though my parents, Francis and Katerina Lyons, traveled a lot on account of my father's position with the government, I called Capri home until their deaths seven years ago.

At first, President McDonough merely offered families the option to send their Talented children to the school. Over time, it became apparent that some parents were reluctant to have their children attend a special school; they didn't want the stigma that many associated with having a Talented child. Instead, these parents chose to homeschool their children if they were unable to hide the abnormalities. If they could hide the abilities, these parents sent their kids to normal schools and pretended there was nothing "special" about them.

This ignited a chain reaction. Parents of "normal" children argued that it was unacceptable because their offspring were at a disadvantage when compared to "Talented" children. These parents claimed that the Talented kids had an unfair edge in every aspect of life, including sports and academics. They argued that the Talented children shouldn't be allowed to attend schools and play sports with the "normal" ones; it simply wasn't fair to those born unaffected by the nuclear contamination.

Parents of non-Talented children weren't the only adults calling for segregation of the Talented. Congress passed the *Mandatory Talent Testing Act* five years after the school's inception. This law required that, at the age of five, every child be tested for special abilities. Any child testing positive was brought to the School. As the first generation of these School-trained children turned eighteen and graduated, it became clear that all of the training and talent development was going to waste, and *Talented Organization of Exceptionally Interesting Citizens* (TOXIC) was born.

TOXIC is an agency within the government that utilizes each child's unique ability in the most advantageous way. Divisions within the TOXIC Agency were created around the most prevalent talents.

The Hunters are aptly named, because their main duty is to hunt both people and information. Morphing, Light Manipulation, and Telekinesis are the most common gifts among Hunters. If another division perceives a threat, a Hunting team is dispatched to neutralize it. When another division stumbles across valuable information, a Hunting team goes to retrieve it. Hunter is the modern term for an ancient profession: spy.

TOXIC's Crypto Division was created for Higher Reasoning Talents (Brains). The Brains spend all their time in front of computer screens, sifting through streams of encrypted communications, quickly decrypting the streams, and analyzing any hidden messages in their heads. They monitor every text, voice or holographic communication throughout the entire United States, and many abroad. Essentially, Brains are the eyes and ears of the Agency; they are the first line of defense against all threats, both foreign and domestic.

TOXIC's Tracking Division is staffed by Viewers – Talents able to remotely observe events taking place anywhere in the world. The more powerful Viewers are better able to control the Talent; they are able to focus their energy when given a picture or a piece of clothing, locate the individual, and give an accurate description of the surroundings. Unfortunately, strong Viewers are rare these days. The one or two Talents that test positive for viewing every year are usually too weak to be truly effective trackers. At best, they are able to track an individual they are physically close to or related to by blood.

The Planning Division is home to the Visionaries, or Talents that see the future. The difficulty with Visionaries is that most cannot control the timing of their visions. The average strength Visionary only has a vision every couple weeks, and it occurs at random. Most are unable to control the target of the vision, as well. The strongest, or Elite level, Visionaries are able to concentrate on one person and see flashes of their future on command. The insight of Visionaries often prevents attacks on our country.

The Interrogation Division is staffed by Talents with varying degrees of Telepathy and Mind Manipulation capabilities. Telepaths and Mind Manipulators use their abilities to question any individual thought to be a threat to the country's safety. Telepaths can easily tell if a person is lying, and manipulators can compel him to tell the truth. The Agency even lends out weaker telepaths and manipulators to local governments to interrogate criminal suspects. Mental Talents have led to swift justice and an expedited legal system. Many years ago the Supreme Court ruled there was no need for a trial in cases where the prosecution has a documented Telepath or Mind Manipulator interrogate the suspect.

There are also divisions within the Agency that are not gift specific. The Research and Development, and Medical sectors, are staffed by any Talent exhibiting a high enough academic aptitude in one of the sciences, biology, chemistry, or physics. Those demonstrating extraordinary physical strengths that aren't accepted into the Hunters, or don't want to be, join TOXIC's Military Division or guard TOXIC's various facilities such as weapons' plants, prisons, and the McDonough School. Some Talents stay on at the McDonough School and help the newbies develop their own abilities. Finally, there are the low-level Talents, some of whom end up in one of the agency's manufacturing plants, assembling anything from weapons to office chairs. The extremely unfortunate, low-level Talents become secretaries, cooks, or cleaning technicians.

I came to live, and attend McDonough after the death of my family. My decision to pledge the Hunters had brought me to my current home, Hunters' Village, at the Elite Headquarters, located approximately one hundred miles west of the nation's capital in scenic Brentwood Springs, West Virginia. If all went according to plan, I would officially graduate in one year, become a Hunter, and find the man responsible for the deaths of my parents. But for now, I would settle for learning to live with my new teammates without killing Erik or dying of embarrassment on account of his constant teasing.

Chapter Five

I wasn't hungry, but I accepted Henri's invitation to have lunch with him before our afternoon practice anyway. Henri was twenty-two and already a full-fledged Hunter after following the usual TOXIC protocol. He had started at the McDonough School, leaving his home in Somerset, Pennsylvania, when he was just five. At seventeen, he'd pledged the Hunters and come to live at the Elite Headquarters. At eighteen, after successfully completing his Pledge year, he'd officially graduated and become a member of TOXIC's most coveted division.

Henri and I chatted comfortably through lunch. In the two weeks since my arrival, we'd rarely spent any time alone, just the two of us. Normally during meals, he lectured me about the nuances of life in the Hunters. But today, he told me a little bit about his family back home in Pennsylvania. Neither of his parents are Talents themselves, and had been shocked, yet pleased to learn he was a poly-morph. His much younger sister, Melony was twelve and also a Talent – a Light Manipulator. He visited her at the School as often as he could get away since neither went home very often.

Most people didn't know about my past, so I let him do most of the talking. At school, I had kept a low profile; not truly displaying my full powers. Telepathy was not uncommon but advanced Mind Manipulation, as I was capable of, was extremely rare. Here, at Headquarters with Henri and Erik, they knew exactly what I was capable of but if it unnerved them, they didn't let it show. Henri had even said he'd requested me specifically because he'd heard rumors of my abilities.

After lunch, we met up with Erik at our designated practice area, Area Thirteen. Today, like every day since I'd been assigned to Henri's team, we worked on three-way mental communication. This skill was the entire reason Henri wanted me as part of his team. I was able to communicate mentally with each of them individually, but he'd thought I might be able to figure out a way for all three of us to hear each other at the same time.

Ordinarily I would've said three-way communication was not possible, but in this case I wasn't the only one in our group with an unusual Talent for a Hunter. Erik is what TOXIC calls a Mimic, meaning he can mimic the abilities of any other Talent he is physically close enough to. When all three of us are together, Erik is able to mimic my mental abilities, and Henri's morphing Talents at the same time. This allows me to communicate mentally with both Erik and Henri, and for Erik to communicate with both me and Henri mentally. The final step, the one we'd worked on every day for the past two weeks, was to establish the three-way link. So far, we weren't having a lot of luck. Henri was becoming frustrated with my lack of progress and Erik's constant threesome jokes, but he was doing a good job of hiding it on the surface. He was too polite to complain out loud and too professional to let his disappointment show. Still, I could feel his patience waning with each passing day.

In addition to the mental training, we also trained physically. I typically spent my afternoons at the firing range, practicing with both firearms and a bow and arrow, or learning to control throwing knives. Once a week, Erik taught me how to fence; I wasn't very good, a fact made more apparent by Erik's phenomenal skill, but Henri insisted it was vital that I train with every weapon available.

After our training that afternoon, we went back to the cabin to shower and change.

"You gracing us with your presence at dinner?" Erik asked as I sat on my bed, drying my hair after my shower.

"Not tonight," I replied, off handedly.

"We're way better company than the Director's son."

"Keep telling yourself that," I scowled. I was used to the way others acted towards Donavon. He wasn't only the son of the Director of the Agency but also shared a last name with the founder of the school. Margaret Ann McDonough was his great-great-great-great-great grandmother, give or take a couple of greats.

"Oh, Talia, come on now, I don't need to tell myself that – there are plenty of girls who tell me all the time," he winked at me.

"Erik," Henri warned, giving him a pointed look.

"What? You know it's true. The only reason people want to hang out with him is because he's the Director's son, and they think that'll somehow get them favors. Probably the only reason he got into the Hunters; he's not even that good."

"Erik. Stop," Henri said through clenched teeth.

"Is that how you feel about me, too? Is that why you wanted me as part of your team?" I rounded on him. I was seething. I might be used to the way people talked about Donavon, but that didn't mean I liked it. It wasn't his fault he was born Mac's son.

"What?" To his credit, he seemed slightly taken aback, like he genuinely didn't know what I was talking about. My anger lessened slightly.

"Mac raised me. I lived with his family until I came here," I said evenly. "Do you think I get special treatment? Do you think I only got here because of Mac? That he called in special favors to get me into the Hunters?"

"Oh, shit. Talia, I'm sorry. I didn't know," he apologized, but Henri was the only one left in the cabin to hear his words.

I was acutely sensitive, maybe overly so, when it came to my relationship with Mac, (those closest to him called him that), Director Danbury McDonough. The crappiest part of being able to read minds: knowing what people really thought about you. Erik's view wasn't the minority opinion; a lot of other students thought I'd only been accepted to pledge the Hunters because Mac had pulled strings to get me in. I wouldn't be surprised to find out a lot of TOXIC Operatives believed that, too. They complained to each other – if I were anyone else I would be working in some remedial Agency position, like food services or janitorial duty. It had been this way since I went to the McDonough School: the whispering when I walked past, the sneers when I answered a question correctly in class, the outright condemnation by all the girls my age when I started dating Donavon. It usually didn't bother me much; mostly the accusations just made me work harder, and I didn't make an effort to correct them.

The truth was that I worked extremely hard to get an invitation to pledge the Hunters. Mac had begun working with me when I first came to the School. Hunters are typically Morphers because their natural Talents give them extremely heightened senses, in addition to the ability to morph into a variety of animals, and in some rare cases, other humans. I will never be able to "learn" to morph since it's not a learned behavior, but fine-tuning my senses was something that could be taught. So I did. I also took extra combat and weapons lessons every day instead of making friends. I felt confident my abilities rivaled those of the best of my classmates when I went to try out for the Hunters. Captain Alvarez, the leader of the Hunters had thought so too; I'd taken the liberty of taking a peek into his head to make sure.

Chapter Six

After the Mandatory Testing Law took effect, several Rebel factions developed in response; they accumulated a strong following, mostly in the southwestern United States. The Rebels staged a small revolt, but the Agency quashed it before it had gone too far. In the end, the *Coalition of Rebel States*: California, Nevada, Utah, Arizona, Colorado, New Mexico and Texas, seceded from the rest of the country and elected their own president. Over the years, the Coalition has served as a safe haven for citizens who championed a country where Talents were suppressed, and hidden, where being Talented was something to be ashamed of. One of the primary objectives of TOXIC is to prevent the Coalition from gaining any more momentum. In fact, Mac's main goal as Director is to defeat the Coalition's leaders and reunite the country.

I was ten years old when my parents, Katerina and Francis Lyons, were killed in an attack by the rebels. My family moved around a lot when I was a child, on account of my father's job as a government scientist. We were visiting the States so that my father could attend an annual meeting with members of TOXIC at the time of the attack. My family always stayed in the same hotel in the same small town in Maryland, about twenty minutes away from the School's campus.

The men in black came in the dead of night. My father and his bodyguard tried to fight them off, but they were seriously outnumbered. My mother hid me in a closet and went to my father's aid, but she was no more a fighter than he was. I watched through the slats in the closet door, terrified as the men in black mercilessly killed my parents. I stuffed my small fist in my mouth, and bit down until I tasted blood, willing myself not to scream out loud. I wanted to close my eyes against the carnage. Instead, I sat frozen, with my eyes open so wide that they began to water, producing tears even before my brain could process what was going on.

My parents' deaths had been quick. One cold metal bullet to the side of my father's head was all it took to steal the life of the man whose lap I curled up in every night before bed so he could tell me a story; the man who brought me cold milk and warm cinnamon sugar cookies when I had nightmares; the man whose warm dark brown eyes and toothy smile lit up the room every time my mother walked in.

My poor mother never stood a chance. A man in black grabbed her from behind before she could even reach my father. A gaping wound appeared across her throat with one flick of his wrist. The man in black tossed her carelessly next to my father's crumpled form, as if she were trash.

I felt murderous. The feelings overwhelmed me, stirring in my stomach and rising like bile in my throat; consuming me. Then the horrible, high-pitched shrieking started; it filled my ears, suffocating all of the coherent thoughts in my brain.

I am still not sure if it was the cold, calculated murder of my father, or the careless disposal of my mother – probably both – but I felt something inside of me snap. One minute, I was hiding in the closet with the silk of my mother's long dresses pulled tight around my face, like curtains trying to block out the brutal scene in the bedroom. The next, I was sitting in the outer room of our hotel suite, surrounded by broken furniture, shattered glass, and the bodies of the men in black. They were all dead.

The heavy black clouds in the night sky matched the darkness I felt building inside me. The rain began to fall through the now-broken windows in fat drops; they came down slowly at first, but it wasn't long before the drops blended together, resembling streams of water falling from the sky. The rainwater was cold – a sharp contrast to the hot tears pouring from my eyes.

I don't know how long I sat there in the rain before a large, blonde man rushed through the open door to the hotel room. I recognized him from meetings with my father, but I couldn't remember his name. He was a large man, with broad shoulders, hair that was cut short, and a tanned lined face from spending time outside over the years.

The blonde man carried a large gun slung over one shoulder, and several smaller ones were tucked at his waist. An entire team of men clamored through the doorway after him. He held up one of his hands, indicating for the men to stay back. He approached me slowly, hesitantly. He was greater than an arm's distance away when he tentatively extended one of his large, gloved hands toward me; I had seen people do the same thing with wounded animals.

"Natalia?" he asked in a soft voice. I couldn't even find the energy to nod my head, I just stared blankly. "Natalia," he repeated, "my name is Danbury McDonough. Do you remember me? I'm friends with your Daddy." I rewarded him with another of my blank stares. "Natalia, are you hurt?" He took my silence as an indication that I was not.

He knelt down next to me and gently untangled my fingers from the folds of my dress. Without thinking, I threw my arms around his neck. He patted me awkwardly on the back, unsure how to react. I dug my small fingers into his shoulders, scared to let go. He carefully picked me up.

"You're freezing," he commented, hugging me close and trying to warm me with his own body heat. I started shaking, actually feeling the cold for the first time. He carried me through the crowd of men huddled in the hallway. The men spoke in low voices to one another as Mac carried me the length of the corridor, and down the stairs to a road car waiting in the parking lot.

"How many are dead?" One man whispered to the shorter man standing next to him.

"There have to be at least ten right there," another proffered.

"Did she do that?" the shorter man asked, in disbelief.

"Impossible, she's a child," a heavily accented voice interjected.

"Does she even have a weapon?"

I could feel Mac's body tense in response to the mutterings of the men.

He placed me in the back seat of the waiting vehicle. I curled into a ball as he covered me with dry blankets. My body and mind were numb, impervious to the rain and cold. He tucked the red and black fabric under my chin. I was vaguely aware that the material was itchy against my skin, but I didn't move it away.

I could hear the soft ping of the raindrops hitting the metal roof of the car, keeping perfect time with the tears leaking on to the soft leather seat and pooling underneath my cheek. I tried to concentrate on the noise instead of the slideshow of my parents' deaths playing on the inside of my eyelids. I was convinced that the images, now seared into my consciousness, would never fade. The feelings I'd had in the closet were now gone, leaving me empty and hollow and tired – so tired. I closed my swollen eyes and willed my own mind blank.

I spent one month at the Medical facility located on the grounds of the McDonough School for the Talented. Mac came to visit me every day. He would keep up a constant, one-sided conversation, never appearing bothered by my lack of response. Every day the medics would draw my blood, hook me up to machines, and talk about my vital signs. Sometimes they talked at me, and sometimes they simply talked around me.

One morning Mac came into my room and instead of sitting in his usual chair in the corner he crouched down next to the side of my bed. He made a point to lock my purple eyes with his own steely-gray ones.

"Natalia, I need to talk to you," he said, in the most serious tone he'd ever used with me, "and I need you to listen very carefully. The medics here say you are physically healthy, and that you can be released." When I did not comment, Mac plunged forward with what, I assumed, was a carefully thought-out speech. "You have two choices. I found an uncle – your father's brother, I think – in Italy, who said he is willing to have you live with him and his family." He hesitated before giving me my second option, but I didn't need to hear him say it; I read the one word, plain as day, out of his mind. Before he could open his mouth to formulate the words, I said my first word in an entire month: "Revenge".

During one of his daily visits Mac had explained to me TOXIC's theory of what happened the night my parents were murdered. They believed that the President of the Coalition, Ian Crane, had ordered the deaths of my family in retaliation for my father's scientific contributions to the study of Talents and what caused our abilities. Mac said our family wasn't the only one the Coalition had targeted, but it was the first time they had left a survivor.

That day I left Medical and went to live with Danbury "Mac" McDonough, his wife Gretchen, and their twelve year old son. I had no personal items, so I followed Mac, empty handed, up the long stone path to a sprawling ranch-style house. Before we reached the bright red front door, it opened and inside stood a tall woman with pretty blonde hair and big blue eyes. Standing next to her was a boy; he looked to be slightly older than I was, and already as tall as his mother. He had shaggy blonde hair and eyes like his mother. He smiled at me and, for the first time since my parents' death, I smiled back.

"Natalia, I would like you to meet my wife, Gretchen, and my son, Donavon," Mac said to me as he gestured to each in turn.

"Natalia," Gretchen greeted me warmly. "I had some clothes made for you, sweetheart. I hope you will like them." I knew I should say thank you, but I couldn't find my voice, so I simply nodded.

"Donavon, why don't you show Natalia to her new room and let her get settled? I am sure she needs to rest," Gretchen said to her son, still smiling down at me.

"'Kay, follow me." I looked up at Mac; he nodded encouragingly, so I followed Donavon. He didn't speak as we wound through the maze that was their house. Finally, we reached a set of double doors in the very back of the house. Donavon opened the doors and led me into a small living area with two overstuffed red couches and a small dark wooden table.

"This is your sitting room," he explained. "Through that door over there is your bedroom and bathroom. My mom hung clothes in the closet, and there are some books on the desk. My dad said you liked reading old books."

"Thank you," I croaked, in a voice that was hoarse from non-use.

"You need anything else?" he asked. I shook my head, and he turned to leave. He hesitated at the door. "Is it true you can manipulate people's minds?" he said it so fast I nearly misunderstood him.

"Who told you that?" I demanded.

"I heard my dad and one of his Hunters talking," he replied, sheepishly. "Dad says you can perform mind manipulation." I just stared, not sure how to react. My parents taught me *never* to talk about my unique abilities.

"So, is it true?" he pressed. After a long moment, I walked towards him. His eyes widened, but he didn't flinch as I reached out and took his hand. I fixed his wide eyes with my own.

"*Yes, it's true,*" I answered mentally. His eyes grew even wider, but he didn't release my hand.

"*Whoa, that's so cool,*" his mental voice replied. "*Can you make anybody hear what you are thinking?*"

"*Only if I want them to; I can make people hear or see anything.*" He smiled.

"*That's so cool,*" he repeated.

"*You're...Not scared of me?*"

"*I don't know how anyone could be scared of you.*"

I looked up into his shining blue eyes and smiled. For the first time in my life, I knew that I had a friend.

The first couple of days with the McDonough family were strange. Mac and Gretchen continually tried to engage me in conversation, but I wasn't ready to talk to them. Mac would come visit me in my sitting room, and talk about my soon-to-be new life at school. I had heard my father talk about the school when he thought I wasn't paying attention. I listened intently to every word Mac said, mentally filing every detail away for later.

While Mac's sole concern was making sure that I understood my new role as a student at school, Gretchen's sole concern was making sure that I never wore the same outfit twice. When I arrived, the closet was filled with elaborate dresses made of raw silk, soft animal hair sweaters in varying colors, and comfortable looking cotton pants. Every day more packages arrived with fabrics that Gretchen had ordered from New York City. She would send for one of the seamstresses from school, and the two of them would spend the day fussing over what new outfits I needed.

Each day, after lunch, Donavon would rescue me from his mother's fawning. I seldom spoke when I was with Mac or Gretchen, but with Donavon I rarely kept quiet. Donavon wanted to know all about the glamorous life I'd led, traveling around the world; he'd spent all his life living at either the School or Elite Headquarters. I hated having to tell him that I spent most of my life inside hotel rooms, and rarely got to see anything cool. Likewise, I wanted to know everything about his life at school with kids and friends. I had little interaction with kids my own age growing up, and even less interaction – none, actually – with Talented kids. In fact, before coming to live with the McDonough's, I didn't know that what I could do was considered a "Talent."

Donavon was what TOXIC termed a Poly-Morph. He was able to change himself into just about any animal. He told me Mac had been teaching him how to morph into other human forms, but he was not even close to achieving such a feat.

Some days, I would spend the afternoon watching Donavon show off, morphing from one animal to another while I giggled and clapped for him. Other days, he would work with me on my abilities. We would hide out in the woods behind his parents' house and see if I could reach his mind. We would widen the gap each day until we could communicate across the entire compound. Other days, we would wander down to the lake on the other side of the woods to play in the water.

Every night, alone in my room, I cried myself to sleep. I had succeeded in almost entirely blocking out the violence that had cost my parents their lives, but that didn't mean I missed them any less. I loved having a real friend in Donavon, and Mac and Gretchen were going out of their way to make me feel like part of the family, but they weren't my family. They would never be my family. I forced myself to repeat the name of the man who I'd learned ordered the death of my family, over and over: Ian Crane. Then, I would promise myself that one day, I would return the favor.

Chapter Seven

I was in a foul mood when I met Donavon in a small café for dinner. He was sitting at a table in the corner waiting for me when I walked in.

Living at Elite Headquarters had a lot of advantages; the biggest, in my opinion, was the abundance of food options. At school, the only place to eat was the cafeteria. They served three strictly regimented meals a day. The food wasn't bad, but lacked imagination and variety, since the school valued proper diet and nutrition above all else. Donavon and I had a unique advantage over the other students at school: Mac and Gretchen lived in a house on the school's grounds. We'd gone up there for dinner quite often.

But here? That was a whole different story. The Hunters weren't the only division of the Agency housed at Elite Headquarters, so it was more like a small town than a training compound. There were cafes and snack shops spread throughout the compound, boasting a variety of foods from around the world. We also had stores that sold everything from toothpaste – in case you didn't like the kind the housekeepers put in the bathrooms – to small electronics.

"Hey," I said, taking the empty seat across from him.

"Want to tell me about it?" he asked, immediately sensing my dark mood.

"No," I replied a little too forcefully, "I don't. Can we just eat?"

"Course." Donavon took a menu out of the holder in the center of the table, and began touching the screen to make selections for both of us. When he was done, he pushed the "Enter" button at the bottom of the screen and replaced the menu.

"Want to tell me how your practice session went?" he asked.

"I'd rather you tell me about your day. I don't feel much like talking." Just then, a woman showed up with two bottles of water. Donavon thanked her.

"I will gladly tell you about my day," he said, once she'd left. He launched in to the events of his day, embellishing a somewhat amusing story to make it hilariously funny. I smiled in spite of myself, not so much because the story was actually that funny, but because I thought it was so sweet of him to go out of his way to try and make me feel better. By the time our dinner arrived I was in a much better mood. Donavon always had that effect on me. I felt safe when I was with him.

"*Arden and Harris went into the city, and won't be back until curfew,*" Donavon said mentally after we had made an entire loop of the compound. Arden and Harris were Donavon's teammates and, therefore, also his cabin mates. If the food options were the greatest advantage of living at Elite Headquarters, then lack of privacy was the greatest disadvantage. At school, every student had his or her own room, making it easy to spend strongly, frowned-upon time with members of the opposite sex. I not only had my own dorm room, but I also had my own suite of rooms at Mac and Gretchen's house, and they didn't mind me and Donavon being alone together.

"*Lead the way,*" I answered.

By the time we got back to Donavon's cabin, we only had an hour until curfew. I took off my shoes and curled up on his bed. Donavon lay down next to me and covered us with a quilt that I recognized from his house; Gretchen had made it for him. I laid my head on his chest. He snaked one arm around my waist and slid his hand up under the back of my shirt, resting it on the small of my back. He lightly ran his fingertips back and forth, sending chills up my spine. I raised my head and stretched up until our lips met. I kissed him softly. He moved both of his hands to my waist and pulled me down on top of him. I kissed him harder. He lifted me up and flipped me over onto my back. I let out a small giggle of surprise. He leaned over me and bent his head, careful to keep his weight off me by holding himself in a push up position. I lifted my head up to meet him halfway. He pulled back, teasing me. I reached up and wrapped my arms around his neck, trying to pull him back down. He was strong, and instead of allowing himself to be pulled back down, he reared his head and shoulders back, lifting me slightly off the bed. I released him and fell on to my back. Thinking I was clever, I gave him a quick jab with the side of my hand in the crook of his right elbow. He wasn't expecting it, and his arm gave out. He fell on top of me, just as I had anticipated. I wrapped my legs around his waist at the same time that he tried to roll himself to one side, afraid that his weight would crush me. When he rolled, I'd already managed to entwine my limbs with his waist. Our combined weight – mingled with the fact we were tangled in his quilt – caused us to roll right off the bed.

I landed flat on my back; Donavon landed square on top of me. The initial jolt of hitting the wood floor jarred my bones. The shock in Donavon's eyes must have mirrored my own. Before either of us could say anything, I burst out laughing at the absurdity of the situation. I was laughing so hard that I didn't hear the door open.

"Oops!" Didn't mean to interrupt," Arden's voice called.

"You're not interrupting anything," Donavon grumbled, clearly annoyed.

"Hi, Talia," Harris waved. I peered around Donavon's considerably larger body and returned his wave. The slightly older boy was standing in the doorway, smirking. It wasn't the first time that Harris had walked in on me and Donavon in a somewhat compromising situation.

Harris had been a year ahead of Donavon at school, and the two had been good friends since childhood. He'd always been my favorite of Donavon's friends.

"Could you two wait outside for a minute?" Donavon asked, agitated.

"No, no, no. You don't need to do that," I said quickly. "I need to get back for curfew." Arden strolled awkwardly to his bed, trying not to look at us. Donavon untangled himself and carefully stood up. He reached his hand down to help me up. I quickly pulled my shirt back down to cover my stomach, and tried to smooth my dark curls in vain. I imagined my hair closely resembled a rat's nest.

Harris barely stifled the laughter escaping his throat. "Don't bother, Tal. It's a lost cause at this point."

Donavon grabbed my hand and practically dragged me out of the cabin. I gave both boys a wave as I passed.

"*Are you mad at me?*" I asked as soon as we were out the door. He stopped short, causing me to run into his back. I could feel the waves of tension rolling off of him.

"*It's not you. I just get frustrated at how little alone time we have together.*"

"*I know. Me, too. It'll get better,*" I promised, even though I knew that wasn't quite true. Usually, younger Hunters and Pledges lived in the cabins for years before being moved to the individual private suites in the apartments that housed the rest of the Operatives at Elite Headquarters.

He started walking again. My cabin was only a short way from his, so it didn't take us long to get there. He kissed me on the cheek before saying goodnight. He started walking away, but I grabbed his hand and pulled him back to me.

"*You aren't getting off that easy,*" I proclaimed. I wrapped my arms around his neck and kissed him. At first, he merely complied but soon he wrapped his arms around my waist and pulled me to him harder. I kissed him deeper. I heard catcalls. Donavon placed me back on my feet.

"*Goodnight, Talia.*" He turned and started walking away. "*I love you.*"

"*I know,*" I replied.

I looked around, seeking out the catcallers. I spotted them sitting outside of a cabin a couple down from mine. I gave them a rude hand gesture before walking into my own.

Neither Erik nor Henri was inside. Weird. It was so close to curfew. Sitting on my bed was a bouquet of flowers made up of vibrant blues, purples and pinks. Attached to the flowers' paper wrapping was a note with one word. "Sorry." They were from Erik. I rolled my eyes, and dropped the beautiful flowers on to my bedside table before climbing into bed. I was so tired that I didn't hear either of the boys come in shortly thereafter.

Chapter Eight

The morning sun streamed in through the window of the cabin, waking me early. I needed to remember to close the curtains before bed. I blinked several times, trying to clear the sleep from my eyes. I stretched, turning my head left, then right. When I looked right, I noticed that somebody had put my flowers in a glass vase with water on the table next to my bed. I smiled to myself. I was about to sit up when a pillow came sailing across the room, hitting me in the face. I groaned.

"Get up. We're all having breakfast together," Henri's voice sounded muffled from where I lay underneath the pillow. I sat up and looked around the room.

"Where's Erik?" I asked, noticing immediately that he wasn't in his bed.

"Shower. He was afraid he would be resigned to taking cold showers from now on if he didn't start beating you in there," Henri replied dryly. "Get up and get ready. We have a lot to do today."

I groaned again, grudgingly rolled myself out of bed, and got ready. The three of us headed to Henri's favorite café for a bread-heavy breakfast. Erik didn't mention our fight from the day before, so I didn't bring it up either.

Over breakfast, Henri outlined different strategies that he thought we should try and reinforced how important it was that we – and by "we" I knew he meant me – nail the three-way mental connection.

After breakfast, I worked tirelessly trying to connect all three of our minds while we ran through combat drills, pushing myself harder than I had been in the previous two weeks. A couple of times I was able to make the connection, but I was unable to hold on. By lunch, I was mentally exhausted; I wasn't sure if I could go another round in the afternoon. Thankfully, Henri had decided we would switch to the mental relaying of messages, which came easier, for our afternoon session. By the end of practice, I was nearly shaking from fatigue. The mental exertion combined with the extreme physical activity just about sent me over the edge.

At school, students were put through rigorous training schedules but nothing like what I'd experienced in my short time here.

"Let's go back and shower and then we can head to dinner," Henri announced after I had tripped over my own feet for what seemed like the hundredth time that afternoon. I nodded gratefully; the only thing I wanted to do was lay down in my bed. I trailed several paces behind the boys on the way back to the cabin and followed Henri's orders.

The boys, thankfully, let me shower first. My shaky legs didn't allow me to stay in the hot spray for as long as I would have liked. Lifting my arms over my head to wash my hair seemed like too much work; instead, I just stood under the water until I was at least somewhat confident that the water had washed out most of the sweat and grime. I dressed in the most comfortable cotton pants and sweater I could find in my bathroom cubby, wound my dark, wet curls into a tight bun, getting ready in record time. I stumbled out of the bathroom, and curled up on top of my bed to wait for the boys to shower and dress.

"Let her sleep."

"The more time we spend together, the faster she will be able to form the connection, and the easier it will be for her to hold," Henri responded, a note of desperation underlying his otherwise calm voice.

"She's exhausted, Henri. You have no idea how tiring using that kind of mental energy can be." Erik said in a firm, low voice.

"She needs to get this. I need her to get this." Henri urged, the desperation in his voice becoming thicker.

"I understand that, but you cannot push her so hard so fast – she'll break under the pressure," Erik replied.

I was shocked that Erik was the voice of caution. I wanted to interrupt them - after all, they were talking about me - but I couldn't muster the energy to speak.

"Let her sleep now," Erik's tone was final. "She's getting stronger by the day. I don't think you should push her."

Henri took a deep breath. "You're right. I'm getting ahead of myself."

"Besides, now we can go into the city for dinner." Ah, that was the Erik I knew. I envisioned Henri rolling his eyes.

Somebody, Erik by the feel of it took the quilt from the end of my bed and covered me gently. I murmured something that I meant to be thanks, but sounded more like grunts and moans. I fell back to sleep before they made it out the door.

The next time I woke up, I felt strong arms encircle my waist, and smelled the familiar sandalwood scent of the soaps Gretchen ordered from somewhere out West. I snuggled closer.

"What're you doing here?" My mental voice was sleepy and a little slurred.

"I saw Erik and Henri on their way to dinner. Erik said you weren't feeling well, so I figured I would come check on you."

"I'm okay. Just really tired. Long day."

"Go back to sleep." Donovan said, smoothing the wet pieces of hair that had escaped my bun back from my face.

"Are you going to stay?"

"For a little while."

"Good." I knew this wasn't really Donavon's idea of quality alone time, but also knew that I would sleep better if he were there. Donavon's arms tightened around me, and he nuzzled his face in my neck. I fell back asleep, smiling.

Donavon coming into my cabin brought back the memory of the first night he ever snuck into my room to sleep with me.

On the eve of my first day as a student, my nerves had refused to let me sleep. I tossed and turned in my too-big bed, hoping that all of the movement would wear me out. It was well past the time where one day ends and the next begins, when I opened my mind and reached out to Donavon. We had worked all summer seeing how far I could stretch my mental reach; the distance between our bedrooms was nothing compared to what I'd achieved.

"Are you awake?" I asked.

"Yup. Are you having trouble sleeping, too?"

"I'm nervous about tomorrow," I admitted.

"Hold on."

Not even a minute later, I heard Donavon's light footsteps in my sitting room. I mentally unlocked the door to my bedroom, prodding it open just a crack for him. He silently pushed it the rest of the way and crept towards my bed, barely making any noise.

The bed springs depressed under his weight as he stretched out on the empty half.

"*Why are you so nervous?*" he asked.

"*I've never been to school before.*"

"*This isn't like a normal school. Everybody there is like you. You'll be fine.*"

"*Mac said nobody would be like me,*" I said accusingly.

"*Well, not exactly like you, no,*" he amended. "*Nobody that does Mind Manipulation. But there will be other kids that can move stuff with their minds, like you, and even one or two that can read minds, probably.*"

"*Really?*" I dared to hope that I was finally going to be normal.

"*Really.*"

"*I won't know anybody.*"

"*You know me, and I know everybody. My friends will be your friends.*"

I grinned in the dark. I couldn't make out his features from where I lay, yet I knew that he could make out mine. He reached out and took one of my hands in his.

"*Open your mind and close your eyes.*"

"*Why?*" I asked, suspiciously.

"*Don't you trust me?*" He sounded a little wounded.

"*Of course, I trust you,*" I answered quickly, afraid that I'd hurt his feelings.

"*Okay, then open your mind and close your eyes.*"

Hesitantly, I closed my eyes – I knew that he would be able to tell if I didn't – and removed the remaining barriers to my mind. He began mentally humming an old bedtime song – one my mother used to sing to me. I didn't know the words, but the melody was soft and comforting; before I knew it, I drifted off into a peaceful sleep.

Chapter Nine

The days quickly began to run together, one day morphing into the next, until I lost all concept of time and days of the week. Each day was the same as the one before. Henri had been right; the more time I spent with them, the easier it was for me to create and hold the three-way mental connection. However, the mental bond didn't come without a price. I was directing so much energy to my mental abilities that my balance and coordination were off, and my other senses suffered. At the end of each day, I swore that every inch of my body hurt, even my eyelashes. But thankfully, I was so exhausted that I fell instantly asleep every night.

"I'm sure you've been wondering why I'm pushing you so hard so fast," Henri said, one morning over a breakfast of fatty strips of bacon and goopy eggs. "It hasn't been for nothing." He paused for dramatic effect.

"Well, don't keep us in suspense," Erik said sarcastically. He clearly knew where this was going.

Henri gave him a pointed look. "Captain Alvarez and Director McDonough have been so impressed with the progress that Talia is making that they have given us our first Hunting assignment."

My eyes grew wide with shock that quickly turned to excitement. As a Pledge, I would be participating in several Hunts prior to my actual graduation from School; I hadn't imagined that it would happen so soon. I knew from Donavon that none of the other Pledges had been assigned a mission yet.

"Tell me all about it," I squealed, not bothering to hide my enthusiasm.

"I don't have the specifics yet, but it's a pretty simple assignment. There is some information TOXIC wants, and we need to retrieve it – preferably undetected. I should know more in a couple of days."

"How does it all work?" I pressed. Donavon had been telling me about Hunting missions since the day I went to live with the McDonough's, but I was so eager that I wanted Henri to tell me all over again.

"The Brains will give us information on the location and the people associated with it. Then, we'll stake out the location for a couple of days. We'll make sure that all of the information we have is accurate and see what else we can learn. After that, we go in and get what we came for."

"Sounds pretty simple," I observed.

"Should be. These assignments are usually given to teams with Pledges. But that doesn't mean that there aren't risks, so keep your excitement in check and take this seriously," Henri warned.

I put everything I had in to training that day. I pushed my mental and physical limits to just-short of their breaking points. My excitement was fueling my adrenaline, and I barely felt fatigued at the end of practice.

After we had finished for the day, I ran straight to Donavon's cabin. Our schedules were so strenuous that I'd barely seen him in the past couple of weeks, and I wanted to tell him that I'd gotten my first assignment. I knocked on his door, impatiently tapping my foot.

Harris answered. "Hey, Tal, come on in," he greeted me, holding the door open. "I was just heading to dinner so I'll leave you two alone." I waved dismissively at Harris as I locked eyes with Donavon. He was sitting on his bed, so I skipped over and gave him a big hug.

"You're in a great mood," he remarked.

"I got my first assignment!"

"Congrats." He sounded tired, and not nearly as enthusiastic as I'd hoped.

"I know I shouldn't be so excited, but this is my first step toward really doing something, you know?" I tried to backpedal, embarrassed by my elation.

"We should celebrate," Donavon answered, trying to match my mood.

"What do you have in mind?"

"How about tonight we go for a picnic dinner down by the lake? Then, tomorrow I'll take you into D.C.?"

I frowned. *"I'm not allowed to go into the city, remember?"*

"I bet if you call Dad, he'll authorize it. We'll worry about it tomorrow, though. Tonight, I just want to be alone with you."

I beamed. I wanted to be alone with him, too. Erik's words about special favors from Mac ran through my head, and I knew I couldn't ask for permission to go to Washington; Mac *would* authorize it if I asked, and I didn't want to give anyone more ammunition against me. I would worry about that tomorrow.

"Let's go," I leaned down and kissed him.

We got hot turkey-gravy sandwiches, cranberry juice, and thick pieces of carrot cake (my favorite) at one of the cafes, and took the dinner and blankets to the lake. The lake here was much smaller than the lake at school, but it was still my favorite place at Elite Headquarters. We ate our sandwiches in comfortable silence, and I somehow managed *not* to spill any of the gravy on my shirt. The sun was going down on the other side of the lake; it was just at the height where it appeared to be sitting half in the water and half out of it. The temperature was perfect, and I felt comfortable in a short-sleeved shirt and light-weight pants. In short, everything about the night seemed perfect.

"Fancy a swim?" Donavon asked after we ate, twirling one of my curls around his finger.

"I don't have a suit," I replied absently.

"You don't need one."

I snapped my head towards him and narrowed my eyes, understanding that by "swim" he actually meant "let's get naked".

"You first," I dared him with a confidence that I didn't feel.

Donavon stood and stripped down to his underwear without hesitation. I tried to wiggle my eyebrows suggestively at him, as I'd seen other girls do when they were flirting with guys, but I felt more like my face was in spasms. It was a warm night, but not warm enough to be standing around practically naked; I could see the gooseflesh springing up across his exposed skin. I suddenly felt very nervous.

"Come on, Tal, your turn."

I hesitated. Donavon had seen me in my bathing suit on numerous occasions, but he'd never actually *seen* me in my underwear. The mental and emotional connections that we shared were more intense than I imagined most people ever experienced in their lives, but our physical relationship was somewhat less evolved. I thought I wanted more, yet something always held me back. I knew that Donavon wanted more. Until recently, he'd made every effort to keep his real thoughts from me. Lately, though, his teenage-boy hormones were overriding his regard for my feelings.

Slowly, I stood and lifted my arms over my head. Donavon gripped the bottom of my shirt in his hands and took his time as he lifted it over my head. I had to remind myself to breathe normally, but my nervousness wouldn't let me. I reached for the drawstring on my pants, but my hands were numb, and I couldn't get the tie undone. Donavon gently pulled my fingers away. He knelt down in front of me and kissed the space just below my bellybutton. I hugged my arms across my chest in an attempt to keep from shaking. I held my breath as he untied the string, and the pants fell in a pool around my feet.

Donavon held his hand out. I uncrossed my arms and took it, stepping out of the black fabric puddled around my ankles. I was trembling from head to toe. I was scared to meet his eyes.

"It's just me, Tal. You don't need to be nervous."

"I know."

"Look at me, Tal." He was still on his knees, so for once, I looked down at him instead of up. He wrapped his hands around my waist; his fingers felt warm against my bare skin. His light blue eyes had clouded over, and become heavy with longing. He looked me up and down, making me more self-conscious.

"So, I kinda assume we aren't actually swimming?" I tried to joke, attempting to mask my unease.

"No, no swimming," his mental voice was husky.

In one motion, he swept me off my feet, and up into his arms. A nervous giggle escaped my lips. He laid me down on the blanket and leaned over me. He covered us both with the quilt he'd taken from his bed. Donavon propped himself up on one elbow, and bent over to plant his lips firmly on mine. I wrapped my arms around his neck, trying to match the intensity of his kiss. He ran the fingertips of his free hand lightly down my side, and the sensation made me shiver. His finger toyed with the edge of my boring cotton underwear; I immediately shrank away from his touch.

Donavon pulled back. His eyes found mine. *"You still aren't sure about this, are you?"*

"I don't know, Donavon." I tried to look away. *"I just don't think I'm ready."*

"It's okay, Tal. I don't want you to do anything you aren't ready for." He may have said it was okay, but I could tell that he didn't mean it. I could hear, and feel, the frustration dripping from each word. We'd been having this conversation a lot lately.

"I'm so sorry, Donavon." I meant it. I *was* sorry. Sorry that we had to keep repeating this same conversation.

"Stop," his mental voice demanded. "*Stop apologizing. It just makes me feel bad. Just give me a minute."* He rolled over on to his back and took several deep breaths. I waited – my whole body tense, for him to say something, anything. Finally, he turned his head back to the side and met my eyes.

"Come here." I crawled into his open arms. We lay like that for hours. He let his hands roam every once in a while – testing the waters, I think. He ran his fingertips along my spine, down my arm, through my hair, across my cheek. While I could still feel his longing bubbling under the surface, I knew that he had no intention of trying anything else tonight. He didn't want to face rejection twice in one evening. I liked being close to him, so I didn't resist.

I don't know what kept holding me back – I loved Donavon. I mean, I think I loved Donavon. From the first time I saw him, I had felt drawn to him. He was more than my boyfriend; he was my best friend; granted, he was my only friend, but still, I knew that I wanted to be with him, and only him.

It must've been a mixture of anticipation earlier, coupled with all the craziness from the past couple weeks that set my nerves on edge, I reasoned with myself. *Next time, I would be ready, or maybe the time after that.*

"*I think we should head back,*" he said after we had been laying there until well after curfew.

"*Do we have to? If Henri is going to be mad at me, he probably already is. So I might as well just stay out. Unless you're tired of me?*" I teased him.

"*I never get tired of you,*" he sounded sincere.

"*Good,*" I smiled, not realizing until just then how worried I'd been about that.

"*But I really should get you back. Henri might be a little upset about you missing curfew, but he'll be furious if you don't come home at all,*" Donavon reasoned, getting to his feet and pulling his rumbled clothes back on. Reluctantly I followed suit.

"*Tal?*" he called hesitantly.

"*Yeah?*"

"*I really do love you. I hope you know that.*"

"*I do.*"

Donavon walked me back to my cabin and kissed me goodbye at the door. I eased the door open as slowly and quietly as I could manage. I slipped off my leather flip flops at the entrance and crept across the wooden floor boards on my toes. I lowered myself into bed, willing the springs not to squeak. I let out a sigh as my head made contact with the pillow. I was sure that Henri would ream me in the morning, but at least I could go to sleep in peace.

"Natalia?" Henri's voice cut through the silence. *Crap.*

"Yes?" I replied, tentatively.

"This is your one pass. Don't miss curfew again." He was trying to sound stern, but I could tell from his mind that he wasn't really mad.

"Thank you," I said quietly, trying to sound humble. "Henri?"

"Yeah, Tal?"

"I'm sorry." I seemed to be saying that a lot tonight.

"I know."

Chapter Ten

"Get up. Get up. Get up," Erik sang the next morning.

"Go away, go away, go away," I groaned, covering my head with a pillow.

"Go away?" he scoffed. "We have a big day ahead of us, and the sooner you get up, the sooner we can get it started."

"It's my day off," I whined.

"We have a surprise for you," he tempted.

"I don't like surprises," I countered.

"It wouldn't be a surprise if you had made curfew last night," Henri cut in dryly. Guilt washed over me. I groaned again, and threw the pillow in the direction that I judged Erik's voice to be coming from.

"Nice. All that sensory deprivation training really paid off," Erik commended me as the pillow hit him with a soft thud.

"Thanks. Now tell me my surprise," I said, sitting up.

"You're so demanding in the morning," Erik teased.

"We're taking you to D.C. for the day," Henri announced.

"I'm not allowed to go to the city. Remember, I'm just a lowly Pledge," I tried not to sound too disappointed.

"I already cleared it with Captain Alvarez, who in turn called the Director, who, of course, said you could go," Henri replied dismissively.

I expected Erik to make a snide remark, but for once he kept his mouth shut.

"Wow. Thanks, Henri." Now I felt even worse about missing curfew the night before.

"You can only come for the day," he warned. "The Director wouldn't budge on letting you stay down there after dark."

"That's okay, I'm just so excited to get to go at all!" I exclaimed, jumping out of my bed.

"Then get ready already so we can leave," Erik urged. I squealed happily and skipped to the bathroom.

I absentmindedly hurried through my morning routine and opened up my mind to find Donavon. I could tell he was awake and in his cabin.

"Hey, guess what?" I sent.

"What?" his mental voice sounded sleepy, so I guessed he'd just woken up.

"Henri cleared it with your Dad; I get to go to the city today!"

"With Henri and Erik?" he didn't sound happy.

"Well, yeah. I guess, so we can spend bonding time, or whatever," I tried to sound offhand, but I was really excited and I didn't want him ruining my mood.

"Oh, well, have fun, I guess," he said, obviously irritated.

"I know you were hoping we could go together, but Henri went through the trouble of going to the Captain and calling your Dad and stuff," I started to apologize.

"No, it's fine. I'll take you another time," he cut me off.

"I'll come find you when I get back," I promised.

"Yeah, whatever." I closed my mind again. He was killing my happy buzz.

Elite Headquarters is located in West Virginia, about a hundred miles west of the nation's capital. The actual compound sat on several hundred acres of what used-to-be farm land, but now boasted the latest and greatest technology that the world had to offer. The compound's stores sell anything a Pledge or Operative needs. In Washington, D.C., you could buy anything imaginable, and probably many things that I couldn't imagine. Erik, like many of the other Operatives, frequented the city bars to pick up girls, but Pledges weren't usually allowed to visit the city, even on our days off. I guess the idea was that Pledges stationed at various other locations weren't able to be afforded the same luxuries, so it wasn't fair.

As a child, my parents and I had traveled constantly, never staying in one location for more than a couple of months. Since coming to live with Mac and his family, my travels had been limited. My relocation trip to Elite Headquarters was the first time I'd left the School's grounds since arriving seven years before. The notion that a real city existed, only a hover ride away, had been driving me crazy.

Donavon had completed his pledge year and graduated from school the year before; since becoming a full-fledged Hunter, he had been taking full advantage of his newfound freedom. Sometimes, he brought me flaky pastries filled with chocolate or strawberry cream from the bakeries. Other times, he brought back lengths of embroidered silks to take home to Gretchen, so she could have outfits made for me. When he was feeling lazy, he just bought trinkets from the street vendors.

Henri had reserved a hover car for the day that he used to drive the three of us the hundred miles into Washington. I kept my face glued to the cold glass, watching as the dense woods surrounding Headquarters gave way to small farms and spread-out houses. We were still twenty miles outside of the actual city when the buildings became more dense and elaborate. The roadways beneath us were packed with bumper-to-bumper road vehicles. From our vantage point in the air, I suddenly saw the city materialize beneath us. I stared down in wonder.

When we reached the outskirts of D.C., we flew straight through the border check point without stopping. Ordinarily, all vehicles – both road and hover – needed to stop, and the occupants were required to show identification. But, since we were in a clearly marked Agency car, we were able to sail through without pausing.

I was overwhelmed the moment we landed. The buildings were tall and packed so close together, there was no space to walk in between – the height restrictions for the structures long forgotten. Most of the buildings were made of diffractive glass that changed color depending on where I stood. The architectural style varied from one building to the next, with no two looking exactly alike. I saw some buildings that were short and square, some tall and thin, and several topped with elaborate sphere-like structures. I even saw one hexagon shaped building that had what appeared to be, a moving walkway that snaked around the periphery, taking people all the way from street level to the pinnacle. A sky railway arched high above the busy ground walkways, connecting one building to the next.

The sky was dotted with small hover cars – this must be their primary mode of transportation, although the streets inside D.C. were just as packed with road mobiles as the beltways surrounding the city. The population must be so great the occupants needed both to get around in a timely fashion.

The men and women walking the streets were dressed in beautiful, albeit colorful outfits. Many of the younger had brightly colored hair that was dyed to match their clothing. I noticed a large number of people with unnatural eye colors like Erik's and mine. It wasn't rare to have untraditional eye colors and, actually, it was so not rare that I was unsure why people still referred to my eye color as unnatural. Donavon had told me it was common for city kids to have their eye pigment altered, or in less extreme cases, wear colored lenses in their eyes.

The older women in Washington's shopping district wore vibrant silk dresses and intricately carved wooden high heeled shoes. Many wore ropes of colored, glass stones around their necks, and varying sizes of adornments in their ears. Some of the wealthier women had glass beads braided into exquisite up-dos or bird feathers crowning their heads.

Working-class men and women pushed their way through the crowded sidewalks, wearing cheaply made business attire in varying shades of gray and navy. They ducked into sandwich shops and greasy fast food joints, trying to find the most expedient place to get food on their too short lunch breaks. All of the women wore makeup. The older women seemed to favor simple shades that accentuated their natural features. Younger women, and even some teenagers, sported makeup so thick that their faces looked more like painted masks, designed to look like a caricature of the wearer underneath.

I felt extremely plain and naked in my boring cotton navy dress, thong sandals, and makeup-free face. At least I had my weird purplish-blue eyes and long spiral curls going for me. I did have more elaborate clothes in my closet at headquarters, but I usually shied away from wearing them since none of the other Pledges or Operatives ever wore anything exciting.

"What do you think, Tals?" Erik interrupted my gazing.

"It's beautiful," I replied honestly.

"Far cry from school, huh?"

"Sure is," I agreed softly.

The boys promised me a tour of their favorite places on the ride over, and I'd been worried that meant I would be spending the day becoming acquainted with the city's drinking establishments. My fears were put to rest when our first stop was a candy store. Erik showed me how to use the computer to design my own taffy flavors, and then we watched as large metal claws pulled and stretched long pieces of taffy, mixing and melding, to create my custom candies.

After the candy store, our next stop was the Air, Space, and Technology Museum. There was a tour starting just as we passed through the entrance scanners; I figured we'd join the group. Instead, we walked straight past the throng of people towards the first exhibit. It turned out that Henri was a frequent enough museum patron that he gave the tour better than any guide could.

For the rest of the morning, I followed the boys in and out of game shops, techie boutiques, clothing stores and several establishments that sold questionably legal merchandise. I tried to take it all in, but I was on sensory overload by midmorning.

After a full morning of shopping, we stopped for lunch at a restaurant that claimed to have "The Best Apple Pie in the District." There were so many cakes and pies on the menu that I considered just ordering dessert for lunch; then decided against spending the afternoon with a stomachache. I'd never heard of many of the dishes on the menu, so I settled on a cold octopus soup with spinach bread. Both the Academy and Headquarters rarely served any seafood, and I didn't want to waste the opportunity.

"What else do you want to see before you need to go back?" Henri asked as we finished lunch.

"Can we see the ocean?" I asked hopefully. I knew the city was not actually built on the ocean – it was about another hundred miles or so east – yet I hoped that since we had the hover mobile it wouldn't be a problem. In a road mobile the trip would take hours, but in a hover mobile we could get there in just a half an hour.

"I guess we could do that," Henri answered with a shrug. "Erik? Any complaints?"

"Have at it. You can take her to the ocean if you want. I think this might be where we part ways," Erik answered.

"Do you have something better to do?" I demanded, for some reason offended that he wanted to run off so soon.

"Actually, I do."

I scowled at him. "Fine. Be that way." I turned to Henri, "You don't mind, do you?"

"No, not at all. Erik, I'll meet up with you later tonight?"

Erik nodded before heading out the door of the restaurant.

Henri led me back to the towering, above-ground parking garage where we'd left the hover mobile, and we set off for the short trip to the beach. Even though it had been over a hundred years since the nuclear reactors had leaked nuclear waste contaminating the planet's oceans, very few people risked swimming. Instead, most people favored lakes and ponds – fresh bodies of water that didn't connect to the ocean. As a result, the Eastern Shore beaches were relatively empty, and we were able to land the hover mobile right in the sand. I impatiently waited for Henri to pop the glass covering; once he did, I kicked off my shoes, and jumped over the side of the car, landing deftly on the balls of my feet in the soft sand.

I inhaled deeply and closed my eyes. The smell of salt water and seaweed filled my nostrils. I inhaled a little deeper and concentrated my mental energy towards expanding my sense of smell. I could pick up traces of fish and kelp, mixed with oil from the fishing boats. I found it weird that people would eat the ocean life, but refused to swim in the water. I exhaled happily.

The breeze coming off the water was cool, but the sand was warm from the afternoon sun. I dropped to my knees and picked up handful after handful of sand, letting it trickle through my splayed fingers. As long as I kept my eyes closed, I could pretend that I was a little girl on the rocky beach of Capri.

When I was very young, before we started moving around all of the time, my family lived in a stone house built into the bluffs overlooking the Tyrrhenian Sea. My mother would take me down to the beach at the base of the bluffs and let me play in the pinkish-orange sand. I would collect bottles of the sand and take it back to the house, where I would painstakingly sort out the pink and orange grains under a magnifying lens. My mother knew that the colored sand was a by-product of the ocean contamination, but she never ruined my fantasy by letting me in on the secret.

The sand on the beach at the Eastern Shore was not pink or orange but rather a dark brownish black. The water here was a dark, muddy brown, a stark contrast to the clear, sparkling water of the Tyrrhenian Sea. I kept my eyes closed, and walked towards the sound of the waves lapping the shore. I heard Henri calling my name over the breaking of the waves, warning me not to get in the water. I ignored his counsel, and walked until I could feel the water swirling around my ankles. I stood, inhaling the salty spray until my feet had sunk so deeply in to the wet sand that Henri had to help me out.

As the sun began to sink lower behind us, I knew my time at the beach had to come to an end. Mac had said I needed to be back by dark, and I didn't want Henri getting in trouble on my account.

Henri and I rode back to Headquarters in silence.

"Thanks for today," I said sincerely, when we pulled into the parking bay of Elite Headquarters.

"You deserve it, you've been working so hard."

"I still appreciate it. It was nice of you to go to the trouble of getting permission from the Captain and all to let me go," I didn't want him to think I expected special treatment because of Mac or Donavon or whoever else.

"It wasn't a big deal; after all, being practically related to the Director does have its perks," he winked at me to let me know he was, at least partially, joking.

I smiled. "I'll see you later."

I jumped out and watched as he took off back to the city to join Erik for the evening.

Chapter Eleven

I didn't go back to my own cabin; instead, I went directly to Donavon's. I raised my hand to knock, just as the door opened.

"Hey, you," Donavon smiled as he leaned down to kiss me softly. "You smell like the ocean." He buried his face in my mass of dark brown curls and inhaled deeply.

"Henri took me out to the beach after we roamed around Washington," I smiled.

"You okay?" Donavon had seen my sand collection; it was one of the few things Mac had managed to rescue from the hotel room where he found me.

"Yeah, I'm good," I replied honestly. "You look nice," I commented as I pulled back from his embrace, really looking at him for the first time.

"You think? Would you come home with me if you met me at a bar?" he teased.

"Absolutely. But if you stay here, you don't even have to spend money for me to go home with you," I teased.

"Tomorrow, I'm all yours. Tonight, I promised Harris and Arden a little team bonding."

"I see." Now it was my turn to be irritated.

"Are you mad?"

"No, of course not," I lied.

"You're lying," he accused.

"I'm not mad. I just don't like that I have to stay here while you get to go have fun," I tried to smile.

"You hate going out with groups of people, anyway," he reasoned.

"But I like being with you," my voice was just short of a whine.

"And I love being with you," he said softly. "And all day tomorrow that's what I plan to do, okay?"

"Okay," I whispered.

"Don't worry, Tal, I'll make sure he behaves," Harris said sticking his sandy blonde head out through the door.

"I'm not worried, Harris," I said, pulling myself together.

"Good, 'cause we have to go. Come on, Donavon, kiss her goodbye so we can leave."

"Start walking, Harris. I'll catch up."

Harris squeezed my arm as he walked by and I gave him a nod goodbye.

"*I love you.*" Donavon said as he bent down to kiss me again.

"*I know.*"

I headed back to my cabin in a far worse mood than when I'd left that morning. The bottom of my dress was still damp from the ocean, so the first thing I needed to do was change. With Donavon gone, I didn't really have any friends around, so there wouldn't be any messages on my communicator. Our communicators were actually portable, but I never took mine anywhere, since no one besides Donavon and Mac ever called me. Unlike my dorm room at school, that was equipped with all of the latest technology

TOXIC had to offer, the cabins at Elite Headquarters were barebones. The idea was that, as Hunters, we spent a lot of time in less-than-ideal situations, and we needed to be accustomed to boredom.

As I crossed Hunters Village, I noticed a tall, gangly girl with unnaturally bright red hair coming out of the woods. Her eyes were large and bright green, and the oversized yellow plastic glasses that she wore seemed to magnify her eyes giving her a bug-eyed appearance. The Agency performs corrective eye surgery on all students, so I knew the glasses were purely decorative.

"Hi!" she greeted me with an enthusiastic wave.

I glanced around, unsure she was actually speaking to me. I was the only other person in the vicinity. I returned her wave uneasily and waited for her to get closer.

"I'm Penelope. Well, Penny, actually. Everybody calls me Penny," she said, sounding a little out of breath.

"Talia," I replied cautiously, not sure what to make of her.

"You're a Pledge, right? A Hunter Pledge?"

"Um, yeah." *Obviously*, I thought. *I live in Hunters Village. Be nice*, I chastised myself. She was just trying to be friendly.

"Cool. I am a Crypto Pledge. I know most of the Operatives are in the city tonight, and a bunch of us Pledges were going to get together and hang out."

"Cool," I replied, for lack of something better to say.

"You want to come?" she asked, her eyes were like big green saucers as she looked at me expectantly.

I started to shake my head and tell her thanks, but no thanks, when instead I said, "Sure," before I could stop myself.

"Great! The others are already down by the lake starting a bonfire. I'll wait if you want to get some warmer clothes?" she suggested, scrutinizing my wet dress.

I gave her a small smile; still unsure what made me agree to this, and led her to my cabin. Donavon was out with his friends having fun, probably getting drunk, so I should enjoy myself, too.

Penny followed me through the doorway and made herself at home on my bed while I searched for something to wear. I grabbed a gray sweater, jeans, and a pair of beat-up tennis shoes, and ducked in the bathroom to change.

"Ready?" Penny asked brightly when I emerged.

"Sure," I smiled tentatively.

Penny kept up a constant stream of chatter as we wound through the woods on an unlit, dirt path. I led the way down to the lake since my eyesight was inevitably better than Penny's, on account of all the sensory training I'd done.

The flames and distinct aroma of campfire greeted me before we made it to the lake. I could hear the low hum of voices, but the people were still too far away to make out exactly what they were saying. Once we drew closer, I saw a strange mix of Pledges huddled around the blaze.

Only two groups of Pledges were housed at Elite Headquarters, the Hunters and Cryptos. The two couldn't be more different. Every Talent was classified as either Extremely-Low, Low, Mid-range, High, Extremely-High or Elite Level. The only thing Hunters and Cryptos had in common was that they both required a talent ranking of Extremely-High or better. The Hunters mostly have physical abilities, trained in combat and weapons, and are frequently Morphers. Cryptos, or Brains as they are often called, are all mental. Most Cryptos have a gift that TOXIC calls Higher Reasoning. Higher Reasoning Talents are like human computers. They are able to perform calculations in their heads, analyzing large quantities of information in seconds to determine the likely outcome of any situation and hacking just about any techie device.

There were fifteen Hunter Pledges, including myself. I had no idea how many Brain Pledges were housed at Elite Headquarters, but there were about twenty sitting around the fire. I followed Penny to an empty blanket set up near the fire and took a seat.

"No Donavon tonight, Talia?" quipped a short, stocky Hunter Pledge named Laris as he handed me a bottle filled with pink, fruity-smelling alcohol, similar to the one he was drinking from.

"Not tonight. He's in the city," I replied thinly. I accepted the drink and took a nervous sip. I had never been a fan of Laris, and I knew for a fact that the feeling was mutual. He was antagonistic and combative, which made our personalities incompatible.

"Donavon McDonough?" Penny asked excitedly.

"Um, yup," I took another sip of my too sweet drink.

"Are you friends with him?" Penny's eyes grew even larger; I wouldn't have thought it possible.

"More than friends," Laris interjected, suggestively. I shot him a nasty glare.

"Oh. My. God. Are you dating the Director's son?" Penny was so delighted that she was bouncing, splashing her own drink down her shirt, and not noticing.

"Yeah, sorta," I mumbled.

Most of the Pledges sitting around us were now listening to our conversation. I was starting to feel uncomfortable, and I wanted to direct the attention elsewhere. I didn't actually know many of the people at the fire, so I honed in on the one person I did know – Laris. I concentrated my thoughts in his direction and willed him to stand up and start dancing. Given more time, I might have thought of something more original, but I panicked. Thankfully, my plan worked, and everybody turned their attention to Laris. He looked a little confused, but continued gyrating to music that was only playing in his head, eating up the attention. I nervously sipped my drink.

"So, how do you like it here? Isn't it so much better than being at school?" Penny asked, returning her attention to me.

"Yeah, it's loads better than being at school," I smiled at her. I took another sip of my drink. "The food here is so much better," I elaborated trying to keep up my end of the conversation.

"Totally! And the dorms are even more techie than the old ones," she exclaimed.

"You're so lucky. We're stuck in those old-fashioned cabins," I lamented. I took another sip, already starting to feel a little buzzed.

"Oh, right! Oh, my god, you totally have to come see my room. You will love it! I have all these cool gadgets and stuff. Some I haven't even figured out yet, but I'm sure I will. Maybe you could help! I mean, you'll be using some of it once you, like, start going on Hunts and stuff!"

I wasn't sure if it was the alcohol, or if Penny was always like this. I took another sip of my drink, enjoying the buzz.

"Thanks, that would be really cool." That was *definitely* the alcohol in me talking. I'd never gone out of my way before to make friends. In fact, Donavon was the only real friend that I had. So, my sitting here with Penny, agreeing to hang out again, was next to a miracle. The even bigger miracle was I was actually enjoying myself. Something about Penny put me at ease. She was genuinely nice, and her friendly, outgoing personality seemed to rub off on me in a way nobody else's ever had. I found myself laughing, and even gossiping, with the other Pledges.

"I heard your Team Cap got you permission to go into the city today," another Hunter Pledge, named Jon, said to me at some point after my second (maybe third?) drink.

Oh, great, I thought. I was actually enjoying hanging out with these people, and now they were going to think the worst of me.

"Um, yeah, but you know, it was just for the day. Mac said I couldn't stay at night," I mumbled. I realized my mistake immediately. I always referred to the Director as Mac, but I was one of the few, and I was definitely the only Pledge that did.

"What's it like?" Jon asked.

"It was cool. I didn't get to see any of the bars or anything. We just went shopping," I tried to downplay it.

"You're so lucky. I'm from Johnson City, Tennessee and I've never been anywhere bigger than that. I asked my Cap if I could go with them, and he said no way," Jon drawled in a thick southern accent.

"Henri's pretty cool about stuff," I muttered, wanting to change the topic.

"I know! My older brother knew him in school, and I had hoped I would get assigned to his team when I got here. Guess you're the lucky one."

I smiled and nodded.

"No, she's lucky 'cause she shares a cabin with Erikson," a blonde girl, whose name I couldn't remember, slurred. I laughed a little too loudly.

"Does he sleep naked?" another girl inquired.

"Nope," I giggled. "But he does sleep without a shirt," I added, happy that the topic had changed to something else besides my relationship with Mac.

"Oh. My. God." Penny shrieked. "I'm totally jealous."

Discussions of Erik dominated the conversation for several more minutes until the boys in the group couldn't handle it any longer; they thankfully moved on to somebody I didn't know.

The rest of the evening went by in a blur. I spent most of the time talking to Penny, but I also chatted with Laris and a couple of the other Hunter Pledges that I knew from school. I don't remember exactly how many of the fruity pink drinks I had. Since I had never had alcohol before in my life, I knew it was too many, but I didn't care. I was really having a good time.

Before I knew it, somebody announced that we needed to get back before curfew. Penny, my new best friend, and I giggled as we made our way back up the dirt path, holding on to each other to keep from falling down. Once we reached the clearing with my cabin, I began tiptoeing, which was not easy since my balance was already off kilter. Penny and I said our goodbyes, and I watched her skip off with a group of Crypto Pledges. I reached the door to my cabin and used my mind to shove it open since I wasn't feeling coordinated enough to turn the knob. I pushed it a little too hard, and the door flung open with a bang; I nearly collapsed in a fit of giggles.

I tried to be quiet as I walked in, but every step that I took caused the floorboards to creak. Remembering the door, I used my mind to close it behind me. It banged shut, again much more forcefully than I'd intended. I cringed. Then I tripped over nothing, probably my own feet, and fell over giggling, crawling the rest of the way to my bed. I heaved myself up into my bed, and fell back on to my pillows with a sigh of relief. The excursion across the room had left me exhausted. I closed my eyes, and had almost succumbed to the alcohol induced slumber, when I felt somebody playing with my shoes.

"Henri? I'm sorry, did I miss curfew?" I mumbled.

"No, you didn't," the voice didn't belong to Henri.

The person was trying to take my shoes off, but every time he touched me, it tickled, and I started giggling again.

"Relax, Tal. Let me take your shoes off."

A hand firmly gripped my ankle, and I finally felt my shoes part ways with my feet. I heard footsteps, and then water running in the bathroom. A quilt was pulled up around my shoulders. I felt a hand pushing down on the bed as my savior knelt beside me. I pried my eyes open, and saw beautiful turquoise eyes staring back at me.

"There's water right here on your night stand," Erik said. "Just yell if you need anything."

"Your eyes are the same color as the Tyrrhenian Sea," I mumbled. Erik laughed softly.

"Maybe one day I'll see if that's true," he whispered.

I smiled, "Mmmm. It's pretty there."

"Close your eyes and go to sleep, Tal."

"That sounds like a good idea."

"Night, Tal."

"Night, Erik."

Chapter Twelve

A pounding in my head woke me up the next morning. My tongue felt thick and hairy, and my olfactory senses were assaulted by the smell of stale campfire. I lay awake for several minutes, but refused to open my eyes, instinctively knowing that would make my head hurt worse. The sunlight streaming through the window made the back of my eyelids a reddish-orange. I moaned and covered my face with a pillow.

"Drink the water, Natalia," Erik demanded from across the room. He sounded irritated.

"Water?" I croaked.

"The water I left next to your bed last night. Remember?" No, I didn't remember that, but I reached blindly towards my nightstand. My hand closed around a glass, slippery with condensation. I grabbed it, and without opening my eyes, sat up just enough to drink the entire glass, spilling a minimal amount down my shirt. I replaced the glass on the nightstand and fell back on to my bed. The springs on Erik's bed squeaked loudly as he got up. I groaned. Erik's bare footsteps sounded louder than normal as he padded across the room. He took the glass and trudged in the direction of the bathroom. The water run for several seconds, and then Erik turned it off and made his way back to me. He set the glass down heavily. I cringed.

"Drink it," he ordered.

I opened my eyes for the first time and immediately regretted it. I squinted up at Erik and took in his disheveled bed-head and naked torso. It wasn't the first time I'd seen him shirtless - he normally slept in just his boxers - but for some reason, this was the first time I appreciated exactly how great he looked without his shirt on. Snippets from last night's conversation about Erik danced through my head, and I blushed. He gave me an odd look.

When I didn't reach for the water, Erik picked it up and handed it to me. "Drink it," he repeated. I took it and gulped down my second glass of the day. The liquid sloshed in my stomach, making me queasy, so I lay back down.

"Oh, no, you don't. You're getting up and getting dressed so I can take you to Medical."

"Why?" I whined. "I'm not sick."

"Because you're dehydrated. That's what's giving you the splitting headache. The Medics can give you fluids to rehydrate you. You'll feel better in no time."

"Why do you care how I feel? You don't think I should suffer for my sins?" I asked suspiciously.

"I do think *you* should suffer, but I don't think I should have to."

I stared at him blankly.

"Have you ever been drunk before, Talia?"

"No," I answered grudgingly. I don't know why, but I was embarrassed to admit to him that I was a hangover virgin.

"Well, for the sake of those around you, don't make a habit of it. You're projecting your hangover onto me."

Obviously, I knew that I could force my will onto others, but I'd never accidentally transferred my thoughts or feelings to another person. I briefly wondered if I could do it to anybody, or if Erik were unique because I spent so much time communicating with him mentally. Or maybe it was because he could mimic my Talents, making a connection easier.

"You're killing me, Tals," he said tiredly.

"I'm sorry," I mumbled. "I'm not doing it on purpose."

"I know," his voice softened. "But I can't seem to block you. I didn't have the pleasure of getting drunk last night, so I'm not really up to paying the consequences this morning."

"I'm sorry," I said again. I clamored out of bed and trudged to the bathroom. I peeled off my sweater from the night before, and suppressed the urge to vomit as the smell of campfire overwhelmed me again. I quickly changed in to clean clothes and wound my tangled curls in to a bun away from my face.

"Tal, we're just going to the Medical building. You don't need to impress anybody," Erik called, from the main room, sounding quite annoyed.

I opened the door and smiled apologetically, "I'm sorry."

"So you've said. Come on," he ordered, gesturing for me to follow him.

"Where's Henri?" I asked, noticing for the first time he wasn't there.

"He spent the night in the city," Erik replied shortly, ushering me out of the cabin.

"Henri met a girl?" I did nothing to hide my shock. Henri was so responsible and controlled. I couldn't imagine he was the type to pick up a girl at a bar and go home with her.

"Not exactly," Erik didn't elaborate.

"Did he meet a boy?" I joked.

Erik abruptly stopped walking, and turned to face me.

"How did you know that?" he demanded.

"I didn't," I stammered. "I just figured if he didn't meet a girl, then maybe he met a boy."

Erik gave me a hard look.

"I don't see what the big deal is," I continued.

"It's not a big deal," Erik sighed. "He's just a really private person and doesn't want everyone discussing his personal life."

"I won't say anything," I promised quickly.

"I know. He'll probably tell you, anyway. And he didn't meet a boy at a bar. His boyfriend, Frederick, lives in D.C. They've been together for a few years now. He usually spends a couple of nights a week down there with him, but with you being here, he wanted to seem available and stuff, and be around at curfew, so he hasn't been staying the night."

I wasn't sure how to respond, so I didn't.

We walked the rest of the way in silence. When we entered the Medical building Erik, went directly to the receptionist and said something to her in a low voice. I saw her nod, and then he turned and waved me over. I followed Erik down a back hallway, into a room where a chubby, young Medic was sitting with his feet propped up on a desk, playing with his communicator.

"Hey, Zach," Erik greeted the guy. "I need a hangover shot."

Zach smirked, "You got it."

"Zach and I were friends at school," Erik explained, turning his attention to me.

"Hey," I said to Zach.

He gave me a small nod of acknowledgement, then got up and grabbed a couple vials from the cabinet. He mixed several serums together, and then filled a syringe with his concoction.

"Hop up on the table, big boy," he said to Erik.

"Not me. Her," Erik replied pointing to me. I climbed onto the table and turned my head away from the needle as Zach silently injected me with his mixture.

"Thanks," I mumbled.

"Happy to help," he grinned.

"Yeah, Zach, I owe you one. I'll catch up with you later in the week," Erik thanked him.

"Sounds good. Feel better," he directed his last statement towards me. I smiled at him and let Erik lead me out of the room.

No sooner had we walked out of the Medical building then –

"Talia!" a high-pitched voice squealed.

Erik groaned, rubbing his temples.

"Hey, Penny," I said, smiling as she ran towards us with her fire engine red hair flying behind her.

"Oh, my gosh, I feel so crappy this morning!" she exclaimed. "Note to self, sugary drinks hit you hard."

"Ha ha, yeah," I agreed.

Erik groaned again.

"Oh, Penny, this is Erik. Erik, this is Penny," I said, introducing them to each other. Erik just nodded at her.

"Oh, my gosh, hi!" Penny extended her hand to Erik. Erik shook it hesitantly. "I've heard so much about you; all of the girls in the Crypto unit talk about you all the time!"

Erik wasn't even fazed. "I seem to have that effect on girls," he said dryly.

"I was thinking maybe we could do something later?" Penny said, turning to me.

"Um, sure. Why don't you send me a comm," I replied, referring to the messages we sent each other using our communicators.

"Great! Well, then, I'll talk to you later!" Her excitement was draining what little energy I had. "It was so cool to meet you!" she said to Erik.

"Likewise." Erik looked amused. I wondered if girls normally acted like this around him.

"I see you made a friend," Erik said sounding slightly more amused after Penny walked away.

"Yeah, I guess I did," I smiled.

"Don't look so surprised. If you gave people a chance, you would have a fan club, too."

"I give people a chance," I retorted defensively.

"No, you don't," he laughed. "You're stuck in your own closed-off world with Donavon." He said Donavon's name like it was a dirty word.

"I gave you a chance, didn't I?" I joked.

"You didn't have a choice," he pointed out.

I was thinking about what he said as we walked a couple of yards without speaking.

"Tal! I've been looking all over for you," Donavon called, jogging over to us.

"Oh, shit," Erik muttered. "I'm going back to the cabin." He started walking away.

"Erik?" I called after him. He stopped walking. "Thanks for everything. And really, I am sorry."

He smiled, turned back around, and kept walking.

"*What happened last night?*" Donavon's mental voice demanded.

"*What are you talking about?*" I sent back cautiously.

"*You were drunk.*" It wasn't a question.

"*I had some drinks with friends,*" I tried to keep my mental voice even.

"*What friends? You haven't been interested in making friends in the seven years I've known you.*"

"*No,*" I corrected. "*I haven't had any interest in being friends with your friends."*

"What's wrong with my friends?" his mental voice was shouting.

"Nothing is wrong with your friends, except that THEY'RE YOUR FRIENDS. Like Laris, since I assume that's how you know I was drinking last night."

"Yes, that is, in fact, who told me. Laris was worried, so he left me a comm. How do you think I felt when I came home last night to find out that my girlfriend was so drunk that she couldn't walk herself home?" he demanded.

"Oh, Laris was worried? Worried?!? No, I doubt he was worried. He just couldn't wait to call and tell you all about it!" I was so frustrated and angry that I was close to tears.

"Don't be mad at Laris. I sent you a ton of comms last night and this morning, and you didn't return any of them. What were you doing? What happened after you went back to your cabin? And why were you drinking in the first place?"

"What the hell are you talking about?!?! Nothing happened after I went back to my cabin. I passed out. And why is this such a big deal? Weren't you drinking last night?"

"Yes, I was drinking. But I drink. You don't. And I don't appreciate you getting drunk for the first time without me."

"This is ridiculous, Donavon. I don't understand why you're so pissed. I didn't do anything wrong. I'm going back to my cabin. I cannot deal with you right now." I started walking away.

"Back to your cabin, or back to Erik?" Donavon screamed after me.

"What?" I rounded on him. *"What does Erik have to do with this?"*

"I just find it a little convenient that Erik came home early last night. The first night he has ever left the city bars without a girl on

his arm, just so happens to be the first night you ever get drunk?"

"Have you lost it? I REFUSE to dignify that with a response."

I stomped towards my cabin. My head started throbbing again, but this time, it was from the blood pounding in my ears and not from my hangover. Donavon called my name, but I didn't care.

I ran straight through Hunters Village and down the same path I'd led Penny the night before. I didn't stop until I reached the water's edge. A cold sweat was running down my back, and sticking my shirt to my skin. My breath was ragged, and no matter how hard I tried, I couldn't get it under control. I fell to my knees on the shore in front of the water with rocks biting into my skin through my thin pants.

The audacity of Donavon to accuse *me* of inappropriate behavior infuriated me. I had refused to cry in front of Donavon, but now tears of frustration poured hot and angry, down my cheeks. I jumped to my feet and began pacing along the bank of the lake. My head was spinning so fast the world around me blurred into a collage of colors, made worse by the tears obscuring my vision. For a brief moment, I hated myself for letting Donavon affect me so profoundly, and in my rage I wasn't paying attention to my feet, and I tripped. I was caught off guard, and my superb reflexes failed me. Unable to get my hands out to break my fall, my forehead struck the trunk of a felled tree with a loud crack.

Dazed and disoriented, I laid in the dirt as the lake's water lapped against my legs until I felt strong arms lift me from the ground. I didn't have the energy to speak, so I settled for resting my head against the hard chest of my savior. My barely-conscious brain hoped that it was Henri; I couldn't stand having Erik save me twice in one day.

"She's soaked," I heard Henri's voice comment.

"What's she doing out here?" Erik sounded perplexed.

"Who knows? Let's just get her back and dry her off," Henri replied.

I tried to speak, but found it difficult to form words over the pain in my head. I tried to focus on the rhythm of Henri's footsteps, but I had passed out before we made it more than a couple of steps.

I woke up in my bed sometime after the sun had set. I was wrapped in several blankets, including Henri's quilt. Frantically, I flipped the covers back and looked down at myself; I was dressed in dry clothes. I shot up and looked around the room in a panic. Erik chuckled from the corner of the cabin.

"How are you feeling?" he asked, looking concerned.

"Who dressed me?" I demanded, ignoring his question.

"I did," Henri said, coming through the door to the cabin.

"I helped!" Penny's voice came from somewhere behind Henri, but his massive frame blocked her out.

"Don't worry, Tal, I promise I didn't enjoy it, you're not really my type," Henri joked.

"Thanks," I smiled, feeling more than a little humiliated.

"Penny and I brought dinner, so I hope you're hungry," Henri continued, ignoring my discomfort.

"What are you doing here, Penny?" I asked, then immediately felt bad since she'd obviously been helpful earlier.

"She was blowing up your communicator, so I answered and she insisted on coming over," Erik answered for her.

"She proved very useful when it came to getting you cleaned up and dressed," Henri said pointedly.

"Did everybody see me naked?" I asked, completely mortified.

"Unfortunately, I didn't have the pleasure," Erik quipped.

"You must be hungry. Take your pick," Henri said, changing

the subject. He held out four wrapped deli sandwiches, and I grabbed one at random. Henri handed one to Penny and took the other two to the table, sitting opposite Erik. Penny sat on the end of my bed and spread out her dinner.

We all dug in, and the room was quiet except for the sound of crinkling paper and chewing.

The four of us spent the night hanging out, playing cards and talking. I was able to put the fight with Donavon out of mind and actually enjoy myself. I couldn't actually remember the last night that I had so much fun.

Sometime just before curfew, Henri offered to walk Penny back to her apartment.

"Thanks for tonight," I said to Erik after they'd left.

"No big deal," he looked uncharacteristically embarrassed.

"Yes, it is. I'm sure you and Henri would have preferred going out in the city, instead of spending the night with me and Penny."

"Nah, I needed a break. And Penny's cooler than I would've thought. A little hyper, but nice," he sounded amused when he talked about Penny, and a brief jolt of something that I thought might be jealousy hit me. I quickly dismissed it.

"Thanks all the same."

"Night, Talia," he called, pulling the covers up and turning to face the wall.

"Night."

I closed my eyes and tried to go to sleep, but my mind was replaying the fight with Donavon. I briefly contemplated reaching out to him. He hadn't left me any communications, so I figured he was still mad. We never fought, so I didn't know what to expect.

Curiosity finally got the better of me, and I opened my mind. Donavon was in his cabin, and he was definitely still seething; my good mood vanished. I closed my mind and again willed myself to fall asleep. I had never actually attempt to force my will on myself, so I doubted it would work, but to my surprise, I was fast asleep before Henri returned.

Chapter Thirteen

The next morning, I was up bright and early and back to training. We spent the morning in the usual way, working on our mental connection. By lunchtime, I was mentally exhausted but felt good about our progress. I'd successfully maintained the connection the whole morning, and my physical strength had barely waned. Thankfully, our afternoon schedule included a session with the Brains.

Erik and Henri had both been trained extensively in the use of the portable electronic devices, so the training was just a refresher for them. I spent the first half of the afternoon just learning how to use a portable computer. An older Crypto named Bhen demonstrated, no less than five times, the sequence I needed to follow just to log in. Next, he showed me the appropriate technique for typing on the keyboard. I thought he was treating me like a moron until I tried it myself and realized that only every fourth letter or number I hit registered. He showed me again.

Sometimes on Missions, Hunters were compromised, necessitating a hasty retreat. In rare cases, leaving behind belongings, like Crypto gadgets, couldn't be avoided. The tools held so much vital data that it would be disastrous to TOXIC if it fell into enemy hands. The only way to prevent this was to put biometric fail-safes on all of the devices. Prior to departing for each Hunt, Cryptos would program scans of each team member so we were the only people who could access the equipment.

"What am I doing wrong?" I begged him, frustrated when I still couldn't get it.

"You need to be sure that your whole finger hits the key, so the tiny sensor has enough time to register your fingerprint. If the computer can't register your print, it won't type the letter," he explained. "It's hard at first, but you'll get used to it." I looked at him doubtfully, but kept at it, refusing to admit defeat.

Next, we moved on to heat scanners. He walked me around Headquarters, letting me scan buildings and observe the images that displayed on the screen, showing outlines of all the people inside. While I'd never actually used a heat scanner before, it was far more simple than typing; much to my dismay, we didn't spend too long with it.

For any other Pledge, the day would've ended with Bhen teaching me to use the ear pieces that most Hunters employed to communicate while on a mission. Since that was not necessary, on account of our built-in telecommunication system, he taught me to use a medical body scanner instead.

The body scanner allowed us to see a person's organs and innards through clothing and skin. That way, if one of us were injured, we'd be able to assess the internal damage. Bhen let me run the scanner over his mid-section so I could see his kidneys, stomach, intestines and all that other good stuff. I also ran the imager over his legs and arms to see the bones – it was oddly fascinating.

By the end of the afternoon, my brain was buzzing with all of the newly-acquired knowledge. The new technologies I'd been acquainted with unnerved me. As if all of the other things I had to remember weren't enough, now I had to learn to use all of these new contraptions too? Maybe I'd ask Penny for help with the portable computer; the one she used every day had the same fingerprint-scan technology.

That evening, the three of us sat on the wooden floor of our cabin, pouring over floor plans and intel that the Cryptos had accumulated for our upcoming mission. A lot of the time was spent with Henri explaining to me how to read the intel documents since they mostly looked like gibberish to the untrained eye, which mine was. When I finally crawled into bed, long past midnight, my eyes were red-rimmed and dry from all of the laborious staring; my muscles were knotted from sitting in the same, hunched-over, position for so long.

Donavon hadn't even attempted to talk to me all day. I didn't reach out to him, either. I felt that I was owed an apology, and my stubborn nature demanded that I not be the first one to crack. Right before I drifted off to sleep, I opened my mind, just to take a peek in to his, to see if he were thinking about me, and feeling sorry about the way he'd acted. Unfortunately, he was asleep.

The rest of the week progressed in the same manner: mental communication training, practicing with the gadgets, studying intel. By the end of the week, I felt pretty comfortable with all three.

Several days before we left, I visited Medical, where Erik's friend, Zach, taught me very basic first aid. Mostly, it was "simple stuff": stitching up a cut, making a tourniquet, splinting a broken bone. It made me nauseous. The thought of inflicting injuries that drew blood didn't actually bother me; that was what I'd been training for. But dealing with the aftermath? That made me queasy, as if my intestines had turned to eels swimming in my stomach. I was positive that even if "push came to shove," I'd never be able to perform any of these acts without losing my breakfast, lunch, and dinner.

Donavon and I didn't speak all week; it was the longest I'd ever gone without seeing him, talking to him, and touching him. I felt lost without the comfortable mental connection that I had grown accustomed to. Sure, he left me a couple of messages on my communicator, but they were brief, and none contained an apology. I kept promising myself that I would wait for him to come to me, heart-in-hand, to say he was sorry. But without fail, every night before bed my resolve weakened and I opened my mind to search for Donavon. Since we were up so late going over intel, he was always asleep.

At the end of the week, we were for scheduled two days off to relax and catch up on our sleep before we set off for our mission.

After we had finished the last day of training for the week, both Henri and Erik left immediately for the city. Henri, I presumed, was going to spend the night with Frederick. Erik, I assumed, was going to see if he could find a nice warm bed with a nice looking city girl. I planned on spending the night hanging out with Penny and her friends. I hoped that Laris wasn't there – I didn't need any reminders that Donavon still wasn't talking to me. I also didn't want any tattle tales running back, reporting my every cough and sneeze to him.

I decided to eat alone in my cabin since Penny had a training exercise that would run through dinnertime. I was sitting at the small table in the cabin, eating my meal and reading a book, when I heard a soft knock on my door. I figured it must be Penny, so I called for her to come in. Instead of opening the door, Penny knocked again. I opened my mind as I walked to the door, and abruptly froze, mid-step. It wasn't Penny on the other side of the door – it was Donavon. I was suddenly nervous. This was what I'd wanted, him coming to beg me for forgiveness, admitting he'd been jealous and irrational, conceding that he'd overreacted just a tad, right? But what if that wasn't what he wanted? What if he were here for Round Two? Would he really wait an entire week before coming to yell at me again?

"Talia, I know you're in there; I can feel you," Donavon called through the door, sounding impatient.

I sighed. *There's no time like the present to get this over with,* I thought. I willed the door to open, keeping my feet firmly on the floor. The door swung open, but Donavon didn't enter.

"Can I come in?" he asked, tentatively.

"I suppose," I replied tersely.

Donavon shuffled in, his eyes preoccupied with his sneakers, and sat at the table I'd just vacated. I turned around to face him, but made no move to sit down. After a long moment, he raised his head and met my eyes. We stared at each other for what seemed like an eternity, but I didn't want to be the one to break the silence.

"Tal, I'm so sorry," Donavon finally said, his voice wavering slightly.

"I don't know how you could accuse me of...Well, I don't even know what exactly you were accusing me of!" I yelled. So much for calm and collected.

"I just freaked out, Tal. Erik has such a reputation, and no girl seems immune to him. I know I was wrong. I'm so sorry. You have to believe me," his blue eyes were pleading with me.

I purposely kept my mind blocked, refusing any mental communication; I didn't want to feel his emotions. But the look in his eyes broke my resistance, and I dropped my guard. I could feel how much he cared about me, how sorry he was. His emotions were so strong, they nearly overwhelmed me. Before I'd made a conscious decision, my feet were already moving me towards him.

Our lips met, his arms wrapped around my waist, and I lost my fingers in his hair. He stood up, careful not to break contact with me, and lifted me up by the waist. I wrapped my legs above his hips as he walked with me to my bed. He carefully sat me on the edge and gently pushed me back until I was flat on my back, and he was leaning completely over me. I disentangled my fingers from his hair and ran my hands up under his shirt, over the smooth skin of his back. He broke away just long enough to yank his shirt over his head. Donavon leaned back down, placing one hand next to my head as he dropped his lips back to mine. His other hand toyed with the edge of my tank top. He slowly ran his thumb across my stomach, my muscles tightened and trembled. I looped my legs around his waist again and pulled him towards me. He laughed as he collapsed on top of me. He pushed my tank top higher until there was no clothing separating our stomachs.

"Skin to skin," I whispered.

"Skin to skin," he whispered back. I loved the way his skin felt against mine, warm and reassuring.

He worked my tank top up and over my head. I started shaking harder. Donavon's lips found mine again, and I relaxed against him. He reluctantly pulled back from me and stared hard into my eyes. He smoothed loose pieces of hair back from my face. He leaned down again, but instead of kissing me, he laid his cheek against mine and fluttered his eyelashes against my cheekbone. My whole body tingled, every synapse firing. I giggled, partially because his eyelashes tickled and partially out of nerves. He replaced his eyelashes with his lips. He dropped kisses from my jaw bone down my neck and onto my collarbone.

"Hey, Talia, are you – " Penny stopped mid-sentence. She'd opened the door without knocking. "Oh, my gosh! I'm so sorry." Penny's face flamed to match the color of her hair. Donavon used his chest to cover me while I scrambled to find my tank top.

"It's okay, Penny," I called around Donavon. "Just give me a minute."

"I'll wait outside. I'm sorry," she apologized again.

I burst out laughing as she closed the door, a little relieved at the interruption.

"Oops," I smirked.

"Get dressed before she barges back in here," Donavon said handing me my tank top; at least he was smiling.

We spent the evening with Penny and the other Pledges. We sat by the lake again, but this time I refrained from drinking. I enjoyed myself, and was pleased to see that Donavon did, too. He walked me back to my cabin at curfew and kissed me goodnight outside. I wasn't surprised to find my cabin empty when I went inside. I got ready for bed and crawled under the covers, then I opened my mind.

"*Wanna come cuddle?*" I asked when I could feel Donavon, awake, in his cabin.

"*Are you cabin mateless?*"

"*Sure am.*"

"*Be there in ten.*"

I smiled to myself and counted to ten in my head. When I reached ten, I mentally pushed the door open, and right on cue, Donavon hurried through. He wore blue and white plaid pajama bottoms and a white t-shirt stretched tight over his broad chest and biceps. His blonde hair was slightly mussed. He must have been in the middle of changing when I called to him. I held the covers up invitingly, and Donavon kicked his shoes off before climbing in. He smelled like soap and the spearmint mouthwash that Gretchen buys. I snuggled close to him, embracing the familiar, comfortable contours of his stretched out body, and closed my eyes.

"'Night, Donavon."
"'Night, love."

Chapter Fourteen

The first time I woke up the next morning, Donavon's arms were still tight around my waist, his warm, even breathing tickling the back of my neck. It was relaxing to be at peace with Donavon again. The second time I woke up was a different story.

"Get out," Erik growled, his turquoise eyes blazing with anger, his hands balled into fists by his sides. Stale alcohol seeped out of his pores as sweat dotted his forehead.

Donavon jumped out of bed, but stood his ground.

"I said, get out," Erik repeated, his voice low and threatening.

"What're you so upset about?" Donavon demanded, trying to keep his voice even. "You weren't here, and she was lonely."

"She is a Pledge. She isn't allowed to have visitors after curfew, you know that," Erik shot back through gritted teeth, never taking his eyes off of Donavon. I wished that, they would stop talking about me like I wasn't there.

"Oh, come off it, Erik. You had girls back in your cabin all the time when you were still a Pledge. The stories are legendary." Donavon rolled his eyes and relaxed his stance.

"Just get out," Erik shouted, losing whatever control he'd been hanging on to.

"Fine. Whatever." Donavon tried to sound flippant, but I could tell he was unnerved by Erik's intensity. He turned and kissed me on the top of my head, picked up his shoes, not bothering to put them on, and sauntered out of the cabin.

I waited until I heard the soft click of the door closing into place before I rounded on Erik.

"How dare you!?" I screamed, not bothering to pretend that I was in control of my emotions.

"Tal, calm down." He no longer sounded angry, just tired. I clamored to stand up on my bed, nearly tripping over the tangled blankets. Even standing on top, I was barely eye-to-eye with Erik.

"No, I will most certainly not calm down. You had no right to barge in here and demand that he leave. This is my room, too. And don't call me 'Tal' like you are my friend." The anger and embarrassment were warring inside of me, both just waiting to get out. The anger over Erik acting like he had a right to throw Donavon out of my room; and the embarrassment over being caught in bed with Donavon, and by Erik of all people. It wasn't like we were doing anything; we were fully clothed, after all. But still, something about Erik being the one to find me and Donavon in bed together was humiliating.

"Tal, calm down," Erik urged, his voice low and pleading.

"I am calm," I spat, even though I clearly wasn't. I clenched my jaw so tightly that it hurt. My face was only inches from Erik, and I was seized by an impulse to shove him back, away from me as his closeness was suffocating. I raised my hands to do just that, but Erik's lightning-fast reflexes had his fingers encircling my wrists before I made contact.

"I'm sorry. I overreacted," he whispered, his face still too close to mine. I began to relax slightly, the anger ebbing away.

"What's wrong?" Henri asked, walking in the room and taking in the sight of me and Erik locked in the odd embrace. I tore my eyes away from Erik's to look at Henri, and my anger returned full force.

"Erik thinks what goes on in my room is his business," I fumed, yanking my wrists free of his grasp.

"It is my business, when it takes place in my room," he answered, refusing to take his eyes off me.

"Well, it is kind of our business, Talia," Henri said evenly.

"No, it's not!" I shrieked, rounding on him now.

"Natalia you need to *calm* down," Erik insisted, reaching for my wrists again. I crossed both arms protectively over my chest, effectively thwarting his effort. I felt his nervous energy as his fingers brushed my forearm.

"It is. It may not seem fair to you, and maybe it's not, but what happens in your private life could affect us, so that makes it our business," Henri kept his voice calm, taking his visual cues from Erik. I guess he reasoned that Erik was the resident expert in irrational females.

"I don't ask about your personal life," I spat.

"It's not the same. I know it's a double standard, but our private lives don't affect you the same way yours affects us."

"That makes no sense," I argued.

"Do you understand how much time goes into training a new Hunter?" Henri asked, seemingly switching topics.

"A lot," I conceded. Henri's distraction gave Erik the opening that he needed, and he gently laid a hand on my arm, drawing my attention back towards him. I flinched initially, but calmed a little when I looked into his eyes, and I let him keep his hand there.

"Exactly. And if something were to happen that made that training go to waste, it would be pretty crappy, right?" I didn't understand where he was going with this.

"Right," I answered slowly.

"Well, if you got pregnant, that would kinda make all this time and training useless," Erik said quietly.

"What? But we weren't doing anything!" I wailed, but all the fight had gone out of me.

"Yeah. So, that makes it kind of our business what goes on in your private life," Henri said.

"So, I can't have a boyfriend?" I whispered.

"No, you can," Henri answered quickly. "We just want you to understand the consequences. Granted, Erik might've overreacted a little," he added, giving him a hard look.

I looked back at Erik, his hand still resting on my forearm. A wave of emotions hit me, and I knew that his reaction had nothing to do with any possible "consequences." I opened my mouth, and started to say something to that effect but quickly snapped it shut.

"Right. I understand," I muttered instead, turning towards the bathroom.

The whole scene was mortifying. Talking about this with the two of them was too embarrassing, particularly since I hadn't actually done anything that could lead to me getting pregnant. Ever. I walked into the bathroom, shutting the door noisily behind me. I collapsed on the floor. I could still hear them talking in the other room. I turned on the water and climbed into the hot spray.

The humiliation over what had just transpired wasn't the only reason I needed to collect my thoughts. The intensity of Erik's emotions was also wreaking havoc with my mind. I'd, of course, been attracted to Erik since we'd first met; he *is* hot. I can't imagine a girl who wasn't attracted to him. Regardless, Donavon was my boyfriend, and that was that. Being attracted to somebody was a lot different than having real feelings for them...Right? I mean, I didn't, and couldn't, have feelings for Erik. Besides, Erik might like me now, but he had a short attention-span, and I would be surprised if it lasted. I spent my whole shower trying to compose myself.

When I finally opened the bathroom door, they were both sitting at the table, eating. I took a deep breath and launched into my carefully prepared speech.

"I promise you won't find Donavon in our cabin during non-visiting hours if you, in turn, promise *never* to speak about my sex life again. I promise to make sure my private life doesn't affect either of you, as long as you promise to pretend like this conversation never happened." I could feel my face burning with embarrassment. I kept my eyes focused on an ant that was crawling across the floorboards.

"Agreed, and we're sorry that this conversation had to happen like this," Henri smiled at me and nudged Erik.

Instead of apologizing, Erik asked hopefully, "Any chance you could promise to get rid of your boyfriend?"

"Sorry, not part of the deal."

Erik shrugged, "Breakfast, then?"

I grinned, relieved. "I'm starving."

Since I had the day off, I decided to play it safe and spend it with Penny. We spent most of the time in her room playing with all her gadgets. She had been right, there were quite a few she had no idea how to use. Even the two of us together couldn't seem to figure it out. We talked about Donavon, and a Crypto Operative she had a crush on. She asked what it was like to live with two guys, and I complained about how lucky she was to have such a nice, big room to herself. We painted our toe nails bright orange, I was beginning to realize that wasn't just Penny's hair color but more like her whole color scheme.

Penny insisted on doing my makeup. I normally only wore makeup when I went with Mac's family to a political event that required me to dress up. Penny, however, wore makeup every day, and seemed personally offended that I didn't share her affinity.

Somewhere between applying the orchid eye shadow and the cherry never-been-kissed lip gloss, I learned Penny's life story. Penny hadn't started at the McDonough School at five, which was customary. She told me her parents had given her up when she was still a baby. Instead of getting lucky and being adopted, she'd been shuttled from foster home to foster home until finally coming to live at Mrs. Gubbard's Home for Girls when she was twelve. Her extremely elevated intelligence hadn't gone unnoticed. Once she realized Penny wasn't normal, the house matron had immediately contacted TOXIC. Just weeks after arriving at the home, she was moved once again, this time to a permanent domicile – The McDonough School.

Penny's story made me feel a kinship for her. I wondered if maybe I'd instinctively known when I met her, that first night, that we had something in common, as I was oddly drawn to Penny from our first encounter. Up until now, I'd thought that maybe she'd just come along at a time in my life when I really needed a friend, kind of like with Donavon. Now I thought it must've been that I knew on some level we had something in common; we were both orphans.

I wanted to take a quick look into her head, wanted to see if she felt it, too, but decided against the intrusion. I knew I wouldn't want somebody invading my most painful and private memories.

Somehow, I, too, found myself recounting my own tragic past. I gave Penny the abridged version of events that led to my own enrollment at the school. I hadn't shared my story with anybody, even Donavon. Donavon knew, of course, but Mac had been the one to tell him. More likely, he overhead Mac talking to Gretchen. He did have a penchant for eavesdropping.

That evening, I had dinner with Donavon, and then we took a walk around the grounds. Even though my upcoming mission was supposed to be easy, I was starting to get nervous. I wanted to spend as much time with him as I could before I left, but I still made sure to be in long before curfew. I didn't want to risk upsetting Henri after our conversation that morning.

Erik was the only one there when I walked into my cabin two hours before midnight. He informed me that Henri always spent the night before he left with Frederick and that he would be back early the next morning. I wished for the umpteenth time that day I could spend the night with Donavon, but after the morning's showdown I wasn't about to take the chance. I lay in my bed, tossing and turning, well in to the night.

The anxiety of my first Hunt was making me restless, and preventing sleep. I wanted to seek out Donavon's mind, but decided against it; talking to him in my head would just make me more desperate to be physically close to him.

Sometime shortly before sunrise, Erik turned on the light next to his bed.

"You should be sleeping. We have a couple of big days ahead of us," he lectured.

"I'm sorry, did I wake you up?" I apologized, feeling bad, but secretly a little glad that he was awake, too.

"No, not exactly. It's more like you haven't let me sleep."

"I'm sorry," I repeated, actually feeling guilty now.

"It's okay, I was just as anxious before my first mission," he mumbled.

"Did you keep Henri up all night?" I inquired, hopefully.

"Well, no," he admitted. "But I also don't have the ability to project my thoughts and feelings onto the people around me. Well, I don't usually," he amended. Henri was probably doubly glad that he weren't here if I was projecting my anxiousness onto Erik, making him jittery, too. Having to deal with both of us would be pretty irritating.

"How do I force myself to sleep?" I moaned.

"You probably won't be able to," he conceded.

"So, what do I do?"

"Get up and put on your workout clothes," he suggested.

"What? How is that going to help me sleep?"

"You should go for a run or something. It'll tire you out, and you really need to get some sleep before we leave tonight."

I sighed and pushed the covers off me. I trudged into the bathroom to change. Running was low on the list of things I wanted to do right then, but I was willing to try anything that would help me sleep. When I emerged, I was surprised to see Erik sitting on the edge of his bed dressed in matching Agency-issue workout clothes, tying the white laces on his mesh tennis shoes.

"Ready?" he asked, without turning around.

"You're coming?" I didn't bother to mask my surprise.

"I'm up," he answered simply.

We set off at a quick pace on a trail through the woods. We maintained the pace, without speaking, for over an hour.

As we ran, I focused my energy towards my olfactory sense. I breathed in the intoxicatingly sweet fragrance of the small, white flowers that grew on the base of the trees, the fresh smell of dew on the leaves, and even the earthy musk of the dirt. I could make out the heady scent of Erik's sweat mixed with his deodorant, it was so distinctly male. I inhaled deeper without thinking twice, taking in as much of his aroma as I could. Suddenly, I realized what I was doing and quickly redirected my energy.

I switched my concentration to my sense of touch. The morning was cool and damp, and I could feel the tiny droplets of cold water that hung in the air on every surface of my exposed skin. I felt the trickle of cold sweat as it traced a path from the base of my skull down my back. I felt the tiniest pebbles as my feet pounded out a steady rhythm along the path.

I narrowed my eyes and refocused my energy to my sight, blocking the rest of my senses. I could see the beads of condensation on the too bright leaves. I could see the minute details in the bark of the passing trees. When I turned my head to look at Erik, I could see his long, thick eyelashes framing his beautiful eyes. I lost my footing and stumbled slightly. Erik looked down at me as I quickly strained to right myself.

"Okay?" he asked, raising his eyebrows questioningly. I caught a glint in his eyes and knew that he had caught me looking at him.

"Yup," I grunted, embarrassed.

Closing my eyes, I tried to regroup. I directed my energy to my hearing. The pounding of my feet against the dirt was almost deafening. I could hear the thudding of my heart against my chest, just a microsecond faster than Erik's. A small bumblebee flew next to my ear, and the flutter of its wings filled my head. I relaxed as my stride fell into a rhythm with the steady burbling of a stream somewhere in the distance to my right.

I continued to cycle through my senses, expanding each one in turn, throughout the entire run. Over the years, the routine had become second nature. The familiarity comforted me, and the anxiety that had been dampening my thoughts all week gave way to confidence. I could do this. I was ready for this mission.

Mac had begun teaching me to sharpen my senses six months after I came to live with his family. I would run blindfolded to improve my hearing. He would have me wear earplugs for entire days to improve my eyesight. Some days, Mac would deprive me of two of my senses at once, pushing the remaining ones to their limits. It was a gradual process, but eventually, I was able to tune in to each individual sense by drawing on my mental energy, and focusing it towards one sense.

The same principle worked with my mental abilities. Mac taught me to draw all of my energy towards my telecommunication abilities, strengthening and fine tuning my natural Talent.

Erik was right – when we got back, I was exhausted. I showered quickly and then got back in my bed, promptly falling asleep.

Too soon, I woke to Henri gently shaking my shoulder.

"Tal, it's time to get up," he said softly.

"Hmmm," I replied drowsily.

"You need to wake up and pack. We're leaving in two hours."

The bed rose as his weight left. This was it; I was finally going on my first Mission. My confidence from earlier remained. I was ready.

I rolled over and stretched. I pulled myself out of bed and began packing a small bag with only essential toiletries and several days' worth of the most non-descript clothing that I owned. Bags containing the weapons, tech devices, and specialized clothing that we needed for our mission would be waiting for us at the hover plane.

I had finished my packing, and was pulling on knee-high black boots over a thick black adapti-suit made of an impenetrable material that protected my skin from the elements, glancing blows and would slow down a blade and even a bullet, when I heard the knock on the door. As soon as I heard the knock, I knew that it was Donavon. I dove for the door, but Erik got there first.

"I should've guessed it would be you," he greeted Donavon icily as he opened the door.

"Just wanted to say goodbye to Tal," he held up his hands, indicating that he didn't want trouble.

I walked over, grabbed his hand, and ushered him out the door. I slammed it shut behind me.

"Sorry about that," I said to him.

"I don't want to talk about him," Donavon leaned down and kissed me. "Seriously though, Natalia, be careful."

"Don't worry, Donavon. I'll be fine," I promised.

"I know, but I can't help but worry about you," his voice was husky.

"Wrap it up, Tal. We gotta go," Erik called, walking out of the cabin with his bag over one shoulder and mine over the other.

I stood on my tiptoes and reached up to kiss Donavon goodbye.

"*I love you, Tal.*"

"*I know, Donavon,*" I gave his calloused hand one last squeeze before turning to follow Erik and Henri, only allowing myself to look back once.

Chapter Fifteen

When we arrived at the hangar, it was a bustle of activity. Three black backpacks sat at the base of the steps leading up to the underbelly of a mid-sized camouflage hover plane. One of the bags was distinctly larger than the other two. Henri grabbed that one and climbed the steps into the plane. Erik and I followed suit. I took a seat in one of the oversized chairs and waited while Henri spoke to a man who I assumed must be the pilot. My apprehension from earlier hummed behind my confident exterior.

"Move all the stuff you brought from the cabin into the black backpack and then strap yourself in," Henri instructed, his voice serious. I did as I was told. The atmosphere was so charged that I could nearly feel the tiny sparks of electricity. No one spoke again until we were in the air.

"The plane will drop us off in a rural area approximately fifty miles outside of Mexico City. There is a road car there that we will use to drive to a safe house approximately twenty miles outside the city. The laboratory we are looking for is on the border of the actual town," Henri explained. We had, of course, gone over all of this numerous times, but I nodded my head and listened. I knew Henri was anxious, and reciting the plan helped calm his nerves. I tried to prevent his feelings from intensifying my increasing unease. I had to stay focused. I had to sustain my composure.

The flight took several hours, most of which I slept. I was still tired from my sleepless night; the brief respite wasn't sufficient. We finally touched down in a small clearing in the middle of nowhere. The humidity engulfed me as soon as the craft door opened. Thankfully, the Hunting suits had temperature regulators, so it only took seconds for the interior of my suit to adjust, returning to a comfortable level. My hair was another matter; my dark curls absorbed the moisture in the air immediately, and expanded exponentially. I fished a bandana out of my bag and used it to contain my hair. I tightened the straps on my backpack until they fit snugly against my body, and climbed down the shiny metal steps. As soon as all three of us deplaned, the steps retracted and the plane rose silently flying off into the inky-black night sky.

This was it; we were actually here. I was a bundle of nervous anticipation. Breathe, focus, I reminded myself. You can do this. You *can* do this, I repeated over and over again in my head.

I followed Henri and Erik out of the clearing and into the surrounding woods. The trees were thick, and I had no idea how Henri knew where we were going. When I opened my mind to him, I could feel his senses on overdrive. We only walked for a couple of minutes before we reached the most dilapidated barn that I'd ever seen; the heavy wooden doors protested loudly when Henri pulled them open. I walked several paces behind Henri and Erik, afraid the barn would collapse once we entered. My senses were not quite as good as the boys – since theirs came naturally with their Talents – so it took my eyes several additional seconds to adjust to the pitch black barn interior. Once my eyes could distinguish shapes, I realized that the barn wasn't nearly as unstable as it looked. In fact, there were large support beams holding the roof and sides up in an odd configuration which gave off the impression that the building was falling in on itself. I stared up in wonderment.

In the middle of the barn were several road vehicles. Henri selected a small rusted looking one with a layer of grime covering the windows and got in the driver's seat. I opened the back door and climbed in, leaving the passenger seat for Erik.

The interior and the exterior were a study in contrast. The outside looked like that of a vehicle that had been sitting in an abandoned barn for years while the inside looked the crypto bank at Headquarters. The seats were soft, black leather and the dash and the doors were covered in buttons that lit up in a rainbow of colors when Henri powered up the car. The backs of the headrests and center console were equipped with small touchscreen computers. I stared, wide-eyed, at all the gadgets.

Henri drove out of the barn and turned down a path situated between two large trees.

"Talia, eat something from your pack," he ordered after we'd been driving for a couple minutes. His tone was serious, and he was in charge, so I obliged without comment, even though my stomach was so knotted that I doubted any food would fit.

"I want to stop by the safe house and make sure everything is copacetic, then we'll go locate the laboratory while it's still dark. It's probably about ten miles from the house to the location, and we are going on foot so make sure you have the energy," he continued.

I found several bags of dried fruit in my pack, and started munching on them noisily. I don't know how long it actually took us to arrive at the safe house, but it felt like forever. Every passing minute compounded to my mounting anxiety. When we finally pulled up out front I was saddened to see that it looked much like the barn on the outside – extremely run down. I don't know what

I'd expected. I knew we wouldn't be staying at a four-star hotel, but I'd hoped the rumors of the poor living conditions on Hunts were exaggerated; they weren't.

"Only mental communication from now on, understood?" Henri's mental voice filled my head. Both Erik and I nodded.

"Erik, go around back. I will go in the front. Talia, stand guard outside. Keep your mind as open as you can." I nodded again, swallowing over the lump of sugary fruit lodged in my throat.

"Get your weapons ready and be on full-alert," he continued.

I immediately rummaged in my bag and withdrew a belt with eight knives fastened to it. I threaded it through the belt loops at the waist of my suit. Next, I strapped two larger daggers to the outsides of each of my legs, blades running the length of my thighs. I could feel my heart beating in my throat. I was suddenly terrified. It wasn't until I actually strapped the weapons belt around my waist that reality hit me. I was actually in the field. This was *not* practice. The weapons were real. I could really die. I started to panic.

Erik reached back and put his gloved hand over my mine, *"Just stay calm, you're going to do great. Remember your training and focus."*

I nodded, and gave him the closest thing to a smile that I could muster. Inhale. Exhale. Repeat.

I waited for Henri and Erik to get out of the car before opening my own door.

"Count of three," Henri said once we were all standing outside of the vehicle. *"One. Two. Three."*

Erik silently jogged around to the back of the house. Henri moved deftly towards the front door. I positioned myself outside of the entrance that Henri had just disappeared through. I closed my eyes and opened my mind wider. I had a strong connection with both Henri and Erik. I couldn't feel a flutter of mental activity anywhere in the immediate vicinity, which calmed me slightly.

Several minutes had passed before Henri called, *"All clear."*

"Ditto," Erik responded.

"All quiet out here," I tried to make my mental voice calm, but it came out frantically.

I could feel both Henri and Erik moving through the house, emerging a full minute later.

"I'll take the lead. Erik, take the rear. Tal, stay between us."

Henri took off at a steady jog through the woods. I focused on his back, and kept my mind as open as I possibly could, casting the net wider and wider as we ran. I couldn't feel anything human in the woods, but I didn't honestly expect to since it was the middle of the night.

Sweat drenched my hair, soaking the bandana that I'd used to tie it back from my face. The rest of my body was covered by the suit and remained, surprisingly, nice and cool. Henri's strides were much longer than mine, but I was surprised to find that it wasn't that hard to keep up with him. It took us over an hour to reach the location. I felt the distinct buzz of a human brain when we were still about three miles out.

I cannot read minds without an established relationship. It only takes a couple of exchanges with a person to establish a relationship that allows me to probe their mind, but if I've never met a person, I can't just read his thoughts. I only get a murmur of brain activity letting me know there is a human in the vicinity.

"I can feel someone," I announced.

"How far?" Henri inquired.

"Maybe three miles. I'm not really sure. The buzz is faint."

"I can feel it, too, but just barely," Erik chimed in.

"Talia, take the lead," Henri ordered. Great. Following Henri was comfortable and mindless; leading the way added a level of responsibility that I wasn't ready for. Henri was in charge, so I silently jogged ahead of him and stretched my mental net. I honed in on the buzzing and followed it to the edge of the woods.

I went to step out of the wooded cover, but Henri placed his hand on my shoulder, holding me back. The three of us crouched down in the leaves, and I pulled the focus from my mind and redirected my energy to my eyesight. It took longer than I would've liked, but finally the buzzing dulled and I could see a house that I recognized from the intel. I could also see the source of the buzzing – he was sitting in the dark by the front door. He looked as though he was sleeping, but I knew better. Sleeping minds don't buzz.

"How many total do you feel awake, Tal?" Henri asked.

"Just the one."

"Can you tell how many are sleeping?"

"No, I'm sorry," I responded regretfully, feeling as though I'd let him down.

Henri unhooked his backpack and searched inside for something. He pulled out his communicator and a heat scanner. He attached the communicator to his wrist and the scanner to his communicator. His communicator gave off a faint glow that wasn't visible from more than a couple of feet away.

"There are ten inside," he said.

"Ten?" Erik sounded surprised. *"I thought there weren't supposed to be more than a handful of them at any given time."*

"That's what our intel said, but who knows. We aren't going in tonight, anyway. Hopefully, there won't be as many tomorrow or the day after," Henri answered him.

Henri spent the next couple of minutes collecting heat images of the house and the surrounding areas. Then he repacked the devices in his bag.

"Erik, we should morph. Why don't you give your bag to Tal," Henri said. Erik took off his boots and all of his weapons, packed them in his bag, and then handed everything to me. I draped his long rifle across my chest and secured his backpack to my front. Henri also removed his boots and weapons and handed me his back pack.

"Tal, after we Morph, strap the extra packs to my back and then get on Erik, and he'll carry you back."

I desperately wanted to argue with him, to tell him that I could make the run back, but the first thing that Henri had taught me was not to argue with the person in charge, it could get us all killed. Unfortunately, our minds were so connected that they both heard my mental struggle just as clear as if I'd been speaking out loud.

"Okay, Henri," I finally agreed, ashamed that he'd heard me warring with his authority. Both boys transformed into large wolf-like dogs. The suit's material stretched to conform to their new body shapes. I'd seen it plenty of times over the past several months, but it never ceased to amaze me. I quickly fastened the packs to Henri before climbing on to Erik's back and winding my hands into the fur around his neck. The boys took off at a breakneck speed into the woods. I clung to Erik as we weaved in between trees in the dark, thankful Henri had chosen a wolf form when he morphed.

Henri was a Poly Morph, like Donavon, and could, therefore, transform in to any animal of his choosing. Like most Poly Morphs, Henri favored one animal in particular, an extremely large bird, since it made the most of his tremendous wingspan and was the fastest way for him to travel. The trouble with his bird-morph was that I had yet to master riding it. In practice, we had been working on me riding on one of them while they were in bird form, but I tended to fall off more often than not, and I never would've been able to stay on while Erik flew through the dense trees of this forest.

Even not in in bird-form, it took considerably less time to get back. I jumped off of Erik's back as soon as we arrived in front of the house. I unfastened the packs from Henri, and watched as the forms of both boys rematerialized in front of me.

Henri silently led the way into the house. Immediately, I noticed that, like the barn, the house was designed to look more decrepit from the outside than it, in fact, was. It was nowhere near luxurious on the inside, but it was clean, and all of the walls and staircases appeared more intact than I'd guessed. I was relieved. As soon as we closed the door, I pictured all the doors and windows from the floor plans and mentally locked them. The sound of all the locks clicking simultaneously into place was faint, but both boys heard the noise. I felt safe for the first time that night.

"We're going to sleep in shifts," Henri announced, speaking out loud for the first time in hours. I hadn't realized what a toll maintaining the mental connection was taking on me until it was broken. I sagged with relief at the reprieve.

"I'll take the first watch. The bedroom is upstairs. Both of you need to get some sleep. Erik, I'll wake you up in a little while," Henri continued.

Exhaustion was beginning to set in as I followed Erik up the stairs. There were three rooms on the upper floor; one was a bedroom and one was a bathroom, while the third room looked like a command center. There were touchscreens lining the walls, and panels decorated with buttons and switches. I walked directly to the bathroom and took off my suit, replacing it with my pajamas. My skin was immediately thankful to be free of the constricting material and allowed to breathe. I quickly brushed my teeth to erase the fuzzy film. Sleep couldn't come fast enough.

Erik was standing awkwardly in the bedroom in his pajamas when I walked in.

"There's only one bed. If you want me to sleep on the floor, I will," he offered.

"The floor is wood; not exactly comfortable," I observed. "Haven't you ever been on a Hunting team with a girl?"

"Yeah, Henri and I had a girl as a floater before he asked to have you permanently assigned to us," Erik confirmed.

"Did you sleep in the same bed with those girls?" I asked.

"It never came up."

"Just don't grope me in my sleep and I think we'll be okay," I replied dryly.

"I don't plan on it, but I make no promises," Erik's eyes twinkled mischievously in the darkness.

I rolled my eyes and climbed into bed. Erik headed towards the bathroom. I was vaguely aware of him climbing into the bed a couple minutes later, but I didn't have the energy to speak.

There were no windows in the bedroom, so I had no concept of time when I woke up. I was lying on my side facing the wall, and I could feel a hand on my hip. The sheer size of the hand indicated to me it belonged to Henri. I gently removed his appendage and slid down to the end of the bed, to go in search of Erik. I didn't have to go far. I found him in the command center watching surveillance of the perimeter surrounding the safe house. He was sitting in one chair with his feet propped up on a second. He was eating something from a bag that looked disturbingly like dehydrated meat.

"Hey. What time is it? Why didn't you wake me?"

"It's not that late. I was going to let you sleep for another couple hours." He looked over his shoulder at me. The light pouring in the window caught his eyes causing the turquoise color to look even more unnatural, and gorgeous, than normal.

"You don't have to coddle me," I retorted, snappier than I meant. My awareness of him when we were in close proximity irritated me, and I irrationally blamed him, as if he could help being ridiculously good-looking.

"I'm not coddling you. You're expending a lot more energy than either me or Henri, and it's your mental powers that we are counting on to keep us connected when we go inside that house. You have to be at your strongest." His reasonable response irked me further.

"I'm not really tired anymore. I'm really hungry, though," I said changing the subject.

"There's some stuff in the kitchen cabinets. None of it's expired or anything, but a lot of it is less than appetizing. It's smart to conserve the stuff in your pack, in case we have to hide in the woods somewhere."

I made my way downstairs and rummaged through the kitchen cabinets. Erik was right; nothing in there looked edible. I finally settled on mixed nuts and canned peaches. Taking my meal back upstairs, I sat with Erik, and let him explain how all the buttons and switches on the panel worked.

"Did you guys get enough sleep?" Henri asked when he finally wandered in a couple of hours later. Erik and I both nodded. "Good. I want to scout out the town, so go get dressed – no suits, just regular clothes."

I nodded and headed to the bathroom to do as I was told. I chose tight-fitting jeans and strapped a knife to each of my calves, covering them with knee-high black boots. I secured the knife belt around my waist and covered it with a loose-fitting white cotton shirt. I strapped on my backpack and wrapped myself in a light-weight jacket to hide the pack from view. When I was ready, I walked downstairs to find Henri and Erik both dressed in loose-fitting dark jeans and black shirts with their jackets covering their packs, as well.

We piled into the road car and followed a decidedly roundabout set of dirt roads that eventually led us to the town. There were several blocks of white stone buildings, no more than four or five stories tall. All of the structures were completely open air with no doors or windows. I wondered how they kept the rain out. One look at the cloudless sky had me doubting there was much precipitation here. The streets running through the city were narrow, barely wide enough for one vehicle. The walkways were the same white stone as the buildings, and the streets were a mix of gray, black and white stones. I assumed the white buildings and walkways were to keep the city as cool as possible in account of the extreme temperatures.

I'd noticed the heat and humidity the day before, but neither had affected me because I was wearing my suit. Today, wearing normal clothing, the heat was nearly unbearable. I found myself wishing that I had packed shorts. Both Elite Headquarters and School were in moderate climates, so the temperatures never came close to the heat here. Capri is on the water, so despite being closer to the equator, there is always a nice breeze that makes the temperature more bearable there.

Henri parked the car just outside of the city, and we walked the short distance on foot. I could feel the sweat dampening my shirt. My knife belt began to chafe against the slick skin of my hips and stomach. I stole glances at both boys, and found them oddly unaffected by the soaring temperatures.

Henri had told me to stay close to him just in case there was trouble, but nobody gave us a second look as we wandered through the crowded streets.

I was unsure what Henri expected to find out by spending the day roaming the tiny town, so I concentrated on my surroundings. It was apparent that the town was poor. Most of the shops sold fabrics or meats and cheeses. I saw one store that sold beautiful metal plates, bowls, and jewelry with each piece individually crafted – no mass manufacturing here. Most of the road vehicles I observed looked much like ours on the outside, but I doubted that any of them contained the interior comforts our vehicle offered. I only glimpsed a few hover vehicles all day, and those I did see didn't glide silently through the air; they created a great deal of racket, making them stand out.

After scouring every inch of the town for something only known to Henri, we walked about half a mile to the house we'd scouted the night before. We kept our distance for fear of being seen.

"Erik, I want you to go check out the surveillance system. Talia and I will stay down here and keep watch," Henri instructed. Erik nodded and began to undress. I turned around, my cheeks flushing, even though he didn't appear to be modest. I felt Erik morphing behind me, and I turned around just as he completed his change into a small black bird. I tried to follow the bird's movements through the treetops, but he moved so quickly that it was impossible to keep up. I opened my mind, and tried to get a feel for how many people were in the house. All that I could tell was that there were at least a handful. Henri busied himself with snapping images of the surrounding area. In the daylight, the house looked almost inviting. I stored the mental image away for later, hoping that it would comfort me later that night.

Erik was only gone for a couple of minutes. After landing, he quickly morphed back and dressed.

"I found all of the cameras that our intel suspected. I looked around for additional ones, but didn't find anything," Erik reported.

"Let's head back and go over the heat images from last night, and the ones that I just got. We can finalize the plan and hopefully take action tonight, so we can be out of here by tomorrow," Henri replied, satisfied. With that, we returned to the vehicle, and Henri drove us a different roundabout way back to the safe house.

Henri insisted that I get more rest before the evening. I hated to admit how exhausted I was from spending the day in the hot sun, but after a cold shower I climbed back into the bed and fell instantly to sleep.

When I woke from my nap, it was dark outside. Henri had made the executive decision we would not go in that night, and instead perform another stakeout, so I suited up; we hid in the woods, using the trees as cover, for most of the night. Henri took images of all the men coming and going. We observed the guards posted outside to determine when the least number of people would be awake and alert. We left with just enough time to make it to the safe house before dawn.

When we got back, Henri confirmed that tomorrow night would be *the night*. I was still wired from the night's activities, so I offered to take the first watch. I diligently monitored the surveillance feeds and munched on dried fruit and hard chunks of cheese while Henri and Erik slept. I promised myself that the first thing I'd do when we returned to headquarters was eat a hot meal, consisting of only fresh foods.

Around midday Henri woke up, and I gratefully climbed into bed with Erik. He didn't move when I flopped down next to him. The night before, I'd been so spent that being close to Erik –

sharing a bed with Erik – hadn't fazed me. I was tired today, but my body hadn't been subjected to the same mental rigors, and exhaustion didn't prevent my awareness of Erik's warm presence next to mine. I wedged myself close to the wall, as far from Erik as I could manage. Still, I could feel his body just inches from mine, making it hard to sleep. I needed something else to focus on, anything else...the intel; I would concentrate on the intel. If I mentally reviewed all of the tedious details from the reports, maybe I could bore myself into sleep. It must've worked because I was soon dreaming about eating dehydrated chicken strips on a pebbled beach while I watched Erik play in the frothy waves.

Chapter Sixteen

When I woke up several hours later, I was anxious and jittery. Just thinking about what the night entailed made me twitch. I was on a rollercoaster ride of emotion; part of me couldn't wait a minute longer to put my skills into action, but the saner part of me was near hysteria. A list of "what ifs" materialized in my head like a grocery list. Imminent death was shelved right next to egregious bodily harm.

I took a cold shower, hoping to drown my fears. My hands shook as I pulled on my adapti-suit. My fingers fumbled while I wound my hair into a tight bun at the base of my neck and covered my head with a black bandana. I knew that I should eat something, but the butterflies in my stomach made me reconsider. When I finally joined Henri and Erik in the control room, I was vibrating like a too-tight guitar string, fraught with tension.

"Ready?" Henri asked. I nodded, unable to unclench my teeth.

The ten mile jog to the house seemed to take less time than it had the previous two nights, my mind was so consumed with the upcoming task. We weren't running particularly fast, but my heart was pounding loudly in my chest. I assumed that Henri and Erik could hear it with their heightened senses, but neither said anything.

Erik had an uncharacteristically serious look on his face. Henri's expression was grim. I could feel Henri's confidence in my Talent, but I also felt his uneasiness about how I'd react if there were trouble. It didn't help with my nerves. I wanted – *needed*, to prove my worth; not just to Henri, but to everybody who'd said that I didn't belong here, and also to myself.

We settled in to wait for our moment once we reached the spot in the woods just outside of the area the cameras surveyed. I lay down in the leaves on my stomach, and tried to even out my breathing. The three of us sat motionless, not speaking, for hours. I filtered their thoughts from my own while still holding the connection, each boy's apprehension weighing heavily on my already-overburdened mind.

"*It's time,*" Henri announced, finally. "*Erik, you're on.*"

"*See you guys shortly,*" I caught a hint of a smile, and felt his trepidation turn to giddy anticipation as he rose. I clung to that emotion, letting it overtake my fear.

Erik silently morphed into the small bird. He took off towards the treetops, and while I couldn't see or hear him, I knew that he was taking out the security cameras. Several minutes later, the black bird flitted down. Instead of morphing back into a human, he morphed into the large wolf-like dog from the other night. He scurried off in the direction of the house; Erik would go create a distraction, hopefully causing the guard to leave his post so Erik could take him out.

There was only one door to the house, so once the guard was gone, Henri and I would be clear to slip in. Henri had determined that the laboratory was located on the second floor of the house, and we needed to get in and take images of all the research. If all went well, Henri and I would be able to go up the stairs, collect the data, and leave the house undetected. The plan was to return to the safe house, and be on our way and out of the region before sunrise. We knew that the next guard wasn't scheduled to come on duty until morning, so no one was likely to find the incapacitated guard until then.

I heard Erik start barking in the woods, far to the right of where Henri and I stood. The guard hesitated at first, so Erik moved into the clearing and barked louder. The guard finally went to chase him off.

"*Now, Talia,*" Henri said. His anxiety was gone, a calm reassurance taking its place.

"*Right behind you,*" I responded, thankful that my voice mirrored his calm tone. A coil of thrill unwound in my stomach, invigorating my limbs. I was ready. I could do this. I would do this.

I followed right on Henri's heels. I was vaguely aware that Erik had ceased barking as we entered the house. There were no lights on inside, but my sensory training, combined with the fact I'd memorized the layout of the house, made finding the staircase easy. Sweat stung my eyes; I wiped it with the back of my gloved hand. Henri and I crept up the stairs and to the end of the hallway. I stationed myself outside of the door while Henri entered the lab to photograph the research. My breathing was even as I slowly scanned the corridor for signs of mental activity. Henri had been in the room for several minutes when I heard a scuffle downstairs.

"*Trouble downstairs,*" Erik grunted through the bond. My mouth went dry. A clammy sheen covered my face. This was *not* part of the plan.

Henri came rushing out of the room. I met his brown eyes and saw the same alarm that I felt. We ran back down the hallway and flew down the stairs, my feet barely making contact with the carpet. Somebody had turned on the lights, and I could see Erik sparring with two men. I reacted without thinking, adrenaline starting to pump through my veins. I grabbed two knives off of my belt, throwing one at each of the men. Both knives struck their targets. Satisfaction surged through me as one landed in the shorter man's thigh and the other cut the upper arm of the taller one. When I mentally summoned the knives back to me, I was already in motion. The first man had fallen when the knife struck him, and I went for him. Henri went for the taller one. I deftly hit the man in the temple, and he crumpled to the ground, knocked out.

All of the noise had woken the rest of the men in the house, and they were now flooding into the foyer. Panic gripped me. We were outnumbered. We were going to be killed or, worse, captured. I needed to do something. I needed to restore our advantage. I needed to focus. I needed to breathe. I greedily gulped the stale air, filling my lungs, my eyes darting around the space for a sign of what to do. The lights, I thought. A thread of hope pulled through the quilt of dread.

I concentrated on the overhead lights until they exploded, blanketing the room in darkness. It was a risky move but, I figured that our heightened senses would give us an advantage in the dark, and just then we needed all the help we could get. My eyes adjusted in seconds. The men from the house floundered in the dark, and relief washed over me. We weren't out of the weeds yet, but we'd definitely gained ground.

I closed my eyes and focused my energy to my hearing. I moved through the room, depending solely on my ears and my mental abilities. I quickly sunk my blade into the mid-section of the first man I encountered. Flecks of sticky, dark liquid dotted my glove. I suppressed the urge to retch. Keep it together, I chastised myself. He stumbled to his feet. I brought a fist and the blunt end of my knife, slick with his blood, down on his head. The cracking sound it made reverberated through the room, and blood spurted from his new wound. His knees buckled. I swallowed my disgust and hit him again. He stayed down that time.

Before I had time to congratulate myself on my victory, another figure collided with me, knocking me to the floor. I let out a small grunt of surprise as I landed on my back, and instinctively crossed my arms protectively over my face. The man's fists rained down on me, but luckily he couldn't see well enough to hit anything vital. He got in one good punch to the side of my head, my ears rang, and I coughed and sputtered, blood filling my mouth. The metallic taste reminded me that I needed to take the offensive; I couldn't play his punching bag.

The man was straddling me, his bulk pinning me to the floor. His weight was compressing my lungs, and I couldn't catch my breath. The room started spinning around us. Getting him off of me was the only thing that mattered. I used the only weapon I had, my head. I strained my neck muscles and flung my forehead towards his, head butting him. My vision blurred slightly, but I summoned my mental energy to throw him off of me, chiding myself for having not thought of it sooner. He flew backwards, landing several feet away in a crumpled heap. I scrambled to my feet, my chest aching from the sudden influx of air. *Erik, Henri*, I thought weakly. They were both still fighting with their own combatants. I didn't waste time assessing my injuries; I threw myself back into the fray.

With the cover of darkness, the three of us were able to even the numbers. I heard movement on the stairs, and I moved toward the noise. I heard three loud pops. I froze mid-step, a fresh wave of panic overcoming me. Someone had a gun. Time seemed to stand still. The bullets headed straight to where Erik was standing over a man kneeling before him.

"NO!" I shrieked, mentally, unable to get the word past my lips.

All of the mental energy I was expending caused me to shake with fatigue, and I didn't know how much I had left in me. But I couldn't let those bullets hit Erik, so I gathered my waning strength and froze the projectiles mid-flight. I almost cried with relief. The gun fired again, but I also managed to stop the second round of bullets. Rage filled me. Stop the gun from firing, I ordered myself.

Fury consumed me as I rushed to the man on the stairs, praying that he would at least need several seconds to reload, but not caring if he didn't. He didn't bother reloading, he just threw the gun at me. I deflected it with my mind and literally dove at him. I knocked him backwards, his spine connecting – I hoped painfully – with the steps underneath him. I wanted to make him hurt. I needed to make him sorry that he pulled that trigger.

When I came down on top of him, I felt a sharp pain pierce my side. I screamed in shock. I reached down, my fingers closing around the handle of a dagger; it was sticking out of my side. I gasped. Panic paralyzed me. These suits were supposed to be impenetrable, how could this happen? I'd been so concentrated on the gun that I hadn't even noticed a knife. My eyes sought those of the man lying underneath me, and his astonishment mirrored my own.

Strong arms pulled me to my feet; I knew instantly that they belonged to Erik. He leaned me against the banister. My knees were shaking so badly that I couldn't stand on my own. Erik moved past me. He reached for my waist and pulled one of the knives free. I averted my eyes as Erik plunged the blade into the man's exposed neck. I brought my hand to my mouth, stifling the strangled cry that was fighting its way out. Erik turned to face me, with murderous rage burning in his eyes. The intensity that was radiating off of him both terrified and thrilled me. He reached for me, and I collapsed into his arms.

"*Get it out. Erik, get it out,*" I yelped hysterically, reaching for the end of the dagger myself. My hands were shaking so badly that I couldn't grip it.

"*No! We need to get you somewhere safe first. If you pull it out now, you'll lose too much blood,*" Henri exclaimed, coming up behind me. "*We need to get out of here now. Most of these guys are still alive, just unconscious.*"

Erik scooped me up in his arms, running out of the house, and to the woods. Once we were a good distance into the trees, he set me down gently on the forest floor. I was disoriented, my vision hazy. Henri dropped to his knees and morphed instantly. Erik fastened all three of our packs to Henri's back and then turned to me. "*I'm going to morph. Can you climb on my back by yourself?*"

"*Yes,*" I answered, even though I wasn't actually sure that I could.

Erik morphed into the large dog and dropped down to his stomach making it easier for me to crawl onto his back. I wrapped my arms around his neck, trying to position myself so that the blade handle wouldn't bump into his back. The two enormous animals took off into the night.

Every breath that I took sent a fresh wave of pain through my side. I wanted to reach down, and see how much blood was soaking through my suit, but I was afraid that I'd fall off if I let go of Erik's neck. I took ragged, shallow breaths in time with Erik's paws beating against the dirt. I needed something to distract me from the pain, so I tried to count Erik's footsteps, but my mind was spinning too quickly to keep up.

The combination of the moonless night and the speed at which we were moving made it impossible for me to actually see our surroundings, but after a time I was positive that we'd passed the safe house. Erik and Henri showed no signs of slowing. I wanted to say something, but I had yet to manage mental communication with either of them in animal-form.

The pain was becoming too much, and I thought there was a chance that I might actually pass out. Fear enveloped me. I wanted Donavon. I instantly scolded myself for being so weak that I needed a boy to comfort me. It was just a little knife wound, after all, right? The pain was so intense; spreading from my side, down my left leg, and across my stomach. One minute icy-cold fear shook me. The next, my skin was on fire and sweat bathed my face.

I gave up caring whether I appeared weak, I reached out to find Donavon's mind, but I couldn't even catch the faint buzz of his mental activity from such a great distance. I tried harder, opening my mind and expanding it little by little. It was a lost cause; I now knew definitively that my mental net did not span thousands of miles. I guess that even I have my limits.

After what seemed like forever, Erik came to a halt. I gratefully rolled off of him and promptly passed out.

"Stay with me, Tal. You need to stay with me," Erik urged, frantically shaking my shoulder.

"I'm here," I mumbled, reaching my hand towards the sound of his voice.

"Open your eyes," Henri ordered harshly. I tried desperately to obey, but couldn't manage more than small slits. I felt Erik pick me up again. The sound of his footsteps changed as the ground underneath segued from dirt to something smoother, concrete maybe.

"Where are we?" I choked out.

"The Barn," he replied, tersely.

He shifted me slightly as he walked up a set of stairs. I winced, but managed to keep in the howl climbing in my throat. He set me down on a hard mattress at the top of the stairs. I heard Henri come in after us, and then the space filled with a faint blue glow. I managed to open my eyes wide enough to see Henri flipping switches on a panel that was similar to the one in the control room of the safe house. The computers hummed quietly as they sprang to life.

Henri started pulling gadgets out of his pack and setting them on the floor next to the mattress.

"I need to take off your suit so I can do a body scan, and see if the blade hit any of your organs before I take it out. The imager won't work through the material," he said quietly, searching my face for a sign that I understood him. I nodded that I did. He unzipped the suit down to my waist, and slipped the imager underneath the parted fabric, next to where the knife was piercing my skin. His hands were surprisingly soft, and his touch was light as he probed the area surrounding the knife. The sight of the cold gray handle protruding from my flesh made me dizzy. I looked away as bile rose to the back of my mouth. I searched the room for something to focus on, and found Erik standing a couple of feet behind Henri, his arms crossed, nervously chewing his thumbnail. He met my eyes and locked me in a stare. The pain dulled slightly. I breathed out, and felt the stomach acids trickle back down.

"Good news. It went cleanly through without hitting any organs," Henri smiled at me. I tried to smile back, but I couldn't tear my eyes away from Erik. "I'm going to take it out, but I need to test your blood for poison before I can sew it up. It should only take a minute." I gave another barely perceptible nod. Henri stood to get what he needed to test for the poison, and Erik moved forward, dropping down to kneel next to my head. Concern rolled off his body in waves.

"Give me your hands." His voice was not unkind but had a firm, authoritative feel to it; I couldn't stop myself from complying. He laced his fingers with mine and the pain dulled a little more.

"Ready, Tal?" Henri asked, bending back down. I nodded and gritted my teeth.

"Open your mind and focus on me, Tal," Erik said in the same firm tone. Still helpless to say no to him, I submitted. The pain didn't totally subside, but it did lessen considerably. Henri placed one hand on my hip and one hand on the end of the dagger. In one swift motion, he extracted the long, hooked blade. I'd expected blinding agony, but it didn't come. There was an odd sensation as it moved through my muscles, but otherwise my body felt almost numb. My eyes were still locked on Erik's, and when his face contorted and his eyes filled with tears, I understood what he was doing. I admonished myself for not having realized it earlier.

"No!" I shrieked. I tried twisting away from Erik, but he had a firm grip on my hands, and Henri was holding clean towels firmly to both my stomach and back, immobilizing my body. I managed to break eye contact, and the moment I did a hot, burning pain shot out in every direction from the wound. I gasped as the pain spread, writhing on the bed as hot tears filled my eyes. Erik refused to let go of my hands. He was so much stronger than I was, and in my weakened condition, I couldn't even put up a real fight. He pulled them behind my head and held my face in a vice grip with the muscles in his forearms.

"No," I repeated, this time with much less conviction.

"Tal, stop. You need to relax and stay still. He can't give you painkillers, this is the only option that you have," Erik's face was only inches from mine, his breath hot against the cold sweat covering my face.

"Your blood is clean. I'm going to sew up your cuts now," Henri interrupted. "I need to take your suit completely off so that I can get to your back."

Erik quickly worked my arms out of the suit and pulled it down to my waist. I thought I would be more embarrassed, lying half-naked, but the pain was excruciating and I found decorum the least of my concerns. I ground my teeth, and tried to fight the feeling of nausea that was quickly overtaking me. Erik grabbed my hands again and pinned them back behind my head. His elbows dug into my collarbone, but I barely felt it over the pain radiating through my side. He rested his forehead against mine, and I had no choice but to look into his eyes.

Erik may be able to mimic my abilities, but he can't match my strength. I'd had years to perfect my Talents; he's had only weeks to work with them. I knew that I could've fought against his mental invasion, but my resolve was weak from the events of the night. While I wanted to be strong, and not let him do this, I wanted for the pain to stop more. I stopped fighting him and opened my mind, the pain easing immediately. I felt myself losing control as Erik took over, but I was beyond caring. In the end, Erik pulled all conscious thought from my mind. The pain completely dissolved.

"Ready?" Henri's voice asked, from a place that sounded a million miles away.

"Yeah," I heard myself say, in a mechanical voice that sounded nothing like my own.

I felt disconnected from my body; my alternate reality consisted only of Erik's eyes. Some part of me felt the tug of the thread that Henri used to stitch my wounds. While I felt no pain, Erik's eyes filled with tears. I watched in wonder as they filled to the brim, and then slowly cascaded down his face.

"I can give you something now, Talia, that will make you sleep for a while," Henri's faraway voice came again.

"Okay," I said in my mechanical voice. I became aware of my arm as a dull chemical sensation spread from the crook of my elbow, making it heavy.

"*Sleep, Tal.*" Erik's mental voice was heavy with exhaustion.

"*I think I will,*" I replied drowsily as I closed my eyes.

Chapter Seventeen

I fluctuated between varying levels of consciousness. Sometimes, I enjoyed a dreamless sleep. Sometimes I dreamed only of crying turquoise eyes. Other times, I thought that I might actually be awake, but I couldn't be sure. During one of my seemingly-conscious periods, I thought I heard Henri and Erik talking.

"I never thought I would see the day," Henri teased, his tone light even though I somehow knew that the underlying mood in the room was heavy.

"What day?"

"The day that Erikson Kelley would genuinely care enough about a girl to ease her pain instead of causing it."

"I'm offended! I always try to comfort girls in pain," Erik responded, with mock indignation.

"Yeah, girls suffering from broken hearts who need a shoulder to cry on, and a body to keep their bed warm," Henri laughed.

"Comfort all the same, buddy."

"Seriously, Erik, what you did for her was really amazing. The mastering of her Talents alone was pretty impressive, but taking the pain...WOW."

"I would do the same for you," Erik sounded embarrassed.

"Really? Really? You'd take the pain of having a blade that had run completely through your side being pulled out and the wounds stitched up, without any painkillers or anesthetic for me?" Henri demanded.

"Of course, I would. I would even suck the poison out of a wound for you," Erik's voice had a light joking tone.

"Ew, no way, man. If I somehow get injected with poison, or bit by a poisonous snake, or whatever, promise me that you won't stick your mouth on my skin. I've seen some of the women your mouth goes home with, and I'd rather take my chances with the poison," Henri laughed. There was a dull thud, and then Henri saying "Ouch," followed by Erik's laughter.

"Erik, promise me one other thing," Henri said, his voice turning serious again.

"Sure, what?"

"You need to put aside any feelings that you have for Talia."

"I don't have feelings for her, Henri," Erik insisted, his voice so low that I thought I might have misunderstood him.

"Okay. You want to play it that way? Fine. Just remember one thing – she has been dating the Director's son for practically her whole life, and I don't see that changing anytime soon."

"Donavon's an ass," Erik said emphatically.

"You know I don't disagree with you there, but that doesn't give you the right to mess with his girlfriend."

"Wouldn't be the first time I've slept with another guy's girlfriend for that reason," Erik tried to lighten the mood.

"Talia isn't really the kind of girl that you have a one-night-stand with," Henri switched tactics.

"What makes you think that it would be only one night?"

"Because you're you. You've never had more than a one-night stand. You're not the only one who cares, and doesn't want to see her hurting."

"I'm not the one you have to worry about hurting her," Erik said quietly. Henri gave a loud sigh, and I imagined him slowly nodding his head.

"Yeah, I know you're not," he replied. "Just promise me that you'll leave it alone?"

"Whatever, man."

"Erik, you've been different since you met her," Henri insisted.

"She makes an incredible first impression; there aren't too many girls who can kick my ass," Erik mused.

I smiled at the memory.

The first time I'd met Erik was at my Placement Exams for the Hunters. The last scoring phase was a five-round spar. Five rounds of hand-to-hand combat against members of the Hunters. No weapons were allowed, only Talents and raw physical fighting. Oddly, of all the rounds of qualifying tests to become a Hunter Pledge, this was the one that I had dreaded the least. I knew that most, if not all, of my opponents would be male. I knew that Mac had personally selected the best fighters. I also knew that most of them would be Morphers. Most importantly, I knew that none of my opponents would be prepared for what I could do. The first four I had beaten because my Talent was stronger, not because of my combat skills. I'd used my mental abilities to dictate their moves for them. I'd choreographed the blows, the final act ending with my victory before they realized what was happening. I was cocky by the time that I got to the fifth competitor. I knew that being last meant that he was the best, but I hadn't known that he was a Mimic.

At first, he'd fallen prey to my mental manipulation like the others, but he quickly realized what I was doing, and was soon using my own abilities against me. I'd never met a mimic, or another Elite-Level Manipulator, so I was unprepared. I was already drained from expending so much mental energy on the previous fights, and when I realized that I would have to fight him for real, I panicked. I had never envisioned a future where I didn't become a Hunter, and I wasn't about to let him change that. I went at him with everything I had, and then some.

Our fight had been dirty, "no holds barred" sparring. When it became obvious neither of us would concede victory to the other, Mac declared the match a tie. At the time, I'd been incredulous that I'd have to take a draw for my last fight. Later, on my first day of training at Elite Headquarters, Henri informed me that it was the first time Erik hadn't won. Ever.

"Talia, it's time to wake up," Erik whispered, close to my ear.

"Not ready yet," I replied sleepily. I could feel him smoothing the damp curls that were stuck to my forehead. Why was I so sweaty? Why was Erik whispering in my ear to wake me up? My eyes flew open, and I tried to sit up, but my stomach muscles protested so much, I was barely able to lift my back off of the bed. The sudden and intense throbbing in my side made me fully conscious, like a cold bucket of water to the face.

"Easy," Erik smiled at me. "We have time, you don't need to rush."

"I think I might need help getting up," I said sheepishly.

"Hold still so I can check your stitches, okay?"

"As long as you promise that it won't hurt," I tried to joke, but instantly regretted it when the memory of what he'd done for me surfaced.

His hands lightly touched my bare stomach, and I froze. I felt a jolt of electricity where his fingertips lingered. My whole body was overcome by a pleasant tingly sensation, and my heart started racing. I gasped involuntarily. I felt the blood rush to my face, and I tried to hide my humiliation over my body's reaction.

"Did that hurt?" he asked, his voice laced with concern. "I'm sorry, I'll be more careful."

"No, it didn't hurt," I whispered. "I'm just jumpy," I added lamely.

"I won't hurt you," he promised. I instantly recalled the conversation that I'd heard between him and Henri, wondering if it had, in fact, been a dream.

"Where's Henri?" I asked, changing the subject.

"Packing the car, and getting things ready for us to leave."

"What all does he have to do to get ready for us to leave?" As long as I kept talking, I could ignore my body's involuntary response to Erik's contact.

"Burning all the stuff with your blood on it."

"What? Why? I thought that he said my blood wasn't poisoned?!?" I said frantically, trying to sit up again.

"It's just protocol, Tal," he soothed. "After I get you up and dressed, he'll burn this mattress and the sheets, too."

"Oh, right, protocol."

"Your stitches look good. Let me help you up so I can re-bandage them."

Erik slowly lifted me into a sitting position. I sat on the edge of the bed, wearing only my bra and underwear, feeling more than a little self-conscious. Erik carefully covered my stitches with bandages, and then wrapped gauze around my entire mid-section to secure them in place. He was careful only to touch at my wounds with his long, rough fingers. He handed me a black tank top, and I pulled it on over my bandages.

"Stitches feel okay?" he asked.

"As okay as they can," I answered.

He helped me to my feet and handed me a pair of my loose cotton pants, but I couldn't bend over to put them on myself.

"I feel like a little kid," I lamented as Erik helped me into one leg and then the other.

"No way. You wouldn't believe the number of times I've done this for Henri," he winked at me.

I rewarded his attempt at humor with a small snort of laughter, but instantly regretted it when pain exploded down my left side.

Once my pants were on, Erik guided my feet into leather flip-flops and wrapped a lightweight jacket around my shoulders.

"Ready?" Henri asked, walking through the door.

"Yeah," I smiled. "I'm ready to go home."

"Erik, get her into the vehicle while I finish up with the mattress and sheets."

Erik half-carried me down the stairs from what I now realized was a loft in the barn. Once I was as comfortably settled as I could be in the backseat of the car, he went back to assist Henri finish cleaning up.

I noticed, as soon as we got in, that this vehicle was even nicer than the previous one. For starters, it was a lot bigger and had a lot more gadgets. There was enough fire power in the doors to outfit an army, and the front passenger seat looked like a mobile command center.

Henri opened the driver's side door and hopped in. Erik climbed in the passenger seat and started up all of the monitors and display screens. Apparently, it didn't just look like a mobile command center – it actually was one. We drove through the open barn doors, and I realized that it was dark outside.

"How long was I asleep?" I asked.

"Only about three hours," Henri answered. "We couldn't spare any more time; I wanted to leave while it was still dark." Shame washed over me at his unspoken meaning. We had to drive because I wasn't in shape to make the trek on foot, or even riding on Erik's back.

"Why don't you lie back down and sleep? It'll be a couple of hours until we get to the pick-up location," Erik added.

"What are you doing?" I asked, nodding towards the monitors.

"Checking in. The Director wants us in constant contact with him. He's worried about you," Erik added. Great, Mac already knew that I'd screwed up my first mission.

I was still in a lot of pain, and woozy from the drugs that Henri had given me earlier. I curled up in the nest of blankets and pillows he'd made in the backseat, and instantly fell back to sleep.

I slept during the entire drive, only waking when the vehicle stopped. Henri parked outside of a large old house. It looked like it had once been beautiful, but had succumbed to neglect and age. The peeling paint revealed wooden boards underneath, and the windows were so thick with grime that it was impossible to tell if curtains hung inside. A white wraparound porch marked the entrance to the house, but I doubted that it would hold my weight, let alone the boys'.

The sun was fully up, shining brightly in the sky, and I guessed it was late morning by the angle.

"Where are we?" I asked drowsily.

"About five miles from the hover plane," Henri answered. "Erik will morph and carry you the rest of the way. It's too risky to drive into town."

"I can walk," I insisted.

"No, you can't," Erik interjected. I gritted my teeth and sighed. I hated to admit it, but he was right. I was weak, and in a lot of pain, and it was unlikely I'd make it the entire way. Even more than I disliked admitting that Erik was right, I hated that he knew how crappy I felt because he was reading it out of my mind. I didn't like having the tables turned on me.

Erik morphed into a large black horse as soon as he exited the vehicle, and Henri lifted me easily on to his back. Once I was settled, the three of us set off towards the town. Erik trotted at a moderate pace, and Henri ran alongside of us, ready to catch me should I fall. Each step sent a jolt of pain up my side, but I knew that this was better than the alternative: walking.

The town was small, with only one real street that was lined with old brick buildings. Erik and Henri both slowed to a walk, and Henri reached up to take my hand. It was early enough that few people walked the street, and to any onlookers, we looked like a man with his wife and their horse.

We were about halfway down the street when I spotted a hover plane with the Agency logo parked, but still idling. As we neared the plane, I noticed the plane's exterior had the telltale sheen of camo-metal. There was a more technical name, but I couldn't pronounce it. The metal was designed so that once we were airborne, it would blend in with the sky and make the plane hard to detect. The metal also contained a chemical coating that scrambled radar, making the plane hard to detect.

Henri gripped my hand tighter and walked up to the plane. Several Agency medics surrounded the ramp that led into the underbelly of the plane, looking anxious.

"We were starting to get worried," a curly blonde Medic called out, sounding relieved.

"Sorry, we got here as quickly as we could," Henri called back.

When we reached the plane Erik did not stop, but instead entered in horse form, his hooves thudding heavily on the metal. A small red-haired boy with freckles waited inside. He gave a small, relieved smile when he saw us.

"Hey, Natalia," he greeted me.

"Hey," I replied. I recognized the boy from school – we were in the same year. I thought that his name might be Chad, but I wasn't sure. He must be a Medic Pledge.

He reached up and carefully lifted me down from Erik's back. As soon as I was off, Erik morphed, causing the Medic Pledge to gasp. I guessed that he'd never actually seen someone morph before.

"Hi there, I'm Erik," he said extending his hand.

"Chad," the red-haired boy stammered, confirming my earlier guess.

There was a bed sitting off to the right, and Erik helped me over to it with his arm wrapped around my waist, careful not to disturb my stitches. Chad followed closely behind.

Once I was settled comfortably with my head on the small, square pillow, he worked quickly, hooking up monitoring devices to my body. There was a cuff on my arm to monitor my blood pressure, several cold plastic leads on my chest to monitor my heart, and sensors to each temple to monitor my brain activity.

While Chad worked, I watched Henri and the remaining medics file through to the front cabin of the plane. Erik stayed back with me, not wanting to get in Chad's way, but refusing to take his seat.

The curly blonde Medic joined Chad at my bedside and introduced himself as Dr. Daid. He patiently listened as Chad quickly briefed him on all my vitals; since I had no idea what my vitals should be, I didn't know if the numbers that he rambled off were normal.

"Take off in five," called a gruff voice from the front of the plane.

"You should get belted in," Dr. Daid said, turning to Erik.

"I'd rather stay back here if that's okay," Erik replied tightly. Dr. Daid nodded, and then turned to collect some supplies that he'd need.

Erik helped me turn to my side, and then covered me with a thin, scratchy blanket.

"How you feeling, Tal?" Henri asked, poking his head back in from the main cabin, his eyes full of concern.

"I think I'll live," I answered.

"Good," he smiled. "It'll be a couple of hours before we get back to Headquarters, but once the Medics check you out, they'll give you something to sleep." Henri turned to Erik, "Come up front when you're done."

"Will do," Erik replied, not taking his eyes off mine.

Chad returned to my bedside with a tray of instruments. He watched as Dr. Daid used an imager, slightly fancier than the one Henri had used, to scan my stomach and back. The images were displayed on a large monitor that was behind the bed. He assured me that the blade hadn't ruptured any organs and that the only real internal damage was a scrape on my lower rib. He touched the screen of the monitor, on an image of my rib, to enlarge the area that he was talking about. I nodded my understanding, but I had no idea what he was actually pointing at.

Next, he removed the bandages. I winced as he touched the area surrounding the stitches. Erik offered me his hand, and I squeezed it hard. The pain made me grip a little harder than I meant to, and a groan escaped Erik's lips.

"Sorry," I sent apologetically.

Erik smiled kindly and rubbed his thumb gently across the backs of my fingers to let me know he didn't mind.

"The stitches look great," Dr. Daid commented. "Whoever did

these has a very steady hand. Once you heal, we'll be able to remove the scar without a problem." He grabbed a white spray bottle off his tray of accouterments and sprayed both sets of stitches. When the droplets first hit my skin, I let out a small scream as a white-hot pain shot through my skin. Just as quickly as the pain had come, it was gone, replaced by a cool, numbing sensation.

"Sorry," Dr. Daid said, sheepishly, "should've warned you." He grabbed a small pen-like object off of his tray and reached for my free hand. Before I had time to ask what he was doing, I felt a sharp prick on the pad of my index finger, and he squeezed a couple drops of my blood into a small vial.

"I'm doing a more complete test for poison," he explained, "the field kit they give you guys only tests for the common ones."

I nodded my understanding and looked over at Erik, who attempted a reassuring smile.

Finally, Dr. Daid took clean white bandages and rewrapped my side. When he was finished, he gave me a cocktail injection of painkillers; an anti-infection medication, and something to make me sleep.

"I'll come check on you a little later," he promised, once he'd finished. Dr. Daid turned his attention to Erik. "You should let her sleep. She'll start to heal faster." He got up, and then made his way to the front of the craft. Erik nodded, but waited for him to leave before speaking with me.

Erik leaned down and whispered in my ear, "If you need anything, I'll be right up front. Just yell, okay?"

"Thanks," I breathed back. The injection hit me hard, and I was already struggling to keep my eyes open. I had drifted off before I felt the pressure of Erik's hand release my own.

Chapter Eighteen

I slept the entire way to Headquarters. When I awoke, I was groggy and disoriented, and both Henri and Erik had to help me down the ramp to exit the plane. When we reached the bottom, I felt them both stiffen. It took me a minute to react to their change in demeanor. When I looked up, I saw Mac standing several feet away with Donavon on one side of him, and, to my surprise, Penny standing on the other.

"Natalia," he exclaimed moving towards me, his long strides closing the gap quickly. "How are you?" His big gray eyes were full of fatherly concern.

"I'm fine, Mac. It could've been worse," I reassured him.

"Did you lose a lot of blood?"

"Um, I don't think so," I replied with confusion.

"No, sir. She didn't lose much. I was able to stop the bleeding pretty quickly, and, of course, I burned everything afterwards," Henri said, stepping forward.

"Wonderful, Operative Reich. Do you have the information?"

"Of course, sir."

"Good. Why don't you and I go back to my room so I can look it over?" Henri nodded. Then Mac turned his attention to me, "Natalia, go lay down, and I will come visit you before I leave."

"Thanks, Mac," I reached out and gave him an awkward hug.

Erik stood frozen, unmoving, next to me. He kept his face blank, an unreadable mask. His mind was barricaded with thick walls I couldn't easily penetrate, but I got the feeling that he was fighting to keep himself in control. I assumed his tension was on account of Donavon's presence, except I swore the air around his body visibly relaxed when Mac left.

I watched as Mac walked away with Henri following in his wake. Once his father was gone, Donavon rushed forward and wrapped me in his arms.

"*I was so worried, Tal,*" he breathed.

"*I'm fine,*" I said, returning his hug. "*I'm just really tired, and I missed you so much.*"

"*I missed you, too.*"

Erik cleared his throat noisily, and I pulled back from Donavon.

"It's been a long day. I'm going back to the cabin. You coming, Tal?" he said.

"I was thinking maybe she could stay in my room for the night?" Penny hurried forward, talking for the first time. "After all, my room is so much nicer, and she can have some privacy and stuff."

"Thanks, Penny, but I don't want to bother you or anything," I replied.

"Oh, it's not a problem at all! It'll only be for a night or two, and it will be fun – like a sleepover." Her bright green eyes were a shining mix of concern and excitement.

Penny had a point; her room was a lot nicer than the cabin, and she even had a huge soaking tub in her bathroom. I felt grimy from head to toe, and wanted nothing more than to lie down.

"Thanks, Penny, that'd be great," I answered honestly.

"See you tomorrow, Tal." Erik left without as much as a word to Penny or Donavon.

The medical cocktail was beginning to wear off slightly, but I still didn't trust my motor skills. Donavon must have sensed my uneasiness because he immediately wrapped one arm protectively around my waist. I leaned gratefully into him, and we headed to Penny's room. It was a slow trip, made slower because I needed to stop and rest several times.

Penny's room was located in the largest of the three housing buildings, and the enormous structure contained ten floors. Workout facilities, an indoor pool, and a room-service kitchen made up the first several levels. The upper floors housed Cryptos, older Hunters, and the Medics. The smaller of the other two buildings contained suites where higher-ups, like Captain Alvarez lived or where Mac stayed when he visited. The third building housed the essential support staff: receptionists, cooks, cleaning staff, etc. Most support staff were low-level Talents who weren't offered a position in one of the Agency's other divisions.

The huge glass doors slid silently apart as Donavon, Penny, and I approached the entrance to Penny's building. We entered the cavernous main foyer, with a glass ceiling stretching all the way to the tenth floor, and skyways bridging the gaps between the east and west wings of the upper levels.

Donavon half-dragged, half carried me to the west elevator bank. Once inside, Penny pressed six, and the elevator shot upwards so fast I thought I might be sick. I scrunched my eyes closed, and leaned further into Donavon for support.

The elevator came to an abrupt stop on Penny's floor. The steel doors parted as a mechanical, female voice said, "Level six." Thankfully, Penny's room was very near the elevator.

"Welcome to my home," Penny said, opening the door using a

fingerprint scanner – no door knobs here. Her greeting was for Donavon. I had been to Penny's room numerous times since she befriended me.

My entire cabin could've easily fit inside Penny's room. The floor was covered in plush, white carpeting that was soft to the touch. The walls were also white, and Penny had hung brightly painted pictures on several walls to liven up the room. Her huge bed was up against the far glass wall. Penny had the glass wall set to show the actual scene outside, but she was able to program the window to any number of outdoor scenes, including snowy mountains, sandy beaches, and flowery fields. My room at Mac and Gretchen's had the same technology.

The bathroom was half the size of the bedroom and made of white marble with grayish flecks. She had a large soaking tub with enough room for four, and a walk-in shower. The pedestal sink and the toilet were also white with gold fixtures.

As soon as we walked through the door I, bee-lined for the bathroom, leaving Penny and Donavon to entertain each other. I turned the gold faucet, and waited while the tub filled with warm water, and added the contents of a small bottle sitting on the tub's ledge to create soapy bluish-colored bubbles.

I tried to remove my clothes, but found the pain too intense when I tried to raise my hands over my head to take off my shirt.

"Donavon?" I called.

"Right outside the door, Tal," he sent back.

"Can you come help me?"

Donavon tried the handle on the door, and I disengaged the lock so he could enter. I sat on the closed lid of the toilet, trying to wriggle my way out of my shirt. Donavon smiled when he saw me tangled in my own clothing.

"Stop, stop, stop. I'll do it," he gently helped me pull my arms

out of my t-shirt, and up over my head.

"I can do the rest myself. Thanks," I smiled at him, taking in his clear blue eyes, and all of a sudden, I didn't want to be alone. The events of the past day and a half hit home. I could have died. I might never have looked into Donavon's eyes again.

"Will you sit in here while I take a bath?" my mental voice pleaded. I sounded desperate. I didn't care.

"Of course," I could tell by the look on his face that I was projecting my thoughts toward him.

"I know you're scared right now," he began, confirming that I was, indeed, projecting. *"It's normal to be scared after what you've been through. These kinds of accidents happen all the time. You'll get used it,"* he continued.

Get used it? I was pretty sure I didn't want to get used to be stabbed.

"Turn around so I can finish getting undressed," I ordered.

"Yes, ma'am," he smirked.

I stood and untied the drawstring on my pants – thankfully, they fell to the floor without any further prompting. Getting out of my underwear was tricky, but I managed. No way was I asking Donavon for assistance doing *that.* The bandages were supposedly waterproof, so I figured I would take my chances and leave them on. I climbed the steps to the tub and lowered myself into the soapy water. My muscles instantly began to relax, and I sighed contentedly.

"You can turn around now," I called to Donavon.

He walked over and sat on the steps up to the tub. *"Want to tell me what happened?"* he asked, batting at the bubbles.

"Not really," I answered, but I found myself launching into the story, anyway. I talked until the water cooled and only a thin layer of bubbles remained on top. I told Donavon everything. Well,

not quite everything. I didn't tell him about what Erik did.

I don't know exactly why I didn't tell him about what happened with Erik. Okay, that's not true, I knew why. I didn't want him to be upset, and I certainly didn't want to further the feelings of animosity between the two of them. I was careful not to think about Erik's involvement in my impromptu medical care, and Donavon seemed oblivious to any holes in my story.

After my bath, I felt a million times better, and unequivocally cleaner. Penny and Donavon helped me into Penny's huge bed, and I sank gratefully into the soft mattress, letting it mold to my body.

"Want to watch something on the screen?" Penny asked brightly.

"Something funny," I answered, even though I wasn't likely to stay awake that long.

"You got it!" Penny replied, a little too cheerfully.

Penny turned on her wall screen using a remote device, clicked through several menus, and selected a romantic comedy about some ridiculous love triangle. I tried to pay attention to the movie, but my thoughts kept straying to Erik. I blamed the drugs. Every time I caught a glimpse of Donavon out of the corner of my eye, I felt guilty, as if I'd done something wrong. I finally fell asleep.

I felt Donavon kiss me on the forehead. *"I'll see you tomorrow."*

I mumbled something unintelligible and fell back asleep.

I slept through the night and for most of the next day. When I woke, I saw Penny sitting at her table working on a small portable computer.

"Hey," I mumbled.

"Oh, good, you're up!" she exclaimed closing her portable. "How do you feel?"

"I've been better," I said trying to sit up. "Are you hungry? I can order us something to eat." That was another advantage of staying with Penny: room service.

"That'd be great. I'm famished," I admitted. I couldn't remember the last time I'd eaten.

Penny used an electronic menu, similar to the ones in the cafes, to order us platters of cheesy eggs, and buttery onion bread, with a pitcher of melon juice to wash it all down. I carefully climbed out of bed, over the mess of blankets and pillows that Penny had used as a makeshift bed the night before, and made my way to the bathroom. It took me longer than normal to complete my morning routine, and when I exited the bathroom I heard Penny thanking the room service delivery man.

We sat at her white plastic table, and I hungrily devoured all of my food, plus half of Penny's.

"I can order you more if you want," she joked.

"Sorry, it's been a couple days since I've had food that's not dehydrated," I replied, embarrassed.

"Want to tell me about what happened?" she asked, her voice softening.

"Not right now," I responded.

Telling Donavon had been one thing; he could at least relate to what I'd been through. Penny lived a very different life, it was unlikely that she'd ever leave the comforts of Headquarters since her Talent ensured her usefulness to the Agency for the foreseeable future.

"I understand." She tried to hide her disappointment, but I knew she was hurt I didn't want to confide in her. She looked as though she might press the issue, but then decided against it.

"The Director's sent several comms. He wants you to contact him as soon as you're up and moving."

"Can I use your communicator?" I asked.

"Course," she gestured to her bedside table, where the device sat.

I called Mac and let him know I was alive. He said that he was staying in the same building as Penny, and would stop by shortly. After we disconnected, I used mental communication to let Donavon know that I was awake. I told him that I would be back in Hunters Village that night and I would come see him.

When Mac arrived, Penny excused herself and left us to talk. He asked me about my injuries, and for a detailed account of the night we invaded the house. He listened carefully without comment, but I could tell that he was taking mental notes. He told me that the medical lab had called him late last night, to confirm that there wasn't any poison in my blood. They did, however, find poison on my suit, around the tear in the fabric. The lab believed that the poison on the blade had allowed it to tear the suit because ordinarily a knife would not have been able to penetrate the material. They determined, luckily, that the suit had absorbed all the poison before the blade made contact with my skin.

I knew that I'd messed up my mission, and I wanted to assure Mac that I'd do better next time, but I didn't know how to broach the subject. I decided to go the apology route.

"I'm sorry. I messed up," I told Mac after he'd finished his spiel.

He gave me a hard look. "These things happen. No Hunter, no matter how experienced, can plan for every possible outcome," he assured me. I did a quick swipe of his mind. He hated when I did that, but I needed to know how poor my performance had actually been. He was disappointed; he'd staked a lot of his reputation on me being Hunter material. I felt bad that I'd let him down.

"You'll do better next time. The important thing is that you're alive," he smiled. He honestly did believe that was what really mattered.

Before Mac left, he told me to go by Medical before the end of the day. He also informed me that I was expected to be back at practice the day after tomorrow. I asked him to send my greetings to Gretchen, and thanked him for coming.

Penny accompanied me to Medical, and sat with me while Dr. Daid looked at my stitches. He informed me that the wounds were healing nicely, and the stitches should dissolve fully by tomorrow morning. He gave me a mild painkiller shot, and ordered me to return the next morning.

After we left Medical, Penny escorted me back to my cabin.

"You should totally stay with me again tonight. You'll be so much more comfortable at my place," she pleaded, once we'd arrived at my door.

"I absolutely *cannot* take your bed again," I argued. "Besides, I'm feeling much better today. As nice as your bed is, I really want to sleep in my own." I actually *was* feeling a lot better, and more than anything wanted to put this behind me, and get my priorities back on track. If I'd let Mac down, I could only imagine how Henri was feeling. My placement scores at school had assured that I would be assigned to the Hunters, but it was Henri who had spoken up and insisted he could make my Talent useful on Missions. No other team captains had been willing to take the risk.

"Well, if you change your mind, just come on back," she smiled and hugged me.

"Thanks for everything, Penny. It means a lot to me," I told her honestly.

"That's what friends are for."

I smiled. "Yeah, friends".

I walked into my darkened cabin, and immediately noticed

that neither Erik nor Henri was there. Part of me was saddened –
the childish part – that they were both gone and not sitting, waiting
on pins and needles for my return. Part of me was also relieved. I
didn't want to see Erik. My feelings were becoming muddled
where he was concerned. I tried telling myself that I had just been
through an ordeal, and I was confusing the gratitude that I had for
all he had done for me with something more.

I assumed that normal teenagers had lived through more than
one crush by the time they were my age. Penny had a new
infatuation every other day, it seemed, but I had yet to have a real
crush, unless Donavon counted, and I kind of didn't think he did.
Looking back, I don't honestly remember how our relationship
went from childhood best friends to teenage boyfriend/girlfriend.

One hot summer day, we'd been sitting, dangling our feet in
the lake. I sat as still as possible because every movement, no
matter how small, caused fresh drops of sweat to leave salty trails
down my back. Donavon sat next to me, skipping rocks across the
lake's glass smooth surface. I used my mental abilities to make the
huge leaves on the surrounding bushes fan us, creating a small
breeze in the otherwise stagnant air.

I was lost in thought when Donavon put his hand on my arm. I
jumped in surprise. When I looked into his eyes, I saw his
nervousness. The physical contact mixed with the intensity of his
emotions made it nearly impossible *not* to know what he was
thinking and feeling. I could hear the internal debate in his head –
he didn't know whether to ask if he could kiss me or just lean in
and go for it. Only seconds passed, but I grew so impatient waiting
for him to make a decision that I leaned over and kissed him firmly
on the lips. It was awkward at first, as I imagine all first kisses are,
but it didn't take long before we got the hang of it.

We never had a conversation about being a couple or

anything. It just happened. Nobody seemed surprised. I hadn't really thought about him like that before our kiss, but afterwards, it only seemed natural that it had happened. I never felt nervous or uncomfortable around Donavon. I also never felt the thrill of an adrenaline rush like the one I got when Erik touched me. I wasn't sure if that was what a crush felt like, but I hated myself for feeling whatever it was. I hated having any feelings for Erik that weren't platonic. It was a betrayal of my relationship with Donavon.

Gratitude, I told myself. Gratitude was the feeling I had for Erik; just gratitude for helping me through a difficult situation.

A vision of his turquoise eyes swimming with tears filled my mind. I shook my head as if to erase the mental picture before my emotions became even more confused.

I went straight to my bed, and was planning on climbing under the covers when I noticed the light on my communicator was blinking. I hit the hologram button and Henri's head materialized, telling me that he was staying in the city with a friend and Erik would likely stay in the city, as well. *Thank goodness*, I thought, kicking off my shoes and climbing into bed. I opened my mind and reached out to Donavon.

"Want to come sleep with me?" I asked. I sort of hoped he'd say no. I really wanted to be alone, but my conscience reasoned that if I asked, it would alleviate some of the guilt I was feeling about Erik

"I'll be right there."

Donavon knocked three times on my door, and then pushed it open. He walked over to my bed without turning the light on, and climbed in next to me.

"Are they going to be gone all night?"

"Yup. Henri left me a message."

"Is he staying with Frederick?"

160

"How did you know about that?" I was surprised.

Donavon shrugged, *"I've hung out with them in the city a couple of times. Frederick's pretty cool. He used to be with TOXIC. It's pretty well known that Henri stays with him before he leaves for a mission, and when he gets back."*

"He used to be with the Agency? Is he a Talented?"

"Technically, he's Talented, but very low-level. He wasn't placed after graduation, and after working a remedial job here for a couple years, he got permission to leave and went to work in the city."

Very interesting. Some people weren't placed in a major division after graduation because their powers weren't strong enough to be of use to the Agency. I hadn't realized that people actually left TOXIC, though. Even a remedial job with TOXIC was better than being off all alone. The Agency provided everything for their Operatives: housing, clothing, food, everything.

"Do you hang out with Erik when you're in the D.C.?" I asked before I could stop myself.

"I have, but not often. He and Harris have been friends since school, so sometimes we all go out together. Why?"

"Just curious," Why did I want to know? Did it really matter? I tried to clear my mind; I was worried that thinking too much about Erik might cause me to project my thoughts about him onto Donavon.

"I'm leaving in a couple of days for a mission," his mental voice was hesitant as he changed the subject.

"Why didn't you tell me last night?"

"I didn't want to bother you with it. It's not a big deal, it should be simple. I should be back in a couple of days."

"Well, I'm glad that we get to spend tonight together, then." I kissed his cheek softly. Another wave of guilt washed over me

when I thought about the reason I'd reached out and asked him to come over. I was lying on my good side, so I rolled on to my back and pulled Donavon's head down, giving him a kiss on his lips this time. *"You'll be careful?"*

"I'm always careful." He leaned in and kissed me again.

We talked well into the night. It felt so good to just spend time with Donavon – I felt like we were back at school, sneaking into each other's rooms late at night. I was so tired, but I didn't want to fall asleep, not yet. I wanted to spend every minute that I could with him since we so rarely had the chance to do this anymore. The more time that I was with Donavon, the less confused I felt about Erik. By the time I finally closed my eyes, I was able to convince myself that any feelings I had for Erik were strictly limited to gratitude. At some point, I fell asleep, mid-sentence.

I woke up when Donavon eased himself out of bed before sunrise.

"Where ya going?" I mumbled, reaching towards him.

"I have an early practice. We have a lot to go over before we leave for this Mission. I also don't really want to be here when Erik gets back," he whispered. He kissed my cheek. "I love you."

"I know," I replied, mostly incoherently. Donavon sighed, and then I heard his quiet footsteps moving towards the door. I was already back to sleep when Donavon closed the door softly behind him.

I was fifteen when Donavon left for his Pledge year with the Hunters. The day before he was scheduled to leave school, we spent the whole day up by the lake. Donavon packed a picnic of cheeses, breads, and jams that he'd borrowed from his mother's kitchen. In between eating, swimming, and making out, we laid on blankets, soaking up the sun. We were drying from our latest swim, watching the sunset, when Donavon rolled up onto his side and leaned over me.

"It's going to be hard at first, Tal, but promise me you'll hang in there." Donavon's blue eyes were clouded with nerves.

"Of course, I will. You promise me that you won't forget me once you're surrounded by all those city girls," I teased.

"I don't think it'd be possible for me to forget you. I literally can't get you out of my head," he joked, leaning down to kiss me softly. He ran one hand along my hip and my upper thigh. I responded by wrapping my leg around his waist. Our kisses became deeper, more desperate. My heart was pounding in my chest, and my stomach was queasy in a good way. Where his skin touched mine, I felt alive. There was barely any material separating us since we were both wearing bathing suits, and where his skin touched mine, it tingled. He moved his mouth from mine and started kissing my neck. I gulped air greedily, trying to catch my breath. His hands were running over every inch of my exposed skin.

"Donavon, I love you," I whispered.

"What?" he pulled back, I'd caught him off guard with my admission.

"I love you," I said in a clear voice. He just stared at me, a gambit of emotions racing through his mind.

"I don't know what to say," he finally responded, pushing my leg off of him.

"I think that this is where you say you love me, too," I said slowly, pushing him the rest of the way off of me. Donavon looked everywhere but at me, refusing to meet my eyes. "I see how it is. You expect me to have sex with you, but you can't even tell me how you really feel about me?" I exploded. By this point in my short life, my temper was already part of my trademark.

"I don't know, Tal. I mean, I'm only seventeen, how do I

know if I love you?" I felt as if I'd been punched in the stomach. All of the air rushed out of my lungs. I focused my energy and bore into his mind.

"Talia, don't," Donavon ordered sharply, realizing what I was doing. He scrambled further away from me, and covered his head with his arms like that would help to keep me out of his mind.

"I know that you love me, but if you're too scared say it out loud, fine," I kept my voice as calm as possible even though I was so mad that I could've spit fire. "I'm going back to my room. Don't bother coming to say goodbye tomorrow." Tears filled my eyes and threatened to spill down my cheeks.

I grabbed my clothes and ran from the woods, leaving Donavon alone by the lake. Donavon tried to reach out to me several times that evening, but I blocked his attempts.

Very early the next morning, I heard a knock at my door. I knew that it was Donavon the moment I heard the tapping.

"*Go away,*" I sent, still reeling from the night before.

"*Tal, open the door,*" Donavon's mental voice commanded.

"*No.*"

"*I'd really rather say what I have to say to your face.*"

"*Well I'm not letting you in so you can say whatever you want from out there.*" My irritation was obvious.

"Natalia, I love you. I've loved you from the moment I first saw you, when I was twelve. I'm sorry that I was too scared to say it yesterday." His voice was soft, but my hearing was acute enough that I could hear him through the door, and he knew it. I mentally pushed the door open. Donavon ran over and fell on his knees next to my bed. I threw my arms around his neck.

"*I love you, Tal,*" he pulled me tight against his chest.

"*I know, Donavon.*"

Even though he'd finally said those words, I was stubborn and still hurt from his earlier rejection. We both knew that it would be a long time before I said those three words to him again.

Chapter Nineteen

Something crawled in my ear. I swatted at it. I felt it again, slithering down my neck this time. I reached to scratch the place where it had been, when I heard stifled laughter.

"Erik, you'd better be out of my arms' reach when I open my eyes, or I'll make you sorry," I grumbled without opening my eyes.

"Won't be hard, your arms are pretty short," Erik teased.

I opened my eyes and rolled over to face him. I groaned at the dull ache in my side.

"Think you're funny?"

"Sure do," he smirked.

"Did you meet a nice girl in the city?" I asked, changing the subject.

"I met a girl who was nice to me," he did his eyebrow wriggle. I felt another stab. This one was something akin to jealousy, and I immediately hated myself.

"I'm sorry I asked." I only hoped he didn't know how sorry I actually was.

"Where's your boyfriend? I expected to find him here since we left you all alone last night." Erik's tone changed to one of mild disgust.

"Why don't you like him?" I demanded.

"It's not really so much that I don't like him," he replied, evasively.

"Then what is it?" I was perplexed by the animosity between them.

"We're just not compatible, I guess," Erik mumbled, looking uncomfortable.

"You don't have to date him. I just wish you'd be civil to him."

"For you, Talia, I would do anything," he bowed gallantly.

"So you'll be nice to him?" I pressed.

"You said civil. Nice is pushing it," he warned.

"Civil," I agreed. "Thank you, Erik."

I got up, dressed, and made my way over to the Medical building. The Medic removed my bandages and confirmed my stitches had dissolved. I was now left with two thin scars, one on my stomach and one on my back. The skin was tender and pinkish. I was amazed by how quickly the wound had healed. The Medic used a laser scanner, passing it over my scars again and again, fading the raised skin until it was non-existent. When he was done, the skin was still discolored, but he assured me that too would fade in a few hours. My internal damage would take a little longer to heal, but cosmetically I was good as new.

I felt better about the Erik situation after spending the night with Donavon, but I was still hesitant to return to my cabin. Spending the night with Donavon had reminded me why I loved him, but just seeing Erik made me think and feel things I didn't understand. Both Donavon and Penny were working, so I took the opportunity to have some alone time, finally. I strolled, leisurely around the compound. For the first time in months, I was completely alone. Not just physically, but mentally, too. I'd forgotten how nice it was to be by myself with my own thoughts.

I hadn't realized how heavily everybody else's stresses were weighing me down until they were gone. Henri was overwhelmed by his position as team leader. He constantly worried that he was too young to be in such a high position. He worried I wouldn't perform in the way he had hoped when he'd requested me as part of the team. He worried that I'd get hurt, and Mac would blame him.

Erik maintained a carefree attitude on the surface. He was indifferent to the Agency and the war with the Coalition. If it were up to him, he wouldn't have gone to the McDonough School. Unfortunately, like every other Talented child born in the United States, he hadn't had a choice. He mostly worried about how long he'd be able to keep up his city going party boy and Agency Operative lifestyles. He also worried about disappointing Henri by not taking his responsibilities seriously enough. But most of all, he worried about me.

Maybe my feelings for Erik were only a reflection of his feelings for me, I mused. I hoped so. If Henri's feelings could affect me, then surely Erik's could too, right? After all, my mind and Erik's seemed to have a strong connection, even stronger in some ways than my connection with Donavon. I could project my thoughts, my feelings, and my will onto anyone, but Erik was the first person I'd subconsciously done it to.

I wandered in the woods, relishing the blissful emptiness in my head. I sat by the lake and skipped stones over the water's surface. I lay down in the dirt, not caring about my clothes, and let the sun warm my face. I closed my eyes, and the back of my eyelids lit up, bright reddish-orange from the sun's rays. It reminded me of Penny's hair. I was so glad I had a girlfriend to talk to about my boy problems. As the thought crossed my mind I smiled wider; I had boy problems! How very normal of me.

I felt different my whole life, mostly because I *am* different. Going to the McDonough School and meeting other kids like me had made me begin to feel better. Yet, I still felt different because I never bonded with the other kids, never actually made friends. But now, for the first time, I had a boyfriend, a crush, and a best friend to talk to about my boy problems. I couldn't remember a time when I'd felt more content.

After my quiet afternoon at the lake, I still wasn't ready to return to my cabin. I lounged in the grass outside the Crypto bank, feeling slightly stalkerish, waiting for Penny to finish work for the day.

"Do you have dinner plans?" I asked when Penny finally emerged from the Crypto bank.

"Would you mind going back to my room to eat? The kitchen is making sweet potato ravioli. It's my absolute favorite."

"Sounds perfect," I smiled.

I trailed Penny up to her room, and made myself comfortable on her bed while she ordered dinner. I aimlessly flipped through the movies on her wall screen without actually reading any of the descriptions.

"What's on your mind?" Penny asked after I failed to answer a question she'd posed three times.

"It's nothing, I'm still just a little out of it from the last couple of days."

"Erik?" Penny guessed.

"What? Why would Erik have anything to do with anything?" I retorted, defensively.

"I've seen you two around each other, Tal; it's obvious he likes you. And everyone talks about how Erik has changed since you got here," Penny said, rolling her eyes.

"It's not like that. He just sees me as a younger sister or

something," I mumbled even, though that wasn't entirely true, considering the conversation I'd heard between him and Henri. "Besides, I have a boyfriend – you know, Donavon," I added hastily.

Penny looked doubtful. "How do you feel about him?" she asked softly. I knew that she was talking about Erik.

"I don't know," I answered honestly. "Sometimes, I think that maybe I have a little crush on him." My cheeks burned with embarrassment. I quickly looked down at my hands, but it was too late to take it back.

"A little crush?" Penny snorted.

"I don't know! I've never really felt like this about anybody. I spend so much time in his head, it's confusing. You don't understand," I added hastily.

"You spend just as much time in Henri's head as you do in Erik's," she reasoned. "Why is Erik different?"

I gave her a long, searching look. "Henri has a boyfriend, so that's not an issue."

"Hmm, well that explains the difference," she laughed. "What about me? Do you go in my head?" Her question took me by surprise.

"No, no, of course not," I stammered.

"I understand if you do," she said quickly. "I mean it's your Talent and stuff, and it's really cool. I just, you know, was wondering." Now it was Penny's turn to blush.

"I'd never go in your head, Penny," I assured her. "You're my friend, and I know it's a huge violation of someone's privacy to do that."

She smiled. "Thanks."

"I think that's why most people are afraid to be close to me. They're scared I'll read their thoughts, learn their secrets," I continued.

"Do you read most people's minds?"

"Not if I can help it. Unfortunately, some people are really strong projectors, and I end up hearing their thoughts without meaning to," I explained. "It's risky, too. When I read someone's mind, I have to open up my own, so in the process they have an open window into my head. They can then see my thoughts and feel my feelings. It makes me completely vulnerable," I continued.

Just then, the kitchen aide knocked on Penny's door, delivering our dinner. Over ravioli, the conversation turned lighter. We talked about Penny's less complicated boy problem – her crush of the week: Randell. The evening ended up being exactly what I needed to relax.

When I finally hurried through my cabin door, just before curfew, Henri was the only one there.

"Hey, how're you feeling?" he greeted me with a grin.

"Good," I answered truthfully, "I'll be ready to practice tomorrow."

"I'll take it easy on you," he winked at me.

I smiled and made my way to the bathroom to perform my nightly bedtime ritual of washing my face and brushing my teeth. I took my time in the bathroom, and when I emerged, Henri's light was out, and Erik's bed was still empty. Even though I'd stayed at Penny's all night to avoid seeing him, I was still disappointed Erik wasn't back.

After getting into my bed, I opened my mind and found Donavon awake in his cabin.

"Hey, I'm sure you're busy getting ready for tomorrow. I just wanted to say goodnight," I sent to him.

"Are you coming to see me off tomorrow morning? We're leaving just before sunrise."

"I'll be there."

"Good. Night, Tal."

Sleep didn't come until after I heard the cabin door open, and the squeak of the springs in Erik's mattress compressing under his weight.

I was up, dressed, and waiting outside Donavon's cabin the next morning when he emerged with Arden and Harris. I couldn't help but grin when I saw him; he gave me a small smile in return. He took my hand as we walked across the compound, and gave it a little squeeze when we neared the hover hangar.

I gave Arden and Harris quick hugs and wished them luck before they boarded the hover vehicle, leaving Donavon and me to say goodbyes alone.

"Be careful," I pleaded.

"There's no reason to worry. I've been on a ton of these, and this is a quick one – nothing serious."

"I'll miss you."

"I will miss you, too, Tal. I love you, and I'll see you as soon as I get back."

I stretched up on my tiptoes and kissed him, hard. I stood, watching his back as he boarded the hover plane. I stayed in the hangar until the plane flew into the early morning sky.

Whenever Donavon went on a Mission, I worried about him, but this was the first time I'd actually been here at Headquarters to see him off. Now that I'd been on a Hunt of my own, I knew the risks, and knew how much potential danger he would be in.

I was wide awake, so I decided to swing by Medical, and become officially cleared. Dr. Daid was on duty and declared me completely healed; he promised to put a note in my file so I could return to training.

By the time I left Medical, the sun was up, and I needed to get back to the cabin to meet the boys for practice. Henri and Erik were both up and getting ready when I walked in the door.

"Did your boyfriend get off okay?" Erik asked, trying to sound uninterested.

"*Donavon* got off just fine. How'd you know that's where I went?"

"Harris said they were leaving on a mission this morning. You weren't here when I woke up, so I figured that you'd gone to say goodbye," Erik answered.

"Have you eaten?" Henri interrupted.

"Nope, waited for you guys. But I did go to Medical. They said I'm cleared to train."

"Good to hear; let's get to it. The Captain left me a message this morning. He has a couple of upcoming Missions already scheduled for us."

"Really?" I was shocked. I'd figured my abysmal performance would put me on the sidelines for a while.

"Yeah. Despite the whole getting hurt thing, which, by the way, is always a risk and does not mean that you're a bad Hunter. You did really well. Everyone was impressed," Henri praised me. I knew that he didn't actually mean "everyone"; Mac clearly wasn't impressed.

"Wow, thanks," Henri's approval meant almost as much.

"Don't let it go to your head," Erik teased. I shot him a death look, and he had the good grace to feign fright.

The first day back at practice was surprisingly easy. Once we started moving, my tight muscles stretched and loosened. My side was sore, but it felt much better than I'd anticipated.

We worked steadily the entire day, and I felt a sense of fulfillment when we finished for the afternoon.

Donavon's Mission ended up taking longer than he'd

predicted. As the days passed without word from him, I became increasingly more anxious. I called Mac's communicator morning, noon, and night. He assured me everything was okay and I would be the first to know if something went wrong. Every night, lying in my bed, I opened my mind and tried to reach out to him, even though I knew he was too far away.

Chapter Twenty

During the days, I trained harder, and longer, than I had before our Mission to Mexico City. At night, I spent time doing girly things with Penny: painting our nails, dying Penny's roots, watching movies on her wall screen, and avoiding Erik. On my first day off since Donavon had been away, I received permission – thank you, Henri – to go to Washington for the day. Just like last time, I was required to return before dark. I knew Mac was already playing favorites by letting me go, but I decided to see just how far his fatherly feelings for me went, and I begged him to let Penny go, too. To my surprise, he grudgingly agreed.

Seeing the city with Penny was an entirely different experience than seeing it with Erik and Henri. Penny was from the District originally and knew all the "best" places to shop. We spent over an hour in a store that sold every shade of nail polish ever made. Penny carefully picked out only colors that would clash horribly with either her bright hair or too green eyes. Next, she dragged me through aisle after aisle of a huge makeup and perfume store, stopping every so often to test a color of eye shadow or lipstick on the back of my hand. She loaded my basket with shades that "brought out the color in my eyes" or "matched my skin tone."

After makeup, we moved on to hair. I drew the line at dying

my hair, but agreed to let the hair stylist braid purplish-blue pieces of hair in with my own brown curls to "accentuate my eyes." I even let her talk me into buying two hair accessories; one made of beautiful black and deep green feathers that fastened to the side of my head, and the other was a tight web of large, shiny creamy pearls and crystals that bounced the colors of the rainbow on the walls of the store when I twirled. I had no idea where I would wear either of them, but I got caught up in the moment and I knew that Gretchen would love to have outfits made to match both.

Henri had only agreed to let us go shopping by ourselves if we promised to meet him at his favorite restaurant in plenty of time to make it back before dark. When we walked in, the tidal wave of blue overwhelmed me; the booths were dark blue leather, the tables and chairs were powdery-blue plastic, and the floor was royal-blue linoleum. Even the walls were painted pale blue, and decorated with blue-toned pictures. We were greeted by a short man with frizzy blue hair and big blue eyes framed by long blue eyelashes. He wore a pair of blue and silver stripped overalls with a silver shirt underneath. He didn't speak, so much as grunt, that we should follow him. He led us to a booth in the back where Henri was sitting and chatting with the most beautiful man that I'd ever seen.

The man sitting next to Henri had fine, pale blonde hair that swept across his forehead and fell just above his perfectly shaped eyebrows. He had big, light brown eyes that shone with amusement as he conversed with Henri. His skin was fair and flawless over his delicate features. I instantly recalled what Donavon said, and wondered what his Talent was.

"Hello!" Henri greeted us.

"Hi," Penny and I said in unison.

"You must be Frederick," I said warmly, extending my hand

to him.

"It is a pleasure to meet you, Natalia," Frederick replied, smiling and shaking my hand. "And you must be Penny?" He turned towards Penny and offered her his hand.

She shook it enthusiastically. "Yes, I am."

Penny and I climbed into the booth and picked up the blue menus before I realized that there was a fifth place sitting. My stomach gave a small flutter – I knew who the place setting was for.

"Sorry I'm late," Erik apologized, hurrying up to the table and confirming my suspicion.

"Don't worry, Tal and Penny just arrived," Henri dismissed his apology.

Erik slid into the booth, squishing me between him and Penny. His leg brushed against mine and, even through my pants, I felt a slight jolt, my stomach doing a little flip flop. I blushed and fumbled with my menu as both embarrassment and guilt washed over me.

After the initial awkwardness that I felt when Erik had arrived, dinner turned out to be a lot of fun. Henri ordered a bottle of Berry Blue Wine for us to share, but I restricted myself to only two glasses. I didn't want a repeat of the campfire night, but the wine eased my tension and I relaxed. All the food came out, and unsurprisingly, it was all blue. When I looked in the mirror in the blue bathroom, I noticed that my tongue and lips were tinted blue.

Frederick kept up friendly conversation throughout the entire meal. He told us funny stories about work – he taught at the city school – and the people and students that he worked with. He told us about all of the places that we had to visit in the city, which I was assumed was for my benefit since the others had probably been to most of these places. Apparently, the Blueberry wasn't the only color-themed restaurant in the city. Every color in the rainbow, and some in between, shared the distinction. Frederick also told us about a bar that's made entirely of ice: the booths, the stools, cups, plates, everything was made of ice and the patrons had to wear special clothing so that they didn't get frostbite. Similarly, there was a bar called The Grass Is Always Greener that was decorated to look like a grassy meadow; grass and flowers grew out of the dirt floor, and the ceiling was painted to look like the sky at midday. I was not sure if it was the wine or Frederick's infectious good mood, but by the time he finished describing the places, I was dying to go.

Much too soon, Henri announced that he needed to return Penny and me back to headquarters.

"You stay, I'll take them back," Erik piped up.

"Really? Are you sure?" Henri asked, raising his eyebrows.

"Yeah, I was thinking that I'd head back to the cabin, anyway. I don't mind taking them."

"Thanks, Erik." Then turning to me and Penny, he added, "I'll see you ladies tomorrow." We finished saying our goodbyes, and Penny and I followed Erik in one direction while Henri and Frederick set off in the opposite one.

The wine had gone to my head, and I wasn't drunk as much as giddy. As a result, on the way home Penny and I recounted every minute of our shopping day in full detail. Erik was a good sport, even asking questions to encourage our chatter. We landed back at Headquarters just after sunset, and Penny and I agreed to spend the night playing with our new purchases.

"Tal, can we take a walk?" Erik asked quietly as I made to get out of the vehicle.

"I'll take our things up to my room, just come up when you're ready," Penny offered.

"Thanks, Penny, see you soon," I smiled nervously.

"You bet. Thanks for the ride, Erik!"

I watched Penny walk off towards her building, both arms loaded down with our purchases. I fidgeted uncomfortably, waiting for him to say something.

"So, you wanted to take a walk?" I asked awkwardly, shifting my weight from one foot to the other.

"Let's go down to the lake," he offered.

I followed Erik without speaking, through the densely packed trees that lined the path down to the lake. I would have opened my mind and tried to read Erik's thoughts, but the alcohol was making it hard for me to concentrate. At least I was going to blame the alcohol for my concentration problems. I also thought that Erik might be intentionally blocking me out.

When we reached the lake, Erik sat on a large log. I hesitated before tentatively sitting down, careful not to touch him. We sat for several minutes in uncomfortable silence.

"Why are you avoiding me, Tal?" he asked bluntly.

"I'm not avoiding you. I see you all day, every day," I countered.

"Yes, but at night, you keep running off to be with Penny."

"This is the first time I've ever had a girlfriend, Erik. I'm making up for lost time," I reasoned.

"Making up for lost time?" he gave me a short laugh. I shrugged. "We should talk about what happened in Mexico City," Erik continued, when I didn't respond.

"There is nothing to talk about. I messed up. I got hurt. End of story."

"First of all, you didn't mess up; these things happen. All of us have been injured on a hunt. On one of my Missions, when I was still a Pledge, I broke my leg jumping from a roof that was higher than I thought. Henri had to carry me home." Erik paused and gave me a pointed look. "But we both know that's not what I am talking about." I could feel Erik's eyes boring into me, but I refused to turn and look at him.

"Erik," I started quietly, "you're right, I *have* been avoiding you. Since getting back, I have just been confused about things," I said honestly – too honestly. Talking about my feelings didn't come naturally to me. The fact that I was doing it now was unusual – maybe I was drunk.

"Confused about what things, exactly?" Erik's voice was low, and there was a hint of something I couldn't comprehend.

"Just things," I answered, my voice rising an octave. "Like you and Donavon," I blurted out. Crap. I should *not* have said that. Note to self, no more alcohol, even in small amounts. I started to stand, but Erik grabbed my wrist, and pulled me back down.

"Let me go, Erik," I pleaded in a low voice.

"No, Tal. I want to talk about this."

"Erik, either let me go on your own or I will force you to," I threatened him in a voice just above a whisper. Physically, Erik was much stronger, but my mental abilities always seemed to improve when my emotions ran out of control, and tonight they were like a speeding train without brakes. I knew that my mental Talents would trump his physical ones, and if he didn't remove his hand, he would be sorry. He must've known it, too.

Erik released my wrist and I took off into the woods, leaving him sitting alone. I sped through the woods, and into Hunters Village. I ran through the Village, but stopped in my tracks when I noticed Donavon's cabin lights on.

"Donavon?" I called.

"Hey! I just went by your cabin, but you weren't there." He threw open his cabin door and ran out to meet me. I jogged

towards him and leapt up into his arms. As soon as his arms were around my waist, I felt the familiar, safe feeling that being with him always invoked.

"Sorry, your dad gave Penny and me permission to go into the city for the day, and we just got back."

"No worries, Tal. You're here now."

"I missed you so much, Donavon." I found his lips and kissed him softly. When I pulled back, I saw Erik coming out of the woods. He stopped abruptly when he saw me and Donavon entangled in each other's arms. I was torn – part of me wanted to run to Erik, but I suppressed the urge.

"Wanna come in and hang out for a while?" Donavon asked.

"Of course, let me just send Penny a comm and tell her I'm not coming over."

"Oh, if you have plans with Penny, then go ahead over there. I'm really tired, anyway. We'll spend the day together tomorrow," he promised.

"Tomorrow," I agreed, relieved. Truth be told, I didn't want to be with Donavon right then, not when my wrist was still burning from where Erik had grabbed me.

Once in Penny's room, I dutifully played with my new purchases. I painted my nails with purple polish and sat still while Penny experimented on me with different shades of eye shadows. Penny was her bubbly self, and I felt guilty that my heart wasn't in it. I kept thinking about Erik and what might've happened if I hadn't left when I did.

I got back to my cabin after Erik was asleep, and left again in the morning before he was awake. I knew that I would have to face him eventually, but I was happy to prolong the inevitable.

I spent the whole next day with Donavon. We played in the lake with Harris and Penny and some of Donavon's other friends, including Laris. My thoughts never strayed to Erik, and his beautiful eyes, his generous mouth, his shirtless torso. Okay, maybe once they did – or twice.

"I hate that this day has to end," Donavon moaned as we lay side by side on a blanket next to the water.

"We don't need to go anywhere for a while," I replied, rolling over on my side to face him.

"I've got to shower and get ready."

"Get ready for what?" I demanded.

"I promised that I would go into the District with Harris and Arden."

"I see."

"You're mad," he observed.

"I just figured that you'd be spending the night with me since you just got back," I argued.

"Would you rather I not go?" he offered, but I could tell that he didn't mean it.

"No, you go. It's fine," I snapped. Why was I picking a fight with him?

"Tal, I'm not going if it upsets you," he said, trying to pull me to him.

"No, go," I relented. "I'm not mad, just disappointed." I tried to reign in my irrational anger.

"I'll bring you back a good present," he tempted.

"Are you trying to bribe me?" I scowled, letting him pull me down into his arms.

"Only if it's working," he smiled, and his whole face lit up.

"It's working," I grinned.

In the end, I was relieved that Donavon was spending the night in the city with Harris and Arden. I felt guilty about being relieved, but I felt even worse about being with him when I couldn't get Erik out of my head.

Chapter Twenty-One

Erik and Henri were both gone when I got back to my cabin; a fact for which I was grateful. I showered, dressed, and curled into my bed with a book. Penny and some of the other Pledges had invited me to hang out in Penny's room, but I really wanted to take advantage of this rare opportunity to be alone.

I must have fallen asleep while reading because I woke with a start when the door to the cabin flew open and slammed against the wall. I shot up in my bed as Erik stormed through, with Henri hot on his heels. Something was wrong – Erik was holding a bloody cloth to the side of his face with one hand, and had a bag of ice in the other.

Henri went straight for the medical kit in the bathroom as Erik threw himself on his bed.

"What happened?" I exclaimed, jumping off of my bed and running over to him.

"It's nothing, Tal. I just got in a little scuffle with an asshole at the bar." He refused to meet my eyes, and I could tell by the tone of his voice that he was hiding something.

I reached up, and pulled the hand holding the cloth away from his face. I gasped at the cut across his cheekbone, with a bruise already blossoming around the edges. I looked over the rest of him;

his shirt was torn and I could see red patches across his chest and stomach. The knuckles of both his hands were bloody, and several nasty red scratches ran the length of his arms.

"Who did this?" I asked tightly.

"I told you, just some asshole at the bar," Erik said, through clenched teeth.

"Look at me," I demanded. He shook his head and refused to lift his eyes. I opened my mind, and tried to reach into his.

"Stop!" he screamed jumping back. "Don't you dare, Natalia. I've been through enough tonight, I don't need you playing around in my head, too."

"I'm sorry," I stammered, stumbling backward off of his bed, regretting overstepping my bounds.

"Tal, why don't you sit over there so I can clean Erik's cut," Henri said quietly, gesturing to the chair in the corner of the room. I nodded and moved clumsily back out of the way.

"Erik," I tried again. I couldn't help myself.

"I don't want to talk to you right now," he cut me off.

"Did I do something wrong? I don't understand."

"Not everything is about you!" he shouted. His words stung, and I felt the prick of tears in the corners of my eyes.

Out of habit, I did what I always do when I'm upset; I opened my mind to find Donavon, and was shocked to learn he was in his cabin. I had no idea if it was after curfew, but I didn't care either. I grabbed my shoes and ran out the door.

"Talia! No!" Erik yelled after me, but I ignored him.

"Let her go, she's going to find out soon enough," I heard Henri say to him.

I suddenly felt sick to my stomach, and I hesitated at the door to Donavon's cabin. I had an awful feeling about what I would find behind that door. I raised my hand and rapped three knocks in fast succession. Harris opened the door a second later.

"Hey, Tal," he said, a little too loudly.

"Hey, Harris, is he in there?" I asked, even though I already knew he was.

"Um…yeah. He's here, but I'm not really sure this is really a good time." He filled the entire doorway, preventing me from seeing into the cabin.

"Let her in," I heard Donavon's muffled voice from inside.

Harris gave me a pity-filled look, but moved to one side. I walked to where Donavon was sitting with ice wrapped in a cloth pressed to his mouth. His shirt was torn and bloody, and one of his eyes had swelled almost completely shut, leaving only a slit of blue visible.

"Why?" I demanded.

"I don't want to do this with you right now, Tal." Donavon sounded tired.

"Why?" I repeated louder. Both Harris and Arden were there, watching and listening, but I didn't care what they thought about me.

"Erik was being a jerk and I said something. Then one thing led to another, and we got into a fight," Donavon wouldn't meet my eyes. For the first time ever, Donavon was lying to me. What I didn't know was why. I could push my way into his head, but a part of me was afraid what I might find.

"Fine, if that's all, then I'm going back to bed." I turned and walked to the door.

"*Tal, wait!*" I turned around and met his eyes. "*I love you.*"

The look in Donavon's eyes said he was scared. I didn't have to dig in to his mind to know what he was scared of – he was scared of losing me. A familiar surge of emotion washed over me. I felt awful for letting Erik affect me the way that he had. I felt ashamed about the way that I'd been acting. Most of all, I felt guilty.

"I know, Donavon. I love you, too," I walked back over to him and gently kissed him on the cheek.

When I left Donavon's cabin, I didn't go back to my own. I couldn't face Erik. What had I done? What had I started? Erik had never liked Donavon, but now they were getting in physical altercations? If anyone in charge found out about this, they would both be in huge trouble, and it would all be my fault. When had I become the kind of girl who played boys against each other? Let boys fight over her?

It was cold outside, and I wasn't really dressed appropriately for the rapidly decreasing temperature. I hugged myself and tried to will the cold away. I sat on one of the wooden benches that surrounded a fire pit in the center of Hunters Village, and counted the stars in the night sky. I don't know how long I sat there, but I had lost count several times before I heard footsteps behind me.

I knew it was Erik before he spoke. "Tal?" he hesitated when he was still several feet from the bench.

"Hi, Erik," I replied, without turning around.

"Can I sit with you?" he sounded nervous.

"Are you sure you want to?" I mumbled.

The bench sagged slightly under his weight as he sat down, careful not to touch me. "It's cold out here, why don't you come back to the cabin?"

"I'm sorry, Erik," my voice was barely audible.

"Sorry? For what? It's not your fault your boyfriend sucks."

"Sorry that you got in a fight because of me." I tried to keep my voice from trembling.

"Do you love him, Tal?" Erik caught me by surprise – I hadn't expected him to be so bold.

"Of course, I do," I snapped, but I didn't even believe my own words. "I do love him," I repeated, this time with more conviction and more for my benefit than Erik's.

Erik hesitantly reached for my hand, and when I didn't pull away, he grasped it firmly in his own. "I just don't want to see you get hurt."

"Donavon would never hurt me," I said evenly. I was the one hurting him. Did Erik not see that? I met his eyes.

"You sure about that?" Erik asked. I looked at his bruised face and wanted more than anything to comfort him. I raised my hand slowly toward his cheek, but let it drop before my fingertips could brush his skin.

"Positive," I answered.

Erik nodded sadly and got to his feet, pulling me with him, "Let's get you to bed."

I let Erik lead me back to our cabin. I curled up in my bed when we got back. But even with all of my blankets, I couldn't shake off the numbness that had taken over my body.

The next couple of days were awkward at best. Everyone wanted to talk about the fight between Donavon and Erik. Nobody knew they'd been fighting about me since the only other person from the Agency there had been Arden. Henri had been with Frederick until Erik messaged him, needing a ride back to Headquarters, and Harris never left the cabin.

Penny pressed me for details, but I couldn't tell her what I didn't know. Besides knowing that they got in a fight about me, I didn't know how it had started or ended. I saw the aftermath, and that was plenty; I didn't really want to know more. I wanted for it all to go away.

Captain Alvarez called both boys into his office, but thankfully, only issued stern warnings to each. If Erik had gotten in a fight with any other Operative the penalty would've been stiffer, but no one wanted to risk angering Mac by punishing his son. Since neither would admit who'd started the fight, Captain Alvarez was hesitant to hand out unequal reprimands.

Our training sessions became longer, more intense. Erik was friendly, not going out of his way to avoid me, but he rarely joked around and he seemed distant most days. Every chance he got, he went into the city and stayed until well after curfew if he came home at all. Henri insisted I just needed to give him time. I wanted to believe him, but I was afraid my silly crush on him had ruined everything.

"Maybe you should have me transferred," I suggested to Henri at dinner one night after Erik had gone to D.C. for the third night in a row.

"No," he answered firmly. "For months, we have worked to get where we are, and I'm not throwing that away. Erik just needs some time."

"I messed up, though, didn't I?"

"No, you didn't do anything wrong," Henri said, emphatically. "Honestly, the reason he's staying away is not what you think. Erik just does this sometimes." He was lying to make me feel better, but I nodded as if I understood what he meant, anyway.

Donavon was a different story. He clung to me like a drowning man does to a life raft, waiting for me when I was done with practices, and then insisting I eat dinner with him almost every night. After we'd eat, he would refuse to let me out of his sight until he deposited me at my door, minutes before curfew. Instead of going into the city on his nights off, Donavon chose to stay at Headquarters with me and Penny. When we were alone, he was careful not to get too physical, saying he knew that I would let him know I when I was ready.

Soon, Donavon was at my side every minute that I wasn't training. When we weren't physically together, he was sending me thoughts. I wanted to block him, but I knew that would upset him too much. I longed for the blissful days when Henri's worries bogged down my mind. Now, I couldn't even make space in my head for Henri's thoughts because Donavon's constant mental rambling left no room. Training was my only reprieve from his relentless intrusions. I felt justified in blocking him, in order to concentrate on my mental connection with Erik and Henri.

Honestly, it was all becoming a little over the top, and I started to feel smothered. So, when Henri announced at breakfast one morning that we had been given two back-to-back Hunts that would keep us away for at least two weeks, possibly longer, I was relieved.

Space from Donavon was not the only reason that I wanted to get away from Headquarters. I was eager to correct the mistakes that I'd made in Mexico. I was desperate to prove that I belonged here; that I had what it took to be a Hunter. No matter how many times Henri told me that Hunters get hurt all the time, and I hadn't messed up, I couldn't really believe him. I knew that the hard part had been getting accepted to pledge the Hunters, but if I didn't prove my worth in the field, I still might not graduate.

We flew out before sunrise the next morning. I'd said goodbye to Donavon the night before because I didn't want him coming to the hangar with Erik there. A bleary-eyed, bushy-haired Penny did show up at the hangar to say goodbye and wish us luck, and I was grateful for her presence.

I had mixed feelings about leaving Donavon. I was, of course, relieved to be away from him for a couple of days, but I was also uneasy about spending so much time alone with Erik without the constant reminder of my boyfriend. I was nervous that my irrational fixation with Erik would return. No wonder that Donavon was scared to leave me alone; if I couldn't trust myself to keep my distance from Erik, how could he?

The first of the two missions was an abandoned warehouse in a Coalition town just over the border. The town belonged to the Coalition, but the Agency had a number of loyal followers there. TOXIC had become aware of the warehouse when it was still occupied by Coalition forces, but it was deemed an unnecessary risk to check out – or so that was what our intel said. Our mission was to search the warehouse for any sign of what was once manufactured there. The Agency believed it was just physical weapons – guns, swords, knives – but we needed to be sure they hadn't been making biological or chemical weapons, as well.

Even though this mission was technically on enemy territory, it was considered extremely low risk since it was doubtful that we'd come in contact with any members of the Coalition. The atmosphere on the flight was far less tense than the ride to Mexico for our first mission had been. Still, I could barely sit in my seat, but it was more out of anticipation than nerves. Erik and Henri talked and joked for almost the trip, and Erik even went out of his way to include me in the conversation. Finally, things were starting to get back to normal between us.

Once we landed and deplaned, we walked the short distance to another dilapidated-looking barn, where Henri chose a vehicle to drive into the town. We didn't wear our adapt-suits but rather regular clothes, although we all had weapons concealed underneath.

Instead of going to an abandoned safe house, we drove straight into town and parked behind a small, well-maintained house. There was nothing remarkable about the building; nondescript, was the best word for it. This safe house had no command center like the previous one, but, thankfully, it did have a fully stocked kitchen and two small bedrooms. I took one of the rooms and the boys shared the other. Henri explained that we would scope out the area surrounding the warehouse after nightfall to ensure that it was indeed abandoned. As long as all of our intel was correct, we'd be able to go in the next night, gather the necessary information, and be on our way.

This sort of fact-finding mission was the norm for Hunters. TOXIC knew that the Coalition was becoming stronger by the day recruiting followers to aid in the battle against the rest of the country; we didn't know was how much progress they were actually making.

Intel, gathered daily, informed us that they were developing technology to rival ours. It was important for our side to learn exactly how far they'd come in reaching that goal, but the locations of their research and development plants were hard to get an accurate fix on. I assumed that they'd developed at least some form of masking technology, similar to ours, to scramble satellites so that we couldn't pinpoint their whereabouts.

These fact-finding Hunts ranged in difficulty – our mission ranked pretty low on that scale. Privately, I assumed that it was because of my performance on the last one that we'd been relegated to mediocre assignments. However, I actually didn't mind. The important thing for me was to do well. As long as I successfully completed my part, I'd be given positive marks, and that was all that mattered. I needed to do well on all of the remaining Hunts in order to graduate and actually become a Hunter for real; becoming a Hunter was the only thing that truly mattered.

We were off in full Hunting gear as soon as the sun set. We spent the night watching the warehouse, and blessedly saw nothing worth noting. We returned to the safe house just before sunrise the following morning, and I was happy to sleep the day away.

At nightfall on the second night, we once again set off in our Hunting gear. We watched the warehouse for another couple of hours and, not seeing anything suspicious, made our move.

I opened myself up to both the boys' minds, absorbing their thoughts and feelings. Their excitement and the thrill of the hunt filled me, consumed me, causing adrenaline to surge through my veins. I felt invincible. I was ready for whatever came. Unfortunately or fortunately, depending on how you look at it, in the end what "came" was nothing.

Once inside, we quickly assembled all of our equipment and combed the warehouse. I used a chemical detector to sweep the area while Erik and Henri looked for evidence of the types of physical weapons that might have been made there. I found only a trace amount of a chemical associated with the manufacture of ammunition, and immediately uploaded my findings, sending them back to Headquarters. Erik and Henri found spare parts for several different models of rifles but nothing impressive – nothing like the artillery the Agency manufactured. Henri finished up by taking images of every inch of the warehouse. We were back at the safe house well before the sun started peeking over the horizon.

Henri told us that we weren't scheduled to leave until after dinnertime, so I went to lie down, but found it impossible to sleep. Even though the mission had proved ridiculously easy, I was on a success high.

Erik's easygoing nature from the plane was gone. He was standoffish toward me and careful to keep his mind guarded when it wasn't necessary for it to be open for communication. When our minds were connected, I couldn't help myself; I risked gently probing into his psyche. He knew me better than I'd thought; he'd known that I would try, and all of my attempts were met with resistance.

Our third mission was much deeper into Coalition territory – the southernmost tip of California. Our only objective was to confirm that a man, believed to be a high-ranking member of the Coalition, had a residence in San Lucas, California. The most time-consuming part was actually traveling there; we weren't able to take any hover vehicles because the skyways in that area were highly restricted. We had to travel a great deal of the way by road vehicle, and an even greater distance on foot – or, rather, hoof, as it turned out. I took it as a good sign that Erik didn't insist that I ride on Henri instead of him.

The mission went off without a hitch. We were in and out in less time than anticipated, and Henri contacted Headquarters so that they could send a hover plane to meet us early. The rendezvous was close to the safe house we'd stayed in for our first mission.

We retraced our trek from the previous day without incident.

I was riding the crest of a victory wave when we landed back at Headquarters. The time apart – and, if I was honest, Erik's coldness toward me – had made me long for Donavon and his comforting presence; I couldn't wait to see him. I wanted to surprise him, so I opened my mind long enough to confirm that he was in his cabin, but didn't call out to him.

I jogged the whole way back to Hunters Village with a big grin on my face. I realized a moment too late that something was off. My hand was already turning the knob to Donavon's door when a sick feeling filled the pit of my stomach. My mind was still blocked, yet instinctively, I sensed that there was something inside his cabin that I wasn't going to like. I pushed his door open using my mind. The interior of the cabin was dark, but it took only seconds for my eyes to adjust. For the first time in my life, I regretted my training.

My eyes narrowed in on Donavon's bed. Long blonde hair spilled over the side, and a girl's shocked voice let out a gasp as I burst through the door open. Donavon sat up so fast, you'd have thought someone set fire to his mattress. He jumped off of his bed, taking a blanket with him. He hastily wrapped the material around his waist, but he was otherwise naked. I was vaguely aware of the girl saying something, but I couldn't hear her over the ringing in my own ears.

All of the air in the room vanished, making it hard for me to breathe. The wind began to pick up, blowing leaves and twigs through the open doorway behind me. I locked Donavon's eyes, so full of shame and fear, with my own and bore into his mind.

"Tal, no, please, don't," he moaned softly.

He started walking toward me, one hand extended in my direction, the other holding a fist full of blanket at his waist. I used my mind to hold him in place, rooting his feet to the floor and stopping his advance.

I felt the cold rain drops coming through the open door, splashing my back. Donavon tried to shove me out of his head, but I pushed with everything I had. He was no match for me. I found what I was searching for – the fight with Erik. I saw through Donavon's eyes as he kissed another girl, a girl who was not me. I saw as Erik walked over to him, demanding to know what was going on. I saw as Erik hit him in the mouth. I wanted to pull out of his mind; I couldn't stand to see this, but I was in too deep to extricate myself. I watched the fight play out between the two of them. I felt something inside of me freeze and then shatter into a million pieces. My heart.

Donavon was still fighting against my mental invasion. He started walking toward me again, and I used my mind to throw him back against the cabin wall. He landed with a thud, and I heard the girl scream as Donavon moaned. He tried to get up, but I pinned him to the floor. One of his arms was hanging limply at his side. Blood trickled down his cheek as the light in his eyes slowly faded to unconsciousness. I caught movement in my peripheral vision as the blond moved from the bed to Donavon's crumpled form. I didn't think twice before mentally throwing her back down on the mattress, holding her in place. She whimpered, but was powerless to do anything more.

I refocused my attention on Donavon; he was slowly regaining consciousness. I dove into his mind, and he started shrieking like a scared child. The blonde's whimpers grew louder as she watched Donavon writhing in pain on the floor. He grabbed his head with both hands. I wasn't sure if he thought that would help to keep me out, or to keep his thoughts in.

I dug through Donavon's mind, searching frantically for every memory involving the girl. I pulled on and discarded his memories, like his mind was a dresser drawer and I was looking for a matching pair of socks. He struggled harder the deeper I went unlocking memories and thoughts that he'd worked so hard to keep from me.

Finally, I pulled out of Donavon's head when I couldn't handle it anymore. Feelings of betrayal and pain swirled inside of me, fighting to get out. Thunder boomed, rods of electricity streaked across the night sky. A huge explosion reverberated through the cabin, blowing the windows inward and spraying the entire room with shards of glass. A sliver sliced open my cheek, and then my entire world went black.

Chapter Twenty-Two

My head throbbed, feeling about eight times its normal size. Wincing, I tried to lift my cheek from the rough material that was scratching my skin. A large hand gently smoothed stray curls away from my face, as I attempted to open my swollen eyes.

"It's okay. You're okay," Erik's deep voice cooed. Pain radiated from my skull down through my entire body. I groaned, but finally managed to open my eyes. Scenes from Donavon's cabin invaded my mind. Erik's voice brought on another emotion, almost stronger than the pain – humiliation. Burying my sticky face in my shaking hands, I withdrew from his touch. Erik was the second-to-last person that I wanted to see right then.

Stupidly, I'd assumed that Erik had fought Donavon over his feelings for me. How could I have been such an idiot? He hadn't actually been fighting him because of romantic feelings, but because Donavon was, in fact, an ass. He'd just been defending his partner. I was even more mortified by the fact that he'd let me believe that fight was actually over me.

The betrayal and embarrassment became too much. My body trembled uncontrollably with silent sobs. Erik wrapped his arms around me, and I didn't pull away. Instead, I clung to Erik's shirt as hot tears scorched my skin. He rocked me while I quivered, overwhelmed by hurt, humiliation, and exhaustion. The ache in my chest made it hard for me to breathe. I longed to retreat to the darkness from which I'd just woken.

"Close your eyes," Erik murmured into my hair. His voice was firm and authoritative. "Sleep, Tal. Go to sleep," he repeated softly, his voice commanding. I obeyed, over the stinging protests of my eyeballs.

Unfortunately, the blackness didn't come. Colorful dreams of Donavon laughing and kissing the faceless blond played in my subconscious. Rage filled me as I recalled the images of me attacking Donavon, screaming and clawing at his shocked expression. I wanted to physically hurt him the way that he'd hurt me. I continued to shriek while my fists pounded his chest. Cold water dripped, from the crown of my head, down my face. Rough fingers encircled one of my wrists as I raised it to strike Donavon again. I struggled against my attacker.

"Get off of me," I screeched hysterically. "Get off me."

"Talia," a sharp voice hissed in my ear. "Wake up."

I blinked rapidly, trying to adjust to my current surroundings. My cabin. I was back in my cabin. Erik, not Donavon, was leaning over me, his hands pinning my wrists next to my head. I thrashed against his weight, but he refused to release me. Finally, my body stilled – nightmare. Donavon and the girl were just a nightmare. I struggled to sit up in my own bed, Erik's eyes alive with alarm. I brushed at the water that was actually dripping down my face. My fingers brushed a small bandage on my cheek. The sound of exploding glass filled my ears, and a stinging sensation tingled the nerve endings under the bandage. The memories flooded my mind; it wasn't a nightmare.

A damp cloth was leaking water into my sheets, the wetness seeping into my thin pants. Erik tentatively released my wrists and picked up the offending rag and slowly wiped my forehead.

"Hey," he said, giving me an uneasy smile.

"Hey," I muttered, not meeting his eyes; I couldn't stand to see the look of distress there again. We sat in uncomfortable silence for several long moments.

"Are you hungry?" Erik finally asked. "I can get you something to eat."

"No, don't feel much like eating," I mumbled.

"Can I get you anything?" He let his hand and the towel drop back to my mattress.

"No, thank you," I said, in a small voice. I hesitated. "Why didn't you tell me?" I finally demanded, regretting the words the second they were through my lips.

Erik didn't answer immediately. He looked away, the wall next to my bed suddenly becoming so intriguing that he couldn't tear his gaze away.

"I didn't think that I was the right person to tell you," he said carefully, measuring his words.

"You let me think that you got in a fight with him over me? You thought that was better?" I demanded, hysteria rising in my chest.

"At the time, I thought it was better. In retrospect, probably not the best move."

"How long has it been going on?" I grabbed his shoulder, forcing him to meet my gaze.

"I honestly don't know." He opened his mind to me, showing me that he was telling the truth.

"Had you heard things? Is that why you hated him so much?" I pressed, looking in to his head, instead of at his face, for the answer.

"Well...Yes. I'd...heard things. But I've never liked him, even at school."

I saw snippets of memories dance through his mind. A much-younger Erik and Donavon trading insults in the School's practice gymnasium. Donavon, his hand resting on the small of a blonde girl's back, ushering her through a crowded bar, Harris' gray-blue eyes pleaded with Erik to mind his own business when he tried to follow them.

"I see." So, everyone knew but me. Awesome. My humiliation deepened, squeezing my lungs like a vice.

"Tal, I'm so sorry – sorry this happened, sorry that you had to find out this way, sorry that I didn't tell you. Sorry that I lied to you." The words tumbled from his mouth, tripping over each other to get out.

"Sorry that you let me be self-absorbed, and think it was all about me?" I prompted. Rage boiled, hot and unpleasant, in my stomach. I wanted to lash out at somebody. I wanted to pummel something, and the pillow next to me took the brunt of my fury.

"I did get in a fight with him because of you," he snapped, anger clouding his features. "I flipped when I saw him with her; I wanted to kill him." The intensity of his words unnerved me. In that moment, I honestly believed if Arden hadn't been there, Erik might've killed Donavon.

"Right, but you let me believe that it was because you cared about me or something," I spat back. Pity flashed through his turquoise eyes, fueling the flames of my ever-growing rage.

A knock at the door cut me off before I could say anything that I might regret later. I looked at him in alarm. Erik shot up to answer the knock. I didn't open my mind because I was afraid that it might be Donavon. I might kill him if I saw him right now. It wasn't Donavon; it was worse: Mac.

"Director McDonough," Erik greeted him in a tone just south

of respect.

"Mr. Kelley," Mac nodded, ignoring Erik's inflection.

"Hi, Mac," I mumbled.

"Natalia," he didn't sound happy. "Mr. Kelley, could you excuse us for a moment?"

Erik nodded, but waited until I gave him the okay before stepping through the open doorway. "*I'll be right outside, Tal.*"

Mac walked over and took the place on my bed that Erik had just vacated. He didn't say anything for several minutes. I shifted uncomfortably on my slightly soggy sheets.

"How much trouble am I in?" I asked when I couldn't stand the silence anymore. I figured there would be repercussions for the property damage, at the very least, not to mention the fighting.

"No trouble, I already took care of it." He wouldn't look at me. Relief washed over me; Mac's position as my de facto guardian did have its advantages.

"Thank you," I replied, quietly.

"You don't need to thank me. While I cannot condone your actions, I cannot say that I blame you either. Donavon and the girl were not harmed." He added the last part almost as an afterthought.

"I wish that I could say that's a good thing," I blurted out. A hot flush crept up my neck and spread across my cheeks. I probably shouldn't have said that out loud.

Mac actually laughed. "I warned him not to make you mad."

That wasn't exactly the response I'd expected. Mac knew that I had a temper, but I wasn't aware that he thought it warranted a warning. I almost wished he'd yell at me; admonish me for my rash behavior. If he scolded me, at least I would have another outlet for my bursting emotions. Instead, it was almost as if he understood why I'd done what I'd done. Worse, it was almost like he'd expected something like this to happen. I wasn't sure if I should be angry that Mac thought so little of my self-control; I guess, in light of my actions, he was justified in assuming that I couldn't control myself.

Neither of us spoke for several agonizing minutes. Just when I thought that he might leave without another word, he spoke, his usual no-nonsense demeanor back in place.

"I have lined up several more missions for your team in the coming weeks. You've done exceptionally well in your training, and I think that it would be good for you to take this opportunity to refocus. I know that right now this seems like the end of the world, but you are smart and I am sure when you take a step back you will realize this is for the best. We are still a nation at war, and there are more important things that need your attention." To anyone else, his words would have seemed harsh and uncaring, but I knew that he wasn't saying it to be cruel. Mac believed in TOXIC and the Delegation. He was right – there were more important things for me to worry about. His words shamed me; here I was concentrating on my love life when, in the grand scheme of life, it was inconsequential.

Mac was also right about me feeling as if it were the end of the world. I couldn't help myself. Donavon's betrayal did feel like the end of the world, at least the end of mine. How was I going to keep going when Donavon had been the only reassuring presence in my life since my parents' deaths?

When I finally summoned the ability to speak, I fought to keep my voice even. "Thank you. You're right, I would really like to concentrate on work." As I said the words, I knew that they were true. Of course, I desperately wanted to crawl under my comforter and never see the light of day again. However, I had a duty, and I would not further disgrace Mac by shirking my responsibility to the Agency. I couldn't even imagine what the people that Mac answered to thought about me attacking Donavon, but I am positive that it didn't reflect well on Mac. And there was no way I would lend any more credence to the commonly held belief that I didn't belong here.

"I have you scheduled to leave in a couple of days for a week-long mission. I've made arrangements for the three of you to be moved to the apartments. Your personal belongings will be in your new rooms when you return."

What? Teams with Pledges were never housed in the apartments.

"You don't need to do that," I argued. "I don't want special favors or anything."

Mac raised his eyebrows. "You don't? I didn't even make provisions for Donavon to go to the city when he was a Pledge, let alone one of his friends."

"That was different," I mumbled, embarrassed.

"I'm not doing this just for you; I think that it would be best to put some distance between you and Donavon for a while, at least until you both calm down. If you are living in the apartments, you won't see each other. Both of you will concentrate better this way," he reasoned. Mac is nothing if not practical. "Your friend Penelope is housed in the west wing, is that correct?"

I nodded.

"Good, you will be on the same floor, as will Mr. Reich and Mr. Kelley." His thin lips smiled, but his gray brown eyes remained cool. "I have to take care of some business; I just wanted to be sure that you were okay." He got up to leave. "Oh, I have some packages for you from Gretchen. I will have them sent to your new room."

"Thanks, Mac."

He nodded, then turned and walked out of the cabin.

I sat alone for several minutes, contemplating Mac's words. The reality was that I'd chosen this life; I'd chosen to be a Hunter. The luxury to heal my broken heart in peace wasn't one that I'd be afforded. Normal teenage girls, even Talented ones, would be allowed to mourn their loss, but I was not normal. I was a Hunter – well, almost a Hunter, anyway. Hunters weren't supposed to let emotion cloud their judgment. Mac wouldn't be the only person I'd be letting down if I didn't pull myself together.

Erik materialized in the cabin doorway, followed by Penny, interrupting my mental pep talk.

"Hi, Tal," her tone was unusually subdued.

"Hey, Penny." For some reason, seeing her brought on a fresh wave of tears, and my earlier resolve vanished. She rushed over to me and threw her arms around me in a huge hug.

"It's okay," she soothed. "It's okay."

Thankfully, news spreads fast at Headquarters – particularly when you destroy an entire cabin – so Penny already knew what happened. I don't think that I could've managed the words to tell her myself. I heard the cabin door open and shut quietly, signaling Erik's departure. I was crying so hard that I started hiccupping. Eventually, my tear ducts ran dry, and I just shook with dry, retching sobs. Penny sat there, holding my head to her shoulder, and smoothing my tangled curls. She never really said anything, but I didn't need her to – just knowing that she was there was enough.

My dreams were filled with images of Donavon making out with the faceless blond girl. I couldn't shake the pictures out of my mind. I would wake up crying, and for several blissful moments, I wouldn't be able to remember why I was so upset. Then reality would set in, and images of Donavon – half-naked, jumping out of his bed – would tear through my consciousness, and the floodgates that held my tears back would break.

The nights seemed to go on forever, alternating between vivid nightmares and harsh reality.

The days that followed passed in a blur. I slept, I trained, and I slept. I only ate when Henri made me. Everything tasted like sand. I spent most of my free time with Penny, but the constant look of concern and pity in her eyes was almost too much to bear. I knew that if I read her mind, it would match the look in her eyes, so I refrained.

Erik and Henri were no different. Both went out of their way to be nice to me. Henri made it a point to go easy on me during practices, treating me as if I were a china doll. At first, I was grateful – I didn't have the energy or the desire to train – but it wasn't long before I began to feel pathetic. I'd always hated showing weakness, and now I was sitting back and letting everybody treat me like a child. Instead of getting angry with them, I became angrier at myself. I was angry for letting Donavon have such a hold on my life that his absence nearly destroyed me; angry for letting myself be taken advantage of, angry for letting everyone coddle me. I'd never felt so utterly worthless in my life.

After my parents' deaths, I'd been furious. Mac had offered me the opportunity to join the McDonough School, to replace my grief with purpose and to avenge their deaths. I'd given everything I had to training – honing my existing abilities, developing new ones, and channeling my feelings towards a goal.

At first, for the month that I had been in the Medical Ward at the school, I'd felt so alone. I'd never spent more than a day or two away from my parents, and then the only company I had was the medics that came to take my blood and check my vitals and, of course, Mac. Unfortunately, Mac was no substitute for my parents. My parents had been warm and caring. Mac was straight to the point and matter of fact. While over time, he became in many ways like a surrogate father, he was impersonal and cold compared to my warm and loving parents.

When I left the Medical Ward, I met Donavon, and from that day on, I'd counted on him. Until now, he had never let me down. Donavon hadn't replaced my parents either, but overnight, he became everything to me – my best friend, my family, and, eventually, my boyfriend. We shared everything, and, thanks to my mental capabilities, we even shared our innermost secrets, thoughts, and desires. I doubted that people who spent an entire lifetime together died knowing as much about each other, or feeling as close to one another as I'd felt to Donavon. Or so I'd thought.

Donavon's betrayal was made worse because it made me doubt myself, and my Talents. Before, I'd felt secure in the notion that I could tell who to trust by using my abilities. Yet Donavon had been able to keep a monumental secret from me, and I hadn't even guessed that something was wrong. I felt like a fool when I thought about how many people probably knew Donavon's secret while I, who could read his every thought, had been oblivious.

I would've been convinced that Erik was restraining himself from saying "I told you so," but I frequently connected with his mind, and what I found was even worse – sympathy. Outside of practices, I kept my mind closed; I didn't want to know what others thought or felt about me.

The anger and resentment built steadily in the days that followed the incident with Donavon until one day, I finally snapped during practice. Henri had us doing two-on-one sparring drills. He was in the center of the sparring mat, blindfolded while Erik and I took turns attacking him from different angles. Erik barked commands into my head, but my lack of concentration made me flounder in most of my attempts. Erik's frustration at my inability to focus, mixed with pity, crashed through his mental barricades and saturated my subconscious. The haze that I'd been living in for days cleared. My self-control shattered like a thin layer of ice.

Instead of attacking Henri, I rounded on Erik, launching myself through the air. He was so surprised that he didn't have time to defend himself. I collided with him, my momentum knocking him, to the ground. I landed on top, my legs straddling his waist. I pulled my right fist back to hit him, but I hadn't broken the mental connection before attacking, and he read the move right out of my mind. He caught my fist in mid-air, stopping the assault. Not missing a beat, I drew my left back and hooked him in the side of the head. He barely noticed. He wrapped his large hands around my waist and hoisted me up and over his head. I rolled neatly to my feet and turned just in time to see him crouched low, the long sinewy muscles in his arms coiled like twin snakes ready to attack. His eyes were black and alive, two coals burning with excitement. I felt electricity course through the connection, fueling my own desire for the fight.

"STOP!" Henri bellowed, throwing off the blindfold, but it was too late. I was like a lioness on a hunt; I smelled the prey and nothing could change my direction.

Erik didn't spare him a glance before hurtling towards me with a speed and ferocity that I was unprepared for. I leaned to my right just in time to avoid a direct hit, but one of his corded arms caught me around the waist, slamming me onto the mat. The air rushed from my lungs, but I managed to roll on my side before he could get himself on top of me. I was on my feet before he was, and I didn't waste the opportunity. I kicked him as hard as I could in his midsection. He barely slowed his ascent. I raised my leg to kick a second time, but he was too fast. His long fingers encircled my ankle and managed to throw me backwards across the mat using a combination of his own physical strength and my mimicked telekinesis. I scrambled to my feet, anticipating another attack.

"Talia! Erik!" Henri shouted, trying to get our attention.

Erik glanced sidelong at him. Then he looked back at me. His lips parted slightly, revealing his perfect white teeth, his canines looking sharper and pointer than I remembered. I could feel the thrill emanating off of him in waves and my own pores soaking up his excitement.

"That all you got, Tal?" he taunted. *"You know what? I do pity you. Your fighting skills are abysmal."*

I knew that he was mocking me, purposely provoking me now. He knew that I would rise to his challenge. I let out an inhuman scream, a jumble of all of the unspoken emotions ripping me apart from the inside out as I ran full tilt towards Erik. I'm not sure if it was the screaming or if Erik read it out of my head, but he ran at me just as I ran towards him. When we were still a couple of yards apart, we both leapt, crashing with a thwack in flight. We fell on to the mat, our arms and legs wrapped oddly around one another as if we were doing some bizarre dance. We began to roll around, punching and kicking at any exposed area on the other. He would use my mental powers to throw me across the room, only to have me use them to pull him back towards me to go another round.

Erik was, no doubt, the better combatant, but today, I was in a rage-driven haze, and for the first time in days, I felt alive. The physical pain made me forget about the emotional battering I'd taken only days before. The adrenaline steeled my frazzled psyche. I was like a junkie; I wanted more. Erik's desire encouraged my own, and I fed off of the thrill that the fight provoked deep within him as it bled through the connection.

Henri had given up trying to stop us and positioned himself against a wall, clucking his disapproval.

Eventually, my stamina started to weaken. Erik pressed his advantage. There would be no more coddling from him, no mercy. I tried to use his resilience to reinvigorate my tired and aching body, but he was waning, too. He pinned me underneath him, straddling me, squeezing my ribcage with his thighs; I tried to physically fight him off. Too much more mental exertion and I'd pass out. I was starting to see black spots, my already-labored breathing and short arm span were doing me no favors. I summoned all of my remaining strength, and mentally flung him off of me, since I knew that I was on the verge of unconsciousness either way. I heard him hit the ground with a thud. I blinked furiously at the spots dotting my vision, trying desperately to hold onto awareness.

The dots grew smaller and smaller until I was left with a clear view of the glass ceiling, high overhead. I was too tired to move, almost too tired to breathe. My body throbbed from being thrown and pummeled. I knew that I would be *very* bruised tomorrow. My breath was still coming out in labored gasps, and I didn't hear Erik crawling his way across the padded floor until he was nearly on top of me.

"Concede," he wheezed, flipping down beside me.

"Never," I muttered. Out of the corner of my eye, I caught the slight upturn of his mouth as his lips curved into a smile. We lay side by side trying to catch our respective breaths for several long minutes.

"Feel better?" he whispered in my ear, his voice so soft that a strong gust of wind would have taken it away had we been outside.

I turned to face him. He had been careful not to hit me in the face, but I had not responded in kind; the right side of his face was puffy and red from several lucky shots that I'd landed. I reached over, lightly running my fingers over his swollen skin.

Exhaustion was weighing on my eyelids. If I could have, I would've closed them right then and there, falling into a deep and satisfied slumber. The brief determination that I'd mustered after Mac's spiel in the cabin several days before returned, full force. Now, more than ever, I knew that I was meant to be here, to be a Hunter.

The release of so much pent up aggression gave me hope that I would, in fact, be able to get past Donavon's betrayal. The anger and hurt were still there, just not as intense. While I was still having trouble catching my breath, the iceberg in my chest was starting to thaw, just a little. My stomach even grumbled, and I realized that I was actually hungry. I had no idea how long this adrenaline high would last, but I was willing to do just about anything to hold on to it.

"Thanks, Erik," I finally whispered back.

"If you two are done killing each other, can we please get back to practice?" Henri said, his tall body looming over us. He tried to sound irritated at the interruption to our practice, but I could feel his elation at finally seeing me focus my energy on something productive, even if that was attacking my own teammate.

Chapter Twenty-Three

A week after the incident, as I was now referring to my destruction of Donavon's cabin, we finally left for our next mission. I busied myself with the preparations: memorizing floor plans and city maps, reviewing how to use all of the crypto gadgets and even spending a full day shadowing Dr. Daid.

Henri was worried that I wasn't ready. He thought I was too distracted, and a distracted teammate wasn't a risk worth taking; I'm sure that my impromptu death match with Erik hadn't actually helped my cause. At the time, he'd been relieved to see that I had the ability to focus on a task, but he wasn't impressed with my impulse control. If Erik hadn't convinced him to let me go, I doubt he would have. He trusted Erik's judgment, and Erik thought that the best thing for me was to get back to, or close to, a normal life again.

I knew all of this because Henri was a terrible blocker, and a great projector. When our minds were connected for practice, his thoughts flowed easily from his head to my own without a filter. I frequently caught glimpses of the hushed conversations on the topic of my "readiness" between Erik and Henri while we were practicing. I wanted to reassure Henri, but I didn't want him to realize how exposed his mind actually was.

Erik was much better at blocking me from the parts of his mind that he didn't want me to see, and I tried not to push. He was the only person who seemed to believe in me, and I was in no hurry to find out that wasn't true.

We left for the Mission in the middle of the night. After packing my small bag with the necessary clothing from my cabin, I sat on my bed, taking in every minute detail for the last time. When I first arrived at Headquarters and saw the cabin, I'd been devastated. Donavon had been at Headquarters for a year and had told me about his cabin, even showed me pictures, so I thought that I was prepared for the bare-essential living associated with Hunters Village. I'd thought wrong. Donavon's warnings had not prepared me for the small wooden structure that smelled faintly of pine and damp earth.

The main room was just large enough for three beds, three night stands, and a small wooden table that sat three people. The room contained no closets but had shelving alcoves built into the walls next to each of the beds. The bathroom had three small closets for towels, toiletries, and after-shower clothing. The room had none of the techno gadgets I'd grown accustomed to; in the beginning, I'd thought I would never get used to turning off and on the lights manually, let alone using five blankets to get warm instead of setting the temperature regulator on my mattress.

Now that I knew I was looking at my cabin, my home for the last several months, for the last time, I knew that I was going to miss living here. The next morning, day laborers from the city, who came in during the day to perform odd jobs around Headquarters, would be here to pack our things and move them into our new rooms.

"Sure is going to be nice to come back and have a great big bed to crash in," Erik commented when he caught my gaze wandering over the wooden walls.

"Yeah, I guess." I gave him a small smile.

When I walked out of the cabin, I stopped and looked to my right, at the ruins of Donavon's cabin. My stomach clenched uncomfortably. Every time I entered or exited my cabin, I couldn't help but stare at the destruction. I should feel bad, maybe even regret what I'd done, but I didn't; Donavon deserved it. Actually, he deserved worse – way worse. Arden and Harris probably thought that I was crazy, but their opinions were of little significance to me anymore. If they did think I was nuts, than they were in good company.

Workers had already cleaned out the inside and replaced the windows and door; I felt slightly abashed at the thought that somebody else was cleaning up my mess. By the time I returned from my mission, the cabin should be finished. I knew from Penny that Donavon, Harris, and Arden were staying in a suite in guest housing until the cabin was rebuilt.

Erik gently grabbed my arm and steered me towards the plane. Erik and Henri spoke in hushed voices the entire way to the hangar. I remained silent unless asked a direct question. Once on board, I curled into a ball in my seat and fell asleep almost immediately.

Our mission was in Topeka, Kansas. Kansas, like the other states that bordered the Coalition's territory, was of particular interest to the Agency. The Coalition movement had been building steadily, spreading like a fungus, infecting states one city at a time since the Secession of the Western States. Colorado was the latest state to succumb to Ian Crane's rule and the Agency worried that the Coalition had a foothold in parts of Kansas as a result. Our government wasn't naïve enough to believe that Crane didn't have some supporters in every state: he did. The concern with border-states was that they were more susceptible to Crane's influence because the Agency didn't have a great presence in those regions.

In recent years, uprisings in the border states had become more and more prevalent. TOXIC worried that if these rebel factions weren't quashed we would be faced with a full-on revolt, much like the one that Crane had staged when he originally gained control of the handful of states that he currently controlled. While his rebellion had ultimately proved only mildly successful (in school they taught us that he was unsuccessful, but I personally thought that gaining control of seven states was not exactly unsuccessful) the Agency that knew the more states he gained, the harder it would be to defeat him the second time around.

Kansas was one of the few border states that had yet to come under martial law. One of our Crypto teams had learned of a large gathering of supporters taking place in Topeka, and we were going to apprehend the leaders before the meeting could take place. If we were able to take the organizers into custody and prevent the rally, we could, hopefully, prevent a recurrence of trouble that took place in Mobile five years earlier.

In Mobile, almost a hundred citizens died when TOXIC had tried to break up a similar gathering. Since the incident in Mobile, Hunting teams were frequently dispatched to arrest the leaders in advance. TOXIC found that the rebel factions frequently disbanded in the absence of leadership.

Honestly, I wasn't really gung-ho on the whole idea of preventing free speech and all that. (In *The United States v. Brighton*, the Supreme Court had ruled that Talents were a protected class of individuals; therefore, the First Amendment didn't protect salacious speech). Most days, I wasn't even sure that I was completely on board with the *Mandatory Testing Act*. I mean, *forcing* children to be tested seemed a little extreme.

Imprisoning violators, parents who refused to submit their offspring, definitely seemed harsh. Despite that, going to the McDonough School had proved beneficial for me. Prior to meeting other Talented kids, I'd honestly believed there was something shameful about my abilities. My parents, bless them, had discouraged me from exploring my powers. They'd made it clear that I should hide them. Now, I understood that they were probably just scared that untalented people would treat me like a freak, and they didn't want me subjected to taunting and teasing. That same sentiment was likely what drove parents here to risk jail time by violating the Act. I've always wondered if my parents would have submitted me for testing if I'd been born here. I believed that they would have. My father had been friends with Mac so he would've known that I'd be taken care of.

What I was sure of, without a shadow of a doubt, was that anyone who supported Ian Crane was inherently bad. Any man who ordered the deaths of innocent people was evil. Anybody who supported such an agenda was, by association, evil.

Surprisingly, I wasn't the only member of our team that didn't completely back the *Mandatory Testing Act*; Erik worked hard to keep his thoughts about it to himself, but sometimes they leaked out. I never pressed the issue. Speaking openly against the Act was only a couple of steps removed from treason. Normal citizens were given a little more leeway, not much, obviously, but a TOXIC Operative speaking against the Act would lead to traitorous accusations. I'd heard of too-vocal Agency Operatives being charged with spying for the Coalition. The thought of Erik standing trial for spying shook me to my very core.

Like our previous missions, this one went off without a hitch. The misguided leaders of the Coalition rally were a husband and wife. We'd purposely raided their home in the middle of the night, in hoping to prevent a spectacle. However, the stealth proved unnecessary as they came without protest. I'd been shocked when we arrived at their modest, yet well-maintained home. It was in one of those cookie-cutter neighborhoods, where even the hover cars in the driveways matched. I wondered how many of their neighbors would be surprised to learn that they'd been living amongst rebel supporters. I wondered how many of the neighbors *were* rebel supporters.

Erik remained steel-faced through the short endeavor, yet I could tell that he wasn't comfortable. He performed every detail of the mission with the same precision and thoroughness that he did everything, but his mood was heavy, very un-Erik-like. I tried not to dwell on it too much.

After taking the offending duo into custody, we escorted them to one of TOXIC's interrogation facilities, just outside of D.C.'s overcrowded beltway. My first real twinges of unease came when we handed our captives over to the guards at the base. Psychic interrogation was not fun, for anybody involved. The prisoner's minds would be poked, prodded, and searched; every memory examined, every detail of their lives exposed to determine exactly how far their involvement with the Coalition went.

I shuddered at the thought. Secretly, I hoped that their interrogator wasn't very strong. True, they were in league with the man who'd ordered my parents' deaths, but they might actually just be people against mandatory testing, not in support of Crane's more radical agendas. Not everyone who underwent intense mental interrogation made it out unscathed; sometimes, the interrogator went too deep or broke the person's will. I *really* hoped that the interrogator wasn't that strong. I assured myself that it was unlikely they would be. According to Mac, I was the only Mind Manipulator currently with TOXIC who was that strong.

After depositing the violators, we headed back to Elite Headquarters. We were only there long enough to research our next Hunt before setting out again. This quickly became a trend, but I didn't mind; the more time that I spent away from Headquarters, the less chance that I would run into Donavon.

Once there, I headed straight for my new room. I'd expected it to look like Penny's, which it did, except instead of white, the room was decorated in shades of purple. The carpet was the same plush carpeting that covered Penny's floors, but it was a deep royal purple color. The walls were bare but had been painted lavender with white trim. My new bed was covered in a violet and white floral patterned bedspread with matching purple pillows. The plastic chair and table set was somewhere in between the deep purple of the carpet and the lavender on the walls. My meager clothing hung pathetically in the humongous closet, making me think that I might actually take Penny up on her offer to help me buy some new clothes, even though I would likely never wear them. I had a ton of clothes, but I'd left them at Mac's house; there wasn't really a need for my more extravagant outfits here.

My bathroom had a white tiled floor and white ceramic sink, toilet, and soaking tub, just like Penny's. But instead of white walls, my bathroom was lined with purple glass tiles, alternating frosted and clear from floor to ceiling.

I fell in love with my room the moment I stepped foot inside. But I didn't have much time to enjoy its luxuries before I was back at training and gearing up for my next Hunt.

Thankfully, the hours in between waking and sleeping were packed full, and I rarely had time to think about anything except the task at hand. I'd begged Erik to convince his Medic friend, Zach, to sneak me pills that induced a dreamless sleep. He caved, so it was only twice a day that thoughts of Donavon invaded my mind, threatening to pull me back into the darkness and depression that I was still clawing my way out of.

Our missions took us all over Coalition and Agency territory. One day, we were in a small town without running water, in a Coalition state, where they tended to be poor since they no longer received any kind of government funding; the next, in a huge city with techie stores on every corner. Even though I was spending all of my time with Erik and Henri, I felt more alone than ever. All of the previous confusion over my feelings for Erik seemed trivial. I no longer felt anything. My internal numbness wasn't reserved specifically for Erik; I felt indifferent, at best, towards everything except Donavon. I hated Donavon. Nothing excited me anymore, and nothing shocked me anymore, but nothing hurt me anymore, either.

During our actual Hunts, I let my teammates' emotions become my own. I fed on the thrill and excitement that coursed through them, using it to propel my own senses into overdrive. The surge of adrenaline that accompanied the moment before we entered a building, the heart-stopping pandemonium associated with every fight, and the ecstasy of victory when we succeeded filled the void left by Donavon's absence. I soon became addicted to the Hunt.

On the rare occasion that we were at Headquarters long enough to do anything besides get ready for the next mission, I spent my time with Penny. Mac arranged for us to be allowed to go into the city on our days off, as long as we were back before dark. Unfortunately, he balked at authorizing hover lessons for either of us, so we had to rely on the good graces of Henri and Erik, but that wasn't usually a problem.

Penny urged me to buy decorations for my room every time we went into the city, but I never felt like it. I spent so little time there that it seemed silly to hang pictures only the cleaning staff would see. I did let her talk me into buying clothes and shoes to fill my closet. That also seemed silly, but it made Penny happy, and seeing Penny happy made me feel...something.

The best thing about spending time with Penny was not being in her head. It was nice to sit with her and pretend that I was normal. I had no choice with Erik and Henri since I had to connect with their minds for our missions, and, no matter how hard they both tried to keep it from me, thoughts of Donavon and the incident in his cabin came to the forefront while we were practicing. With Penny, I never had to know what she was thinking. When I asked her a question, I waited for her response. I took her answers at face value because I didn't have a reason to suspect otherwise.

I hadn't actually seen Donavon since our break-up. Not living in Hunters Village reduced the risk of me running in to him by accident. I was careful to avoid the cafes that I knew he frequented, and chose to order my meals from the kitchen downstairs instead. When I went into the city, I didn't have to worry about running into him at the kind of places Penny liked to shop. My practice gym was far enough away from his that if I took certain pathways, I knew I was unlikely to see him. Also, I had a feeling that Mac and Captain Alvarez were arranging our missions to ensure that one of us was almost always away from Headquarters, and that suited me just fine.

Chapter Twenty-Four

Before long, our missions became more dangerous and more complex. I knew that this was unusual for a team as young as ours, but Mac insisted that our track record spoke for itself. We received our first Kill Mission just before I was due to formally graduate, and I had conflicted emotions about the assignment. I knew that Kill Missions came with the job, but they were few and far between. They were even less common when one of the teammates was still a Pledge. It wasn't like we escaped every mission without taking some casualties. Our very first mission had been proof of that. But a Hunt where the hunted was another human life, the knowledge that for us to succeed, somebody had to die? I couldn't stomach the thought.

The week before we were scheduled to leave was more hectic and intense than usual. Henri programmed the simulator in our training arena for Kill Scenarios, setting the rubric for situations similar to the one we'd likely face on our mission. The holographic images were incredibly life-like, and when one landed a blow, a jolt of electricity ran through my body. Our trainings were more somber, more serious than usual. The collective mood of our team weighed heavily on me since I absorbed the feelings of both boys.

Henri and Erik had been on several Kill Missions in their time with the Hunters, and neither was eager to repeat the process. Henri tried to treat the assignment like any other, but he couldn't keep the darkness from his mind. Erik, usually so good at pulling off a nonchalant, carefree attitude, tried to keep the sickness that he felt tucked away in the corners of his mind, but sometimes, it slipped out.

For my part, I was secretly glad to have something all-consuming take over my thoughts. The more that I thought about what we were about to do, the less that I thought about Donavon, and anything that kept my mind off of Donavon was a good thing.

Henri painstakingly walked me through every detail of the laboratory where we would carry out our mission. He explained that the target worked late, alone in his lab, and we should be able to get in, complete the mission, get out and be on our way before anybody discovered his body. Henri had a complete bio on the target, but I couldn't bring myself to read it. I told myself that he was a threat to TOXIC, and most likely a Crane supporter. He must be a very bad man. That was all that I needed to know.

Henri spent the night before we left in D.C. with Frederick. His mind had been distracted all day with thoughts of mortality and the prospect of never seeing Frederick again. I kept seeing flashes of past Kill Missions, some that had gone right and some that hadn't. I realized for the first time how close Henri had come to being captured on more than one occasion. Of course, I had heard of horribly botched missions and near misses, but feeling Henri's fear as if it were my own, unnerved me. I finally understood the enormity of the situation. Any initial relief over the distraction quickly dissipated.

I wasn't the only one feeling it; Erik also felt Henri's past experiences mingled with his own. He radiated desire to feel alive, and connected with a person outside of TOXIC, a person who had no idea what he did or who he was. When he got ready to leave for the city that night, I wanted to beg him to stay with me, but I knew I had no right. It would be selfish and unfair of me to deny him the opportunity to find what he was so desperately craving, particularly when I knew that Henri's thoughts and feelings were not the only ones that he was absorbing.

I'd noticed in practices when, in my weaker moments, my fear and trepidation over the task reached a boiling point and spilled over that Erik's mood would plummet even further. I tried to keep my thoughts to myself. I knew firsthand that shouldering the burden of others emotions – especially when compounded by your own – was exhausting, but sometimes, my feelings were just too intense to contain, and they would burst free into the only outlet that I had: Erik.

That night, I didn't want to be alone. No matter how many times I told myself that what we were doing was necessary, I couldn't shake the leaden feeling that was making my insides heavy. This man probably had a family or friends, somebody that would miss him. What was his crime, anyway? What could he have done that was so horrible that he deserved to die?

After tossing and turning for half the night, I got up, having decided to knock on Penny's door. I only made it as far as my own before I heard a soft knock. I paused, not trusting my ears, and waited to see if the knock came a second time. It did. I opened my mind – Erik. I slowly opened the door with my powers. He was leaning against the door frame, his dark hair hanging in his bloodshot eyes, now looking more blue than green, with his shirt half untucked from his jeans. I drank in his disheveled appearance and thought that he had never looked better.

"You're awake," he slurred, his eyes lighting up.

"You're drunk," I replied, matter-of-factly.

He grinned, "Can I come in?"

I swept my arm in a welcoming gesture and Erik stumbled in, headed straight for my bed. He flopped down on the comforter, leaving his feet dangling off the side. I stood uncomfortably in the middle of the room. Since moving to the apartments, we'd had little social interaction. I saw him every day, and even spent most of my waking hours with him, but we hadn't been alone, just the two of us, since everything had happened with Donavon.

"It's very purple in here," he observed.

"It's my favorite color," I replied lamely.

"Makes sense." I failed to see how any of this situation made sense.

"Erik, what are you doing here?" I asked bluntly.

He raised himself up on one elbow and tried to tuck the too-long strands of his hair behind his ear, but didn't respond. I nervously chewed the inside of my lower lip and willed him to say something, anything.

"Don't want to be alone," he finally said in a low voice.

"You could've stayed in the city if you didn't want to be alone," I tried to keep my tone light.

"True," Erik conceded, "but I didn't want to pretend that I was having a good time and that tomorrow was just like every other day." All of his normal bravado was gone. His eyes were unguarded, making him look uncharacteristically vulnerable.

I nodded, "Okay."

"If you'd rather I leave..." he started to get up.

"No, no, don't leave," I said too quickly, making a move towards my bed.

"I don't want to be alone, either," I added quietly.

"I know," he answered.

I really didn't want for him to leave. Any feelings that I may have had for Erik in the past aside, I really wanted to be near somebody, anybody.

I moved slowly towards my bed and sat on the edge, careful not to touch Erik. I could feel my heart beating in my throat, and hoped that Erik was too drunk to notice. He was still propped up on his elbow, and he reached out with his free hand and took mine.

"Thanks, Tal," he whispered. I smiled nervously, not meeting his eyes. His vulnerability stirred something inside of me. I was seized by the desire to comfort him, but I refrained.

He released my hand and reached behind him, grabbing two of my pillows and throwing them to the opposite end of the bed. He kicked off his shoes and flipped his body around so that his head lay at the end of the bed where my feet usually went. I crawled up to my end of the bed and curled up so that my toes wouldn't be too close to his face, even though his much larger feet were resting on a pillow near my head.

I closed my eyes and tried to relax. On the one hand, having Erik there satisfied my need to be close to somebody, easing my tension. On the other hand, having Erik there elicited feelings that I thought no longer existed, creating more anxiety.

Something tickled the sole of my foot, and I instinctively kicked out. Thankfully, Erik's drunken reflexes were still much faster than most normal people's sober ones, and he had grabbed my foot before it made contact with his more sensitive areas.

"Tal, it's your bed, stretch out," he mumbled. "Beside,s you're only half a person, so you barely take up any room," he laughed at his own not-funny joke.

I gave another small kick, but he still had a hold on my foot, so it didn't actually achieve anything. I stretched out my legs and, even though my bed was plenty big enough for both of us, without the need to touch, Erik held on. Erik cuddling with my feet had an oddly comforting quality, and I fell asleep almost instantly.

When I woke up the next morning, I was immediately aware of Erik's absence, and for some reason, it made me feel even more alone than I had before he'd shown up the night before. I quickly packed my mission bag and headed for the hover hangar, my whole body a rope of tightly-kinked knots.

Erik and Henri were both waiting when I got there. The tension in the air was palpable. Nobody spoke. Erik's vulnerability from last night was long gone, replaced by a confident mask that concealed his strained psyche.

Henri was all business. His demeanor lacked Erik's confidence, but contained none of his nerves either. He was cool and collected, and he had cleared his mind of the slideshow of fears that had been playing there all week.

I curled up in my seat and closed my eyes, concentrating on turning off my mental abilities. I managed to reach a meditative-like state, with all of my energy focused on my sense of touch. My fingers traced the contours of the quilted seat cushion, counting the thread. If Erik or Henri thought my behavior was weird, they didn't let on. I didn't honestly care either way; I couldn't handle their feelings on top of my own. It was easier to block it all.

All three of us changed in to our adapti-suits on the plane, and strapped on our weapons, since there would be no time to waste once we deplaned. Erik smudged adapti paint on my face, to make my skin blend in with my suit. It provided my entire body the ability to meld with the surroundings.

We needed to complete this mission very quickly. Once we were on the ground, we'd have two hours to jog the ten miles to the village, do a quick check to verify our intel, complete the mission, and get out. Kill Missions were too risky to linger in the vicinity for very long.

We landed in a small clearing like usual and deplaned in silence. I immediately opened my mind up to establish our mental connection, and we took off at a jog into the surrounding woods. I could feel both boys' minds buzzing with concentration. The suit regulated my body temperature so that my body didn't sweat, but that same couldn't be said for my face. I had to resist the urge to wipe at the moisture dripping down so I wouldn't rub off any of the adapti-paint.

The jog was not strenuous, but the physical activity helped to take the edge off. Or at least it did until the village came into view. Once the surroundings became familiar from the surveillance footage provided by Crypto, my case of nerves returned two-fold. I pulled at the neck of my suddenly too-small suit and gulped air, never seeming to get enough in my lungs.

"Talia, I need you to focus. The sooner we get in there, the sooner we get out. Okay?" Henri's voice was not unkind, but contained an edge telling me that I needed to get myself under control, immediately. He was right; I needed to control myself. I gritted my teeth and concentrated on slowing my breathing. Erik placed one gloved hand on the nape of my neck and applied just a shadow of pressure.

"Be strong, Tal. You've got this," he encouraged.

I took one last deep breath. *"I'm ready."*

The laboratory was on the edge of a small village just over the border, in Coalition territory. On our jog we'd passed several solitary homes, but our best shot at finding the target alone was at work in his laboratory. The lab happened to be in the heavily-populated main village. We didn't even have the luxury of waiting until dark since we needed to catch him before he left for the evening. Our suits and face paint allowed us to blend easily into our surroundings; unless somebody was fairly close, or looked really hard, they wouldn't notice our presence, but I still felt exposed as we moved through the village.

The laboratory was a long sprawling square one-floor cement building. We took cover behind a dumpster that wasn't visible from the street. Henri worked quickly getting the imaging devices out of his bag and taking heat images of the cement building. Erik and I crouched over his shoulder, watching as the images appeared on the tiny display screen. The concrete was thicker than we'd imagined, but we were still able to pull faint images and confirm that the target was inside.

"*Ready?*" Henri asked.

"*Ready,*" Erik confirmed.

"*Ready,*" I echoed, not feeling ready at all. Erik's words rang in my head, "*Be strong.*" *Be strong, be strong, be strong*, I chanted to myself. *You've got this.*

I followed Henri and Erik up to the front gate, and held my breath while Erik punched in a ten digit code. The lock on the gate soundlessly disengaged, and Henri pushed it open, just enough for us to squeeze through. He took the lead, and we flanked his sides. I reminded myself to breathe as I jogged silently up to the main entrance. We navigated the maze of hallways back to where the target was supposed to be. The interior walls were the same thick concrete as the outside of the building, and I suddenly realized that there were probably more people in the building than we'd seen on the imager.

My thoughts were confirmed when two men rounded the corner at the end of the corridor that we were walking down. The hallways were too narrow to hope that we would go unnoticed, even if we flattened ourselves against the concrete walls.

"*Erik, take the left. I'll take the right. Talia, move on to the target,*" Henri ordered.

The men didn't see us until it was too late. Henri and Erik attacked in unison, catching their prey by surprise. I ran through the middle of the fights and continued on to where we'd seen the red outline on the scan, indicating the target. I found the room easily and turned the knob, but it didn't budge. Putting my other hand on the door, I envisioned the locking mechanism. I mentally disengaged all of the bolts and felt the knob turn in my hand. I breathed a sigh of relief, and pushed the door open.

A short, balding man sat behind a large table full of vials and contraptions all holding different colored liquids. He looked directly at me, and dropped the vial that he was holding in his hand. I didn't know how many more might be in the building, but I didn't want to take the chance, so I froze the vial to suspend it in midair before it could shatter on the floor. The guy could see me, but was having a hard time focusing on me since the suit and face paint were obscuring my appearance.

I moved slower than I should have towards him, reaching for one of the knives in my belt.

"TOXIC, right?" the man stuttered.

I didn't respond; I couldn't have formulated words if my life depended on it. My tongue felt thick and heavy, filling the small space between my tightly clenched jaws, and a sour taste ran down the back of my throat. I continued towards him. He backed away as I advanced, knocking over vials as he went. I wasn't fast enough to mentally catch all of them before they hit the ground. So much for not attracting attention. He continued to retreat until his back slammed into the far wall of the room. I quickened my pace until I was standing over the top of him. He fell to his knees by my feet, holding up his hands to shield himself. My reflexes took over and I pounced, pressing my knife to his throat.

"No, please, no," the man begged.

I reached with my free hand into my belt and grabbed the syringe holding the poison. I gripped the syringe so hard that I could feel the skin over my knuckles go tight. The same panic that had seized me outside took over my body again. My chest heaved in and out as I tried to catch my breath. I felt a burning sensation in the corners of my eyes, and willed myself not to cry.

Noting my hesitation, the man started to get up. I pushed the tip of the knife harder against the pale skin of his neck, penetrating the flesh and drawing blood. I closed my eyes and shook my head, trying to erase my misgivings. The man shrunk back even further, pressing himself into the wall. A large hand closed around mine, the one holding the syringe. The hand forced the syringe into the man's bulging blue vein and depressed the plunger. I watched in horror as the man's dark brown eyes dulled and then rolled back as he slumped to the floor.

The hand holding mine pried my fingers away from the syringe that I was still holding.

"Let go, Tal."

I collapsed back against the person attached to the hand – Erik. He wrapped his arms around me, holding me to his chest for a brief second before releasing me, to reach in his pack. I fell to my knees next to the man's lifeless form. Erik pulled out a small scanner, similar to the one that Henri had used to image my body when I got stabbed. He scanned the man's body, and the scanner gave a barely perceptible beep.

"He's dead," Erik confirmed.

I couldn't move. I stared down at the dead man's body, open mouthed. I felt the burning sensation behind my eyes again.

"We need to go now, Natalia," Erik said firmly, pulling me to my feet. He wrapped his arm around my waist and gently pulled me to the door. Henri was standing guard outside. We sprinted out

of the building, the same way that we'd come in, with Henri in the lead. We didn't slow our pace until we reached the edge of the woods.

Henri and Erik quickly shed their weapons and packs and morphed into two large birds. As if on auto-pilot, I mindlessly strapped their weapons to my body and the packs to Henri's back. When I was confident that everything was secure, I climbed on to Erik's back, in the space between his wings, and wrapped my arms securely around his neck. I closed my eyes as the two large birds took off into the now dark night sky.

I had yet to master riding Erik's giant bird form, but I was consistently staying on in practices, so I wasn't really scared flying the distance back to the hover plane. I was in such a state of shock that I don't think I would've cared if I did fall off.

The two giant birds touched down in the clearing, near the waiting craft. I jumped off Erik's back before his talons struck the ground, and ran up the gangplank before either could morph back. I climbed into my seat. I fumbled with the buckles, trying and failing to fit all of the pieces into the right parts. I screamed in frustration when I failed for the third time.

"I got it, Tal," Erik said gently, taking the buckles out of my hands. He deftly fastened the buckles and then got up, returning a moment later with chemi wipes. He gently cleaned the streaked paint off my face, wiping away the silently falling tears with his thumb before he stood. When he finished, he got up and went to clean himself up.

"You did really well, Natalia," Henri said, taking Erik's place next to my chair.

"Thanks," I sniffed.

"I know how hard it is the first time. I'd like to tell you that it gets easier, but it doesn't," he continued sadly.

I nodded as if I understood. He reached out and squeezed my hand before getting up to take his seat. I tucked my knees up against my chest and rested my head on top. I closed my eyes, but I couldn't manage to fall asleep.

The ride back to Headquarters was just as silent as the ride out, but the mood on the hover plane was different. Instead of the stress and tension, the ride back was filled with sadness and remorse. Both Henri and Erik kept stealing not-so-discreet glances in my direction.

When we arrived back at Headquarters, I went straight to my room. Erik, Penny, and Henri all made excuses to knock on my door, but I ignored all of them.

For the first time since our fight, I wanted to reach out to Donavon. Up until now, I'd felt a barrage of emotions towards him, mostly anger and pain, but this was the first time I actually missed him. I lost track of the number of times I opened my mind to seek out Donavon, and it took every ounce of restraint that I could muster to keep me from actually calling out to him. Erik or Penny or even Henri would have come to sit with me, but it wasn't the same. Despite everything, I yearned for the comfort that only Donavon could provide.

I barely slept the night that we got back. I sat in my big bed, clutching an overstuffed purple pillow filled with goose feathers, staring mindlessly out of my huge window at the grounds below. The next morning, I woke up more depressed than when I went to sleep, made worse when I realized that it was the beginning of the Festivis Holiday.

The nation came together every May 13th to celebrate Festivis Day – the day that the government had halted the Coalition's rebellion. I wasn't really sure about celebrating a holiday that marked the split of a country, but I think I might be the only person who viewed it that way. Officially, the government declared that Festivis signified the commitment of the lasting states to remain unified. Given how tenuous the government's hold on some of those states was, I hoped that the celebrations served as a reminder of how great a nation we would be if we stayed unified.

All of the Operatives not training for an active mission were permitted to leave Headquarters. Ordinarily, I would have spent the holiday with Mac, Gretchen, and Donavon, but despite my moment of weakness the previous night, I wasn't ready to see Donavon, let alone stay in the same house as him. Gretchen had sent me message after message, begging me to come home, but I didn't return any of them. Mac had come to see me several times since the incident with Donavon, and passed on more of Gretchen's pleading. I'd told him that I thought it best if I stayed at Headquarters. Mac had assured me that he understood, and, of course, the decision was mine.

My communicator began buzzing early that morning. I groaned and reached out in its general direction. Mac's name flashed across the display screen. I considered not answering, but I knew that he was aware that I was back from my mission, and would likely continue to call until I answered. I fumbled around with the buttons until I finally found the right one.

"Hi, Mac," I croaked as Mac's holographic face appeared.

"Hello, Natalia." Mac sounded slightly disapproving. I hoped that it was because I was still in bed, and not because he'd learned that I cried during my assignment. Mac didn't approve of crying.

"Happy Festivis, Mac," I mumbled into my pillow.

"Yes, Happy Festivis. There will be lots of parades and celebrations going on in the District over the next couple of days. I've arranged for both you and Penelope to attend any that you wish. Please don't overdo it; no other Pledges have been afforded the same privileges."

"Thanks, Mac," I replied, brightening slightly as I propped myself up on my elbow. "Tell Gretchen that I said hi and I will see her at my graduation."

"Yes, I will...Speaking of graduation, I heard that you completed your first Kill Mission yesterday."

Oh, no, here came the lecture.

"I don't want to talk about it," I said quickly.

"Natalia, you knew that this was part of the job," Mac said flatly. Guess he had heard about my breakdown.

"I know," I replied tightly, gritting my teeth.

"You'd better get used to it, and fast. You graduate very soon. Once you are a full Hunter, Kill Missions will be more prevalent."

"I know," I repeated, an edge to my voice.

"Do you still want to be a Hunter, Natalia?" Mac demanded.

"Of course, I do!" I exclaimed, scrambling into a sitting position.

"Good. Start acting like it," he retorted bitterly. I sighed. His words were laced with unspoken innuendo. I had chosen to be a Hunter. I'd worked towards this goal every day since I went to the McDonough School. I knew what the Hunters did before I came here, I'd just been unprepared for the difference between knowing what Hunters did, and actually doing it. Now I knew. I just had to get used it.

"Your solo mission is just around the corner," he continued. "It is supposed to be a formality, but if you do not perform well, you will not become a Hunter. Nothing that I can do will change that."

I don't know if he meant it as a threat, but that's how I interpreted it. I winced. I'd never truly considered not becoming a Hunter. That was not an option.

I'd chosen the Hunters because that was the only chance I'd have to find the man responsible for my parents' deaths. Most mental Talents work in psychic interrogation, but I knew that would never be enough for me. I didn't want to interrogate the man who ordered my parent's execution. I wanted to hunt him down; I wanted to kill him. The realization hit me hard. I guess I did have a killer inside me.

A myriad of excuses for Mac were on the tip of my tongue, but Mac didn't want excuses. Mac wanted results. Besides, he already knew that I'd been distracted after the incident with Donavon – I think that was kind of the point of this phone call.

"I understand," I said instead.

"I hope that you do. I hope that you're taking your position seriously."

"I am," I protested, louder than I meant to.

"Good, because if you fail your solo mission, I won't be able to save you," he warned.

"I'm not asking you to," I replied coldly.

"Enjoy the holiday," Mac said, letting me know that the conversation was over.

"Whatever," I spat back.

"Goodbye, Natalia." My communicator made a loud buzzing noise, and then Mac's holographic image disappeared.

I screamed in frustration, rolling over on to my back. I pounded my fist against the mattress. It was childish, but I was furious – mostly with myself. I needed to be more focused. I needed to become more desensitized to what we were doing. TOXIC was important, and what we were doing was important. The Coalition killed my parents. They deserved anything that came their way. I pounded the mattress with my fist again, this time in determination. I climbed out of bed and headed to my bathroom, vowing that I'd be stronger next time. Next time, I wouldn't falter. Next time, Erik wouldn't have to do it for me.

Chapter Twenty-Five

There was an insistent pounding on my door when I exited the bathroom a short while later. I pulled the tie on my fluffy bathrobe a little tighter as I opened my mind. It was Penny. Should've guessed. I mentally forced the door open, and Penny's lanky form tumbled through, red hair first.

"Hey!" she exclaimed.

"Hey, Penny," I smiled.

"I just heard," she said excitedly.

"Heard? About what?" How I cried like a little girl during a mission? Yeah, I didn't need to hear about that, I was there.

"The Director gave us permission to attend the Festivis celebrations in the city!" Penny could barely contain her enthusiasm.

"Oh, right, Mac mentioned that." Before Mac had lectured me about my dedication to becoming a Hunter, I'd been really excited about attending the celebrations as well, but now it didn't seem so important.

"We totally have to find our most city girl looking outfits!" Penny seemed immune to my indifference.

"I'm not really sure I'm up for going," I started. Penny's face fell, and her bright green eyes clouded with disappointment.

"We don't have to dress up," she offered, looking hopeful.

"It's not the dressing up, Penny," I assured her.

"Then what is it? I've always wanted to attend Festivis Day celebrations," Penny pleaded. "At the orphanage, we were only allowed to watch the parade go by, but they never let us leave to take part in any of the activities."

"I'm sure some of the other Cryptos are going, right? Why don't you go with them?"

"Because I want to go with *you*!" She gave me one of her big toothy smiles and batted her eyelashes, exaggeratedly at me.

"I don't know, Penny . . ."

"I *promise* it'll be fun." She could tell my resolve was weakening and pounced on the opportunity. "If you aren't having fun, you can just tell me, and we'll come straight back," she promised.

It wasn't as if I were going to train today anyway, so I nodded. "Deal."

Penny's fervor was contagious, and before long I was almost as amped to go as she was. Penny took a quick inventory of my closet and dismissed all of my day-to-day clothes as too boring. She pulled out the silk garment bags that contained my most recent gifts from Gretchen, and littered their contents across my bed. I could practically see the wheels turning in her overly-analytical Crypto head as she ran her fingers over the fabrics.

Finally, Penny held up a long, sleeveless dark green dress made of chiffon. The straps of the dress fastened over the shoulders, with two large interlocking gold hoops on each side. The dress was cut in a deep V in the front and back, and a thin slip of a light green see-through material was all that prevented my skin from exposure. The waist of the dress was cinched with a wide belt that was the same lighter green shade as the slip and was embroidered with gold and dark green flowers. The skirt of the dress was floor length, full and flowing. A small gold hook was sewn into one side of the skirt so I could hold the bottom of the dress off the ground when I walked.

"This is amazing!" she squealed. "You are going to look amazing in it!"

"Thanks. It was a present from Gretchen. I think she always wanted a daughter," I mumbled, embarrassed.

"Now we just need to decide on your makeup." She scrutinized my features, and I suddenly felt very self-conscious under her intense gaze. "Stay right here. I'll be right back." With that, Penny was out the door. She was only gone for a couple of minutes, but when she returned, her arms were laden with garment bags of her own, and huge boxes that I had a feeling contained makeup.

Penny dumped all the stuff on my bed and pulled one of the chairs from my breakfast set into the middle of the room.

"Sit," she ordered, her eyes glittering with excitement.

I obediently sat in the purple plastic chair and closed my eyes, giving my appearance over to Penny. While I still wasn't fully committed to the idea of going into the city, I began to warm to the idea. After the nightmare mission, maybe blowing off a little steam would be good for me. Maybe, dare I hope, I would even have a good time. Celebrating Festivis Day in the city with Penny had to be better than the alternative – wallowing in my own self-pity.

For the next hour or so, I opened my eyes when Penny said open, I puckered my lips when Penny said to pucker, I tilted my head when Penny said to tilt, and I tried not to flinch while Penny tugged and wound my hair around my head.

"Done!" she announced proudly after she zipped up my dress.

"Can I look in the mirror now?" I asked, although I wasn't

sure I actually wanted to. If Penny's makeup was any indication of what she found attractive, and I kind of assumed it was, then I probably looked ridiculous.

"Of course! You're totally going to love it!"

I grimaced. Somehow I doubted that, but for Penny's sake, I'd have to pretend.

I was shuffling my way towards the bathroom, trying not to step on the hem of my dress, when I heard a knock at the door. I looked at Penny, alarmed. She gave me a quizzical look in return.

"I don't want anybody to see me like this," I mouthed.

Penny rolled her eyes and moved towards the door. I knew before she opened it that Erik was on the other side. He was dressed from head to toe in black, making his turquoise eyes shine like two small, perfectly matched gems. His black dress pants fit perfectly. The black, leathery belt threaded through the loops looked shiny and new, and his black dress shirt gave off a slight shine when the light hit it. His ensemble was completed with a black dress jacket.

"You girls almost..." Erik trailed off when he saw me standing in the middle of the room. "Tal, you look..."

"Ridiculous?" I finished for him.

"No, no, you don't look ridiculous. You look amazing," his eyes traveled the length of my body slowly, leaving me feeling flushed and oddly thirsty. The memory of Erik's hand brushing my stomach to put on my bandages suddenly invaded my consciousness, and the same tingling sensation that captivated me then washed over me tenfold now. I let out a shaky breath, silently praying Erik hadn't felt it, too.

"Thanks," I mumbled, reaching up to smooth my hair self-consciously. I pulled my hand away in horror when I felt feathers covering one side of my head. Blood rushed to my cheeks, but thankfully, Penny had put so much makeup on my face I didn't think either of them could tell.

"I just need to get myself ready, we'll only be a minute," Penny said to Erik.

"Are you going with us?" I asked, confused.

"Who'd you think was going to drive you?" he smirked. I hadn't honestly thought about it. Any Operative who hadn't left the compound for the holiday would be going to the city celebrations, and all the Pledges that were still here would likely be trying to sneak into the city. I guess I'd just figured we'd beg a ride off one of them.

"Thanks." I smiled at Erik.

"No problem. I'll wait downstairs with Harris and Henri, just come down when you're ready." Erik made no move to leave, instead staring at me with a glint in his eye that made my head spin.

"The sooner you leave, the sooner Penny can get dressed," I said, trying to keep my voice even.

"Right," he spun on his heel and strolled to the door. Once he was gone, I let out a breath I hadn't realized I was holding, and felt the circulation return to my extremities as the pounding in my heart quieted.

Penny gave me a knowing look, but kept her mouth shut for once. She hurried into the bathroom and, in record time, applied smoky gray and black shadows with flecks of gold over her eyelids and blood red gloss on her thin lips.

She held up three simple dresses for me to choose from. They were all the same basic style; one-shouldered sheaths that hung to the middle of her calf, one in black, one in electric blue and one in lemon yellow. I saw her glance enviously towards the rest of my elaborately-styled dresses strewn about on my bed. I wanted to offer her one, but given our considerable height difference, they would never fit her. Instead, I pointed to the electric-blue one and watched as she slipped it over her head.

I smiled. "You look beautiful."

She returned my smile. "We'd better go before the cavalry returns."

I quickly programmed a request for room maintenance to clean the mess that Penny and I'd left behind as we scurried out the door.

As Penny pushed the down button for the elevator, I glimpsed my reflection for the first time in the metal doors. Penny had smoothed my curls into a sleek bun on one side of my neck. I did indeed have gold feathers decorating the opposite side. She had dusted green and gold shadows over my eyelids, and a pink blush on my cheeks. She'd informed me, with a smirk, that the blush was called *First Kiss*. The pale pink gloss on my lips added very little color, but a whole lot of shine. I smiled at my reflection. I definitely looked like a city girl.

Erik, Henri, and Harris were waiting for us in the lobby when we emerged from the elevator. I hadn't seen Harris since my fight with Donavon, and I had no idea what he thought of me; he was, after all, one of Donavon's best friends.

I gave the boys a tight smile and busied myself with fastening the hook on the skirt of my dress to the thin gold bracelet fastened around my wrist.

"We're ready to have a totally awesome time!" Penny announced in greeting.

"Good, let's get going," Henri laughed at her enthusiasm.

Penny and I followed the boys through the apartment lobby and out into the cool day. To my surprise, Erik fell back and offered me his arm as I hobbled unsteadily on the wooden shoes designed to be worn with the dress. Penny shot me a not-so-subtle look before hurrying forward to catch up with Henri and Harris.

"How ya doing after yesterday?" Erik asked, in a quiet voice.

"Better," I lied. My earlier conversation with Mac may have confirmed that I had a killer instinct lurking somewhere deep within, but every time I thought about the man in the laboratory on his knees, begging for his life, I felt disgusted with myself. I wasn't sure if there was valor in revenge, but I did know that there was nothing heroic about what we'd done yesterday. I tried to remedy that by pushing those thoughts to the darkest, cobweb-laden corner of my mind.

"Good," he answered, with an easy smile. There was no doubt in my mind he knew I was lying. "You're going to love the city celebrations," he said, changing the subject. "The floats in the parade are awesome, and the street vendors sell great food. You're seriously going to love it."

I'd never seen Erik so animated before. I'd felt his thrill, his fear, his anxiety, and even his self-loathing after he plunged the needle in the scientist's neck, but never genuine happiness. I smiled, letting his exuberance become my own, my mood lifting until I, too, wanted nothing more than to celebrate Festivis. I listened intently as he babbled on about the festivities during the entire walk to the hangar and for most of the ride into the city.

The city celebration was everything he'd promised and more. The streets had been shut down to vehicles, leaving street vendors plenty of room to set up.

Our small group, plus Frederick, who had met us at TOXIC's city hover hangar, made our way from one street vendor to the next, stopping to sample the delicacies. I ate pork and pineapple skewers from one, and a caribou dog wrapped in a cornbread bun from the next. Penny and I split candied plums and spiced apples from a dessert vendor, and cashew and pistachio crisps from a nut vendor. Erik insisted I try a bite of his black bear and bean burrito, and despite the feeling that my stomach had already stretched beyond its capacity, I ate half.

The exotic food vendors were only outdone by the performers dancing through the streets, and the elaborate floats. Each float held a small group of representatives from each state. Even the representatives from the smaller, and usually poorer, states were dressed in their finest silks and satins, with brightly colored jewels adorning their bodies and elaborate head toppers. I marveled as the street performers flipped and tumbled through the air, twirling fire batons and sharp swords.

The atmosphere in the nation's capital was lively and energetic. Residents from cities all over the country had come to D.C. to celebrate Festivis. People toasted each other in the streets, randomly hugged and kissed strangers, and broke into off-key verses of the National Anthem.

The mood was infectious. I was careful not to drink too much of the burning, brown liquor that a drink vendor handed me when we walked by, but the couple of sips I had spread warmth and happiness through me. Before I knew it, I was dancing and singing off-key with the rest of the celebrants. I wasn't the only one who appeared to be enjoying myself; Erik refused to dance with me, but he hooted and hollered as Penny and I danced circles around him. Henri and Frederick were holding hands and singing at the top of their lungs to the District's state song, which was blasting out of speakers mounted on the buildings. I'd seen Henri relax, and even joke with Erik, but I'd never seen him truly enjoy himself before now. Harris drank several cups of the brown liquor, and kept making excuses to touch Penny's arm or lean in closer than necessary to whisper in her ear, sending her into a fit of giggles.

Penny was basking in Harris' attention, and I loved seeing her so happy.

When we finally got tired of contending with the crowds on the street, we ducked into an eatery called Igloo; the entire inside was made of ice. I recalled Frederick telling us about this place, and was excited to see it firsthand. I was still stuffed from all of the food I'd sampled, so I only ordered a hot chocolate. It came out topped with huge fluffy marshmallows and, at Erik's insistence, spiked with several shots of cocoa liquor. The boys somehow found room for cold squid noodle salad with beef and cooked carrot skewers also served cold, with frosty mugs of beer to wash it all down.

"I think it's time I took you girls back," Henri said regretfully to me and Penny after all of the food and drinks were gone.

"No one will notice if they aren't back before dark," Harris commented, slurring his words a little bit. He reached over and rubbed his large, calloused hand down Penny's arm, and she let out an excited titter.

"The Agency notices everything," Frederick said darkly. It was an awkward moment – something about the way he said it made me uneasy. I looked around, but nobody else seemed concerned; maybe there'd been too many shots in my hot chocolate.

"The Director was very clear about wanting them back before dark. I don't want him taking their privileges," Henri said, giving Frederick a pointed look. Guess I wasn't the only one who'd noticed.

In the end, everybody came back with us to Headquarters, except Frederick. Henri promised him he'd come back after he dropped the rest of us off. Penny disappeared with Harris as soon as we landed. I was a little nervous about letting her go off with him when they'd both been drinking, but she seemed so happy that I didn't want to burst her bubble. Henri turned right around and headed back to Frederick's apartment in the city, leaving me and Erik standing together, alone, outside the hangar.

"Walk you back to your room?" he asked, offering me his arm.

I smiled and circled my arm underneath his.

"Do you think Penny will be okay alone with Harris?" I wondered.

"He's a good guy, Tal. She'll be fine."

"You're a good guy, and I wouldn't leave a drunk friend alone with you," I teased.

"I'm offended!" Erik bristled. "I've always been a perfect gentleman to you."

"Yes, you are," I agreed quietly, suddenly struck with the thought that I might not want him to be such a gentleman.

What is wrong with you? I scolded myself. *You just got your heart broken by the boy you've been in love with since you were ten. It's way too soon to be thinking about another guy.*

I couldn't rid myself of the overwhelming amalgam of feelings when I was alone with Erik. In practice I was aware of him, but not like I was *aware* of him when it was just us. And we were touching.

"Have fun today?" Erik probed, mistaking my sudden change in mood for sadness.

"I did, it was everything you said it would be." I tried to give him a genuine smile, but when I looked up in to his eyes, my stomach muscles tightened, clenching so forcefully that I grimaced.

Erik walked me all the way to my door. He waited patiently while I pressed my palm to the sensor next to the door. The green light came on, indicating the scanner had confirmed my identity. I walked in, looking back over my shoulder when I didn't feel Erik following.

"Don't you want to come in?" I asked, trying not to sound too disappointed.

"I don't know...I'm still pretty worn out from yesterday. I should turn in early," Erik's voice was tight.

"Oh, okay," I nodded, giving him a half smile. I wanted to open my mind to see what he was really feeling and thinking, but Erik was the only person I'd ever subconsciously transferred my thoughts and feelings to. My emotions were so out of control, I worried if I opened my mind, I wouldn't be able to contain my thoughts and feelings to my own head.

In one quick, fluid motion, Erik moved from the doorway into my room. He wrapped one of his rough hands around the side of my neck, rubbing his thumb along my jaw bone. My breath caught in my throat, and the room started to spin around us. He placed his other hand on the small of my back, right below the bottom of the V in my dress. I could feel his warm hand through the thin material. He leaned down, his turquoise eyes holding my purple-blue ones.

I bit the inside of my lip so hard, I tasted blood. The pain cleared my head just enough to remember to breathe, preventing me from passing out on account of the lack of oxygen. I wanted him to kiss me so badly that I could taste the desire, mixed with the blood in my mouth. I wanted to know how he felt, I craved the mental connection. I reached out to his mind. I felt raw desire, so primal that it felt more animal than human. I could hear his mental struggle over whether to kiss me, and I wanted to reassure him. I wanted to beg him to kiss me. I wanted to plead with him not to let this moment end. I wanted to tell him so many things.

The agonizing seconds of anticipation before you dive head-first off of a cliff are only outdone by the actual free fall itself. I was done agonizing; I was ready to jump, I wanted the free fall. Erik tilted my face gently towards his. I closed my eyes as he leaned down, knowing this would be the moment we went over the edge. As Erik touched his lips gently to mine, I felt a crackle of electricity shoot through our lips and straight down to my toes. It was the strongest sensation that I'd ever experienced. Even with everything that Donavon and I had shared, we'd never had a kiss like this. I'd never felt anything like this when I was with Donavon.

Erik abruptly pulled back, and my eyes popped open. He gave me a look I didn't understand. He leaned back down, but instead of pressing his lips to mine again, leaned in until his lips were right next to my ear. I thought I was going to faint when his bottom lip brushed my earlobe.

"Good night, Natalia," he whispered.

I blinked. His hand was no longer on my back. His thumb gave one last gentle brush across my cheek, smearing something wet, and then he was gone. I wanted to call after him, but I couldn't breathe, let alone speak.

As if Erik's hands had been the only thing holding me upright, I sank to the floor almost immediately after he broke contact. I watched him walk out and close the door quietly behind him, not once looking back. Once he was gone, I wiped my fingers across my cheeks and realized the something wet he'd smeared were my tears.

Disappointment washed over me, wrapping my body in a cold embrace. Had I done something wrong? Why did he leave? I felt hollow inside. Why had I cried when he kissed me? I wanted him to kiss me, wanted it more than I've ever wanted anything in my life. Why was I still crying? I didn't know exactly, and that made me sob harder.

There were still two more days of festivities, but I didn't feel like going into the city the next morning. Thankfully, Penny was so hungover the next day that she wasn't feeling up to making the trip either. We lounged in my room, eating greasy potato pancakes and cheesy eggs for breakfast instead. Penny delighted in telling me the blow-by-blow of her evening make-out session with Harris.

"He's totally a good kisser," she said, for the tenth time that morning. I gave her a genuine smile. Penny usually crushed on boys from afar and, while she had a lot of boy friends, she'd never had a *boyfriend*.

"I'm glad you had a good time," I replied honestly. I genuinely liked Harris, even if he were one of Donavon's friends. He'd always been nice to me and, last night, after the initial weirdness had worn off, he'd treated me just like he always had before I destroyed his cabin. Hmmm, yeah, I probably wouldn't have blamed him if he did think I was a little nuts. Sane people didn't destroy whole structures when they were angry.

"I did! And he even sent me a message this morning to ask if I wanted to have breakfast or something, but my head hurt so bad I totally wasn't up for getting dressed and doing my hair all cute." I laughed. Penny's red hair was sticking out every which way, and she still had dirt smudged on her face from rolling around with Harris the night before. She was wearing a thread-bare, standard issue McDonough Athletics t-shirt I estimated she had owned since she first started at school, and gray sweatpants speckled with nail polish and hair dye.

"What about later? Are you going to hang out with him tonight?" I asked, trying to match her enthusiasm.

"I don't know! Should I?"

"I don't know," I laughed. "Do you like him?"

"I don't know! I liked kissing him, does that count?"

"That counts," I confirmed.

"Did you do anything after we got back?" she inquired.

"No," I said, a little too fast and a little too emphatically. My pulse quickened, and my face flushed just thinking of Erik's face so close to mine, his hands touching me in a "more than just a friend" manner.

"I'll take that as a yes," Penny laughed, flipping from her back to her stomach so she could see my face.

"It wasn't a big deal. Erik just walked me to my room," I refused to meet her eyes.

"And?" she pressed, her eyes shining with excitement.

"And nothing," I replied, trying not to let my voice sound too dejected.

"But you wanted there to be an 'and'," Penny nodded her head knowingly.

"I think I do," I buried my face in my hands.

"Are you embarrassed?!" Penny exclaimed her green eyes growing larger. "He's totally hot. Every girl I know talks about him; any of them would trade places with you in a second!"

"Why? He barely even kissed me," I whined. Last night, I'd been upset about the situation – had I done something wrong? I wasn't the most experienced kisser - Donavon was the only person I'd ever kissed - but Erik hadn't even given me a chance to show him how much of an amateur I actually was. Did he not feel the same current of electricity when we touched? The sensation was so overwhelming, I thought for sure that it had to be our combined reactions I felt. Did he regret the kiss?? He must – that was the only explanation.

"Barely?" Penny squealed. "Barely kissed you? So he did

actually kiss you?"

"Sorta," I muttered, humiliated all over again.

"How do you sorta kiss somebody? Did his mouth touch yours or not?"

"It sorta did," I mumbled, my breakfast squirming in my stomach, making me wish that I hadn't eaten so much.

"What happened after he sorta kissed you?" Penny questioned, her expression hungry for every detail.

"Nothing," I said, clearing my throat.

"He didn't say anything? He just left?" Penny looked incredulous.

"Yeah, he just left," I confirmed. "I think he regretted doing it," I added in a small, humiliated voice.

"He didn't regret it, give it time," Penny said wisely. She flopped back down on the bed.

"Penny?" I asked hesitantly.

"Hmmm?"

"Can I ask you a question?"

"Totally."

"Is it wrong to have feelings for Erik? Donavon and I just broke up. It feels wrong."

"No way, Tal. For starters, you and Donavon broke up like months ago. It's not too soon to have a crush on Erik. It only feels wrong because you've never had a crush on anyone besides Donavon. Trust me, I have crushes on people all the time. You'll totally get used to it by the third or fourth one."

Had it really been months since the fight? I guess it had. In the days following the incident, time had slowed until the seconds ticked like dripping molasses. I even tried to will time to speed up, but to no avail; I guess even my superior powers had their limits. Now, looking back, I realized the last several months had flown by. Even so, the emotional and mental lacerations left from Donavon's betrayal were still smarting. Every time I thought the gashes had scabbed over, I remembered that...that blonde, and a dull ache started in my chest, growing steadily stronger until I thought my heart might explode all over again.

"Thanks, Penny."

Chapter Twenty-Six

Penny returned to her room to sleep off her hangover after breakfast, and I took the opportunity to make good on my promise to Mac. I headed to the workout arena and spent the afternoon training with the simulator. I set the simulator to "random" and pulled on a suit and a Sim headset. The Sim headset had an ear piece and goggles. The ear piece acted like a team leader, feeding me audio instructions regarding the randomly selected Sim scenario. The eye goggles kept scrolling coordinates of my location within the Sim scenario and mission statistics I needed to be aware of. Henri once told me that the simulator is programmed with over a thousand different Sim scenarios; despite my best efforts, I only made it through four.

After my afternoon with the simulator, I headed to the indoor target range and set up a handful of practice dummies for myself. I intended to rotate through the targets, alternating between my throwing knives, a scoped rifle, and a handgun. Throwing knives have always been my specialty; knives were far easier than bullets for me to control with my mind.

The weightless tungsten carbide blade, in contrast with the heavy steel handle, felt natural, like an extension of my own small hand. I closed my eyes, envisioning the space just slightly to the right of center on the target's chest. I released the knife in my left hand first, directing the dagger blade over handle as it twirled through the air and sank deep into its mark. I liberated the one in my right hand just as the first made contact. I summoned two more knives that had been lying by my left foot. I didn't wait this time, launching both simultaneously. I beckoned the next two, and let them both fly the instant my fingers closed around the cool handles. When I finally opened my eyes again, ten knife handles protruded from the dummy's chest, the blades embedded to the hilt. Satisfaction washed over me.

I held my left hand out to my side, parallel to the ground, and bid the rifle to rise. The heavy barrel sailed towards my outstretched palm. My fingers curled delicately around the cylindrical shaft as I tapped the orange glasses from the top of my head down onto the bridge of my nose. I ran my finger over the sensor on the sidepiece, activating the simulated targets. In the same motion, I tossed the gun lightly in the air, catching the handle in my left, my index finger sliding neatly into the trigger, and the butt of the gun landing heavily on my left shoulder. A little showy, I know, but what I lacked in actual skill, I liked to make up for in finesse. Reaching for the barrel with my right, I cupped the bottom to steady the rifle. I squinted one eye, peering through the sight with the other. I pulled the trigger ten times in fast succession as ten Sim targets danced across my vision. Several of the targets disintegrated when I fired at them, but over half were still standing when I dropped the gun against my left side. I touched the sensor on the sidepiece again, and my Sim statistics digitally appeared on the left lens. Kills: 4. Wounded: 3. Misses: 3. Overall score: 55%. Yeah, I sucked.

I hit the sensor a third time, and a countdown appeared on my left lens, counting down from ten. I extended my right arm, calling a handgun resting close by while tossing the rifle to the floor with my left. The handgun flew through the air, landing hard against my palm. In the same motion, I brought my left hand to grip the opposite side of the pistol handle. A "one" appeared on my lens, and I readied myself to fire. I breathed evenly, in and out, in and out. Focus. I concentrated for all I was worth on each individual bullet as it spun through the rifled barrel of my gun. I felt the bullet explode through the end as the gun powder residue blew back, coating my white knuckled hands. I tried to guide the bullet's trajectory towards the intended victim. Once I emptied the entire clip, I lowered the handgun and hit the sensor to display my Sim statistics. Kills: 3. Wounded: 7. Misses: 0. Overall Score: 65%. Slightly better, but nowhere near good enough. Feeling only slight dejected, I reloaded.

I poured myself into my bed sometime after midnight. I couldn't muster the energy to shower, so I settled for peeling off my workout clothes, damp with sweat and reeking of gunshot residue.

I woke up early the next morning, feeling a renewed sense of purpose and determination. I pulled on black mesh tennis shoes and headed to the woods, as fast as my short legs would carry me. I performed sensory honing drills as I ran, cycling from one sense to the next without skipping a beat. I could still hear Mac's words pulsing in my head, as though he were running alongside me, screaming in my ear. *Do you still want to be Hunter, Natalia?* I ran harder. *If you fail your solo mission, I won't be able to save you.* I ran harder. *You have two choices, Natalia.* Revenge, I screamed to myself. I pushed harder. *Do you want your parents' deaths to be for nothing, Natalia?* My chest constricted, and my lungs seared as I inhaled and expanded my lungs until they felt as though they might burst, willing my body to outrun Mac's words in my mind.

Erik hadn't sent me a message or come to see me at all the day before, but I hadn't actually thought he would. Regardless, I would have to see him the following day and while I was still confused and hurt over what happened several nights ago, I really wanted to see him. Donavon would be back from his parents' house the following morning, and I really didn't want to see him; I had yet to run into him, but I knew it was only a matter of time.

I hated him because of what he'd done to me; I was sure of that, I think, but I was starting to wonder if I'd ever truly loved him. The feelings I was developing for Erik were so different, so much more intense than anything I'd ever experienced with Donavon. But could I really hate him if I'd never loved him? After all, hate is love's counterpart, right? At seventeen, did I actually know what love meant? I know that I knew hate; I hated the man who was behind my parents' murders. I'd loved them, the type of all-consuming, unconditional love that you only feel for those who share your blood.

I couldn't wrap my head around all of this, and it hurt to try. If it weren't for my feelings for Erik, I never would've doubted the feelings I'd had for Donavon. Even though we were young, I'd thought Donavon and I were family. We'd shared so much. He'd been the first person to like me, let alone say that they loved me, mental abnormalities and all. Now, I was left wondering if any part of it had been real.

Instead of going back to my room after my run, I jogged straight to the practice arena. I had programmed five Sim scenarios at random before I suited up, purposely choosing scenarios that listed firearms as necessary weapons. I strapped the knife belt around my hips, holstered two handguns to my thighs, and slung the strap of a scoped rifle across my chest. I caught a glimpse of my reflection in a glass-paneled wall and jumped back, unnerved by the steely eyed soldier staring back at me.

As soon as I walked onto the arena floor, the lights slowly dimmed until I was left standing in total darkness. I lowered the Sim glasses into place and tapped my ear piece, causing it to activate. A fluorescent white light appeared overhead as the Sim scenario materialized around me. I found myself in a dimly-lit hallway, with water trickling down the cement walls surrounding me. I ran one gloved finger horizontally across the stream. My finger, safely ensconced in the soft leather, felt wet when I pulled it away.

"End of the hallway, make a right," a mechanical voice said into my right ear. I took off at a jog, expanding my senses as I went. The Sim scenarios were often more difficult for me than a real Hunt; I had to rely on normal, albeit superiorly trained, senses to guide me. I couldn't feel the minds of the opponents in the scenario because they were holographic images and not real people. Fortunately, the holograms still made noise when they moved, so I heard the two men before they rounded the corner at the end of the hallway. I dropped low into a crouch and reached for the gun strapped to my right thigh. I didn't hesitate before I pulled the trigger once, moved the gun millimeters to the left, and fired again. Both holograms fragmented before breaking down completely. I straightened, and covered the distance to the end of the hallway in record time. I turned to the right and slowed slightly, waiting for my next instruction.

"Third door on left. Proceed to the top of the staircase, and turn right," the mechanical voice said.

The mission statistics started scrolling several inches in front of my left eye. Disposed: 2. Remaining: 20. Ammunition: 95%. Time remaining: 28:04. Target: Unacquired. Health: 100%.

I'd just passed the second door on my left when I heard the

soft thud of footfalls behind me. I spun on one foot and dropped down to the other knee. As I turned, I reached down to my knife belt and grabbed a handle in each hand, releasing both before my knee hit the dirty concrete floor. Both blades struck the lead hologram, and he crumbled into nothingness. The two men behind him kept coming for me, and I grabbed for the gun that was snug against my right leg. I wasn't fast enough. Both men squeezed their triggers, several rounds hurdling towards me in the narrow corridor. I fell backwards, flattening myself against the hard ground and blindly returned their fire.

Unlike in real life, I couldn't mentally stop these bullets because they weren't bullets at all – they were electrical impulses. If one struck me, my suit would register the hit and fire tiny, painful electrical impulses into the injured area until the simulation ended. One of the holograms' bullets found my right shoulder and I felt the tell-tale shocks attacking my skin. The bullet must have only skimmed me because the impulses didn't penetrate into my muscles, but remained superficial. They still hurt.

I cocked my head to the left and fired my gun again, squeezing off six quick rounds into the still standing holograms. Both flickered, and then disappeared. I scrambled to my feet and took off in the direction I'd been going before the interruption. The mission statistics flashed again. Disposed: 5. Remaining: 17. Ammunition: 80%. Time remaining: 25:04. Target: Unacquired. Health: 95%.

I found the door and pushed. The stairwell inside was pitch-black. I felt the stairs under my feet, rather than seeing them. I misjudged the height of the first step and banged my shin hard, against the lip of the second. I swore loudly. I cautiously climbed the remaining stairs, and pushed open the door on the landing.

I stumbled noisily through the doorway, and into a brightly-lit meeting room. Five holographic men sat around what looked like a conference table. Their heads snapped to stare at me in unison. Crap. If I'd been quicker, I might have been able to creep silently along the length of the wall without being noticed. Now, not so much. I did a quick sweep of the room. Two armed men stood several feet back from the table, one on each side, blocking the exits. A huge glass window was on the opposite side of the table from where I stood.

One of the exit guards raised his huge gun and fired. I dropped to my knees and covered my head as shards of holographic wood rained down on me from the splintered door I'd just come through. The second guard raised his gun to fire. I tucked and rolled as the ground exploded where I'd just been kneeling. I felt a deep shock in my left arm as one of the guards' holographic bullets found a home in my bicep. The electric pulses cut all the way down to the bone, rendering my left arm useless. Gritting my teeth against the unpleasant sensation, I gripped the handle of a handgun with my right hand and fired across my body, towards the guard on my left. I mentally yanked three knives from my hips, and sent them whooshing through the air towards the right guard. Both fell to pieces, within seconds of one another. The men at the table appeared unarmed. *Not a threat*, I decided. I darted to my right in a low crouch, tried to protect my head, and dove through the now clear right door.

I rose to my feet and flattened myself against one of the walls, waiting for my next instruction.

"Turn right. Target, end of hallway," the mechanical voice informed me.

The mission statistics obscured my left eye's view a second later: Disposed: 7. Remaining: 15. Ammunition: 65%. Time remaining: 19:52. Target: In sight. Health: 75%.

I sprinted for the door at the end of the corridor, cradling my left arm to my chest as the electrical impulses fired, painfully, over and over again. I wanted to bust the door down mentally, but I knew that wouldn't work. When I reached it several seconds later, I turned the knob with my right hand – locked. Of course it was. I flashed to a different mission, a real mission, where the knob had refused to turn. I shook my head to clear my thoughts. I raised my right arm above my head, clenching my hand into a tight fist, and steeled myself against the impending impact. I brought my elbow down as hard as I could on the knob. I heard a sharp crack and felt pain radiate outward from my funny bone. Crap that hurt worse than I'd anticipated. I looked down; the holographic door knob was dangling uselessly and the door was slightly ajar. I pushed it open the rest of the way and stepped into the room.

A scientist stood behind a table full of beakers and brightly colored vials. Was this really happening? I shook my head again. It was like déjà vu, except this had actually happened. I gritted my teeth and raised my throbbing right arm, pointing the gun levelly at the scientist.

"Kill," the mechanical voice ordered. Icy fear pumped through my veins for the first time since starting the simulation. I hadn't intended to program any Kill Scenarios.

I swallowed over the lump in my throat. The man held up his hands in surrender. His head was bent when I walked into the room, but now he raised it until his hard gray eyes met mine. He looked nothing like the balding man from my actual mission, he actually reminded me a little of Mac. I sneered at him before pulling the trigger, without hesitation. I fired a single shot. It buried itself in the space between his knitted eyebrows; he then disintegrated.

"Vacate the premises to complete the mission," the

mechanical voice ordered. Several inches in front of my right lens a floor plan of the simulation appeared, "X"s marking the exits. The closest one was back in the conference room. I spun on my heel and tore from the room.

Disposed: 8. Remaining: 14. Ammunition: 62%. Time remaining: 14:52. Target: Acquired. Health: 55%.

I weighed my options. Fourteen potential combatants remained in the simulation. My left arm was basically useless. I could barely move it. My right arm throbbed, and my fingers were twitching too badly to get off any more steady shots. I needed to reach the nearest exit and get out if I wanted to complete this mission successfully.

I retraced the steps I'd taken just minutes before, and found myself back in the now empty conference room. I tapped the side of my glasses to bring up the floor plan with the marked exits again. I reached out and tapped once on the "X" that marked an exit in the conference room. A mini floor plan of the room that I was now standing in took shape, in front of my right eye. The "X" was on the huge picture window. I walked over to the picture window and looked out. The room I was in appeared to be thirty stories high, maybe more, overlooking a city I thought might be D.C. I wasted several long moments contemplating my next move. I was actually still in the arena, not thirty stories above the nation's capital, and, therefore, if I did jump out this window, my fall would not be nearly that far. I also knew I was probably on the top level of the practice arena, and jumping out of this window would, in reality, be jumping over the rail that surrounded the observation deck; it would still be a solid five-story fall.

Footsteps pounded up the stairs from the basement behind me. I made a snap decision. I wasn't strong enough to fight off any more attackers. I fired the remaining bullets in my gun at the window, my hand shaking so badly that I was just glad my target was an entire wall. The holographic glass shattered in front of me. The footsteps grew louder. I backed up several feet, took one last deep breath, and sprinted the short distance across the conference room, throwing myself over the side.

I let the glorious rush of adrenaline engulf me for several seconds before I mentally slowed my falling body, floating the rest of the way to the arena floor. I landed on my back with a soft thud. The Sim scenario evaporated around me as the lights in the arena came back on. I waited for the final mission statistics to appear in front of my glasses.

Final Statistics: Disposed: 8. Remaining: 14. Ammunition: 53%. Time remaining: 10:31. Target: Acquired/Deceased. Health: 55%. Overall Score: 86%. Overall Rank in Accordance with Attempts: 1/2136 attempts. I beamed. *Not too bad*, I thought smiling to myself. *Not too bad at all.*

When I finally returned to my room that night, my body ached from the physical abuse. My mind buzzed from the strain of my attempts to direct bullets firing from the gun barrel thousands of times. Despite all of that, I felt alive, invigorated, and most of all, happily exhausted.

Mac was right about one thing – my solo mission, also known as "the-mission-I-needed-to-complete-before-I-could-actually-graduate-from-school," would be coming up soon. I decided to continue my early morning runs and sensory training, even when our regular training schedules resumed after the holiday. I also kept up with the extra nightly Sim sessions.

Chapter Twenty-Seven

Erik treated me as if nothing had happened after the Festivis Celebration. That, of course, brought on a rush of fresh worries. He definitely regretted kissing me. Maybe I'd misinterpreted the entire situation? Maybe he'd never actually wanted to kiss me to begin with. Except, I'd read his feelings right out of his mind, and he *had* wanted to kiss me. Had I been too drunk to read his mind correctly? Maybe I'd projected my feelings of wanting onto him, and he'd only thought he wanted to kiss me.

I spoke to Penny at length about the situation. I was so used to keeping everything bottled up inside, it felt good to have a friend I could talk to about everything. We obsessed over every interaction between me and Erik, trying to decide what it meant. Penny gave me suggestions on "playing it cool"; she urged me to act just as disinterested as he seemed. That was easier said than done. I didn't want to be disinterested. I wanted to dig into his head and find out exactly what he was thinking. Penny thought that might make me appear a little desperate, or, even worse, psycho. Unfortunately, I felt a little desperate, and maybe a little crazy, too. Erik's indifference was infuriating.

Likewise, we talked about every single interaction Penny had with Harris, and what they meant. The two had been hanging out regularly since Festivis. Unfortunately, I was much less experienced when it came to dating than Penny, so I provided little insight into their encounters. Mostly, I just listened, and made the appropriate responses to her musings, but I did assure her he was a nice guy. His dating history wasn't as colorful as Erik's, so that was probably a check in the plus column for him, and I'd hung out with a couple of the girls he'd dated over the years, always getting the impression he treated them well.

I was happy Penny was enjoying her time with Harris, but it also made me uneasy to know she was spending time with Donavon. It wasn't a lot of time, and it was unfair and irrational for me to feel jealous; I didn't want to see him, I wasn't ready. I didn't know what I'd say to him if I did see him. Still, for some reason, I couldn't help but envy Penny's interactions with Donavon. I never told her about my feelings, and she was careful not to mention what little interaction that she did have with him.

Several weeks after the holiday, I returned from my morning run to a comm from Mac. All that he said was to meet him in the main building before practice today. I had a feeling that I knew what the meeting was about: my solo mission. Graduation was only a month away, and I'd started getting anxious because I hadn't heard anything. Every day, I asked Henri if he'd heard anything, but he seemed just as uneasy as I was. Many of the Pledges had already completed their solo missions and were now able to relax, knowing they were going to graduate.

Solo missions were assigned by Mac and Captain Alvarez. Supposedly, the missions weren't assigned in any particular order, but I'd kind of expected Mac to give me mine earlier, rather than later. Although, given our last few less-than-friendly interactions, I presumed he was making me squirm on purpose, by saving mine until so close to graduation. I wasn't the absolute last to receive my assignment, but I was close.

I felt a mixture of relief and apprehension as I showered and changed in record time. I literally ran out of my room. Impatient, I jabbed at the elevator button as if that would make it arrive faster. Once inside, I hit the first floor option, repeatedly pushing the button to close the door until they slid soundlessly shut. My entire body vibrated with anticipation and nerves. This was it. Finally, I was going to prove myself, proving to all of my doubters that I belonged here, and verifying that Mac and Henri's confidence in me wasn't unfounded.

When the elevator came to a stop in the lobby, I didn't bother waiting for the doors to open completely, instead sliding sideways, through the gap, and taking off at a run towards the main building.

"I'm here to see Mac," I panted, to the receptionist.

"Excuse me, dear?" the middle-aged brunette smiled, looking up from her computer.

"Sorry, Director McDonough. I'm here to see Director McDonough," I said, impetuously.

"And who should I say is wishing to speak with him, dear?" her plastered-on smile irked me further.

"Natalia Lyons. He's expecting me," I tapped my foot, impatiently as she pressed a button on her panel communicator, informing Mac that I was here.

"Follow me, dear," she motioned, getting up from her desk.

"No need, I know the way," I waved her off. I took the stairs to Mac's office two at a time. Grabbing the knob of the thick wooden door bearing his nameplate, I paused briefly. Tension rolled through the closed door. I opened my mind. Mac wasn't alone. Captain Alvarez and Henri were both in the room, too. I should've expected as much; Henri was my team leader, and Captain Alvarez was the leader of the Hunters. What I didn't understand was why the atmosphere was so tense. Solo missions were a normal part of the Pledge program, leading up to graduation.

Suddenly, an awful thought occurred to me. What if this weren't about my solo mission? What if I'd done something wrong? What if I were in trouble? Mac knew I'd broken down after our Kill Hunt, but the official report stated I'd been the one who actually performed the kill.

What if they knew I hadn't been able to go through with it myself? That Erik had to do it for me? Was that why I hadn't been given a solo assignment yet?

Closing my eyes, I took a deep breath and braced myself, before turning the knob. The men were talking in low voices, but grew quiet, all three heads turning in unison towards me when I entered.

"Natalia, please come in. Take a seat," Mac greeted me, motioning to the empty chair between Henri and Captain Alvarez.

"Mac. Captain. Henri." I nodded to each in turn as I walked slowly to my chair.

Henri looked uncomfortable, wringing his hands in his lap and clenching his jaw. I opened up my mind and quickly scanned his: he was more than uncomfortable, he was scared. He kept repeating, over and over, in his head, *this is wrong, this is wrong.* My blood ran cold. I was in trouble.

Carefully, I sat on the edge of the empty seat. "You wanted to see me?" I asked Mac, swallowing over the lump that had materialized in my throat.

"Yes, Natalia. As you are aware, you need to complete a solo mission prior to graduation." I sighed heavily, my body sagging with relief – thank goodness this was about the solo mission. I nodded my understanding.

"The Crypto bank received some intel last night about Ian Crane."

I froze. Mac paused and looked directly in to my eyes, searching for understanding. Somehow, I managed to nod jerkily. I knew who Ian Crane was. He was the Coalition's equivalent to Mac, except Ian Crane and the Coalition killed innocent people, people who wanted no part of the civil war over territory...People like my parents. Ian Crane's men had been the ones to invade the hotel and kill my parents. Ian Crane was the name that had kept me awake at night as a child. Ian Crane was the name that I equated with revenge. Ian Crane was the faceless man that I pictured every time I killed a hologram in the Sim scenario. I would not hesitate to kill Ian Crane.

"Ian Crane and his family are arriving in Las Vegas in a week; the preparations for their arrival are already well under way. I need you to go to Vegas, get into the compound where the Cranes are staying, and gather as much intel as you can. I want pictures of everything that you can get your hands on. I want pictures of every single person that Ian Crane meets with. I want pictures of every member of his family," Mac's voice rose an octave with every statement. *"And if you get an opportunity, I want you to kill Crane."* Since Mac added the last part mentally, I figured it wasn't part of the official assignment.

No wonder the tension in the room was so thick; this mission was not an ordinary solo Hunt, it was huge and extremely dangerous. Ian Crane was rarely, if ever, out in public. He spent most of his time on heavily guarded compounds, much like Elite Headquarters and the School's grounds. He seldom spent any time in a city where he would be vulnerable to attack. Mac lived in a similar manner. All of TOXIC's facilities were heavily guarded, even more so when Mac was around. He never stayed more than a night or two in any city, and he traveled with a specialized guard of Agency Operatives.

"What exactly am I supposed to do?" I squeaked.

"This will not be a stealth mission. You will find one of his men and convince him to bring you to the compound. You'll need to keep up this cover for as long as possible. You'll fill the man's head with whatever is necessary to keep him happy; just be sure that he continues to take you into the compound and that he does so without attracting too much attention to either of you."

The lump in my throat had grown so large that I nearly choked on my spit when I tried to swallow. I'd never actually been trained in deception. Controlling a man's will was dangerous and consumed a great deal of mental energy. Hopefully, I could find a weak-willed victim. *Mac must really believe in me if he's willing to take such a big risk*, I thought. Pride filled me, nearly seeping out of my pores. I had no doubt that I should be concerned about the dangers, but just then, I didn't really care. Mac's approval meant the world to me, and if he were willing to take the risk, then so was I.

"TOXIC is already arranging an apartment in the city for you; you'll be based there during the mission. Over the next week, techies will be here to outfit you with the latest technology that we have to offer. I trust that you understand how important this mission is? And why you were chosen?"

I nodded. I definitely knew how important this mission was. Part of the problem with the Coalition was that, outside of Ian Crane, TOXIC didn't really know who the leaders were. Ian Crane was the figurehead, but there had to be plenty of other decision-makers. If the Agency could take out the leaders of the Coalition, we could make major headway in ending this war and reunify the country.

I also knew why I'd been chosen. This couldn't be a stealth mission – it was unlikely that anyone could successfully get by all of the security around the Crane's residence. Given that, someone who could control other people's minds was necessary, someone to convince her way on to the complex: Me.

"Good," Mac continued. "You will practice with your team as usual, unless I send you a communication to the contrary. Henri will excuse you whenever it's needed so that you can become acquainted with the tech you will be using, and any intel the Cryptos are able to gather."

My eyes shifted to Henri. He gave me a tight smile and a small nod that I thought was supposed to be reassuring.

"I don't want to keep you from practice any longer," Mac dismissed us.

"Thank you," I said quietly, getting up from my chair. Henri stood next to me and gave a small nod to both Mac and the Captain. He placed one of his large hands on my back, gently guiding me out of the room.

Henri kept his arm wrapped tightly around me the entire way to the practice arena, but remained mute. I didn't need to read his mind to know that he thought this was a suicide mission. When I did read his mind, I could tell that he was shocked, and more than a little angry that Mac would put me, of all people, in such a dangerous position. He was also chiding himself for not speaking up.

There was no doubt in my mind that Mac cared a lot about me, but Mac also cared a lot about TOXIC, ending the war, and reuniting the Nation. The Coalition's influence grew every day. My recent missions with Henri and Erik had proven that; we'd been sent to disband way too many rallies in recent months.

Despite that, I firmly believed that Mac wouldn't risk my life.

He was confident in my abilities, and that I'd be able to use my mental manipulation to gain access to Crane's complex. Once inside, he had faith that I could elicit the information he wanted from the necessary minds, and gather all of the data that he needed.

Part of me was terrified about the threats of the upcoming mission; I'd be a fool not to be scared. Still, the rest of me was bursting with satisfaction at being selected. A mission of this importance would almost never go to a team with a Pledge, let alone be assigned as a solo mission. Sure, I might feel a lot more confident about my chances at success if this were a normal team Hunt, but a team would draw too much attention. One lone girl would appear less threatening, and was less likely to cause alarm.

It was obvious that Erik already knew the instant we walked into the practice arena. The look on his face told me exactly how he felt about it; he was even less pleased than Henri. The practice was intense, charged with unspoken anger (Erik), anxiety (Henri), and nerves (me).

I stuck to my now-daily routine and headed to the target range after our workout. To my surprise, Henri joined me, quietly correcting minor issues with my technique and stance. Patiently, he coached me through Sim scenarios using our mental communication. He was doing it because he was worried about me. He didn't honestly think I was ready for such an assignment, but I wasn't offended. He was probably right. But I had one week to become ready; I had no choice.

The following day, a techie from one of TOXIC's special Technology Development sections arrived at Headquarters. I left practice halfway through to spend the afternoon familiarizing myself with the equipment.

Techno Talents, or techies, had an unquantified gift for technology. They could develop and configure any type of technological device. The techies spent all of their time at TOXIC Research and Development facilities, coming up with new technologies and ways to implement them.

The techie's name was Blaine, and he told me he'd graduated from the McDonough School ten years before. His almost entirely gray head of hair, and the deep creases at the corners of his muddy-brown eyes made him look much older than his twenty-eight years. He'd been stationed at the main techie outpost outside Philadelphia since graduation, with his wife and three children, only one of which exhibited any Talent thus far. His eldest son, Brine, the Talent, would be starting at the school the following year.

Blaine began practice by giving me a pair of eyeball lenses, and I carefully put one in each eye. Every time that I blinked, a tiny imager affixed to the surface of the lens would take a picture. Once I took all of the pictures that I wanted, I was to put the lens into a special compartment on a handheld communicator. The pictures would instantly upload, and I could view them on the small display screen. Admittedly, the lenses were pretty cool.

Next, Blaine handed me a second set of lenses that were loaded with facial recognition software. One lens scanned facial features and if the person were in TOXIC's database, all of their information appeared on the display surface of the other lens. Blaine had me walk around Headquarters to practice using them. I quickly learned that I was going to need a lot of practice. In order to scan a person's facial features, I had to get a straight-on view of their face. At first, I only managed to scan every fourth person. The really tricky part came when I did scan somebody's face, and his information popped up on my other lens. Trying to read the information with one eye, while still walking and scanning with the other eye, was next to impossible for me. I kept walking into things, mostly Blaine, and he promised me that we'd work with the lenses every day until I departed.

That evening, I poured over the first pieces of intel that the Cryptos had compiled. Penny was part of the team that had intercepted the initial communications about Ian Crane's visit to Nevada, so she offered to help me go through the material. Gratefully, I accepted her assistance. I might be proud, but I wasn't arrogant. I needed all of the help I could get.

We'd just ordered room service and were sitting with the intel spread across my purple carpet, when we heard a knock at the door. It was way too soon to be our food, so I opened my mind, then gave Penny a huge smile. Henri and Erik.

"Thought I was supposed to do all the prep work alone?" I called, mentally opening the door for them. Technically, it was a violation for Pledges to receive outside assistance when preparing for their solo assignment. Penny's face reddened; she knew that she could get in a lot of trouble for helping.

"Everybody cheats," Erik grinned. "Obviously, you're not above it since you seem to already have help," he nodded his head in Penny's direction, and she blushed even deeper.

"This is a suicide mission for a Pledge. I'm not letting you go there unprepared," Henri explained, folding his extremely long legs under him as he plopped down on the floor next to me.

"Thanks," I smiled at both of them. I might not be able to have them with me in Nevada, but having them here now would be almost as good.

The four of us worked well into the night, and I could barely hold my eyes open when Henri finally declared the night's session over. Technically, since it was my solo mission, I should be the one calling the shots, but I was so overwhelmed that I was happy to submit to his authority.

Erik lingered after Penny and Henri left. He lounged on my

bed looking perfectly at ease in its mass of purple and white. When I saw him sitting there, I suddenly wasn't tired anymore. Erik patted the bed next to him, and my head filled with the sound of my heart ricocheting off my ribcage. I climbed on to my bed and sat next to him. He wrapped one arm around my shoulders, and I leaned my head against his chest. He rubbed his stubbly cheek against my hair while absently tugging on one of my curls.

"I'm so sorry," he whispered after a moment.

"For what?" Of all the sentiments that I'd expected him to express right then, sorrow wasn't one of them.

"Tal, this mission is really dangerous. A Pledge shouldn't be doing this. You shouldn't be doing this for your solo mission. I'm sorry this happened to you. That you were chosen."

"I'm not," my voice was strained, but I meant what I said. I wasn't sorry that Mac had picked me. This mission was important, and I was the only one that could do it; I felt a certain delight in that fact. "I'll be okay, Erik. You'll see. I can do this."

"I know you can, Tal, but that doesn't mean you should." I opened my mind and could feel his trepidation. Unlike Henri who thought that I wasn't ready, Erik believed that I was capable, but he was terrified of all the "what if's". His level of concern elated me. His arm tightened around me, so I scooted closer to him. I wanted to will him to stay with me like this, holding me all night. I didn't feel safe with him the way I had with Donavon; I felt something that I liked even more. I felt reckless and out of control around Erik, and it thrilled me. I wanted to be close to him so bad that it hurt. I didn't trust myself when I was near him, but I did trust Erik. I trusted him with my life, and I wanted to trust him with...Well, more.

"I should go," Erik mumbled into my hair.

"No!" I said, more forcefully than I'd intended. "Will you just stay for a little longer?" My voice sounded whiny, but I didn't really care.

"Are you sure?" he asked, uncertainly.

I nodded.

Erik kicked off his leather sandals, lying back on my pillows, and I curled up into a small ball facing him.

"Do you want to talk about it?" Erik asked, reaching over to smooth my hair away from my face. His fingers brushed my against my cheek, sending violent shivers through my whole body.

"The mission? No, not really," I shook my head. The mission was the last thing that I wanted to talk about right then.

"Are you scared?" he asked in a soft voice.

"Yes," I answered without thinking. Of course, I was scared.

"Good, fear is good. It'll keep you on your toes. It'll keep you alive." He pulled me to him, and I buried my face in his chest. I inhaled his earthy scent, reveling in the soft fabric of his t-shirt against my cheek. Unlike my own erratic heartbeat, Erik's was steady and strong. He was probably used to lying in bed with members of the opposite sex. Either that or he really didn't have romantic feelings for me. The thought made me shiver, goosebumps springing up on my exposed arms. Instinctively, Erik rubbed his hands up and down my skin, instantly transforming my flesh from icy cold to searing hot.

I wanted him to kiss me, even more than I had the other night, but I was content just to have him hold me. The pounding of my pulse and the buzzing in my mind weren't going to let me sleep, but I closed my eyes, anyway. Erik moved his hands from my arms to my back, gently massaging away all the knots of tension. He tickled the back of my neck with his fingertips, and I giggled into his chest. I wasn't sure if he meant to tease me, but that's what it felt like. When I couldn't stand it anymore, I looked up at him, my eyes locking with his. I pulled myself up so we were face-to-face. His beautiful eyes were indecisive, so I made the decision for him. Risking rejection and humiliation, I leaned in and pressed my mouth to his. His lips were soft, tasting fresh and clean.

He was surprised at first and didn't kiss me back. I panicked. Ashamed, I blushed and pulled away from him. My earlier misgivings returned, and I tried to scramble even further back on the bed. Our eyes met again, and he tightened his arms around me, pulling me to him. He crushed his mouth to mine once again. A small moan escaped me, and he kissed me harder, deeper. I dug my fingers into his biceps and felt his muscles flex. I clung to Erik, convinced that if I let him go, this moment would end, and I never wanted it to end.

When we finally broke apart, I couldn't catch my breath. I could feel my chest rising and falling so fast that it hurt, but in a good way. I could feel Erik's heart pounding along with my own. He gently placed one of his hands on my chest, just above my heart, which only made my breath come even more quickly. He rewarded me with a mischievous grin. He kissed me again, so softly that his lips just barely made contact with my own. I melted into him again, my whole body going limp against his.

"I should go now," he sighed.

"Why?" I demanded, once again scared that he might regret kissing me.

"Because you need your sleep and if I stay too much longer, you won't get any," he chuckled. Relaxing, I grinned at him. He wasn't sorry he'd kissed me. Delight coursed through me at the realization. His eyes were still twinkling with desire.

He brushed his soft lips across both my cheeks and my forehead before climbing over me and out of bed. He pulled my quilt up, tucking it around my body. He leaned down and gave me one last, lingering kiss, before whispering, "Night, Tals."

Chapter Twenty-Eight

The next day, it was back to business as usual. Erik treated me just the same as every day since I'd arrived at headquarters. I'd been nervous about seeing him, but his nonchalant attitude frustrated me, even while putting me at ease. It wasn't like I wanted him to walk into the practice arena and kiss me good morning – that would've been weird – but I also didn't want him acting as if nothing had changed between us. Our relationship had shifted, become more intimate.

If Henri suspected anything, he didn't let on. He pushed me harder in practice, making me repeat every move until he was satisfied. At the firing range, he forced me to run through the Sim targeting schemes, over and over, until I managed to fire Kill Shots each and every time. He barked orders into my head during the Sim, restarting the scenario if I made a mistake. I didn't want to appear ungrateful, but I was concerned that if he kept pushing me this hard I might have a breakdown before the week was over.

Blaine's techniques were much gentler. He patiently led me throughout the compound with my lenses, praising me when I managed to snap solid pictures of the passersby. He didn't even complain when I stepped on his feet. When I apologized, he assured me that I wasn't the only person to have so much difficulty. He was so nice, almost too nice, and I felt bad for being so abysmal at it. I practically missed Henri's tough love approach by the end of our session.

After my exhaustive day of physical and mental abuse, I wanted to slip between my comforter and my sheets and never come back out. Unfortunately, that wasn't a viable option because Penny, Erik, and Henri were already waiting outside my door when I emerged from my too short shower. I tried not to grumble when I opened the door to let them in – at least they brought dinner. Once again, the four of us worked well into the night, analyzing intel, pouring over floor plans, and outlining different strategies. By the end of our session, my eyes were glazed over, and a dull throbbing had developed in the base on my skull. Even Penny's normally happy-go-lucky attitude had diminished over the course of the evening, and when she said goodnight, her voice was strained and tired. Henri's eyelids were dropping, and his shoulders were hunched when he rose to leave with Penny.

Erik stayed after the other two left, but only for a couple of minutes.

I sat on the edge of my bed, and Erik stood in between my knees, his hands kneading the knotted muscles in my shoulders.

"I don't want to distract you right now. I know how much you need to focus," he said, leaning down to kiss the side of my neck.

Closing my eyes, I reveled in the way his mouth moved over my skin. He was right, but I actually had to bite my tongue to keep from begging him to distract me. Despite the words of caution, Erik's lips moved slowly to my jawbone, before gently closing around my bottom lip. Falling onto my back, I grabbed the back of his neck, pulling him down. Erik caught himself before his chest hit mine, planting his hands on either side of my head on the mattress. Our lips locked, and I reached up to touch his face, cupping his cheeks with my hands. He turned his head slightly to kiss the inside of my palm. His gesture was so sweet that I couldn't help but beam, even though my mouth felt empty without his. Suddenly, I felt the blanket under my head tighten, and I saw Erik's knuckles turn white as he balled the comforter in his hands. The thoughts racing through his mind made me both embarrassed and thrilled. While I knew I shouldn't be doing anything to further his desire, I couldn't help it; I wrapped my legs around his waist, and pulled his hips against mine.

My bold move surprised Erik, and he hesitated before his mouth found mine again – the kiss was intoxicating. When he broke it off, my head was spinning so fast that I definitely felt drunk. His lips moved down my neck, then my collar bone, his tongue moving slowly across the tender skin, and I nearly whimpered. Erik trailed kisses to the top of my shirt. Using his teeth, he pulled the neckline down just enough to expose the top of my bra. My hands moved down the back of his t-shirt, exploring the contours of his lean back. One of his hands moved to my waist, his fingers lightly skimming the space where my tank top and pants didn't quite meet, before closing around my waist. His thumb danced lightly across my hip bone.

"You should really go to sleep now," he mumbled, his mouth now in the hollow of my throat.

"I'm not that tired," I gasped, gripping his shoulders tighter, and glad my nails weren't long enough to leave claw marks.

I felt Erik's lips quirk into a smile against my neck.

"You need to save your strength, and I need a cold shower," he said playfully as he raised his face to meet my eyes. The passion in the depths of his irises excited me almost as much as his touch. I knew how much harder my reaction made it for him to restrain himself. Erik was worried about distracting me from my Solo

Mission, but he also didn't want to rush me into doing something I wasn't ready for.

Sighing, I regretfully detangled my legs from his waist. Erik smoothed my shirt back into place, letting the tip of his index finger slip beneath the waistband of my pants to touch the edge of my underwear. Closing his turquoise eyes, he emitted an audible moan as he felt the lacey material. I brought my lips to his and kissed him softly. A pained expression clouded his features.

"Cold shower," he repeated against my mouth.

Not wanting to test his willpower any further that night, I released my death grip on his shoulders.

"I'll see you in the morning," he whispered, gently biting my earlobe as he climbed off me to help me crawl under the blankets. Light as feathers, his fingertips tickled my nose and eyelids, before pressing gently against my lips. They lingered there just long enough for me to kiss the pads.

"Night, Erik," I said in a voice that was barely audible.

"Night, Tal." With that, he left. I fell asleep smiling so big my cheeks hurt.

Every day leading up to my Solo Mission was more grueling than the one before. Henri pushed me harder and further than I'd thought I was capable of. Every time my sore muscles protested, I cursed him silently...And sometimes, not-so-silently. Every time that I complained to Erik, he reminded me that Henri wasn't being callous; he cared, and wanted me to be prepared. I knew that was true, but when I tried telling my blistered index fingers that, they didn't want hear it.

Erik began to tag along on my morning training runs. He never spoke, since he knew that I used the time to cycle through my senses. Even in silence, I appreciated his company. I knew he worried that his presence distracted me – in truth, it did – but sometimes, I really needed the diversion.

When Erik was with me, he consumed my subconscious. When I was alone, the possibility of my impending death took his place; obviously, thoughts of Erik were vastly preferable.

With Henri's continued tutelage on the target range, my confidence rose from one day to the next. He pestered the Cryptos until they programmed the simulator with the floor plan of Ian Crane's temporary home so I could practice navigating my way through the levels.

Blaine gave me a third pair of eyeball lenses, loaded with the floor plan for the home and GPS tracking. He explained to me that, depending on the security surrounding the estate, either the GPS would update the map as I moved through the house, or just the static image of the general blueprint for the entire estate would appear on the lens. Even if it were the latter, that would be sufficient for me to find my way in and out in a pinch. I'd memorized the layout so I wasn't worried, but I did feel better knowing that I had the lenses to fall back on. Blaine spent every afternoon leading me around the compound until I finally stopped running into him while regarding the information on the lenses.

Penny went above and beyond, tracking down all of the intel she could muster. She was almost as worried about me as Erik and Henri were; "almost" only because she'd never been on a Hunt, so she couldn't appreciate how dangerous this one actually was.

In addition to learning to use all of the handheld technology gadgets, there was one other thing that I would likely need to use on my Mission, one I was very excited to train on: a hover vehicle. Since I would be alone on my Mission, Mac had no choice but to authorize driving lessons. Unfortunately, I had so many other more pressing matters to attend to throughout the week, that I only had time for one lesson. It was the very definition of a crash course –

pun intended. Henri showed me how to use all of the buttons and switches on the dashboard, most importantly, the autopilot button. Autopilot took care of every aspect of driving, except for getting into the air and setting back down. I loved the feel of sitting in the driver's seat, holding the wheel in my hands; it made me feel in control, and lately I'd felt so out of control that it was a welcome change.

I tried to keep myself calm, but the closer it came to my departure, the more nervous I became. Every night after the four of us poured over the Crypto intel, Erik stayed after the other two left. We only ever kissed; he wanted to do more and I wanted that, too, but everything in my life was happening so fast, I didn't think that adding losing my virginity before I left for the Mission was such a good idea. Despite that, if Erik initiated something more, I wouldn't hesitate in following his lead. The overload of sensations that I felt when Erik just kissed me was so intense, I couldn't imagine how I'd feel when we finally did more than kiss.

Being with Erik was just so different than being with Donavon; with him, I'd always been wary of getting too physical. Something had always made me hesitant to let him touch me too much, but with Erik, it was like I couldn't get enough of him. I felt like I could never be close enough to him. If anything, Erik was the one holding back; his self-restraint was impressive. I seriously doubted that Erik was used to denying himself, and, as much as I wanted him, I appreciated his effort. In a twisted way, I think it actually made me want him more.

"How are you feeling? Think you're ready?" Erik asked one night. He was absently winding my curls around his long fingers as we lay facing each other on my bed.

"Would you think less of me if I said I was terrified?" I asked, tracing the contours of his face.

"Of course not, I was really scared before my Solo Mission, too, and it wasn't nearly as dangerous as this," he confessed.

"What'd you do?"

"Drown my worries with alcohol and spent the night with a Brain," he replied. I had a feeling he was serious. Irrational feelings of jealousy washed over me, and I wrinkled my nose in disgust at him.

Over the last several months, I'd noticed the way that girls, and even some boys, looked at Erik. I was well aware of Erik's reputation, but I thought, or at least hoped, it might be slightly exaggerated. I knew for sure that girls loved Erik and that Erik loved girls, but I wasn't clear exactly how many girls Erik had loved. Since our first kiss, I didn't just notice when girls looked at Erik, I obsessed over it. I'd never been jealous when it came to Donavon, so I was on unfamiliar ground. I tried not to let Erik see that it bothered me. For the most part, I don't think he noticed, but I also thought that for all his talk, Erik might have been oblivious to the way people saw him.

"Are you suggesting that I do the same?" I tried to joke, coming back to the conversation.

"Absolutely not. I'm suggesting you drown your worries in me," he gave me a lazy smile. Beaming, I returned his grin. I knew why girls fell for him – he had a way of looking at you like you were the only person in the world, and it felt amazing.

"Will you stay with me tonight?" I blurted out without thinking. I wouldn't be training the next day; it was the last day before I was scheduled to leave, and Henri had insisted that it would be better spent resting, instead of going over details that I could recite in my sleep.

Erik's eyes widened with surprise, and he looked slightly uncomfortable. "I'm not sure that's such a great idea. You really need to get as much sleep as you can."

"But we can sleep in tomorrow," I suggested, hopefully.

"It's not that I don't want to, Talia," he started, correctly interpreting the undertones in my voice. "I definitely want to spend the night right here with you, sans clothing," he grinned from ear-to-ear and waggled his eyebrows. I rolled my eyes, even as my heart leapt at his not-so-subtle overture. "Besides, aren't we spending the evening together in the city tomorrow?" Mac had given Penny and I permission to go into the city after dark, as long as we returned by curfew, so Henri and Erik were going to take us out for dinner and drinks.

"But we won't be alone tomorrow," I pointed out. I was being childish and pouty, but I really wanted him to stay.

Erik stopped curling my hair around his fingers. He took my hand and interlaced his fingers with my own, rubbing his thumb back and forth across the center of my palm.

"I know I'm irresistible and all," he joked. "But seriously, are you sure that you want me to stay?"

"Positive," I replied, in a confident voice that belied my underlying apprehension. I did want him to stay, wanted it more than I could express, but we hadn't spent the entire night together before. Well, technically we'd spent a lot of nights together, just not in the same bed. Alone. Touching. My heart swelled at the thought of waking up in his arms.

"Sans clothing?" Erik teased, but I could tell that he was kidding. I really wanted to say yes, but I wouldn't have been serious and I didn't want the situation to get awkward.

"I want you to have something to look forward to when I come back," I said instead. I'd been lying on my side facing him, and he gently pushed me over onto my back, our fingers still intertwined. He kissed me softly at first, and then harder. The weight of his body – warm and heavy on top of mine – felt amazing, and I pulled him tighter against me.

"You've got yourself a deal, Pledge," he grinned when he finally broke off the kiss. I beamed and leaned up to kiss him again, even though I had yet to catch my breath from the last one. Erik gently pushed me back down and shook his head. "There's no way your clothes are staying on if you keep kissing me like that." I tried to reach up again, and he gave a deep laugh that I could feel reverberate through his body. He rolled off of me, but didn't let go completely. I flipped over, turned my back to him, and curled my body into his. He tightened his arms around me and buried his face in my mess of brown curls.

"Erik?" I said, after a minute.

"Hmmm?" he mumbled.

"Thank you for staying, even though we're keeping our clothes on." I felt him smile since his cheek was resting on my head. "In all seriousness, I really don't want to be alone tonight."

"I know the feeling, Tal. I felt the same way before mine."

I tried to snuggle closer, even though I was already pressed completely into him. I was too amped up to sleep, from the combination of being so close to Erik and my nerves over the Mission. I knew that I was projecting towards Erik, and tried to control it so that he could get some rest. I guess I was doing a poor job of it because he gently detangled himself from me and scooted a couple inches back. I assumed that the physical separation would make it easier for him to block my mind, but I sighed with disappointment. Surprisingly, I felt Erik gently roll up the bottom of my tank top, and I experienced the now-familiar heart pounding, shortness of breath, and crackles of electricity that shot through me when his skin touched mine. I was, of course, nervous as he started to undress me, but I didn't want him to stop. Only he did stop, as soon as he'd pushed the back of my shirt up over the place where my bra would have been, had I been wearing one. Suddenly, a thought struck me: *Did Erik think I was easy because I wasn't wearing a bra?*

"There are lots of words I'd use to describe you, Tal. Easy is not one of them." He lazily traced a design on my back. Blood rushed to my face, and my body went rigid.

"Relax, Tal," he chuckled. He drew undistinguishable shapes up and down my skin. I concentrated on the rhythmic movements of his fingertips and felt my whole body unwind.

"Erik?" I asked after his hand had stopped moving and rested gently on my hip.

"I'm awake," he answered, starting to move his fingers again.

"Can I ask you a question?"

"Sure," his voice was relaxed, but I felt his body tense behind me.

"Why didn't you go home for Festivis Day?" I asked. His teeth ground together. I knew why Harris didn't go home – his parents didn't think being a Talent was a good thing. He'd actually had spent several school breaks with me and Donavon at the McDonough's house. I also knew why Penny didn't go home – she didn't have a real home. Henri never missed an opportunity to spend time with Frederick, so that explained why he'd stayed, but it had been nagging at me why Erik had stayed.

"It's complicated," he finally answered, his words measured.

"Are your parents still alive?" I pressed.

"My dad and both of my brothers are." I could tell that he didn't want to elaborate, and I suddenly realized how little I actually knew about Erik, outside of TOXIC. Then I remembered something that Penny had told me.

"You didn't come to the school when you were five, like most kids, right?" Even as I said it, I knew that I was on shaky ground.

"Neither did you." Well, this was going famously.

"How old were you?" I pried.

"Fourteen." This was like pulling teeth. I should've stopped, but my curiosity was already piqued.

"How did it happen?" I asked.

"It's complicated," he repeated. I considered probing his mind, but thought better of it. Before I could open my mouth to ask another intrusive question that he wasn't going to answer, he pressed his palm flat against my stomach and dragged me into him. He kissed the side of my neck, and I no longer cared that he was being evasive.

"Why the twenty questions?" he whispered, his breath tickling my ear. He nibbled gently on my earlobe. I wriggled closer to him.

"I just want to know you," I whispered back.

"You do know me, probably better than anyone." He kissed my neck again. I craned my head around to find his mouth, and I kissed him softly. I looked into his eyes, more green than blue in the dark. His mind was carefully guarded, and I knew that I wasn't going to get anything out of him tonight.

"Will you tell me one day?" I asked softly. Our faces were so close that my lips brushed his when I spoke.

"One day," he promised, "when you're ready to hear it."

Chapter Twenty-Nine

Penny came over to my room that afternoon so that we could get ready together, for our night out in the city. I selected a simple, long black-and-white floral dress, and a black to keep my arms and shoulders warm. It was another dress that Gretchen had purchased for me that I had yet to wear. Penny helped me put on makeup, just enough that I still looked natural. She selected a black head-topper of floral lace from her collection and fastened it into my long curls. I tried to protest, but Penny argued that we had so few chances to dress up that we might as well take advantage.

For herself, Penny chose a short, navy dress with long, billowy sleeves that wrapped around her slender body and tied on one side of her waist. She managed to sleek her bright red hair into a neat bun, but decided against a head-topper for herself. She looped long chains around her neck and wrists, made of fake gold and pretty glass beads, the same lime-green as her eyes.

I'd seen Penny every night for the last week, but that was strictly business; we hadn't had a chance to talk about anything except my upcoming solo Hunt. Penny correctly surmised that I didn't want to talk about that today, so instead, she filled me in on all of the details of her rapidly-progressing relationship with Harris. Neither was ready to call the other boyfriend or girlfriend, but they were definitely into each other and moving in that direction.

Penny gently pressed me for details about Erik.

"Is it obvious?" I asked.

"Well...Yeah. It's totally obvious when we're all together. He can't take his eyes off you. It's totally hot," she laughed.

"Do you think Henri knows?" I worried. Dating, or whatever we were doing, wasn't against the rules or anything, but I worried that Henri still might disapprove.

"Um, I know he knows," she answered. "Don't worry. He is cool with it." I smiled. Hopefully, that was true.

"I'm so totally jealous," Penny continued, with a pout.

I laughed. "Jealous? You have Harris!"

"I know, and it's not like I like Erik or anything. Well, I mean I do like him, he's really cool, and obviously hot, but I don't like him like him," she rambled.

"Then why are you jealous?" I laughed again.

"Because every girl talks about him! He's like the closest thing to famous that we have here!?!"

I didn't respond right away. That was the problem – I didn't want a bunch of girls crushing on him. I didn't want him to have his pick of girls because then he might not pick me.

"Harris won't be able to keep his hands off of you in that dress," I teased, changing the subject.

Penny blushed, "You don't look so bad yourself."

Erik was waiting for me in the lobby, with Henri and Harris in tow. He looked amazing, as usual, wearing jeans and a navy-and-white gingham button down. His sleeves were rolled up, showing off his muscled forearms, and the white of the shirt contrasted nicely with his tan skin. His dark hair was getting long, and he kept running his hands through it, in a fruitless attempt to push it out of his eyes. I had to resist the urge to run over and kiss him the moment we stepped off of the elevator.

"Hey," Harris said to Penny, his whole face lighting up with a smile as we approached. She returned his smile with a high-wattage one of her own. He bent down to kiss her on the lips, and jealously twisted knots in my stomach as I watched their interaction. I knew that Erik wouldn't kiss me in public and, in truth, I didn't want him to; I definitely wasn't ready for everyone to know about whatever was going on between us. Still, it hurt that Erik treated me the same way now as he had previously, before we'd started rolling around in my bed together.

"Ready to start the celebration?" Erik asked, a mischievous glint in his eyes.

"Celebration? Shouldn't we wait to celebrate until she gets back and well, you know, actually passes her solo Hunt?" Penny asked, looking perplexed.

"Nah, we always celebrate before the Solo Mission – it's just a formality, anyway. Once a Pledge gets his solo assignment, it's pretty much a given that he – or she – will graduate," Harris explained to her.

"But, I thought Talia's Hunt was like super dangerous and – "

"Tonight is a celebration of all her hard work to this point," Erik cut her off, shooting her a warning look. Erik and Henri knew about my assignment because they're my teammates, and Penny knew about it because she was part of the Crypto team compiling the intel. No one else knew the specifics of my assignment, and I wanted for it to stay that way.

"Thank you, Erik," I smiled gratefully up at him. He gave my shoulder a small squeeze, something that he does in public all the time, but he rubbed his thumb across my collarbone before letting go, and I shivered as goosebumps erupted all over my body. Erik suppressed a laugh and blood rushed to my face, coloring my cheeks with embarrassment.

"Let's get this celebration started," Henri said, speaking for the first time. I could tell that he wasn't in a festive mood, but he was trying for my sake.

Henri had been agonizing over my assignment all week, and even tried to talk Mac out of sending me alone, begging Mac for us to go as a team. He'd also been arguing with Erik because Erik refused to speak to Mac, as well. Henri hadn't actually told me any of this; he was such a strong projector that I'd learned it in practice, when my mind was open to him.

I'd been careful to keep my personal reasons for wanting this Mission to myself. Erik wasn't fooled; he could tell that there was more to it than I, or Mac, was letting on. He was aware that this assignment was personal for me, but he wasn't intrusive enough to ask me outright. I guess we both had our secrets.

Frederick was already at the restaurant that Erik had selected when we arrived. He jumped up when he saw us approaching the table, and instead of giving Henri a hug, he folded me in his slender arms.

"I hear that congratulations are in order," he said excitedly to me.

"Thank you," I smiled back at him.

Henri ordered pitchers of lemon flavored mixed drinks for all of us to share.

"You'll love it – gives you a nice drunk, but you won't have a hangover tomorrow," Henri promised.

Our little group drank all of the pitchers that Henri ordered, and then several additional ones. I tried to eat enough to soak up the alcohol, but I was having such a good time that I let myself drink more than I had the first night I'd met with Penny.

Harris and Penny both had so much to drink, they kept touching and kissing, but in a cute way, not a gross, making-everybody-around-them-sick-to-their-stomach way.

Erik sat next to me, and kept reaching under the table to tickle my side or run his fingers over my leg when nobody was looking. The more I had to drink, the harder it was to keep a straight face when he touched me.

"Stop," I mentally pleaded with him when he ran his fingers lightly over the crook of my elbow, taking my breath away so that I couldn't answer a question that Frederick asked.

"You like it," he insisted.

"They're going to know."

"Tal, everybody sitting at this table knows – you have the worst poker face."

"What's that supposed to mean?"

"Every time that I get close to you, the look on your face is a dead giveaway," he laughed out loud.

"Mighty full of yourself, aren't you? Maybe whatever look I have on my face has nothing to do with you," I shot back, trying to sound indignant.

"Trust me, I know that look. Lots of girls give me that look."

"Maybe if they know," I gave a pointed glance around the table, *"it's because of the look you have on your face when you are around ME,"* I gave him a smug smile.

"You might be right about that," he conceded. *"Let's just say that it's a good thing you're the only one who can read my thoughts."*

I gave him a light shove in the chest and attempted a disapproving stare, but it was hard when, in reality, it thrilled me.

I'd been so engrossed in my mental conversation with Erik that, I didn't notice that everybody else at the table had stopped talking. At first, my alcohol-muddled mind thought that it was because they were watching our exchange. Unfortunately, I was wrong. I followed the direction of their frozen gazes, and saw Donavon standing several feet from our table, staring at me.

My stomach dropped, and I had to fight the urge to be sick. I'd known that I would have to see him again one day, I'd just hoped that the day would be WAY in the future.

I stared straight at him, the alcohol giving me courage that I otherwise lacked. After several long seconds of awkward silence, Donavon finally spoke.

"Congratulations, Natalia. My dad told me that you leave for your solo Hunt tomorrow." He spoke to me but looked at Harris, the only friendly face for him at our table.

"Yes, I do," I replied tightly, refusing to accept his sentiments. Erik's hand tightened on my leg.

"*Please be safe,*" he mentally added. I closed my mind off to him completely before I was tempted to reply, and turned my back on him.

"Nice to you see you guys. Harris, I'll see you back at the cabin later tonight." I didn't know if it were wishful thinking, or my newfound love of overanalyzing everything that guys said and did, but I swear he emphasized the fact he planned on returning to his cabin tonight – i.e. not staying with the blonde slut in the city – for my benefit.

Donavon's presence put a damper on my celebration. Penny made an effort to get us back on track, by ordering Electric Shock shots, but I wasn't in the mood anymore. Erik was good at affecting a care-free attitude, but the way his fingers dug painfully into my arm told me that he wasn't pleased. I tried to take part in the conversation, but I couldn't concentrate; I kept thinking about Donavon. My lack of verbal communication left plenty of time for me to down several more glasses of the lemony drinks, and I was completely toasted by the time curfew rolled around.

Penny asked if I wanted her to stay with me when we got back to Headquarters, but I insisted that it wasn't necessary. She wanted to spend more time with Harris, and I wanted to spend the night with Erik.

I clung on to Erik's arm as I stumbled to my room. He would've carried me. I think he actually offered several times, but I refused, arguing that I was perfectly capable of walking on my own. Of course, I wasn't, but Erik indulged me. He even sat crossed-legged on the floor of the elevator with me, when the ride made me too dizzy to stand.

It took me three tries to scan my palm to open the door to my room. Erik smirked, but waited patiently since I demanded that he let me do it on my own.

Once we were inside, I gave up my independent act and fell into Erik's arms. He scooped me off of my feet and carried me to my bed.

"Did you have fun tonight?" he murmured into my hair.

"Yup!" I nodded my head vigorously as he settled me on my pillows.

He slid my shoes off of my feet, before kicking off his own and climbing in after me. He leaned over and bent his head down until our foreheads touched. I giggled as I reached up to pull his lips to mine. He hesitated for a brief second, then gave me one of his toe-curling kisses. I boldly reached for the waist of his pants to un-tuck his shirt. I ran my hands over the hard muscles of his stomach and back, and I felt raised, puckered flesh, marking scars from past Hunts that hadn't been removed.

His heart was pounding against his ribcage in time with my own, he pulled away from the kiss just long enough to pull his shirt over his head, and I stared in amazement as his muscles rippled with even the smallest movement.

I looked up into his eyes, and I saw the same indecision that I had the other night. I reached my hand out to him, and he took it with only a little hesitation. He lowered himself down on top of me again, careful to balance most of his weight on his free arm. He never took his eyes away my mine as he released my hand, and reached up behind my neck to untie my dress. He slowly pulled it down. With one shaking hand, I reached up and traced the lines of his face. He gave me a giant grin and pulled the dress the rest of the way down.

My mouth was dry, my hands trembling, and clammy. I couldn't stop quivering with the mixture of nerves and anticipation. Waves of heat spread over me every time that his skin made contact with mine. I bit the inside of my cheek to keep myself from saying something that I might regret. Erik's eyes crinkled and his mouth quirked into a smile, enjoying the effect that he was having on me.

Once my dress was nothing more than a pile of gauzy fabric on the floor next to my bed, Erik sat back, looking me up and down. It'd always made me nervous when Donavon looked at me without any clothes on, but something about the way that Erik's eyes drank in every detail made me feel special, and I didn't mind at all.

A flicker of something that I couldn't pinpoint flashed across Erik's eyes. He hesitated, before bending down and kissing me, slowly, softly. I wrapped my arms around his neck, pulling him closer to me, but I feared that he would never get close enough to satisfy me.

I'd never felt this way with Donavon, who I'd been so convinced I loved. Donavon, who I'd defended anytime that Erik spoke ill of him. Donavon, who I'd trusted, and who had made me question everything that I thought I knew in my life.

Suddenly, Erik stopped kissing me. He backed away, stumbling backwards off of my bed.

"This is wrong, I can't do this," he stammered.

"W-w-w-what?" I stuttered, hot tears pricking the corners of my eyes. "Why?"

"You're drunk, Talia. It would be wrong."

"Drunk?" I repeated. He had a point - I was drunk, but I would've wanted him even if I were sober. Since I *was* drunk, I actually said, "It doesn't matter. I would still want you if I were sober. I mean I do want you when I'm sober."

"No, this is wrong," he said firmly, shaking his head.

I scrambled off the bed and moved towards him, only vaguely aware of the fact that I wasn't wearing any clothes. I reached out to him, but he kept backing away. The tears that had welled up in my eyes were now falling down my cheeks.

"Did I do something wrong?" I sniffled.

"No," his answer was clipped. I did something wrong. I just didn't know what it could be. I cried harder.

"What can I do? Tell me what I did wrong," I pleaded with him. This is when I should have been biting my cheek, so I didn't say something I would regret.

"Natalia, you're drunk. I don't think this is the best time to have this conversation."

How could he do this to me? I might not have trusted myself with him, but I did trust him.

Erik started walking toward me. He grabbed my bathrobe off of the hook on the bathroom door and wrapped it around my shoulders.

"I should go, Tal," he said kneeling down in front of me. My chest was heaving with my silent sobs. I couldn't catch my breath, and my drunken brain feared I was hyperventilating.

"Please stay," I begged. "I don't understand what I did wrong," I cried, but my words were incoherent, even to me.

Erik ran the back of his hand against my cheek and then stood to leave. I shot my hand out and wrapped it around his wrist, forcing him to turn back around and face me.

"What did I do?" I shouted, anger replacing humiliation. "You owe me that much."

"Owe you?" the fury that flashed in his eyes scared me. Under sober circumstances, I probably would've shrunk away from him. "I don't owe you shit, Tal." He yanked his arm, but my grasp was firm.

"I was about to sleep with you, Erik," I screamed.

"Why?" Erik demanded. He yanked harder, and his wrist broke free from my grasp, but he didn't make moves to leave the room again. Instead, he bent down with his face inches from mine.

"Why what?" I asked, confused.

"Why do you want to sleep with me, Tal?" he demanded. His eyes were blazing, and his face was contorted in rage. This time I did shrink away from him.

"I don't know," I stammered.

"To get back at Donavon?" his voice turned eerily calm, and I leaned further back away from him. I knew he had a temper; we both did, but his had never been directed at me. He terrified me, but I refused to back down. I straightened my spine.

"NO," I screamed at him, shoving him hard in his bare chest. "Why would you even think that?"

"You know how amazing it is to be with you?" his voice turned gentle, but his eyes still had that if-looks-could-kill thing going on. "When I'm with you, I can feel how you feel. You project your feelings on to me so strongly that no matter what I do, I can't keep you out of my head. And I don't want, too. It feels too incredible."

"Then what's wrong?" A fresh wave of hysteria rose up inside me, threatening to overtake me again.

"Donavon! There hasn't been one time I have kissed you that you haven't thought of him!" Erik screamed, pounding his hands against my bed, sending me bouncing up and down. If I thought his eerie calm voice was scary, it had nothing on his losing-his-temper voice.

"No, no that isn't true," I sobbed, hugging my knees to my chest. "I want to be with you."

"Yes, Natalia, it is. And I'm not going to be anybody's fucking silver medal." Every apartment in the building was soundproofed, but I wouldn't have been surprised if my neighbors could hear us screaming.

Erik backed away from the bed, grabbing his shirt as he did.

"No!" I screamed after him. "Erik, please!" I briefly considered reaching out to his mind and mentally forcing him to stay with me, but thankfully, all of the yelling had sobered me up enough to realize how terrible that plan was likely to turn out.

Erik paused near the door, and hope filled me. Then he pressed his hand to the interior sensor and the door swung open. My strangled cries filled the room when he walked out.

Curling up on my bed, I sobbed until I had no tears left to cry and my throat was so raw that it felt as though it were bleeding. I choked on my sobs and dry-heaved over the side of my bed. I dreaded falling asleep because every time I woke again, I'd have to relive the pain and embarrassment of what had happened.

Chapter Thirty

When I finally dragged myself out of bed the next morning, my eyes were so swollen that I could barely see. I wandered into my bathroom, only to find that I actually looked worse than I felt. The purple color of my eyes wasn't identifiable in my reflection. Makeup streaked my cheeks and across my forehead where I'd smeared it rubbing the tears away. My loose curls were tightly knotted and sticking out all over my head. I groaned.

I had several hours until I was due at the hangar for my flight to Nevada. I should've spent that time doing last minute preparations for my Hunt, but I lacked the energy. I had a horrible headache that I wanted to blame on the alcohol, but I remembered that it was supposed to be hangover-free, so I correctly attributed it to my uncontrollable hysteria over what had happened with Erik.

I filled my oversized bathtub with water as hot as I could bear, added scented oils that Gretchen had sent me. I plastered a cucumber-carrot cream over my entire face and slipped over the edge of the large tub and into the steaming water. The cream was one of Gretchen's own concoctions; she used to slather the tangy-smelling lotion on both mine and Donavon's injuries when we were younger to reduce swelling. It worked wonders, and I hoped it would do the same for my puffy eyes.

Floating in the scented water, I tried to clear my head of Erik, of Donavon, and of anything else that didn't directly relate to my upcoming assignment. It was a fruitless endeavor. I couldn't erase Erik's accusations from my mind. Did I really think about Donavon that much? I guess I did, but most of my thoughts weren't exactly friendly. And really, what did Erik expect? Donavon was the only guy that I'd ever dated. The only guy I'd ever kissed. The only guy that I'd ever done anything with that a teenage girl does with a teenage boy. Of course, I was going to think about Donavon, right? I didn't still have feelings for Donavon, unless hate counted, right? Even if I did, was it really fair for Erik to expect me just to turn off my feelings for Donavon, even after what he'd done to me? And why was Erik fishing around in my head while we were making out, anyway? I didn't reach into his head. Sure, I opened myself up to his feelings, but that was a lot different than rummaging around in his head to find out how I compared with every girl that he'd done whatever it is he does with them.

My bath ended up being less relaxing than I'd anticipated. When I climbed out of the tub, trailing watery footprints across the bathroom floor, I was less ashamed about the way that I'd acted with Erik, and more enraged about the way that he'd acted with me. Actually, I was more than angry; I was fuming. I threw my necessary belongings into my black regulation backpack with way more force than necessary, roughly packing my clothes and gadgets while muttering to myself the whole time.

When a knock on the door interrupted my angry packing, my stomach was suddenly full of butterflies. I wanted to open my mind to find out who was there, but I wasn't sure if the fluttering in my stomach was because I hoped that it were Erik, or because I hoped it were Donavon. The epiphany made me irrationally angry with Erik, for being right about the whole Donavon thing.

Instead of opening my mind, I used it to throw open the door. The door slammed into the wall, chipping the purple paint; the doorjamb failed to slow its swing.

"Hey," Penny called, tentatively.

"Oh, it's you. Sorry, come on in," I called back.

"Nervous?" Penny asked, jittery herself.

"Huh? Oh, about the Hunt? Of course, I'm nervous, but I'll be fine. It's just a graduation Hunt, after all." I tried to smile at her, but it came out strained.

"You're distracted," Penny said matter-of-factly.

"I. Am. Not. Distracted," I practically growled at her.

"Tal, I know you've done really well on your Hunts up until now," she spoke softly as she slowly lowered herself to the floor to sit beside me. "But you really need your head in the game right now. This Mission is extremely dangerous; I've seen all the intel."

"I've seen it all, too, Penny," I snapped at her, annoyed.

"Is it Erik?" Penny asked quietly.

"Yeah...Kind of," I relented, softening my tone.

"Why don't you tell me what happened?" she suggested.

I gave her a hard look. As angry as I was with Erik, I knew that the minute I actually said the words out loud, I would be reliving possibly the most mortifying experience of my life. I thought it better to remain heated.

I intended to tell Penny I didn't want to talk about it, but somehow I found myself launching into a detailed account of the night before. I stared at my hands the entire time I spoke. The only thing worse than a drunken fight was recounting a drunken fight while sober. I might as well have put it up on my wall screen and played it back in slow motion.

Penny listened without comment. When I finished, I finally

looked up and met Penny's green eyes, hoping to find something that made me feel better. Her eyes were full of concern, but I wasn't exactly sure why.

"Erik will calm down. He cares a lot about you," Penny finally said. She hesitated before continuing. "Do you want Donavon back?" Her voice was so quiet that if I hadn't been sitting right next to her I wouldn't have heard her.

"No. No, I don't," I said with as much conviction as I could muster.

"But maybe it was a little too soon to start something with Erik?" Penny prompted.

"Probably," I admitted.

"He'll be okay when you get back. He just needs a couple of days to calm down," she assured me. I nodded and gave her a real smile. "Now that you've gotten that off your chest, will you please concentrate on your Hunt?" she insisted.

"Yes, I will. You're right – none of this is important right now." Penny's point was valid. This was exactly what Mac had been talking about; if I actually wanted to be a Hunter, I needed to start acting like it. The last thing that I should be devoting energy to was boys.

Penny finished packing my stuff while I reviewed intel again. Together, we made our way to the hover hangar where I would board the craft that would take me to Nevada. We didn't say much on the walk, but it was nice knowing that Penny was there.

Thanks to all of my mental anguish over Erik and Donavon, I hadn't had time to get nervous about my Mission. But as soon as the hangar came into view, my stomach constricted as fear and anxiety set in, twisting my internal organs. I reached over and grabbed for Penny's hand. She gave it a reassuring squeeze, and I gripped hers tighter.

In a couple of hours, I could be face to face with my parents' murderer. In a couple of hours, I might kill Ian Crane, or Ian Crane might kill me. None of these scenarios sounded very win-win to me; in fact, they all seemed like lose-lose.

Best case scenario, I confronted Ian Crane. I didn't know if I'd be able to restrain myself from attacking him, but if I attacked him, my cover was blown. If my cover were blown, I'd better be sure that he died in that attack. If he died, it was unlikely that I'd make it very far before one of his men killed me. If I did somehow manage to Houdini my way out of there, it was unlikely that I'd graduate since my official assignment was information gathering. All in all, the outcome wasn't likely going to be in my favor.

Mac was waiting inside the hangar with Captain Alvarez when we arrived. His face was set in hard lines, his dark brown eyes unwelcoming. At least Captain Alvarez appeared pleased to see me – his dark features lit up with a reassuring smile when he noticed me.

"Do you make it a habit to see off the Pledges on their solo Hunts, or am I special?" I asked sarcastically. I was still miffed over Mac's thinly-veiled threats.

"I happened to be here on business. I thought I would come say good luck, and remind you that if you don't successfully complete this assignment, you won't graduate. Please take this seriously," Mac replied dryly. He must still be irked, too. Stalemate.

"I take every Hunt seriously," I shot back, my temper flaring.

"You've done very well up to this point, Natalia. I am sure this won't be any different as long as you keep focused," Captain Alvarez interjected, defusing the situation.

"I am focused," I said, through gritted teeth. Penny's sharp intake of breath drew my attention away from Mac; her eyes were pained. I looked down at her hand, still enclosed in mine, and her fingers were turning purple from lack of circulation. I hastily released her.

"Sorry," I muttered.

Mac walked over and gave me an awkward hug. I half-heartedly returned it.

"Be careful, Natalia," he said in a low voice. His cold gray eyes found mine, *"You know what you need to do."*

"I do," my voice was so icy that I gave myself a shudder.

Penny turned and leaned down, wrapping her thin arms around me.

"Keep your eyes and ears open, and remember that I'm always there with you. I know you won't be able to hear or see me, but I'll be there on the other end of all your communications," she choked. When she released me, she wiped tears from her cheeks. I gave her hand a gentle squeeze this time.

"Good luck, Lyons. Just remember –when you come back, you'll be a real Hunter," Captain Alvarez engulfed one of my hands in my both of his, shaking it vigorously. *If I returned,* I thought.

"Thank you, sir," I gave him a small nod, suddenly very glad that he was here.

I turned, walking over to my designated hover plane.

"Talia, wait!" Henri panted as he ran into the hangar.

I smiled, "I thought you weren't coming."

He gave me a huge hug, squeezing me tightly, "Good luck, Talia. Be careful," he whispered.

"Thank you, I will. I'll be back before you know it," I tried to make my voice light.

He swallowed. "I know."

"Is Erik not coming?" The words were out of my mouth

before I could stop them, and I hated myself for asking.

"He thought it would be better if he didn't," Henri's voice was kind.

"Of course, he's right. It's better this way," I mumbled, more upset than I should've been.

"We'll *both* be here when you get back, okay?"

I nodded, feeling tears prickling the corners of my eyes. I gave him another quick hug. He grasped one of my small hands in both of his much larger ones, pressing a tightly folded square of paper into my palm. I risked a quick glance before curling my fingers around the pointy edges; my name was scrawled across the front, and underneath my name it read, "For when you're ready to hear it." I gave Henri one last nod and then turned, continuing to the hover plane before he could see the tears swimming in my eyes.

Chapter Thirty-One

The moment that I stepped on the hover plane, my mood shifted drastically. I pushed all thoughts of Erik and Donavon aside and focused all of my energy on the task at hand. Finding that I was too amped up to sleep, I again ran through all of the intel, over and over in my mind. When that became tiresome, I switched to sensory drills. Even still, the nearly four-hour flight went faster than I would've liked.

When the hover plane landed, we were approximately sixty miles from the Nevada border. My backpack was already strapped firmly on my back when the craft lowered into the clearing. I called goodbye to the crew and readied myself as a metal panel in the bottom of the plane began to slide open. Looking down, even in the dead of night, I judged the ground to be about ten feet beneath me. I tensed, my muscles preparing to jump. Once the hole was large enough for me to fit through, I leapt.

Landing in a low crouch, I focused all my energy to my sight; even though the craft was quiet, it was not easy to hear above the dull hum. I drank in my surroundings, my eyes adjusting quickly. I didn't wait for the hover plane to rise back into the night, but instead took off at a run immediately.

I was wearing tight black pants, made of a stretchy material, and a tight black jacket, instead of an adapti-suit. Since this Hunt wasn't covert, an adapti-suit was unnecessary – I wasn't hiding from anybody. Eventually, I would be trying to attract a certain amount of attention to myself.

I would be spotted on my way into town; in the middle of the night, there would be little traffic going through the checkpoints at the Las Vegas city border. If I were to cross in the middle of the day, I'd be less noticeable, but it was safer for the hover plane to drop me under the cover of darkness. Even in the middle of the night, the risk was too great to get any closer than we did.

The soles of my black mesh shoes barely made any noise as I ran through the woods. I followed the map that I'd committed to memory, concentrating my energy on my sense of feel. The ground would change from fallen leaves, where the tree covering was dense, to tightly packed earth with only a scattering of leaves when the trees began to thin. It was there that I needed to switch directions, from south to southwest. Approximately three miles before the tree cover ended entirely, the ground would change again, becoming rockier. Once out of the woods, I would find myself in a small neighborhood.

Unlike my Missions with Henri and Erik, there would be no hover vehicle waiting for me. TOXIC had safe houses equipped with vehicles in this area, but it was too risky for me to try and cross the border in an Agency vehicle. The Coalition states and their residents were poor, so a car outfitted with the latest technology would cause suspicion. Instead, I would "borrow" a vehicle from one of the houses in the neighborhood.

My run through the woods went exactly according to plan. I was feeling confident when I burst through the trees and into a grassy area behind a neighborhood home. Slowing to a walk, I took several deep breaths and willed my pulse to return to normal.

I pulled the hood up over my curls, hoping to obscure as much of myself as possible, now that I was around people.

I refocused my mental energy and expanded my mind, searching for any creatures that were awake in the area. I sensed several animals – dogs or wolves – in the vicinity. Concentrating harder, I pinpointed the exact homes that they guarded, and I made a mental note to steer clear of them. I crept around the house that I was behind, and did a quick scan of the area. I found myself in a cul-de-sac with only six houses. Four homes had animals patrolling their yards. I chose one of the two houses without a security animal and quickly spotted the owner's vehicle in the driveway. Relief flooded through me when I saw that it was a hover vehicle – they make so much less noise than road vehicles.

Crouching low next to the driver's side door, I unhooked my backpack. I set the bag in my lap, and felt around for the residue-detector that attached to my portable communicator. Once I connected the two, I turned on the detector and ran it over the keypad on the side of the driver's door. Five of the ten numbers glowed neon green. I waited as my communicator processed the possible combinations of the five numbers to make up the passcode. Several agonizing seconds passed before the screen of my communicator displayed the top five most likely combination orders. I entered the first one and was rewarded with a soft click as the lock disengaged. Relieved, I eased the door open and crawled into the driver's seat.

Thus far, pure adrenaline had steeled my nerves. But now, sitting in a car that I was about to steal, my apprehension returned. I took several calming breaths and acquainted myself with the vehicle. Mentally disengaging the door lock would have been risky, since the vehicle could have had an alarm, but there wouldn't be a similar risk using my telekinetic powers to start the engine. The intel package had contained an entire section on engines in the most common hover and land vehicles. I'd meticulously studied each and every one. I placed my hand on the dashboard, envisioned the engine for a Y420 Hover Craft – the name was emblazoned on the dash – and mentally engaged all of the pistons. I held my breath as the engine came alive, purring softly.

Gently, I glided the hover vehicle across the front lawn of its owner's home, hoping that nobody inside needed a late night bathroom run. I didn't exhale until I was safely out of the neighborhood and soaring high above fields and pastures en route to the border of Las Vegas. For my first solo driving experience, it was uneventful. I made a mental note to insist that Henri let me drive the Agency hover craft next time we went into D.C.

I cruised at a moderate speed and made it to the border in twenty minutes.

I pushed the button to lower the tires from the undercarriage when I was still about five miles from the border check; seeing as I had yet to master landing, I thought it better to land a safe distance from the actual checkpoint. Hopefully, I'd draw less attention to myself if I crashed.

Once I landed, with only a minimal amount of bumping and swerving, I drove the last five miles to the border in a haze. Sweat rolled down my back, pooling in the fabric at the waistband of my pants. I wiped at beads of perspiration dotting my forehead and upper lip with the sleeve of my jacket. I gripped the hand controls of the vehicle so hard that I knew my knuckles were white underneath my black gloves. I could hear my heart pounding in my chest, and I prayed that the border guard wasn't a Talent. I didn't overly worry about that since Talents were shunned by the Coalition rather than revered. It was unlikely that one would be working as a border guard.

As I approached, I saw that the border was virtually empty. Only one vehicle occupied any of the ten gates. I focused my energy on my mental abilities and slid the vehicle into the rightmost gate.

A short man with a thick mustache leaned out of the guard booth. I panicked, mentally forcing my window down instead of pressing the button. The guard gave me an odd look. I looked into his dark eyes and locked onto his mind.

You saw me press the button to roll the window down, I mentally insisted. If there were cameras at the border crossing – and I assumed that there were – I didn't want to draw suspicion to myself; I wanted the transaction to appear as normal as possible to anyone watching the surveillance footage. His face relaxed, and he smiled at me. I rewarded him with a toothy grin.

"Good evening," I greeted him without breaking eye contact.

"Good evening, ma'am. What is your business in Las Vegas?"

"Family visit," I responded out loud. *Ask me for my papers and then let me through,* I mentally communicated.

The guard continued to smile. "Do you have your papers, Miss?"

"Of course," I smiled, handing him several blank pages stapled together. *Slowly leaf through the pages, then declare everything in order and let me through,* I commanded.

My last vestiges of anxiety were gone, and I felt truly in control for the first time in months, maybe years. I was in my element. I had complete confidence in my mental abilities. Was I too cocky? Maybe, but I'd been able to bend the will of others for as long as I could remember. My parents had discouraged using my Talents against those around me. Mac had discouraged it while I was at school, but he'd always promised that one day I'd be able to use my abilities to their fullest extent. Now I was, and it felt incredible.

The guard made a show of flipping through the blank pages, scanning each in turn as though checking for pertinent information. He handed me back the papers.

Log me in as a visitor – Name: Anna Reynolds – age 22, visiting Las Vegas to see my father, Arnie Reynolds, I ordered. Arnie was a real Las Vegas resident, and he really did have a daughter named Anna, but our intel indicated that she hadn't visited her father since she was five. Hopefully, she wouldn't feel like reconnecting anytime soon.

The guard obediently turned around. I could hear the tap of his fingers hitting the plastic computer keys as he entered the information I'd given him. "Enjoy your visit to our city, Miss," the guard declared, once he finished entering the data.

"Thank you." I locked his eyes with mine, giving him a mental image of the real Anna Reynolds. I held his mind until I was confident that he wouldn't remember a small, freckle-faced girl with curly hair and purple eyes. There was nothing that I could do about the security cameras, but I'd been careful to stay within the confines of the vehicle.

Before the Great Secession of the Western States, Las Vegas had been an entertainment mecca. The Coalition had claimed eminent domain on the land to gain control of the hotel casinos, turning the rooms into mandatory living quarters for Las Vegas residents. Now, most of the residents lived on one street in the very center of the city limits – Las Vegas Boulevard.

After the Coalition had seized control of the small contingency of states that seceded from the rest of the nation, they declared Martial Law. Without their national funding, the states fell into disrepair. The Coalition herded most of their citizens into the cities, and set up border patrols to regulate all incoming and outgoing traffic. The residents lived in poverty when compared with those who resided in states still loyal to the Agency. The Coalition provided all of the necessities for their citizens, but nothing extraneous. Given all of this, it amazed me that people still sought refuge across the borders just to escape the Mandatory Testing Laws.

The Strip extended several miles. Towering forty-story casino-turned-apartment buildings lined both sides of the street, their splendor long forgotten. Cracked neon signs hung across the front of each complex, announcing the name: Caesars, Bellagio, New York, New York, Treasure Island, and The Wynn. An ancient monorail system connected the four miles of the Strip. At this time of night the trains were still, but I assumed they creaked unsteadily across the rickety rails when they ran during the day. Sky walkways allowed the inhabitants to cross the cracked street without having to navigate the uneven pavement below. Road and hover vehicles were rare here – they were too expensive for most Coalition citizens.

After crossing the border, I made for the patch of neon lights that were like beacons in the black of night. Agency loyalists had filed the necessary paperwork to secure me an apartment several miles off the main strip. I flew over the few freestanding homes located inside the border. Without warning, the control panel on the dash started beeping. I glanced down nervously.

"Redirect route. Redirect route," a mechanical voice cut through the quiet car. Shit! What was going on? Not good, not good!

"State reason," I demanded, unsure if the vehicle would respond to my voice.

"Restricted airspace," the mechanical voice answered. I called up the city map ingrained in my mind. Ohhhhh – my current course had me flying straight over Crane's temporary residence. I cut a wide arc to the right, straining to catch a glimpse of the home as I passed.

It was only a matter of time before the owner of my borrowed hover car reported it missing, so I needed to get rid of the car. I scoured the area just past Crane's temporary housing for a hiding place. The land stretching in every direction from the property was barren; there wasn't a single tree to conceal the vehicle from hover cars searching from above. I was forced to double back to an unkempt house about ten miles from the Strip. I was tired, and the thought of running that far to my new apartment wasn't appealing, but the house appeared unoccupied. I didn't think that I would have a better option any closer to the center of the city, so I grudgingly directed the vehicle towards the ground.

After landing, I stashed the car in an empty shed behind the house. I pulled a small bottle of Identiscure from my pack, and sprayed every surface of the interior with the chemical, removing my fingerprints, hair, and skin cells. After replacing the bottle, I strapped my bag onto my back and set off at a brisk jog toward the glowing lights.

Almost an hour later, I arrived at the apartment. I did a quick sweep of it to make certain that I was alone. The apartment was almost as barebones as my cabin in Hunters Village. It had one main room, with well-worn carpeting that stretched from one paint-peeled wall to the next. The tiny bedroom held nothing more than a twin-sized bed, but the sheets at least appeared clean. A small white-tiled bathroom completed the apartment.

Once I was satisfied that the apartment was safe, I stashed my backpack within arm's reach of the bed, undressed and climbed in between the scratchy sheets.

Unlike our safe houses, the apartment didn't have surveillance cameras or a command center; the only electronics that I'd have access to were the ones I'd brought with me. The apartment served one purpose – a place for me to sleep. Many of my devices uploaded images directly back to the Crypto team at headquarters, and that made me feel a little less lonely. Still, the only way that I could directly contact anybody within the Agency would be by activating the sub-dermal tracking chip that they'd implanted in my hip.

The chip was only to be activated in the event of a "true emergency"; the medic who'd embedded it had reiterated this no less than ten times. Any non-emergency messages were to be relayed through TOXIC contacts that were scattered around the city. In return, I had assured him – no less than ten times – that it would take a "true emergency" for me to slice through the layers of skin, muscle, and tendon IN MY OWN HIP to remove the chip. If I somehow garnered the courage to cut myself, I would still need to keep my lunch down long enough to dig the transponder out of my flesh. Needless to say, it was completely unnecessary for him to worry that I might activate the chip for fun.

Waking up after only a couple of hours of sleep, I went directly to the kitchen and rummaged through the cupboards. I stared contemplatively at the contents. On the one hand, there was food. On the other hand, the "food" was dehydrated fruits and meats. Hunger won out, and I grabbed several bags at random. I munched on dehydrated hen strips and sugary apricot along with banana pieces as I explored the space that I now called home.

I hadn't taken stock of the small closet in the main room the night before, so that was next. Inside, I discovered a handful of plain cotton dresses, fashioned in the nondescript style that was common in Las Vegas since the Coalition's takeover. The floor of the closet held three pairs of identical leather sandals, very similar to the ones that I wore around Headquarters. Unlike Penny, clothes held very little interest to me. The dresses were much like my own everyday wardrobe – boring.

I hadn't been truly on my own since...well, ever. Loneliness and longing for Headquarters engulfed me. The sight of the familiar leather sandals comforted me slightly. Running my fingers across the stiff material, I reminded myself that the sooner I completed this Mission, the sooner I could go home. Hopefully, I'd find Crane in the process.

After I had my fill of dried foods, I made my way to the shower. It was still pretty early, and I hadn't gotten much sleep, but I really wanted to get started right away.

After my shower, I selected a sleeveless navy dress from the closet, paired with a thin, brown leather belt and brown leather sandals. I piled my curls on top of my head in a loose bun and popped in the facial-recognition eyeball lenses. I stared at myself in the small mirror over the sink in the bathroom. The lenses masked the purple of my eyes, making them appear to be murky brown.

I laughed at my reflection. I couldn't count the number of times that I'd wished I didn't bear such an obvious Talent mark, but now as I saw myself, looking "normal," I realized that my purple eyes were just as much a part of my identity as my Mental Manipulation. Even though I still looked like myself for the most part, I felt completely different.

I packed a small bag with the necessary imagers and communication devices and set off towards the Strip. There were several nearby bars that Ian Crane's men frequented, but it was too early for that. I decided that I would wander around the city to familiarize myself with my new surroundings.

Leisurely, I strolled the streets. Uniformed Coalition men littered every corner. I had expected as much, but now that I was actually here, witnessing it firsthand, I realized that I'd vastly underestimated the danger I was facing. My arrogance from the day before vanished. With my facial recognition lenses, I scanned every man bearing the Coalition insignia that I passed, hoping to get a hit.

Around dinnertime, I made my way to a pub on the first level of the Bally's complex; the intel listed the bar as a known hangout for Crane's men. I hesitated outside the doors, my pulse quickening. Crane might be inside. I'd played this scene in my head countless times over the past seven years, but now that I might actually come face-to-face with my parents' murderer...I was scared. I was still the little girl in the closet, just a child. The speech that I'd revised in my head numerous times for Crane before I killed him suddenly seemed inadequate. Maybe Henri had been right; maybe this Hunt was too much for me.

No, no, I chastised myself. I was strong. I was brave. I could do this. My combat skills might not be as developed as Erik's, and my analytical abilities might not be as strong as Henri's, but my Talents, my mental abilities, were second to none. I'd learned early on to control my powers; Mac had worked tirelessly to harness my raw power, and convert it to controlled energy. I had been chosen for this Hunt, not because it coincided with my graduation from school, but because I was the only TOXIC member with a chance of success.

With my inner strength reinstated, I entered the pub, my head high as the glass doors slid apart. The interior was dark and smelled of beer and stale cigarette smoke. Quickly, I shut down my sense of smell before disgust could show on my face. I forced myself to walk slowly and confidently up to the low bar. I pulled out a wooden stool and carefully perched on the edge. I crossed one leg over the other, allowing my dress to ride up my leg far enough to attract attention, but not far enough to give away the muscles resulting from my daily physical training. I spent so much time trying to blend in that it felt odd to purposely draw attention to myself.

I caught the eye of a young guy sitting at the other end of the bar. He wasn't overly unfortunate looking, so I gave him the most dazzling smile I could muster. Either he rarely saw girls, or Penny's flirting lessons were paying off because he returned my smile with one of his own.

My left eye lens scrolled quickly through TOXIC's facial database. My right lens displayed the man's bio in barely-distinguishable print. I focused on the feel of the lens in my eye until it brought the words into sharper focus. I found what I was looking for. He was definitely one of Crane's men.

Buy me a drink, I ordered, not breaking eye contact. He signaled for the bartender without taking his eyes off me, and ordered a fruity alcohol drink that I wasn't familiar with. The bartender wasted no time filling the man's order.

Bring it to me yourself, I mentally barked, when the bartender set the drink in front of him. Nerves made my commands stronger than I intended, but that probably wasn't a bad thing. The man slid off the edge of his stool with his drink in one hand and mine in the other, making his way over to me. I kept my smile firmly in place as anxiety twisted my insides.

"You look thirsty," he quipped, handing me the fruity drink.

"Parched," I replied, reaching for the glass.

"Kyle," he introduced himself. Up close, I noticed how young he was; Kyle couldn't have been more than a couple years older than I was. His blonde hair was in need of a good shampooing, and his clothes were slightly rumpled, but his amber eyes were friendly and inviting.

"Anna." I offered my free hand, and he took it delicately in his. I swallowed the urge to flinch and withdraw from his touch. Instead, I plastered a smile on my face.

"Mind if I sit with you?" he asked shyly.

"Be my guest," I squeaked, all traces of my earlier composure gone. Sure, I was still confident in my ability to control him. Now I just wasn't sure that I wanted to.

Kyle climbed onto the stool next to me. I pulled my dress down, covering the leg that I'd exposed in hopes of attracting attention. I wasn't sure that I could mentally handle more than one of Crane's men.

Kyle and I chatted easily over dinner and several more drinks. I used my Talents to convince him that he needed to frequent the restroom, giving me opportunities to pour my drinks out on the grimy floor. I tried my best to act drunk, but I wasn't really sure that it mattered since Kyle was actually drunk. He didn't even need any encouragement from me.

Several of Kyle's associates – also Crane's men – stopped by to introduce themselves to me. I did my best to appear to be a young, drunk girl new that was to the city. I chanced peeking in to several of their minds to confirm they were buying my act; none were overly suspicious.

Offer to walk me home, I demanded as the night wound down.

"Can I walk you home?" Kyle slurred.

"Thanks, I'd like that," I trilled in my best drunk-girl voice. Kyle shot me a genuine smile, and I almost felt guilty. He paid our bill and stumbled off of his stool, offering me his arm. I gritted my teeth and looped my arm underneath his. Flirting with him was bad enough; touching him wasn't really something that I wanted to do.

We walked toward the exit to the pub in a cacophony of catcalls from his cohorts. I resisted the urge to turn around and attack.

My apartment was several blocks away. Kyle rambled drunkenly the entire walk.

Ask to see me tomorrow, I ordered when we reached the street-level door to my apartment. I doubted that any of Crane's men were watching, but I didn't want to make any mistakes.

"Anna, I would love to see you tomorrow," Kyle stated.

"I'd like that, too," I smiled back at him. He leaned in as if to kiss me, and I recoiled, waves of disgust washing over me. He drew back, shocked at my refusal. Crap.

Realizing my mistake, I went with the first thought that popped into my head. I envisioned kissing Erik. I summoned the feelings that his lips on mine evoked, and then projected those feelings towards Kyle.

The sides of his mouth curled into a dopey grin, and his amber eyes had a faraway look. His body gave a silent shudder as a small moan escaped his lips. I really hoped I didn't actually look like that when Erik kissed me.

"That was awesome," he muttered, brushing his fingertips across his bottom lip.

"I thought so, too," I replied quietly.

"I'll see you tomorrow? Seven at the pub?" he asked, without prompting.

"Sure," I whispered.

"'Night." He stood there a moment longer. I wanted to leave. I needed him to leave. I'd been biting back tears since I'd conjured the mental image of kissing Erik, and the associated feelings.

"Leave," I finally ordered, when it became obvious that he wasn't going to on his own.

With that, he stumbled down the street without looking back. I hurried up the stairs to my apartment, mentally pushing open the door to my unit and rushing through. I ran straight for the bedroom, slamming the front door behind me as I went.

Collapsing on the bed, I hugged my knees to my chest and rocked back and forth. Tears leaked around the eye lenses, pooling in the corners of my eyes before falling in tiny streams down my cheeks. Physically and mentally, I could do this. All night I'd easily controlled Kyle, bending and twisting his will like a pretzel. I'd also established tenuous connections with several of Crane's other men – just enough of a link for a quick swipe of their thoughts. I barely even felt tired from my efforts.

Emotionally? I couldn't have been further away. I wasn't sure how I had managed to get through the last several hours. I hated the way I was acting, hated what I was doing. I reminded myself that it was all just a means to an end, and the end was very important.

I sat, curled in a ball on the bed until the lenses began to burn in my eyes, reminding me they needed to come out. Unfolding my legs, I fished out my bag of gadgets from under the bed. I popped each lens out and placed them in their designated compartment in my communicator. I turned the communicator on and searched for an Agency frequency to transmit the facial information I'd collected. I was connected in seconds. I uploaded the images and reached to disconnect the devices. My index finger hovered over the terminate button for a moment longer than it should have.

"I know you won't be able to hear or see me, but I'll be on the other end of every communication," Penny had said to me. I hoped that was true.

I pulled off my dress, disgusted by the beer and grease stains from where Kyle had touched me. I threw it in a crumpled heap in the corner of the tiny bedroom. The apartment was so hot that I decided against wearing anything to bed. Instead, I stretched out on the mattress and tried to clear my mind so I could fall asleep. When that didn't work, I reached in my bag and pulled out Erik's note.

I ran my fingers over the tightly folded white square, tracing the letters of my name with the ragged nail of my right index finger. I chewed nervously on the corner of my bottom lip.

"For when you're ready to hear it," I whispered, reading Erik's words out loud.

I had no idea what to expect when I finally found the courage to unfold the paper. How would I know when I was ready? What about Erik's childhood was so bad that I had to ready myself to hear it? My parents were murdered in front of me; how much worse could it get?

I flipped the note over and over in my hands. I straightened the intricately folded paper triangles that threaded into one another – securing Erik's secrets inside. I couldn't muster the strength to smooth the crinkles and read their contents; I guess I wasn't ready.

Laying his letter on the pillow next to my head, I stared at the small shape until my eyelids were too heavy to hold up.

I woke up with the sun the next morning. I tried to fall back asleep since I had no reason to get up so early, but the morning sun had kicked up the temperature in the apartment until it was uncomfortably hot. Dragging myself to the bathroom, I turned only the cold water knob in the shower. The bite of the frigid water abruptly woke my senses.

I fished a purple dress, much like the blue one that was still crumpled on the apartment floor, out of the small closet and quickly dressed. I wanted to leave my curls loose around my face, but knew I'd be too hot. I settled for piling my hair into a messy up-do on the top of my head. Today, I selected the camera eye

lenses and popped them in one at a time. I debated strapping a
knife belt to my waist, just in case, but decided against it, opting
for just one blade fastened to my left thigh.

Today my goal was to get ground images of the outside of
Crane's compound. I had all of the aerial images and floor plans
that the Cryptos had compiled, but I figured that more intel could
never hurt. There was always a possibility that I'd learn something
new.

Crane's residence was set several miles back from the strip,
surrounded by yards of metal fencing. There wasn't much around
the home, so I needed to be careful to remain unseen.

My dress clung to my sweaty skin as I approached the gates to
the Crane place. There were no guards stationed outside, but the
fence surrounding the property was likely charged with electricity.
I blinked furiously as I strolled the length of the metal cage, my
eyes trying taking in every inch of the exterior. The house itself
was a stone architectural masterpiece. It stood four stories high and
stretched the length of three average-sized houses. Ornately carved
double wooden doors marked the main entrance to the home, and
large glass windows with dark curtains dotted the front face.

I opened my mind as I walked and felt a buzz of activity from
within. There were so many people inside that I couldn't get an
exact count, but I estimated somewhere between twenty and thirty.
I was able to determine that no humans were patrolling the
exterior, but I could feel animal minds. I'm not as good with
animal minds as I am with human ones; I could determine the
general location of the animals, but nothing exact. Pretty much all I
knew was that they were behind the back of the house, and they
were all real animals – no Morphers. I wanted to get images of the
back and sides of the house, but the animals might give me away.

Heading back to my apartment, I felt somewhat dejected. The

images that I'd actually been able to get didn't give me any new or different information.

I flopped onto the uncomfortable blue couch in the living room/kitchen area with several handfuls of dried beef jerky and crystallized purple plums. The food was dry and unappetizing, but I was starving and would have eaten twigs if they were put in front of me just then. I uploaded the images to my communicator, only to confirm that none were useful, and my morning had been a waste. I groaned in frustration.

After I ate, I still had several hours until I was supposed to meet Kyle. I spread out on the bed and tried not to move too much; I didn't want to sweat any more than absolutely necessary. I pulled out Erik's letter again. Staring at his familiar handwriting, I felt a little less lonely. My sweaty fingers smudged the ink as I traced the letters of my name.

An hour before I was due to meet Kyle, I showered again, partially to calm my nerves and partially to get the salty layer of sweat off my body. The sun had already set, and the temperature had cooled slightly, but it was still warmer than I was accustomed to. I opted for another dress, even though I knew that if things went south, the dress was likely to hamper my movements. I selected a relatively short, loose-fitting dress from the closet, in the hopes I wouldn't get tripped up in the skirt part. I elected to go with the weapons belt this time, feeling immediately safer once it was slung across my hips. The dress had pockets in the folds of the skirt, and I cut the lining open, so when I reached into the dress through the pockets, I could easily grab the blades from my belt. I still had the camera lenses in my eyes, but just in case I needed the others, I stuffed them in the small bag I'd carried last night. Erik's letter, still sitting on the bed, caught my attention. On impulse, I grabbed it and threw it in, too. Having it close to me almost made me feel like he was here with me. I took a last deep, calming breath before heading out the door to meet Kyle.

The pub was crawling with Coalition men when I arrived. I immediately went on high alert. Two Coalition men were stationed by the glass doors, searching everyone before they entered. Crap. No way could I let them search me. I could convince them not to, but if other's noticed, the situation could get out of control quickly. I started to panic. What to do, what to do?

"Anna!" Kyle called, walking through the door and pulling me out of the line. "She's with me," he said to his cohorts. The guards each gave me a curt nod. I gave them a thin smile in return, being sure to blink as I looked at each man. Kyle led me to a small table along the wall farthest from the bar. He even pulled out the chair for me. His small, gentlemanly gesture sent a pang of guilt through me. I hated using him; even if he were the enemy, he'd been so nice to me. I surveyed my surroundings, blinking as quickly as I could in order to get as many pictures as were feasible.

"What's going on? Why all the security?" I asked innocently. I already knew the answer; Ian Crane was either here or on his way here.

"President Crane is here," he nodded to something behind my left shoulder.

Snapping my head around, I searched for him, seeking him out. Finally, I locked eyes with him. The room seemed to go silent, as if the only two people who occupied the room were Crane and me. A tidal wave of rage nearly consumed me. I felt rabid, and the only conscious thought I could form was "attack." I felt my nose twitch as my lips curled into a snarl. Clenching my fists at my sides, I dug my fingernails sharply into the fleshiest part of my palms. The pain brought me back to reality. *Focus,* I ordered myself. *Killing Crane in front of all these people is a bad idea.*

SOPHIE DAVIS

I blinked slowly, hoping to get a clear picture of his face. My eyes were dry from wearing the lenses all day, and I felt the one in my right eye slip. I froze.

It was unlikely that Ian Crane's sight was as good as mine so the rational part of me knew that there was no way he'd noticed from across the room. Even if he'd seen see the purple iris, it didn't really mean anything. After all, the Coalition was anti-Talent and, while not all people with off-colored eyes were Talents, many Talents did have distinctly colored eyes. I was willing to bet that many people in Coalition territories wore lenses to hide their true eye color.

I opened my mind to make Ian Crane forget what he'd anything he'd seen, but as soon as I opened it, I snapped it shut again.

When I first went to the McDonough School, Mac had taught me the sense-strengthening exercises that I still used today. In return, I trained Mac's mind. I worked every day with him, teaching Mac to identify mental intrusions and, eventually, to block them. I was willing to bet that, despite Ian Crane's stance on Talents, he'd had similar coaching.

He held my eyes for a second too long to be chance. When Ian Crane finally pulled his gaze from mine, he turned to the man on his right, careful to conceal his lips as he whispered in the ear of the shorter man. The man gave a quick nod and took off towards the door. Panic now warred with my fury. Did he know who I was?

Gritting my teeth, I swallowed over the lump in my throat. Crane thought that there was something not right with me. I couldn't be sure he'd been conditioned against mental intrusions, but I was positive that he could feel that something was different about me; the realization was written all over his face.

Mac had often said that most people can feel exceptionally

strong Talents, and he'd explained that's why most people have some sort of reaction to me. For some, the power that I –or any other strong Talent – exude, unnerves them causing them to shy away from me. For others, the power was like a drug, drawing them to us. By the way that Ian Crane had just looked at me, I knew that he was a mixture of both. I didn't need to read his mind to know that he feared the power he didn't, and couldn't, understand. Yet he also craved it, wanted to be close to it.

Crane knew just by my presence that I was exceptionally strong – that was the only explanation for his interest in me. The Coalition, and Crane by extension, might reject the idea of *being Talented,* but with just one look Crane had confirmed that his inner circle consisted of strong, rare Talents. He was clearly intrigued by them, drawn to them.

Kyle was talking about something that I'd missed entirely, but luckily he seemed oblivious to my blank stares and lack of response. I let him babble about nothing through dinner, being sure to insert the appropriate "oh really" or "you don't say", so he would think that I was paying attention. In reality, I was plotting my next move.

I'd prepared myself to go into Crane's place tonight, but I'd hoped that it was going to be a first, "get myself acquainted" kind of trip. Now it looked more like it would be a quick and dirty, once-over kind of trip. Mac was not going to be happy.

I ran through a mental checklist of the items in my bag; I had all three pairs of eye lenses and my portable communicator. Once inside, I would be able to take as many pictures as times I could blink. If all went according to plan, I wouldn't come face to face with Ian Crane. If I could manage to avoid Crane tonight, I would be able to use Kyle a little longer. If things didn't go according to plan, I would be forced to make a hasty escape from Nevada. My only hope was that I'd be able to take Crane's life with me.

The waitress arrived with our dinner, bringing me back to the present, and out of my head. I forced myself to eat the chunky beef and vegetable stew that Kyle had ordered for me. I was going to need all of my strength tonight, and all I'd eaten today was the dried meats and fruits in the cabinets of my apartment.

Take me back to Crane's house, I ordered Kyle, as soon as I finished inhaling the stew. Kyle immediately threw some money on the table, grabbed my hand, and began leading me out of the pub. Several of Crane's other men watched us wind our way through the crowded tables, but nobody tried to stop us. I took that as a good sign.

Crane himself was holding court in the center of the room. His eyes bore into my back as I walked past his table. Holding my breath, I willed myself to act normal. The urge to attack him was still strong; I gripped fistfuls of my dress in my balled-up hands to keep from lashing out.

Kyle led me out the glass doors.

You overhead us saying that we're going back to my apartment, I directed to the guards as we passed by. I wasn't positive that it took in either man's mind since I didn't make eye contact – not a necessity, but definitely a help – but I did see one guard giving the other a knowing smile out of the corner of my eye.

I was firmly tuned in to Kyle's mind; his every thought was filling my own head, as if he were speaking out loud. His inner monologue consisted mostly of thoughts that simultaneously disgusted me and made me blush. It was odd being connected to the mind of somebody who didn't know that I was there. Sure, I sometimes read the minds of people around me, but I'd learned early on that I really didn't want to hear every thought that passed through somebody else's subconscious.

The connection wasn't strictly one way; opening up my mind to connect with another person also made me extremely vulnerable. I could usually control which of my thoughts the other person saw or heard, but not always. Like with Erik.

Donavon, Erik, and Henri had permitted me to read their thoughts. All three guarded parts of their minds that they didn't want me to have access to. In return, I didn't dig around to find out information that they didn't want me to know. Well, I rarely dug around...in Henri's mind. I admittedly took some liberties with Erik's, but in my defense, Erik could always tell when I was in his mind, and he'd never told me to get out. I thought my connection with Donavon had been more absolute, but seeing as he managed to keep an entire affair from me, I knew there were recesses of his mind I'd never penetrated.

I felt bad openly listening to Kyle's mind. It felt wrong and dirty, as if I'd made him take off his clothes and sit naked while I interrogated him. I had to keep reminding myself that I was one of the good guys, and he was one of the bad guys. He was associated with the people who'd killed my parents and tried to kill me, would have killed me.

Kyle drove us the short distance from the pub back to Crane's temporary residence. I took note of the passcode he entered at the gate as the numbers flashed through his mind. Once inside the barrier, he pulled around to the back of the stone house. I blinked rapidly, turning my head from side to side, taking as many pictures as I could. Kyle parked the vehicle in a small, relatively empty lot behind the house. He turned to face me, one hand on the button that opened the vehicle doors. His thoughts turned anxious; he was having misgivings about bringing a stranger into Crane's home.

I gave him the most dazzling smile that I could manage. *Crane won't mind. I'm just a young girl, I won't cause any trouble,* I coaxed. His face relaxed, and his thoughts returned to indecent. He pressed the button, opening the doors. I walked around from my side and took his large meaty hand in my small one, calloused and scabbed from all my weapons and combat training. I realized my mistake a moment too late. His eyes grew wide as he ran his thumb across the pads of my palm. *I told you that I worked on my parent's farm,* I quickly covered. His face smoothed as he recalled a memory that wasn't his own – the one that I'd just implanted.

Kyle led me up a stone walkway to the back of the house, where a guard stood watch. He had a large scoped rifle slung over one shoulder and two smaller guns holstered at his waist.

"Kyle," he called. "Who's your friend?"

"Hey, Dan, this is Anna," Kyle called back.

"You know that you're not supposed to bring visitors here," his tone was disapproving, "even if they are cute little girls." He slowly ran his eyes up and down the length of my body. I felt the overwhelming urge to shower. Anger and annoyance bubbled up inside of me. Little girl? I understand that at just shy of five feet, I'm small, but little girl? He was lucky that I had yet to get what I came for, or else I would show him who was a little girl. I took several deep breaths to control my temper.

It will be okay just this once, I directed towards both Dan and Kyle.

"I guess it will be okay just this once," they said in unison.

"I will need to search you and your bag," Dan insisted. I had a feeling that this had more to do with his skeevy nature than fear that I might actually be armed.

Not necessary. Just let us in, I ordered. Dan moved aside, letting us pass, but not before giving me another once over. I shuddered.

The interior of the house was dark, but my eyes adjusted quickly.

Lead me to your room now, I ordered more forcefully than I intended. Kyle tripped over his own feet as he set off in the direction of his room at a near-run, dragging me along with him.

As soon as we walked through his room door, I mentally pushed the door shut and engaged the lock. Kyle's eyes widened.

Lay down on your bed and go to sleep, I ordered. *When you wake up, you will remember taking me home.* I filled his head with a distorted mental image of myself. Many of Crane's men had seen us together and could describe me, but conflicting descriptions might buy me some time later.

Kyle obediently laid on top of his blankets. I waited until his breathing fell into an even rhythm before creeping out of his room, locking the door behind me.

I envisioned the floor plans for the house that I'd painstakingly committed to memory. Aware that my time was limited, I headed directly for Ian Crane's office. I blinked rapidly, taking pictures as I jogged silently through the long hallways and up several flights of stairs. I reached the heavy wooden door in under a minute. Placing my hand on the wood panels, I opened my mind, searching for people inside. There was no one. I forced the lock and slid the door open, just enough for me to squeeze through. Mentally, I closed and locked the door behind me. I reminded myself to breathe.

Slowly, I scanned each wall with my eyes. I opened and closed them at a slow, even pace, praying that the pictures would be useful. After I was satisfied, I moved to Crane's desk. I was no Crypto, and my knowledge of computers was limited, but I followed Blaine's instructions for uploading the contents of the computer to my communicator. I connected my portable communicator to the computer, and it turned it on. A screen appeared on the monitor, asking for a password. I typed a sequence of numbers into my communicator and waited while it worked. Blaine had explained that the communicator was programmed with code-cracking software; several agonizing seconds later, a password box on Crane's computer filled with a row of black dots. It beeped loudly, three times, and then "password confirmed" appeared on the blue screen. The screen went blank, then text, numbers, letters and symbols appeared, scrolling white against a now-black background.

Blaine had warned me that this might happen. He'd explained that everything on the computer was likely encrypted, and to just download the information "as is" and let the Cryptos sort it out. I checked the screen of my communicator; the words "download started" appeared, followed by "download in progress."

While the download ran, I rifled through Crane's desk. Most of the drawers were locked, so I mentally disengaged all of the bolts at once and drew them out on their runners. I didn't actually know what, if anything, I was looking for. Mac said to gather as much information as I could, so I began taking pictures of each and every document that I came across. When the download finished, I decided that my next stop would be the basement.

The floor plans included underground dimensions that ran the length of the house. The aerial and satellite images that Cryptos had weren't able to determine what was down there. The most likely answer was a laboratory. Whatever it was, it had to be important to warrant so much protection surrounding it; the Cryptos hadn't been able to get images that were clear enough to determine what was down there because the entire basement was shrouded in some type of image-blocking technology.

Opening my mind, I pinpointed all of the men in the house. I tiptoed, moving as quickly as I dared, from Crane's office down a lengthy hallway, and wound through the levels of the house until I found the door that led to the basement. I paused.

I couldn't feel any active minds behind the door, but it wasn't because there weren't any. When I opened my mind, I met resistance, but not the usual emptiness that indicated an absence of human brain activity. I pushed harder, but it was like pushing against a brick wall. Not good. I placed my hand on the door to the basement, and tried to disengage the lock. Nothing happened. Really not good. I tried once more, for good measure. Nothing. Crap.

At school, Donavon and I had often found our way into restricted areas. Biometrically protected areas, I could handle. Security guards? Not a problem for somebody like me. But actual blocking technology? This was more advanced than anything that TOXIC utilized. The School's security measures were in place to keep out overly curious kids, but nothing like this. Even Elite Headquarters didn't employ such advanced security measures.

Brute force it was. With my mental faculties rendered useless, I had no other option. I was not super-humanly strong or anything, but I did train for physical combat almost every day of my life. The door was definitely alarmed; once I broke the lock, I forfeited any element of surprise that I currently had.

Since I knew the general layout of the basement, I knew that there was an exit to the outside. I weighed my options. Whatever was behind this door was important. I knew that it was important going into the Mission, but the fact there was some type of protection that rendered my Talents useless meant that whatever was down there was *really* important. There was no question in my mind – the risk was worth it. I would just get in, take as many pictures as I could, then make for the exit door. I took several calming breaths, and then backed up several feet. I closed my eyes, cleared my mind, and prepared myself for the worst.

I slipped off my sandals before launching myself at the keypad next to the door. My bare heel made contact, crushing the keypad in one blow. Plastic cut the bottom of my foot, but I didn't feel pain. I pulled the dangling fragments of the keypad from the wall, exposing the wiring. Reaching through the pocket of my dress, I withdrew a knife from the belt around my waist. I began slicing through wires at random, praying that one would unlock the door. I breathed a sigh of relief when the door whined and eased itself open.

Immediately behind the door was a set of metal steps, so steep that I couldn't see the bottom in the dark. I worried for a split second that the security that was in place wouldn't allow me to focus my energy, but thankfully, my fears were unfounded. I concentrated on my sight. My eyes adjusted to the absolute darkness in no time. Fearing that I'd already wasted precious time that I didn't have, I tore down the staircase.

No alarms had gone off when I broke the keypad, but that only meant that they were silent. There was no way that a facility with so much protection wasn't also alarmed.

At the bottom of the steps, I made a snap decision and turned to the right. I ran down the corridor, mentally trying to open the doors lining either side; I was surprised to find that the doors responded to my mental Talents. The protections only worked to keep people outside from getting in. I searched for human minds, but I'd waited too long.

Just as my mind registered a flurry of mental activity in a room just ahead to my right, a huge man stepped through the door. I couldn't stop myself in time. I barreled into him. His hands closed around my upper arms, gripping them so tightly, I knew that

I would bruise. Instinct took over, and I brought my knee up, directly into his groin. He groaned, but didn't release me. His vice-like grip let up just enough for me to maneuver my hand into my pocket. I withdrew the first knife that my hand closed around, and I didn't hesitate when I plunged it into his side.

This time, he released me. His hands sought the wound between his ribs. I took the opportunity to take the offensive. I kicked behind his left knee, his legs buckled and he fell over. I aimed my next kick at his left kidney. He fell over flat on his stomach. I was on his back before he could react. I wrapped my right arm around his neck cutting off his air supply. He reached back, clawing at my face. He tried to pry my arm from around his throat, but he was quickly losing consciousness. When his body finally went limp, I released my hold and eased his head to the floor.

Preoccupied with the large man on the floor, I didn't sense the second man come out of the room until it was too late. I craned my neck at the sound of his soft footfalls, just in time to see the glint of the silver needle before I felt the prick in the side of my neck. I looked up into the bright green eyes of the man holding the syringe. The metallic burn of chemicals filled my veins. So this was how I was going to die...I'd hoped it would be more dramatic. I didn't even lift a finger to save myself before everything went black.

Chapter Thirty-Two

I came to. I wasn't dead, although I kind of wished I was. My head throbbed. A metallic taste filled my mouth – not blood, a chemical of some kind. I wished that it were blood. My vision was fuzzy, and I blinked several times in rapid succession, trying to clear the haze from my eyes. I was still wearing the lenses. Frantically, I turned my head from side to side, getting as many pictures of the room as possible. The room looked as if it belonged in one of TOXIC's medical buildings. Several hospital-type beds were evenly spaced across the wall. Each bed had electronic monitors and a tray of syringes set up next to it. If I ever got out of here, these would be valuable.

I only moved my head from side to side because that was all I could move. I looked down. I was strapped to one of the gurneys, my wrists and ankles shackled to the railings. Two leather straps, one across my chest, one across my hips, immobilized my body. I tugged on the restraints, testing their strength. They were pretty sturdy.

"I don't want to hurt you, Talia," a deep voice boomed. A tall, thin man walked into the room. His salt and pepper hair was closely cut, his coal-black eyes were small and beady in their deep sockets. Three heavily armed guards trailed in his wake.

My blood turned to ice in my veins as I locked eyes with Ian Crane. The chemical cocktail injection must've been playing tricks with my brain because I thought I just heard him call me Talia. He couldn't know my name. He couldn't know who I was.

I was on the verge of a full-blown panic attack; my chest heaved against the leather strap. I inhaled deeply through my nose. When I blew out the breath, it hissed through my clenched teeth.

I mentally slapped myself. Control. I needed to get control of myself. Only then could I gain control of the situation.

"Yes, I know who you are, Talia. Natalia Lyons. And I assume you know who I am?" Crane continued. Who was the mind reader here? When I didn't respond, he pushed on. "Just hear me out, Talia. I think you might be interested in what I have to say."

"I have nothing to say to you," I spat, my temper flaring. Crane nodded to the closest of his armed men. The man began walking towards me.

Fear gripped me again. *I am going to die. I am going to die. I AM GOING TO DIE.*

Long-buried memories clawed their way to the surface of my mind. The shot claiming my father's life rang in my ears. The sight of my mother's life pouring from her neck clouded my vision. I was not going to die this way. I might die tonight, but not before I killed Crane.

I yanked at my restraints, but they remained unyielding. My eyes darted around the room, looking for something, anything to help me. Crane's man was leaning over me.

NO, I mentally screamed at him. He halted. I concentrated hard, filling his head with a noise so high-pitched that usually only dogs could hear it. His hands flew to his ears. He dropped to his knees, blood trickling through the gaps between the fingers of one hand. The other men looked at each other uncomfortably. Crane gave me a smile that didn't quite reach his eyes.

"You are quite Talented, as I believe TOXIC calls it, Talia." The repetition of my name unnerved me, and I snapped. I pushed my mental energies out towards everyone in the room. Crane's men collapsed to their knees around him, shrieking. Only Crane himself seemed unaffected by my abilities, confirming my suspicion that he'd been conditioned against mental attack.

I gave another go at my restraints, this time with my mind. The solid metal shackles split with a screech. I yanked my wrists free, tearing a large jagged cut on my left wrist. I concentrated on my ankle shackles until they tore cleanly down the seams. Rolling onto my feet, I readied myself to attack Crane.

"No need to get physical, Talia. I just want to talk," he said, holding his hands up as if to show me that he didn't want trouble.

"I already told you, I have nothing to say to you," I growled.

"You don't need to say anything. Just listen," his smile faltered for the first time.

"You killed my parents," I said in a low, even voice that was too cruel to be mine.

"Your parents' deaths were a regrettable consequence of war," he argued. If I didn't know better, I'd have thought that the expression in his beady little eyes was pain.

"Consequence of war? Is that what you'll say about my death - it was a consequence of war?" I demanded.

"Isn't that how TOXIC justifies all their Kill Missions?" he asked lightly.

"TOXIC doesn't kill innocent people," I fired back.

"Really? You know nothing about what your Agency does to innocent people," he shouted, his control slipping.

"TOXIC has taught me to use my abilities, to become a more complete person. You and your Coalition would subjugate Talents if you had your way," I screamed back.

"And what do you think your Agency does, Talia? What do you think the Mandatory Talent Testing Law does? It enslaves you." His black eyes burned into me, as if he were willing me to share his views.

"Mac has taught me to use my abilities for good," I argued.

"Danbury McDonough? You think he has taught you to use your abilities? Talia, you don't even realize how strong you are! Or what you are capable of! He has only taught you enough to make you compliant, to make you his minion. Your powers are so much stronger than any Talent I've ever met," he sounded almost reverent when he said the last part.

"Is this where you tell me that you can teach to use my Talents," I asked sardonically. "You wouldn't even know where to begin."

"I already know how to use your gifts better than you do!" he yelled.

"Really? And who could have possibly taught you that?" I demanded, narrowing my eyes at him.

"Your father," he spat.

I was momentarily speechless at the mention of my father. My hands started to twitch, and the primal urge to attack overtook me. I wasn't going to stand here and listen to him tell lies about my family. I lunged for Crane.

"Talia, please listen to me," his tone held a note of desperation. A red haze was already beginning in my peripheral vision; I was beyond listening.

He shielded himself with his hands, but didn't try to fight back. My bloodlust-filled screams mingled with the pained screams of Crane's men, many of whom were still writhing in pain on the floor.

Colliding with Crane, I knocked him to the floor. I landed on top of him, and he grabbed for my wrists to restrain me. He managed to wrap one large hand around my injured arm. I punched him with my free hand, my fist connecting with his cheekbone giving a satisfying crunch. Crane didn't even flinch. I raised my hand to strike again as I heard footsteps behind me. I felt three more men rush into the already too-crowded room. The lead man raised his gun.

"NO!" Crane screamed, but it was too late – the man fired. I deflected the bullets with my mind. He fired again. And again. And again. He emptied the entire clip into the room, but all of his bullets hung uselessly in midair until I let them drop harmlessly to the floor. I turned my attention back to Crane.

"Talia, please," he begged. His eyes grew wide as saucers as he stared at something behind me. I turned to see the first man locked and reloaded, poised to fire again. I went for the gun this time. I mentally yanked it out of the man's hand, but not before he squeezed the trigger with his index finger.

Pain exploded in my back, just above my left hip. A bloodcurdling scream tore from my lips. I stretched my mental muscles to the breaking point, making the men in the doorway fall to the ground, incapacitated. I jumped off of Crane. Pain seared white-hot as I moved.

I was afraid to look at my wound. I needed to leave. I was using so much mental energy, I wouldn't be able to keep it up much longer. I needed to get to safety. I needed to get out of Nevada. I tried to formulate a plan, but the pain was excruciating, preventing me from thinking straight. Erik did me no favors by easing my pain when I'd been stabbed; maybe if I'd learned how to think through the pain, then I wouldn't be so ineffectual now.

A thought struck me. I fell to my knees next to Crane. I

grabbed his already-swelling face and locked his eyes with mine. I tried boring into his mind, but it was like when I mentally tried to reach through the door upstairs. His defenses were even better than I'd first thought. Whoever had trained him was extremely Talented, at least as Talented as I was, maybe even more so.

"Let me in," I growled. Black spots dotted my vision. I worried that I was going to pass out before I broke through his resistance. Pure desperation fueled my last-ditch attempt to break Ian Crane. Just as the blackness at the edge of my vision grew larger, threatening to render me blind, I felt the fight go out of Crane. His mental barriers gave way, sending me toppling into his mind.

I focused on the physical pain, forcing the agony from my mind to his. The pain slowly eased, before disappearing completely. Crane's face contorted. He curled himself into the fetal position, screams escaping through his pursed lips. I sat back on my heels, panting from the exertion.

I watched him for several seconds, our earlier conversation replaying in my mind: his mention of my father. His argument about the *Mandatory Testing Law. You don't have time for this, MOVE.*

I needed to stop the bleeding. I mentally pulled cabinets and drawers open, searching for something, anything – this was a medical facility, after all. I found towels and gauze first. I pressed the towel over the wound, and Crane screamed louder. I used the gauze to hold the towel in place as best I could. Grabbing several extra towels and an extra roll of gauze, I stuffed them into my pouch. The bag was now devoid of my gadgets, thanks, I assumed, to Crane's men.

I bent over one of Crane's men curled in a ball on the floor, unable to do anything but whimper; I divested him of his own weapons. Guns were not my first choice – despite all the target practice – I had horrible aim – but I was desperate and had no idea where my knife belt was. I gave one last look at Crane, a million questions burning in my mind.

"Talia, please listen to me," he urged through my pain.

"You killed my parents," I said softly.

"No, no." He shook his head from side to side. I heard faint footsteps and judged them to be coming down the metal steps.

Two options warred in my head. I desperately wanted to kill Ian Crane, but I also desperately wanted to live to fight another day. I couldn't do both. My abilities were already stretched to the breaking point, and it was unlikely that I'd be able to control more people mentally if the new men caught me.

I may have transferred the pain to Crane, but I was still the one not-so-slowly bleeding to death. I was physically too weak to fight. My only chance of survival was to run, and if I ran, I needed to keep the pain at bay as long as possible. I didn't know how long I could hold Crane's mind. I did know that if I killed him, I wouldn't get as far as the door. I chose self-preservation, a decision that would haunt me for a long time. With one last glance down at Crane, I turned and ran for the exit.

I easily navigated my way through the maze of corridors in the basement, and burst through the door that I knew to be the exit. I found myself at the bottom of a concrete staircase. I ran up the steps without hesitation, my eyes darting from side to side as I tried to get my bearings. I was behind the stone house, not far from where Kyle had parked the vehicle. I ran straight to the parking lot.

Luck was on my side – the first car that I tried was unlocked. I threw open the door and fell in. I mentally started the engine and took off, without bothering to determine whether I was being pursued.

The hover vehicle rose up and cleared the high fence, but a high-pitched wailing noise went off as I passed. If there had been any question about whether there was an intruder at Crane's place, there wasn't now. I pushed the vehicle as fast as it would go. My mental fatigue was threatening to consume me, and I let go of Crane's men's minds. I was positive that I already had a slew of people pursuing me, what was eight more?

I clung desperately to Crane's consciousness. My blood had already soaked through the towel and was working on the fabric of the seat. My head and stomach were woozy. I began to doubt whether I was going to live; I wasn't sure how much more blood I could afford to lose. Unfortunately, I was going to lose at least a little more before the night was over, and not from my gushing gunshot wound.

My only chance of survival was to be rescued; the only way I was getting rescued, since Crane's men took my communicator, was to activate the tracker implanted in my hip. I put the hover vehicle on autopilot and reached for the knife I'd taken off Crane's man. Hiking what was left of my short dress up, I felt for the small lump that marked the tracker. I found it easily, but hesitated. I hated the sight of my own blood.

My knife hand shook as I brought the tip close to my skin I started panting. Scared that I was hyperventilating, I pulled the knife away from my hip and counted to ten. Closing my eyes, I focused on calming my breathing. Then, as if to psych myself out, I swiftly reached across my body and sliced the skin right over the tracker in one motion. It didn't hurt. Well, it didn't hurt me. I hoped that Ian Crane felt like the skin on his hip tore open when I cut myself.

I threw the knife back on the passenger seat. I gritted my teeth, and looked down at the cut I had made, my head beginning to swim. It was a good thing I hadn't actually looked at the bullet hole in my back. Pressing both of my thumbs to the bottom edge of the tracker, I worked it out of my hip. I sighed with relief as the slippery chip slid into my fingers.

I looked through the windshield of the hover vehicle, just as I sped over the city border. I entered my code into the tiny tracker and held my breath until it glowed green, letting me know that the signal had started. Glancing behind me, I was relieved to see that nobody was following me... yet. I risked driving the hover vehicle all the way to the clearing where I'd been dropped off two days before. Had it really only been two days? I needed to get out of the air; I was mighty conspicuous flying a stolen Coalition vehicle.

Not so gently, I landed the vehicle on the edge of the clearing. I crawled out of the car, towards the woods. My hold on Crane's mind was slipping; I couldn't hold on much longer. The tracking signal was on, but I didn't know if anyone would get here in time. I found a shallow hole and collapsed into the soft leaves. My eyes were heavy, and I wanted more than anything to close them, but I knew that if I did, I might never open them again.

When I couldn't stand it a second longer, I did the only thing that I could think of to stay awake – I released Crane's mind. It would only buy me a couple minutes of consciousness at best. I had lost – was still losing – too much blood to hang on much longer. The pain washed over me, but I didn't even have the energy left to cry. The pain was so intense that it was only a matter of time before I passed out. I held onto the pain as long as I could; as long as I could feel pain, I knew I was still alive.

I reached for my small bag and fumbled around inside until my fingers closed around the edges of Erik's letter. I unfurled the blood-smeared pages and began to read. The words swam in and out of focus, disbelief coloring my thoughts. Too late, I realized I wasn't ready to read the words on those pages.

Epilogue

Donavon McDonough ran at full speed towards the woods. He held a tracking device in his left hand. *Not much further now*, he thought to himself. The green dot on his tracker grew stronger, the closer he came to its source. He opened his mind, praying that she'd respond if he called to her. *Talia! Talia!* He mentally screamed. No response came. Fear propelled him rapidly towards his target. He was nearly on top of her before his eyes found her small form.

Her body was obscured by leaves, and he nearly tripped over her. Relief washed over him.

"I've got her!" he yelled into his headset.

Donavon knelt in the leaves next to Talia's limp form. The foliage shrouding her was stained red with her blood. Her normally olive-toned face was pale and waxy-looking. Her lips were dry and cracked. Donavon probed her delicate neck, searching for a pulse. Finally, his fingers registered the weak beat of her heart. *She's alive.* He breathed a sigh. He frantically peeled the leaves away and gathered her in his arms. As Donavon stood with her limp body in his arms, he noticed several pieces of paper scattered underneath where Talia's body had just been. Taking care not to drop her, he bent back down and grabbed the pages.

"I need someone to come cleanse the area," Donavon spoke into his headset again.

"Affirmative," the voice on the other end replied.

Talia was small and weightless in his arms, childlike. Donavon ran out of the woods as quickly as he'd come, trying in vain not to jostle her still body. Talia's chest wasn't perceptibly rising and falling, and he feared the worst. Panic coursed through Donavon when he felt a sticky wetness seeping through his jacket, her blood was already soaking through it. She couldn't die. Her life was worth too much, more than his own. His father had never let him forget that.

Donavon reached the clearing and carried her aboard the waiting plane, full of medics. They rushed over and scanned for her vitals while she was still draped across his arms.

"She doesn't have much time," the medic declared gravely. "She's lost too much blood."

"Then you'd better make some time. She *has to* live," he snapped back. The team of medics sprang to life around him, taking her small body from his arms. Not caring if he were in the way, Donavon knelt next to the gurney. He swore that he saw her eyelids flutter, and he grabbed her bloody fingers.

"Hang in there, Tal. Just hang in there," he sent.

"Move back, sir," one Medic ordered, shoving Donavon aside. He stumbled backwards, as the team of doctors converged on Talia's nearly-lifeless body. Donavon sank into a seat in the corner of the plane, the pages that he'd rescued still clenched in his fist. A word caught his attention: Natalia. Donavon smoothed the wrinkled sheets against his thigh, and began to read the contents.

Natalia,

A couple nights ago, you asked about the circumstances leading to me going to the McDonough School when I was fourteen. I know that you were hurt I wouldn't share my story with you, but I've never shared it with anybody. I've never trusted someone enough with my secret. I've never wanted to let anybody get that close to me.

I'm so sorry about what happened last night. I'm sorry that I let things go so far with you, when I've known all along that you're still upset over Donavon. But you're right, I do know how you feel about me. I've known for a long time how you feel, maybe even before you knew it yourself. I feel the same way. You've captivated me since the first time we met, during your placement exams. I thought that it was just a crush, an odd fascination with a girl who managed to surprise me, but the more time I spent with you, the more I began to realize that what I'm feeling is so much more than a crush. I'd known about Donavon and the girl – her name is Kandice – for a while. I really wanted to tell you, but Henri persuaded me not to. He thought my feelings for you were clouding my judgment, and was afraid that if I were the one to tell you, you might not have believed me. He sensed you were starting to realize that I am falling for you. I stand by my decision. I wish that you hadn't found out the way you did, but I'm glad that you found out on your own. Honestly, I'm not sure you would have believed it otherwise.

I can't put into words how much it pained me to see you hurting so much, but slowly you bounced back, just like I knew you would. You're a fighter. When you finally started to understand that what you're feeling for me is real, I was elated. I tried to hold back, tried to give you more time to grieve, but I was selfish. I want you, so I started something even though I know that you aren't really ready. I was jealous again when I realized that you still think about him when we're together. I want all of you for myself, and when you thought about him last night, my temper got the best of me. I said things that I can't take back, but hope you forgive me. If time is what you need, that's what I'll give you.

You wanted to give me something that you've never shared with anyone, and I want you to know that I don't take that lightly. I also want to share something with you that I've never shared with anyone. Just know that once you've read what I have to say, you might not like it – or me. That's a risk I'm willing to take; I honestly think that you, of all people, deserve to know. So here it goes:

My parents are firm supporters of the movement to repeal the Talent Testing Act. Both my brothers and I were born at home instead of in a hospital because both of my parents are Talents. They were confident that at least one of us would be born Talented, and they didn't want our births on record. I'm the oldest. When I was three, my parents noticed that I was able to replicate both of their abilities. It unnerved them because mimics are so rare. They knew that the Agency would come for me if they ever found out. Both of my younger brothers also exhibited Talent at a young age, although neither is very strong. My middle brother is a mono-morph, and my youngest brother is a low level Brain.

We moved around a lot, staying off of TOXIC's radar. We lived mostly in rural areas and kept to ourselves. I grew up fearing the Agency, and what they stood for, but as I got older, I began to think that maybe my parents were paranoid. I met a girl on one of my grocery runs when we were living in North Carolina. We became close, and I got cocky. I told her all about my abilities trying to impress her. She, in turn, told her parents. Days later, Agency operatives raided our home. Ordinarily, the penalty for refusing to submit children for testing is jail time and a heavy fine. But my parents were proud and fought. My mother was killed in the raid. My father and brothers probably would've been, too, but I knew that TOXIC hadn't come for them; they'd come for me. The man in charge of the Mission told me that I was in no position to bargain, but I could tell he was lying. I surrendered myself in exchange for the lives of my father and my brothers.

Mimics are so rare, and I could tell how badly he wanted me, so I called his bluff. I threatened to take my own life if he didn't agree to the terms of my deal. In the end, he agreed. I offered to go willingly to the School and take my "rightful" place within the Agency. In return, my brothers would be free to attend regular school and live normal lives, and my father wouldn't be penalized. My father and brothers now live in Raleigh and are closely monitored by Agency personnel. Under the terms of my agreement, I'm not allowed to speak about what happened, visit my family, or step out of line. They'll all be executed if I violate any of these conditions.

I've been closely watched since my first day at School, and, truthfully, I'm shocked that the Agency allowed me to become a Hunter. However, my willing sacrifice – and the constant vigilance of those in charge – has proven me to be a loyal Operative. I don't agree with the Mandatory Testing laws, and I don't really care about the Coalition and their rebellion, but I do care about my family's well-being. If that means I have to fall in line and play my part, I will – and I do.

I told you that I'd tell you all of this when you were ready to hear it. I don't really know if you are ready now, but I wanted to share something with you. I also want you to understand that the Agency isn't all that you believe it to be. There are many within it who are corrupt, and the system in general is incredibly flawed.

You had a choice about whether to join this organization. I know that you see it as a chance to right the wrongs in your past, but just remember that the rest of us weren't given the same *option. The Agency is responsible for the wrongs in my past.*

I feel the deeply buried doubt that you keep bottled up inside of you. I'm not saying that you should leave the Agency or anything like that, I just want you to keep your eyes open, and hang on to that doubt. It's unlikely that Donavon is the only one who's lied to you.

I gave this to Henri because I trust him for reasons he'll have to explain to you some day. I gave it to you now because I wanted you to have a chance to read it away from the ever-watchful electronic presence of TOXIC's prying eyes. I know you're too curious not to read this before you return, so we can talk about it when you get back if you want to. If you don't, well, that's fine too. I hope that you'll understand how much trust it took for me to write this, and, even if you believe nothing I say, I hope that you won't share its contents with anybody.

E.

Donavon carefully folded the pages and shoved the note in his jacket pocket. *Decisions, decisions,* he thought, processing the ramifications of giving the defamatory document to his father. There wasn't really a choice in the matter. His family came first; Donavon knew what he needed to do.

Sneak peek at Caged, the second installment in the Talented Saga

Chapter One

The knock at the door came again. Just like the last three times he'd tried to get my attention, I ignored his appeal. Instead, I continued to stare at the metal lock that was barring him from entering.

"Natalia, open the door," his deep voice demanded. Concentrating harder, I watched as the latch switched from the locked to unlocked position. The sound of the lock engaging and disengaging was barely audible to me, but I knew that he heard the click loud and clear. Confirming my thoughts, he quickly tried turning the knob again, just as I re-engaged the lock.

"Natalia," he warned - his exasperation made me smile - "I will break this door if I have to," he said, his voice low and threatening. The harsh tone left little doubt that he would do just that if I didn't quit playing games. With a heavy sigh, I finally relented, disengaging the lock and leaving it that way. He turned the knob so hard the metal screeched in protest – I thought that it might break off in his hand – and then Danbury "Mac" McDonough burst into the room.

I sat on my king-sized bed, propped against the fluffy pillows, my arms crossed over my chest, my legs crossed at my ankles and a smirk on my face. Mac, the Director of the *Talented*

Organization for Extremely Interesting Citizens (aka TOXIC),
stared at me disapprovingly. "Are the games really necessary?" he
demanded, clearly annoyed.

"Am I not allowed any privacy?" I retorted, not bothering to
hide the irritation in my own voice.

"No, you are allowed all the 'privacy' you like, but you are
not allowed locked doors," he said with mock patience.

"Locked doors, privacy, what's the difference?"

"The difference, Natalia, is that if you have a seizure and the
door is locked, those seconds we lose could prove lethal." His
voice was hard, but the tenderness in his eyes touched me. The
steely reserve that I'd been holding on to faltered a little, but I
quickly recovered.

Pasting on a small smile, I said, "I'm fine, see?" I spread my
arms wide to prove my point. He studied me carefully through
narrowed gray eyes, inspecting every detail of my appearance for
signs of damage. I felt like a child under Mac's hard gaze, but
refused to avert my eyes. In addition to my seizures, Mac feared
me so depressed that I might injure myself. His unsubstantiated
anxiety had landed me in weekly therapy sessions with the Head of
Psychoanalysisfor the Agency. "You wanted to talk to me?" I
prompted, when I couldn't take his scrutiny any longer.

"How are you feeling?" he finally asked.

How was I feeling? Where to begin? Expressions like 'lab rat,'
'caged animal,' and 'prisoner' came to mind, but Mac wouldn't
appreciate those responses.

"Fine," I replied shortly.

"Fine?" he repeated lightly, raising one bushy eyebrow in
challenge.

"Fine. Just like I felt fine yesterday. Just like the day before
that. And exactly how I felt the day before that," my voice raising

an octave as I punctuated each word.

Mac continued to look me up and down, as if the only way that he would believe my words was if he couldn't detect otherwise. Returning his stare, I tried to match the cold glint of his gaze with my own. He was careful to avoid direct eye contact, afraid that I might read his thoughts. As if I needed such contact to access his mind. We both knew better, but we also both knew how much he hated the intrusion, which is why I normally refrained.

"I have been thinking, maybe you would like to help out with some of the classes at school?" He said it like it was a question, but I knew that he wasn't really giving me an option. Mac wasn't in the habit of offering choices; he was more accustomed to barking orders, and few people had the nerve to disobey. I used to be one of his sheep, his approval and praise had meant the world to me, but over the last nine months, I'd distanced myself from the flock. Despite that, option or not, I was eager to do something – anything – besides sit in this room.

"Really?" I replied, almost ashamed by how excited the prospect of leaving my bedroom made me. I tried not to let the excitement show, but I could barely contain myself. I had been locked up in this room, in this house, on the same grounds as the McDonough School for months. The only time that Mac permitted me to leave was to make the short trek to the School's medical facility for my daily blood drawing and injections with Dr. Thistler. Even my therapists, Drs. Wythe and Martin, came to Mac's house for our sessions.

Well, maybe locked up was a *slight* exaggeration – the door was only actually locked when I locked it from the inside. And the room wasn't exactly small; it was bigger than most accommodations for teenagers, even bigger than some families' entire homes, and lavishly decorated.

My large bed was covered in a burgundy down comforter with silver embroidered swirls and occupied a space in the middle of my bedroom. One wall of the bedroom was glass, and covered with draperies the same burgundy and silver pattern as the comforter. A mahogany dresser stood about waist high, extending almost the entire length of the wall opposite the bed, and a wall screen for watching movies stretched above it. A third wall contained a roll-top desk made of the same mahogany as the dresser.

Huge black-and-white paintings of icy lakes and snow covered mountains, painted by a well-known artist, hung on the three true walls. Next to the desk were giant French doors, made of the same mahogany with an intricately carved design. Behind the wooden doors sat a walk-in closet that stretched nearly half the width of the room itself. Most of the clothes in the closet hadn't been touched in years (two years to be exact).

The shelf that ran around the top of the closet held many shoe boxes, filled with pictures of me as teenager. My curly chestnut hair highlighted my purple eyes and framed my small face. My smooth olive complexion was marred only by a smattering of freckles across the bridge of my slightly upturned nose. Beside me in most of the pictures was a slightly older boy, a comparative giant, with shaggy blonde hair and clear blue eyes, his skin as light as mine was dark.

The pictures used to decorate the walls and the bedside tables; when I'd moved back into this room, I'd packed them all away, not wanting to see them every day.

"I thought that it would be good for you to get out and rejoin the living," Mac said dryly, interrupting my thoughts and bringing me back to the present.

"Funny, considering you're the reason that I've been denied

access to the "living," I snorted. The fact that our house was so close to hoards of students and teachers, but I was barely allowed to interact with them seemed almost cruel.

"Yes, well, your health has been much better in the recent weeks, and Dr. Wythe seems satisfied that your mental state is stable." *Great*, I thought, *the man who overanalyzes everything has decided that I'm not crazy – that's reassuring.*

"I could go back to Elite Headquarters," I replied, hopefully. I knew that Mac approving my return to the Hunters was about as likely as me rehanging those photos, but I had to try.

"You have not been cleared by Medical," he stated, the annoyance from earlier returning. Lately, we'd been having this conversation a lot.

"Medical doesn't seem to be any closer to *clearing* me than Medical was nine months ago," I snapped angrily. TOXIC had access the absolute latest and best medical research, yet somehow the exact cause of my seizures still baffled them.

Nine months ago, I was a Hunter Pledge, living at Elite Headquarters, located in beautiful Brentwood Springs, West Virginia. The Hunters are a division within a government bureau called TOXIC, simply referred to as the Agency. The Hunters devote most of their time to collecting information about the Coalition, the largest threat to national security. My solo mission, the culmination of the Hunters' Pledge program, had brought me into contact with Ian Crane himself, President of the Coalition and my parents' murderer. Even though my official assignment hadn't been to kill Crane, I hoped to do just that if the opportunity presented itself. When I finally did come face-to-face with him, things didn't go exactly as planned; I'd been injected with an unidentified chemical and shot while trying to flee. The drug lingered in my bloodstream, now causing me agonizing – and, at times, embarrassing – seizures.

The Coalition doesn't believe that being Talented is a good thing. They believe that people with gifts like me are unnatural. Their sole mission is to bring down the Agency and put an end to the training of special children. If Crane gets his way, Talents will be ostracized, forced to return to the days when we had to hide our abilities or face ridicule.

"Natalia, we have been over this. We are doing everything we can. I just need for you to be patient. It is best for everybody if you stay here until Medical can isolate the compound in your blood," he said with exaggerated patience. "Besides, even if Medical clears you, there is no guarantee that the Placement Committee will make you a Hunter."

Mac's not-so-subtle reminder that, in addition to nearly bleeding to death, I'd pretty much botched my solo hunt, stung. The solo hunt was a necessary mission that each Hunter Pledge needed to complete to actually become a Hunter. Mine had been less than stellar. I knew that there was a very real chance that my performance would prevent the Placement Committee from actually assigning me to the Hunters. Despite that, I was counting on my team captain, Henri, going to bat for me when the time came. Henri would, hopefully, assure the Committee that I'd done very well on all of my group missions, and that I was ready to be a full-fledged Hunter.

Still, my proverbial ace in the hole was Mac. As Director of the Agency, he was an important member of the Placement Committee – as far as most were concerned, his word was gospel. If he voted to place me with the Hunters, the others would likely fall in line. At one time, the mutual confidence that Mac and I shared would've left me with no doubt that he would sway the vote in my favor, but the current state of my mental and physical health made it uncertain.

"Fine," I snapped when it became clear that he wasn't going to give me any good news.

"Fine, you will help out with the classes at school?" He clarified.

"Fine, I will help out with the classes at school," I answered grudgingly. Not that helping students at the McDonough School for the Talented was high on my to-do list, but it sure beat twiddling my thumbs in my bedroom.

"Glad that we settled that." He sounded relieved. "Oh, and Natalia? Keep your senses open," Mac added, seemingly as an afterthought. I could tell that this was his real reason for sending me to the school, and now I was intrigued. Maybe this was more like an assignment than a way to get me to stop brooding. At least, I hoped that was the case.

"Why?" I asked suspiciously.

"I am not sure yet, but I think that we might have a leak in the Agency...a spy."

"A spy?" I asked stupidly, my mouth gaping. How could there be a spy in the Agency? Didn't we take extreme measures to prevent things like that?

"After studying your official report from Nevada, I can only conclude that we have a spy. Your identity was compromised. Crane knew who you were and, based on the events in his home, I believe that he was tipped off by an Operative on the inside here. I have been quietly investigating this theory, but have not made any progress. I think that it's time that we took more aggressive measures." He paused, waiting for my reaction. I kept my face impassive while I mulled over his words. I had entertained the notion that my identity had been leaked to Crane, but I hadn't honestly considered that it might be from someone within the

Agency. Now that I thought about it, Mac was probably right. Crane had clearly known who I was, and it's not like I carry identification on me. He'd also been prepared for my arrival. I guess we really did have a spy.

"Are you thinking that one of the teachers or administrators is selling the information?" I asked carefully, gauging his predictably guarded reaction to my question. If Mac had planned to fill me in on all the details, he wouldn't have broached the subject the way that he did. Ordinarily, he was so direct; that he was beating around the bush could only mean that he was intentionally hiding important details from me. When his expression remained unchanged, I once again considered reading his thoughts. After all, the spy – the traitor – who had compromised my identity had nearly cost me my life. Mac's refusal to divulge details infuriated me.

"Could be." He shrugged noncommittally. "Honestly, I'm not sure. Like I said, I've been quietly investigating this using only a handful of trusted Operatives, those that I am positive are not involved. I think that your specific Talents could be useful, since I have all but exhausted my other options."

Great, I'm a last resort. This time, I did read his mind.

His mental barricades were firmly in place, but since I was the one who'd taught him to build the barriers, they were easy for me to knock down. Mac was telling the truth. He really didn't have any idea who the spy was. His inability to make any progress in his search frustrated and scared him. He was afraid that if the traitor wasn't found soon, we would lose more Operatives. But he was most terrified by the certainty that if the interloper got another chance, he would make sure to kill me.

"And you consider me a trusted Operative," I teased, trying to lighten the mood. "I feel so special."

"No need for sarcasm, Natalia. But, yes, I am confident that you are not the leak," he answered.

"Why do you want me investigating at the School?" I asked, a little confused.

"Here and Elite Headquarters contain the Agency's only Crypto Banks, as you know. There are two possible scenarios for how Crane got his information. The leak theory would mean that an individual, obtained access to your assignment information, and sold that information to the Coalition. The other theory is that we have a Coalition spy working in our ranks. Even in that scenario, the individual would still have needed your mission specifics, and the only way to do that would be by hacking the records in the Crypto bank, or bribing a Crypto to do so. If there was a bribe, that would mean we have several traitors in our midst."

"Why me? Why my records?" I asked with alarm. If Mac was right, wouldn't it have been more advantageous to leak large batches of information? Or Hunting missions where whole teams could be captured or killed, instead of just one Operative? And I hadn't even been an Operative when I went on my solo mission, I'd been a Pledge.

"Most likely, because you were going after Crane directly," he answered.

He had been making eye contact with me up until this point, but averted his eyes when he spoke now. He was either lying, or at least only telling me part of his theory. I didn't press the issue this time. If Mac wanted to give me an assignment, I was happy to take it.

"I see. I suppose this is an unofficial mission?" I asked.

"Yes, that would be best. I don't want to cause panic within the Agency or tip off the potential spy by launching a full-out open investigation," he confirmed, meeting my gaze again.

"When do I start?" I asked with a confidence I didn't feel.

"Tomorrow. You will be posing as an Assistant Instructor, which includes living in Instructor housing. I've taken the liberty of matching you with several individuals who raised red flags in our preliminary search. By tomorrow afternoon, I'll have each of their files sent to your communicator."

He seemed relieved I'd agreed. As if I'd had an option. Even if Mac had actually presented this situation to me as though I had a choice, there wasn't one. Ian Crane had killed my parents. Ian Crane had nearly killed me. And whoever leaked my identity and mission specifics to Crane was just as responsible as he was for my current condition.

"I'll pack a bag," I said glibly. Mac gave me a hard look.

"I'll take you over first thing in the morning."

"I'm sure I can find the campus, Mac. I don't need a babysitter." Mac's house - my house - was on school grounds, it wasn't like I had far to go.

"I'll take you over first thing in the morning," he repeated. With that, he turned on his heel and left my room.

"Couldn't even bother to close the door," I mumbled.

"If you want it closed, do it yourself," Mac called from somewhere in my sitting room. I stared at the door until I heard a loud, satisfying THWACK. Gratified, I smiled to myself. My pleasure was short lived. A crack, followed by a thud filled the room. The door had splintered in two when I'd willed it shut. Crap, no more locking the door for me...good thing this was my last night here. Unfortunately, this was also my last night in my big comfy bed. Oh, well, my bed was a sacrifice I was willing to make.

Chapter Two

The steady beeping of the alarm clock grew louder with each chirp. I groaned. The only good part about being medically inactive was *not* having to wake up with the birds. Reaching blindly towards my bedside table, I slapped at the offensive machine. After several failed attempts I finally connected with the off button. I remained lying face down in my bed for several more minutes, my breathing again taking on the steady rhythm of sleep. The beeping anew began.

Ugh, I must've hit the snooze button. Groaning again I sat up, and rubbed the sleep from my eyes as I swung my legs over the side of the bed. When my feet made contact with the cold wooden floor, I swore loudly, wondering where my slippers were. I padded over to the window and threw open the curtains. It was still dark out . . . *awesome.* Suddenly, I wasn't so sure that I wanted an assignment; sleep sounded like a much better option.

Despite my increasing desire to climb back under the covers, I grabbed my robe and made my way to the bathroom attached to my sitting room. I turned on the hot water, waiting for the steam to fill the white-tiled space before stepping in to the walk-in shower. I savored this moment, my last shower without shoes for a while. When I was a student, I'd frequently come up here to bathe, but it was too far to make the trip on a daily basis. The showers at School were definitely NOT my fondest memory from my student days, and I somehow doubted that the teachers' were any better than the students'.

Following the deaths' of my parents when I was ten, I enrolled to the McDonough School for the Talented, located on a secure facility in western Maryland. I'd always known that I possessed the power to hear other people's thoughts and was capable of controlling their minds, but I hadn't known that my ability was called a Talent. I soon learned that Talents came in all shapes and sizes. There were Morphers, people who transformed into various animals; Light Manipulators, those who could turn invisible; Higher Reasoning or Brains, who were like human computers, capable of analyzing information in the blink of an eye; Electrical Manipulators, people who harnessed and controlled electricity; Visionaries, who saw glimpses of the future; and Viewers, who could observe a situation that they weren't physically present in; the list went on.

Our gifts were a result of the Great Contamination, a breakdown of the nuclear reactors all over the world. The United States created the McDonough School to train Talented children in properly using and controlling their gifts. At sixteen, we took placement exams that ranked our abilities and determined the division of Toxic that we would be positioned in after graduation. I'd been selected for the Hunters, the only division that I'd ever wanted to be a part of.

Hunters went on Missions to track down people and information that are a threat to either Toxic or the country as a whole. Most recently, the Hunters have focused on finding and destroying a group that opposes the Talent Testing Act, called the Coalition. They don't believe that being Talented is a good thing, that Talents are abnormal, and that what we are able do is unnatural. In a way, it is, but the skills that Talents possess help to protect the Nation. We have capabilities that far exceed those of average people, allowing us to both prevent crime domestically, and preclude invasion by foreign countries.

The Coalition is so opposed to the testing laws that it staged an uprising, causing seven states to secede from the rest of the U.S. Currently, one of the Agency's main initiatives is to defeat the Coalition before civil war breaks out, hopefully reuniting the country.

"Are you trying to drown yourself?" a woman's motherly voice called as she knocked on the bathroom door.

Sighing, I turned off the water, but didn't respond. I opened the glass door of the shower, the steam so thick that I could barely find my towel and robe. I dried myself off as best I could considering the amount of moisture in the air, then wrapped my heavy terrycloth robe around myself, cinching the tie around my middle. Bending over, I wrapped the towel around my long wet hair. The robe was so long that I had to hold it up, so I wouldn't trip as I made my way back into the bedroom.

When I opened the bathroom door, steam billowed out into the sitting room, forming warm clouds. The woman who had knocked on the door was sitting at the small breakfast table in the corner with a plate of scrambled eggs, thick white toast and a huge carafe of coffee. I sniffed the air and drank in the rich fragrance of imported dark roast.

"Morning, Talia," Gretchen greeted me warmly. Her clear blue eyes were warm and inviting, a sharp contrast to the cold gray ones of her husband. Despite the early hour, her blonde hair was perfectly coiffed and she was already dressed, in black slacks and a royal blue blouse. "I thought that you could use a good breakfast before your first day of school."

"Thanks, Gretchen," I replied, giving her a genuine smile in return. Gretchen had been like a mother to me since the death of my own, as Mac had been like a father to me, and I'd come to love them both deeply. My feelings for Mac had become muddled in the nine months since returning from Nevada, though, he had gone to great lengths to aid me in my physical recovery, and I was extremely grateful for his support. But, I'd also come to realize that there was a lot Mac had been keeping from me. I knew that as Director he was privy to highly classified information that wasn't any of my business, but all the secrets were lessening the steadfast trust that I'd always had in him.

After moving to the U.S. to attend the McDonough School, I'd learned that Mac and Gretchen opening their home to me was a highly unusual practice. Since Mac had been a close friend of my father's, he argued that he owed it to him to watch out for me. Mac had recognized me for what I was, he'd known that I was; a Mind Manipulator the first time we met, because Gretchen was one of the only other recorded Talents with the same ability.

Gretchen had ranked as a Mid-level Talent during her Placement Exams, and been assigned to the Psychic Interrogation Division. But she had no stomach for the unpleasantness associated with questioning suspects, and dreaded performing the interrogations so much that it made her physically ill. She'd requested permission to leave when she was pregnant with their son. Mac wasn't Director then, but he was still well-connected, so her request had been granted. Now, the only role that she played in the Agency was wife to the Director.

When my parents were killed, Mac had offered me the opportunity to learn to use my Talents, something that my parents had discouraged. I'd readily agreed, and Gretchen had taught me all about controlling the powers. She taught me to open up my mind so that I could *hear* everyone around me, she taught me to close my mind to keep out others seeking entrance to my thoughts, she taught me how to create a true connection with another person and about the potential harm in doing so. In no time I'd surpassed her abilities, I was a much stronger Talent than Gretchen. It wasn't long before I could actively enter someone's mind without making eye-contact or touching them. I could control a room full of minds at the time, bending all of them to my will. Thankfully, Gretchen also taught me about what happens when you abuse your power. She explained to me that Mind Manipulators are so rare, because most have driven themselves mad controlling others.

"I bet you're excited, I know how hard these last several months have been on you," she said gently, cutting in on my memories.

I made a noncommittal noise as I began shoveling food in to my mouth.

The eggs were covered in a salty cheese and contained mushrooms and onions, my absolute favorite. The thick white bread was warm, covered in butter and strawberry jam; Gretchen had made both the jam and the bread herself. I sighed happily as I chewed. Gretchen's cooking had been the only other perk of my confinement.

"How are you feeling today?" Gretchen continued, eyeing me over a steaming mug of coffee.

Swallowing the too-big bite of my breakfast, I cleared my throat before answering. "Pretty good, but I'll be better once I'm around other people." Gretchen blanched, setting her cup on the table. "Oh, Gretchen, that's not what I meant! You've been great, it's just been a little claustrophobic being stuck inside my bedroom all day," I tried to backtrack. I hadn't meant to hurt her feelings.

She'd gone out of her way to make me comfortable and without her companionship, I might've gone crazy.

"I understand, dear," she replied, offering me a small smile. "Dr. Wythe called late last night, he's very pleased with your progress." I groaned. I sort of despised my therapist.

In addition to my physical rehabilitation, Mac had insisted that I see a therapist. Dr. Wythe was the same shrink that Mac had sent me to after I'd witnessed my parents' murders, and I loathed discussing my feelings with him; it reminded me of the months that he'd spent grilling me on what I'd seen when the Coalition raided the hotel room where we'd been staying and killed my only family. This time around, he focused incessantly on the conversation that I'd had with Ian Crane following my capture. The therapy was boring and pointless, since he typically disregarded what I said and suggested a version of events that correlated with what the Agency wanted me to believe. It hadn't taken me long to figure out that if I just told him what he wanted to hear, the sessions would end. After I'd agreed that everything said by Crane was a lie, Dr. Wythe declared me healed. He still stopped by Mac's house when he was on campus, but I was no longer required to endure his daily torture.

Though I'd convinced Dr. Wythe that I didn't believe Crane's words, I hadn't convinced myself. I didn't include every detail of our conversation in my official report, leaving out the part where Crane insisted that he'd known my father. I wanted to work through that on my own, wanted to decide if it was a lie without the influence of the good doctor. I wasn't sure what Talents Dr. Wythe possessed, but they seemed like a weaker version of mine. He couldn't read minds like I could, but he had an influence over people, much like my compulsion. His suggestive nature had nearly worked on me in my weakened condition, but my desire to cling to the truth won out.

"Has Danbury told you which Instructors you'll be paired with?" Gretchen continued, a cloud of displeasure darkening her normally bright eyes.

"Um, not yet. He said that he'd have the list sent to my communicator," I said absently, returning to my eggs now that the topic of Dr. Wythe was closed.

Gretchen grew quiet, scrutinizing my table manners. The slight grimace contorting her beautiful features was the only outward indication that she disapproved.

"Danbury is out for a run right now, but he wanted me to be sure that you are ready to go at 6:30," she said, her features reverting back to an easy smile. "I packed a bag of things for you to take to the dorms with you, but call if I forgot anything and I will send it over."

The only response that I could manage was a small nod, since my mouth was full of egg and toast. Gretchen scowled again at my lack of social graces. I swallowed, "this might be the last good meal that I get for a while. You know that the School food is barely edible."

When I was a student, I'd tried to eat in the cafeteria as infrequently as possible, instead sneaking up to have dinner at Gretchen's table. It was just another reason that the other students disliked me.

Gretchen made some small throaty noise that sounded a little like a snort. "The Instructor's cafeteria fare is much better than the students'," she promised.

I spared her a skeptical glance, I'd believe it when I tasted the truth of her words for myself. I quickly scarfed down the rest of my breakfast, gulping my first cup of coffee before pouring a second cup, and sat at my vanity to get ready.

I dried my hair with a blow dryer, then used a big round brush to straighten out all the chestnut strands. When I was satisfied that it was thoroughly dry, I used a flatiron to ensure that no hint of wave remained. Before the last nine months I'd always worn my hair curly, but lately I'd been straightening my locks for lack of something better to do. I'd decided that I liked the straight look – sometimes change was a good thing.

Next, I pulled my hair into a ponytail at the back of my head. I stared at my reflection in the mirror for several minutes, before deciding in favor of makeup. My skin was smooth but uncharacteristically pale for me, thanks to spending the majority of my time indoors. The dark circles under my eyes were a bluish purple, like I'd been on the losing end of a fistfight.

Rising from the vanity, I retreated to my bedroom, where Gretchen had made my bed while I was in the shower. On the end of the burgundy comforter, in two neatly folded piles, sat several pairs of black stretch pants, white soft cotton t-shirts, and a thin gray sweatshirt. Anticipating my lack of appropriate clothing, Gretchen must've ordered me new outfits. Man, I didn't even have to ask, she always delivered.

My first class of the day was a basic skills combat class, so I grabbed a pair of cotton underwear and pulled them on, followed by the comfy-looking stretch pants. As I put on a matching bra, I caught a glimpse of my reflection in the mirror over my dresser. My back was to the mirror, and over my shoulder I could see angry red scars, peeking out, just above my stretchy pants. Unconsciously, I reached behind me and felt the raised flesh of the scar. My fingers felt the hole where the bullet had pierced my skin, and the places where the Medics stitched me up. I flinched as I touched the flesh, even though no sensation came; the Agency doctors said that I may never regain feeling.

They had offered to remove the scar, as was customary, but I was still a little fuzzy on how I'd actually received it, I didn't want to erase the only evidence that it had happened at all. A perverse part of me also liked the reminder that I now owed Crane for more than just my parents' murders.

My recovery had been a long and painful process, including learning how to walk again. I now received a shot every day to stabilize the chemicals that Crane's men had injected, reducing number of seizures that had plagued me since returning from Nevada. Initially, the doctors were unable to develop an effective antidote, and the episodes were so frequent that I spent most of my time in a drug-induced coma. Eventually, the team of researchers created an equalizer that allowed me to function, but it left me tired and weak.

My primary Medical doctor, Dr. Thistler, had treated me after my parents' deaths as well, but my memories of her weren't as clear as those of Dr. Wythe. Mac told me that she'd been one of the physicians to monitor my condition during my previous stay at Toxic's Medical facility, but I'd been too traumatized to be aware of my surroundings. She was nice enough, but her involvement in my life served as a daily reminder that I was sick, and currently unable to avenge my parents. I longed for a day when she would enter the examination room and proudly declare that she'd found a cure. Unfortunately, the more time that passed, the less confident I became that the time would ever come.

"Natalia, are you dressed?" Mac called from the sitting room, snapping me back to reality.

Grabbing for my shirt, I hastily pulled it over my head. I reached for the insanely bright white shoes, and yanked them on as fast as possible. Then I noticed the bag that Gretchen packed for me, with the meager personal items that I was allowed to take to the School, and stuffed the rest of my clothes inside. I slung the small duffel over my shoulder and walked out to the sitting room to meet Mac. I didn't look back on the room that had been like a prison for the last nine months.

Chapter Three

Mac and Gretchen's home was located two west of the School's main campus. Mac drove me the short distance in a road vehicle that he kept on hand for getting around the compound.

"You really don't need to hold my hand and walk me to class," I snapped once we were seated in the car. Though Mac had been like my surrogate father, our relationship had first become strained while I was in my Pledge year. The past nine months had done a little to repair the rift; I was bitter about my current situation and though I knew it was irrational I blamed him.

"I just want to ensure that you make it there okay," he replied mildly, his eyes fixed on the road. I gave him an odd look; did he forget that I had attended to this school for six years? I'd already taken all these classes, and I was fairly confident that I could find them in my sleep. Opening my mind, I risked gently probing Mac's.

"Natalia . . ." he warned. Mac was one of the few people who could detect when I tried to read him, and he effectively blocked most of my attempts. Mac's uncanny ability to block me was my own doing – I'd conditioned him against mental intrusion.

"Sorry," I smiled sheepishly, only sorry that I'd been caught. The stone façade of the administration building came into view several minutes later. Mac pulled the car to a stop in the rounded, gravel drive, and he reached for the bags at my feet.

"I'll have these sent up to your new room," he offered.

Now that I was safely on campus, I figured that Mac would bid me farewell and retreat inside to his office. Instead, he started walking away from the administration building. I quickly followed him.

As we neared the outdoor practice area, Mac sped up. My short legs could barely match pace with his stride. I was so focused on keeping up, that I didn't notice when he stopped; I ran smack into his broad back, my head bouncing painfully off the bottom edge of a shoulder bone. *Smooth, Talia*, I thought to myself. But Mac barely noticed. I stood behind him, my view obstructed by his massive frame, rubbing my forehead and waiting for him to introduce me.

"Director McDonough," a deep voice greeted him respectfully. I froze. The morning was relatively warm, and the thin sweatshirt that I was wearing had caused sweat to dot my forehead and upper lip, but that voice raised gooseflesh on my arms and made the fine hairs on the back of my neck stand on end.

My heart raced, images flashed through my mind: fingers light as feathers on my arms, running up my sides, blue eyes so full of longing and desire, soft lips against mine, wind whipping wet hair in my face, glass shards spraying my cheeks, the taste of blood in my mouth, a big hand gripping both my small, blood covered, ones. *Stay with me Tal, stay with me*, his voice pleaded in my head.

I wasn't entirely sure where that last image had come from, but the other memories were traumatic enough that I didn't dwell on it. I was torn between two overwhelming desires – one was to run all the way back to Mac and Gretchen's house, bury my face in my pillows, and cry myself to sleep; the second was to attack, viciously assault the boy standing not twenty feet from me.

"Donavon," Mac replied, "I have your new assistant," he paused briefly, "You of course know Natalia Lyons." Mac stepped aside, exposing me to Donavon and his students. Paralyzed, I stood in place as the images swam over and over through my mind. My breathing was labored, my heart beating so fast that I thought for sure everyone could see it through my chest. Mac placed his hand on my shoulder, his touch bringing me back to the present. I tried to smile as I glanced at the seated students, hoping that I looked nervous, but not unstable, which is exactly how I felt.

Finally, when I couldn't put it off any longer, I looked directly at Donavon. He was tall like his father, his shoulders broad, body lean, the muscles in his arms and chest were clearly visible through his thin navy t-shirt. His own gray sweatpants were slung low on his narrow hips. His blue eyes looked as shocked as I felt, his shaggy dark blonde hair was messy, like he'd only run his hand through it when he got out of bed that morning. His normally generous mouth appeared thin, his lips pressed together as if he were desperately trying to keep something inside. He was just as beautiful as I remembered, and the feelings swelling up inside of me were just as dark as I remembered.

When Donavon's gaze met mine, the primal urge to strike him was so strong that I had to fight to maintain control. A low guttural growl escaped my pursed lips, as a light breeze kicked up, the air around me grew cold and clouds began to gather overhead. Mac's grip on my shoulder tightened painfully. The wind became stronger and a raindrop splashed my cheek. Mac's fingers bit into my flesh, his nails digging in so hard that I thought for sure they'd torn my sweatshirt. The pain reeled in my rage; the winds died down and the sky slowly cleared. The whole scene occurred in mere seconds.

"Instructor McDonough," I hissed, through tightly clenched teeth. I tried to give Donavon my most angelic smile, but I could tell from the thoughts he was projecting that I looked slightly crazed.

Confident that I wouldn't maim his son – start a natural disaster – Mac's grip on my shoulder released. "I'll check on you later in the day, Natalia."

I nodded, so furious at him for springing Donavon on me like this that I didn't trust myself to speak. He gave a short wave to the class and a nod towards Donavon. "Stop by and see me soon, son."

Donavon gave his father an easy smile. "You got it, Dad."

With that, Mac turned and left me to face his son alone. But I couldn't move, my feet felt as if they were stuck in quicksand.

"Talia, please have a seat. I'm going to demonstrate the skills that we'll be working on today, and then we'll break off into pairs to work on them," Donavon said to me, his voice full of unspoken tension. His intense gaze penetrating straight through my skin, piercing my heart.

So many questions burned hot and ugly inside of me. *Why did you cheat on me? Why didn't you have the decency to apologize? Why didn't you ever try to talk to me after everything happened? What are you doing here now?* Yet when I opened my mouth, nothing came out, my unspoken questions handing in the air like a thick fog. Donavon's gaze remained on me.

Until nine months ago, I had trained for hostile situations. Now, looking into the face of the boy who had broken my heart, I could barely contain my emotions or my powers. *Get a grip, Talia,* I scolded myself. *He's not important. You don't care about him, and he doesn't care about you. Sit down and act like a normal human being.* Heeding my own advice, I slowly eased myself on to a cushy mat at the back of the class. Donavan reluctantly dragged his eyes from me and began his lesson.

He began reviewing basic offensive maneuvers, nothing too complicated or advanced. *This must be a remedial class,* I thought to myself. When it was time to break in to partners I walked around the periphery, observing the students. I made small corrections in technique when I saw fit, but I was still so distracted by coming face-to-face with Donavon that little else mattered.

During my stay at Mac's house, I hadn't been allowed visitors or communication with anyone besides Mac, Gretchen, and the select Medicals that came to treat me. No one had even mentioned Donavon, let alone told me that he was teaching at the School. Though, the more I thought about it, maybe Gretchen had tried – she'd been nervous and tense when we'd talked over breakfast this morning. Looking at Donavon now, all I could think was that she really should've tried harder.

When I'd left for Nevada, Donavon had been an Elite Operative, same as me, and was stationed at the Elite Headquarters in West Virginia, same as me. He'd also been my boyfriend since I was thirteen, but it ended when I'd caught him naked in bed with another girl.

It now made perfect sense that Mac had insisted on accompanying me that morning. He must've known that, best case scenario, the moment that I saw Donavon, I would leave. Worst case scenario, I would cause my own natural disaster right then and there. He'd been right; without Mac's painful presence, I likely would've done something drastic. I'd always lacked impulse control, but lately my temper was more easily provoked, and reining it in had become harder.

Finally, after what felt like an eternity, Donavon called class to an end. Grateful to escape his unwelcome presence, I turned to leave with the students.

"Talia, can I have a quick word?" Donavon called after me. I briefly considered refusing to speak to him, but then thought better of it. I'd have to face him eventually, now was as good a time as any. Since this assignment wasn't exactly voluntary, it was unlikely that Mac was going to let me opt-out, just because I didn't want to work with Donavon.

I'd stopped in my tracks when he called my name, and twisted my neck to meet his gaze.

"Hey, Donavon, you got a second?" a female voice rang out from across the paddock. Despite the distraction, Donavon's eyes remained locked with mine, pain and regret visible in their cerulean depths. His mind was unguarded, and the thoughts and feelings that poured freely tore open the wound that his betrayal had created.

"Um, sure," he called regretfully to the approaching woman.

I snapped my head to face forward and swallowed the rage and bitterness that threatened to rip from my throat in an animalistic scream. His gaze bore into the back of my skull.

"*I had no idea*," his mental voice said inside my head. Willing myself to remain composed, I closed my eyes, slowly exhaled, and counted to three.

When I opened my lids, I forced one sneakered foot in front of the other, away from the boy who'd broken my heart. I could hear the soft murmur of Donavon and the woman conversing, but their words were indistinguishable over buzzing between my ears. A loud, satisfying crack filled the morning air, followed by two strangled yelps as a large limb landed a foot from where Donavon and the woman stood. Pausing briefly to relish in my childish antics, I smiled, continuing to walk away. Maturity had never really been my strong suit.

Instead of going to my next class, I ran to the Headmistress' office. I barely noticed the lush green lawn or perfectly manicured flower beds that decorated the School's grounds. I could not believe that Mac had done this to me – what was he thinking? Force an interaction between me and Donavon? Was he crazy? Mac was the one who'd continually insisted that my mental state was fragile, what made him think that being around Donavon was a good idea?? Donavon's betrayal had nearly destroyed me, and now, when I was more vulnerable than I'd been in my entire life, Mac was forcing me to relive that pain. What was wrong with him? I continued my mental rant the entire way to the administration building.

ABOUT THE AUTHOR

For more information on Sophie Davis and the Talented Saga, visit Sophie's website, www.sophiedavisbooks.com

To contact Sophie directly, email her at sophie.davis.books@gmail.com.

You can also follow Sophie on twitter, @sophiedavisbook.

Thank you for taking the time to read Talented. Sophie loves feedback, and any reviews posted to goodreads.com, amazon.com, barnesandnoble.com, ibooks.com, or any other retail site where Talented is sold, are greatly appreciated.

Made in the USA
San Bernardino, CA
13 April 2014